BORDERS®
CLASSICS

FREDERICK DOUGLASS

Narrative of the Life of Frederick Douglass

and Other Writings

BORDERS®
CLASSICS

Please direct sales or editorial inquiries to:
BordersTradeBookInventoryQuestions@bordersgroupinc.com

This edition is published by
Borders Classics, an imprint of Borders Group, Inc.,
by special arrangement with
Ann Arbor Media Group, LLC
2500 South State Street, Ann Arbor, MI 48104

Printed and bound in the United States of America
by Edwards Brothers, Inc.

Quality Paperback ISBN13: 978-1-58726-344-6
ISBN10: 1-58726-344-0

10 09 08 07 10 9 8 7 6 5

CONTENTS

NARRATIVE OF THE LIFE OF FREDERICK DOUGLASS, AN AMERICAN SLAVE

Written by Himself

Preface

In the month of August, 1841, I attended an anti-slavery convention in Nantucket, at which it was my happiness to become acquainted with Frederick Douglass, the writer of the following Narrative. He was a stranger to nearly every member of that body; but, having recently made his escape from the southern prison-house of bondage, and feeling his curiosity excited to ascertain the principles and measures of the abolitionists—of whom he had heard a somewhat vague description while he was a slave—he was induced to give his attendance, on the occasion alluded to, though at that time a resident in New Bedford.

Fortunate, most fortunate occurrence!—fortunate for the millions of his manacled brethren, yet panting for deliverance from their awful thraldom!—fortunate for the cause of negro emancipation, and of universal liberty!—fortunate for the land of his birth, which he has already done so much to save and bless!—fortunate for a large circle of friends and acquaintances, whose sympathy and affection he has strongly secured by the many sufferings he has endured, by his virtuous traits of character, by his ever abiding remembrance of those who are in bonds, as being bound with them!—fortunate for the multitudes, in various parts of our republic, whose minds he has enlightened on the subject of slavery, and who have been melted to tears by his pathos, or roused to virtuous indignation by his stirring eloquence against the enslavers of men!—fortunate for himself, as it at once brought him into the field of public usefulness, "gave the world assurance of a MAN," quickened the slumbering energies of his soul, and consecrated him to the great work of breaking the rod of the oppressor, and letting the oppressed go free!

I shall never forget his first speech at the convention—the extraordinary emotion it excited in my own mind—the powerful impression it created upon a crowded auditory, completely taken by surprise—the applause which followed from the beginning to the end of his felicitous remarks. I think I never hated slavery so intensely as at that moment; certainly, my perception of the enormous outrage which is inflicted by it, on the godlike nature of its victims, was rendered far more clear than ever. There stood one, in physical proportion and stature commanding and exact—in intellect richly endowed—in natural eloquence a prodigy—in soul manifestly "created but a little lower than the angels"—yet a slave, ay, a fugitive slave—trembling for his safety, hardly daring to believe that on the American soil, a single white person could be found who would befriend him at all hazards, for the love of God and humanity! Capable of high attainments as an intellectual and moral being—needing nothing but a comparatively small amount of cultivation to make him an ornament to society and a blessing to his race—by the law of the land, by the voice of the people, by the terms of the slave code, he was only a piece of property, a beast of burden, a chattel personal, nevertheless!

A beloved friend from New Bedford prevailed on Mr. Douglass to address the convention: He came forward to the platform with a hesitancy and embarrassment, necessarily the attendants of a sensitive mind in such a novel position. After apologizing for his ignorance, and reminding the audience that slavery was a poor school for the human intellect and heart, he proceeded to narrate some of the facts in his own history as a slave, and in the course of his speech gave utterance to many noble thoughts and thrilling reflections. As soon as he had taken his seat, filled with hope and admiration, I rose, and declared that Patrick Henry, of revolutionary fame, never made a speech more eloquent in the cause of liberty, than the one we had just listened to from the lips of that hunted fugitive. So I believed at that time—such is my belief now. I reminded the audience of the peril which surrounded this self emancipated young man at the North—even in Massachusetts, on the soil of the Pilgrim Fathers, among the descendants of revolutionary sires; and I appealed to them, whether they would ever allow him to be carried back into slavery—law or no law, constitution or no constitution. The response was unanimous and in thunder-tones—"NO!" "Will you succor and protect him as a brother-man—a resident of the old Bay State?" "YES!" shouted the whole mass, with an energy so startling, that the ruthless tyrants south of Mason and Dixon's line might almost have heard the mighty burst of feeling, and recognized it as the pledge of an invincible determination, on the part of those who gave it, never to betray him that wanders, but to hide the outcast, and firmly to abide the consequences.

It was at once deeply impressed upon my mind, that, if Mr. Douglass could be persuaded to consecrate his time and talents to the promotion of the anti-slavery enterprise, a powerful impetus would be given to it, and a stunning blow at the same time inflicted on northern prejudice against a colored complexion. I therefore endeavored to instil hope and courage into his mind, in order that he might dare to engage in a vocation so anomalous and responsible for a person in his situation; and I was seconded in this effort by warm-hearted friends, especially by the late General Agent of the Massachusetts Anti-Slavery Society, Mr. John A. Collins, whose judgment in this instance entirely coincided with my own. At first, he could give no encouragement; with unfeigned diffidence, he expressed his conviction that he was not adequate to the performance of so great a task; the path marked out was wholly an untrodden one; he was sincerely apprehensive that he should do more harm than good. After much deliberation, however, he consented to make a trial; and ever since that period, he has acted as a lecturing agent, under the auspices either of the American or the Massachusetts Anti-Slavery Society. In labors he has been most abundant; and his success in combating prejudice, in gaining proselytes, in agitating the public mind, has far surpassed the most sanguine expectations that were raised at the commencement of his brilliant career. He has borne himself with gentleness and meekness, yet with true manliness of character. As a public speaker, he excels in pathos, wit, comparison, imitation, strength of reasoning, and fluency of language. There is in him that union of head and heart, which is indispensable to an enlightenment of the heads and a winning of the hearts of others. May his strength continue to be equal to his day! May he continue to "grow in grace, and in the knowledge of God," that he may be increasingly serviceable in the cause of bleeding humanity, whether at home or abroad!

It is certainly a very remarkable fact, that one of the most efficient advocates of the slave population, now before the public, is a fugitive slave, in the person of Frederick Douglass; and that the free colored population of the United States are as ably represented by one of their own number, in the person of Charles Lenox Remond, whose eloquent appeals have extorted the highest applause of multitudes on both sides of the Atlantic. Let the calumniators of the colored race despise themselves for their baseness and illiberality of spirit, and henceforth cease to talk of the natural inferiority of those who require nothing but time and opportunity to attain to the highest point of human excellence.

It may, perhaps, be fairly questioned, whether any other portion of the population of the earth could have endured the privations, sufferings and horrors of slavery, without having become more degraded in the scale of humanity than the slaves of African descent. Nothing has been left undone to cripple their intellects, darken their minds, debase their moral nature, obliterate all traces of their relationship to mankind; and yet how wonderfully they have sustained the mighty load of a most frightful bondage, under which they have been groaning for centuries! To illustrate the effect of slavery on the white man—to show that he has no powers of endurance, in such a condition, superior to those of his black brother—Daniel O'Connell, the distinguished advocate of universal emancipation, and the mightiest champion of prostrate but not conquered Ireland, relates the following anecdote in a speech delivered by him in the Conciliation Hall, Dublin, before the Loyal National Repeal Association, March 31, 1845. "No matter," said Mr. O'Connell, "under what specious term it may disguise itself, slavery is still hideous. *It has a natural, an inevitable tendency to brutalize every noble faculty of man.* An American sailor, who was cast away on the shore of Africa, where he was kept in slavery for three years, was, at the expiration of that period, found to be imbruted and stultified—he had lost all reasoning power; and having forgotten his native language, could only utter some savage gibberish between Arabic and English, which nobody could understand, and which even he himself found difficulty in pronouncing. So much for the humanizing influence of The Domestic Institution!" Admitting this to have been an extraordinary case of mental deterioration, it proves at least that the white slave can sink as low in the scale of humanity as the black one.

Mr. Douglass has very properly chosen to write his own Narrative, in his own style, and according to the best of his ability, rather than to employ someone else. It is, therefore, entirely his own production; and, considering how long and dark was the career he had to run as a slave—how few have been his opportunities to improve his mind since he broke his iron fetters—it is, in my judgment, highly creditable to his head and heart. He who can peruse it without a tearful eye, a heaving breast, an afflicted spirit,—without being filled with an unutterable abhorrence of slavery and all its abettors, and animated with a determination to seek the immediate overthrow of that execrable system—without trembling for the fate of this country in the hands of a righteous God, who is ever on the side of the oppressed, and whose arm is not shortened that it cannot save—must have a flinty heart, and be qualified to act the part of a trafficker "in slaves and the souls of men." I am confident that it is essentially true in all its statements; that nothing has been set down in malice, nothing exaggerated, nothing drawn from the imagination; that it comes short of the reality, rather than over states a single fact in regard to *slavery as it is*. The experience of Frederick Douglass, as a slave, was not a peculiar one; his lot was not especially a hard one; his case may be regarded as a very fair specimen of the treatment of slaves in Maryland, in which State it is conceded that they are better fed and less cruelly treated than in Georgia, Alabama, or Louisiana. Many have suffered incomparably more, while very few on the plantations have suffered less, than himself. Yet how deplorable was his situation! what terrible chastisements were inflicted upon his person! what still more shocking outrages were perpetrated upon his mind! with all his noble powers and sublime aspirations, how like a brute was he treated, even by those professing to have the same mind in them that was in Christ Jesus! to what dreadful liabilities was he continually subjected! how destitute of friendly counsel and aid, even in his greatest extremities! how heavy was the midnight of woe which shrouded in blackness the last ray of hope, and filled the future with terror and gloom! what longings after freedom took possession of his breast, and how his misery augmented, in proportion as he grew reflective and intelligent—thus demonstrating that a happy slave is an extinct man! how he thought, reasoned, felt, under the lash of the driver, with the chains upon his limbs! what perils he encountered in his endeavors to escape from his horrible doom! and how signal have been his deliverance and preservation in the midst of a nation of pitiless enemies!

This Narrative contains many affecting incidents, many passages of great eloquence and power; but I think the most thrilling one of them all is the description Douglass gives of his feelings, as he stood soliloquizing respecting his fate, and the chances of his one day being a freeman, on the banks of the Chesapeake Bay—viewing the receding vessels as they flew with their white wings before the breeze, and apostrophizing them as animated by the living spirit of freedom. Who can read that passage, and be insensible to its pathos and sublimity? Compressed into it is a whole Alexandrian library of thought, feeling, and sentiment—all that can, all that need be urged, in the form of expostulation, entreaty, rebuke, against that crime of crimes—making man the property of his fellow-man! O, how accursed is that system, which entombs the godlike mind of man, defaces the divine image, reduces those who by creation were crowned with glory and honor to a level with four-footed beasts, and exalts the dealer in human flesh above all that is called God! Why should its existence be prolonged one hour? Is it not evil, only evil, and that continually? What does its presence imply but the absence of all fear of God, all regard for man, on the part of the people of the United States? Heaven speed its eternal overthrow!

So profoundly ignorant of the nature of slavery are many persons, that they are stubbornly incredulous whenever they read or listen to any recital of the cruelties which are daily inflicted on its victims. They do not deny that the slaves are held as property; but that terrible fact seems to convey to their minds no idea of injustice, exposure to outrage, or savage barbarity. Tell them of cruel scourgings, of mutilations and brandings, of scenes of pollution and blood, of the banishment of all light and knowledge, and they affect to be greatly indignant at such enormous exaggerations, such wholesale misstatements, such abominable libels on the character of the southern planters! As if all these direful outrages were not the natural results of slavery! As if it were less cruel to reduce a human being to the condition of a thing, than to give him a severe flagellation, or to deprive him of necessary food and clothing! As if whips, chains, thumb-screws, paddles, bloodhounds, overseers, drivers, patrols, were not all in dispensable to keep the slaves down, and to give protection to their ruthless oppressors! As if, when the marriage institution is abolished, concubinage, adultery, and incest, must not necessarily abound; when all the rights of humanity are annihilated, any barrier remains to protect the victim from the fury of the spoiler; when absolute power is assumed over life and liberty, it will not be wielded with destructive sway! Skeptics of this character abound in society. In some few instances, their incredulity arises from a want of reflection; but, generally, it indicates a hatred of the light, a desire to shield slavery from the assaults of its foes, a contempt of the colored race, whether bond or free. Such will try to discredit the shocking tales of slaveholding cruelty which are recorded in this truthful Narrative; but they will labor in vain. Mr. Douglass has frankly disclosed the place of his birth, the names of those who claimed ownership in his body and soul, and the names also of those who committed the crimes which he has alleged against them. His statements, therefore, may easily be disproved, if they are untrue.

In the course of his Narrative, he relates two instances of murderous cruelty—in one of which a planter deliberately shot a slave belonging to a neighboring plantation, who had unintentionally gotten within his lordly domain in quest of fish; and in the other, an overseer blew out the brains of a slave who had fled to a stream of water to escape a bloody scourging. Mr. Douglass states that in neither of these instances was anything done by way of legal arrest or judicial investigation. The "Baltimore American," of March 17, 1845, relates a similar case of atrocity, perpetrated with similar impunity—as follows:

> SHOOTING A SLAVE
>
> We learn, upon the authority of a letter from Charles County, Maryland, received by a gentleman of this city, that a young man, named Matthews, a nephew of General Matthews, and whose father, it is believed, holds an office at Washington, killed one of the slaves upon his father's farm by shooting him. The letter states that young Matthews had been left in charge of the farm; that he gave an order to the servant, which was disobeyed, when he proceeded to the house, *obtained a gun, and, returning, shot the servant*. He immediately, the letter continues, fled to his father's residence, where he still remains unmolested.

Let it never be forgotten, that no slaveholder or overseer can be convicted of any outrage perpetrated on the person of a slave, however diabolical it may be, on the testimony of colored witnesses, whether bond or free. By the slave code, they are adjudged to be as incompetent to testify against a white man, as though they were indeed a part of the brute creation. Hence, there is no legal protection in fact, whatever there may be in form, for the slave population; and any amount of cruelty may be inflicted on them with impunity. Is it possible for the human mind to conceive of a more horrible state of society?

The effect of a religious profession on the conduct of southern masters is vividly described in the following Narrative, and shown to be anything but salutary. In the nature of the case, it must be in the highest degree pernicious. The testimony of Mr. Douglass, on this point, is sustained by a cloud of witnesses, whose veracity is unimpeachable. "A slaveholder's profession of Christianity is a palpable imposture. He is a felon of the highest grade. He is a man-stealer. It is of no importance what you put in the other scale."

Reader! are you with the man-stealers in sympathy and purpose, or on the side of their down-trodden victims? If with the former, then are you the foe of God and man. If with the latter, what are you prepared to do and dare in their behalf? Be faithful, be vigilant, be untiring in your efforts to break every yoke, and let the oppressed go free. Come what may—cost what it may—inscribe on the banner which you unfurl to the breeze, as your religious and political motto—

No Compromise with Slavery! No Union with Slaveholders!!

WM. LLOYD GARRISON

Boston, May 1, 1845

I

I was born in Tuckahoe, near Hillsborough, and about twelve miles from Easton, in Talbot County, Maryland. I have no accurate knowledge of my age, never having seen any authentic record containing it. By far the larger part of the slaves know as little of their ages as horses know of theirs, and it is the wish of most masters within my knowledge to keep their slaves thus ignorant. I do not remember to have ever met a slave who could tell of his birthday. They seldom come nearer to it than planting-time, harvest-time, cherry-time, spring-time, or fall-time. A want of information concerning my own was a source of unhappiness to me even during childhood. The white children could tell their ages. I could not tell why I ought to be deprived of the same privilege. I was not allowed to make any inquiries of my master concerning it. He deemed all such inquiries on the part of a slave improper and impertinent, and evidence of a restless spirit. The nearest estimate I can give makes me now between twenty-seven and twenty-eight years of age. I come to this, from hearing my master say, some time during 1835, I was about seventeen years old.

My mother was named Harriet Bailey. She was the daughter of Isaac and Betsey Bailey, both colored, and quite dark. My mother was of a darker complexion than either my grandmother or grandfather.

My father was a white man. He was admitted to be such by all I ever heard speak of my parentage. The opinion was also whispered that my master was my father; but of the correctness of this opinion, I know nothing; the means of knowing was withheld from me. My mother and I were separated when I was but an infant—before I knew her as my mother. It is a common custom, in the part of Maryland from which I ran away, to part children from their mothers at a very early age. Frequently, before the child has reached its twelfth month, its mother is taken from it, and hired out on some farm a considerable distance off, and the child is placed under the care of an old woman, too old for field labor. For what this separation is done, I do not know, unless it be to hinder the development of the child's affection toward its mother, and to blunt and destroy the natural affection of the mother for the child. This is the inevitable result.

I never saw my mother, to know her as such, more than four or five times in my life; and each of these times was very short in duration, and at night. She was hired by a Mr. Stewart, who lived about twelve miles from my home. She made her journeys to see me in the night, travelling the whole distance on foot, after the performance of her day's work. She was a field hand, and a whipping is the penalty of not being in the field at sunrise, unless a slave has special permission from his or her master to the contrary—a permission which they seldom get, and one that gives to him that gives it the proud name of being a kind master. I do not recollect of ever seeing my mother by the light of day. She was with me in the night. She would lie down with me, and get me to sleep, but long before I waked she was gone. Very little communication ever took place between us. Death soon ended what little we could have while she lived, and with it her hardships and suffering. She died when I was about seven years old, on one of my master's farms, near Lee's Mill. I was not allowed to be present during her illness, at her death, or burial. She was gone long before I knew anything about it. Never having enjoyed, to any considerable extent, her soothing presence, her tender and watchful care, I received the tidings of her death with much the same emotions I should have probably felt at the death of a stranger.

Called thus suddenly away, she left me without the slightest intimation of who my father was. The whisper that my master was my father, may or may not be true; and, true or false, it is of but little consequence to my purpose whilst the fact remains, in all its glaring odiousness, that slaveholders have ordained, and by law established, that the children of slave women shall in all cases follow the condition of their mothers; and this is done too obviously to administer to their own lusts, and make a gratification of their wicked desires profitable as well as pleasurable; for by this cunning arrangement, the slaveholder, in cases not a few, sustains to his slaves the double relation of master and father.

I know of such cases; and it is worthy of remark that such slaves invariably suffer greater hardships, and have more to contend with, than others. They are, in the first place, a constant offence to their mistress. She is ever disposed to find fault with them; they can seldom do anything to please her; she is never better pleased than when she sees them under the lash, especially when she suspects her husband of showing to his mulatto children favors which he withholds from his black slaves. The master is frequently compelled to sell this class of his slaves, out of deference to the feelings of his white wife; and, cruel as the deed may strike anyone to be, for a man to sell his own children to human flesh-mongers, it is often the dictate of humanity for him to do so; for, unless he does this, he must not only whip them himself, but must stand by and see one white son tie up his brother, of but few shades darker complexion than himself, and ply the gory lash to his naked back; and if he lisp one word of disapproval, it is set down to his parental partiality, and only makes a bad matter worse, both for himself and the slave whom he would protect and defend.

Every year brings with it multitudes of this class of slaves. It was doubtless in consequence of a knowledge of this fact, that one great statesman of the south predicted the downfall of slavery by the inevitable laws of population. Whether this prophecy is ever fulfilled or not, it is nevertheless plain that a very different-looking class of people are springing up at the south, and are now held in slavery, from those originally brought to this country from Africa; and if their increase do no other good, it will do away the force of the argument, that God cursed Ham, and therefore American slavery is right. If the lineal descendants of Ham are alone to be scripturally enslaved, it is certain that slavery at the south must soon become unscriptural; for thousands are ushered into the world, annually, who, like myself, owe their existence to white fathers, and those fathers most frequently their own masters.

I have had two masters. My first master's name was Anthony. I do not remember his first name. He was generally called Captain Anthony—a title which, I presume, he acquired by sailing a craft on the Chesapeake Bay. He was not considered a rich slaveholder. He owned two or three farms, and about thirty slaves. His farms and slaves were under the care of an overseer. The overseer's name was Plummer. Mr. Plummer was a miserable drunkard, a profane swearer, and a savage monster. He always went armed with a cowskin and a heavy cudgel. I have known him to cut and slash the women's heads so horribly, that even master would be enraged at his cruelty, and would threaten to whip him if he did not mind himself. Master, however, was not a humane slaveholder. It required extraordinary barbarity on the part of an overseer to affect him. He was a cruel man, hardened by a long life of slaveholding. He would at times seem to take great pleasure in whipping a slave. I have often been awakened at the dawn of day by the most heart-rending shrieks of an own aunt of mine, whom he used to tie up to a joist, and whip upon her naked back till she was literally covered with blood. No words, no tears, no prayers, from his gory victim, seemed to move his iron heart from its bloody purpose. The louder she screamed, the harder he whipped; and where the blood ran fastest, there he whipped longest. He would whip her to make her scream, and whip her to make her hush; and not until overcome by fatigue, would he cease to swing the blood-clotted cowskin. I remember the first time I ever witnessed this horrible exhibition. I was quite a child, but I well remember it. I never shall forget it whilst I remember anything. It was the first of a long series of such outrages, of which I was doomed to be a witness and a participant. It struck me with awful force. It was the blood-stained gate, the entrance to the hell of slavery, through which I was about to pass. It was a most terrible spectacle. I wish I could commit to paper the feelings with which I beheld it.

This occurrence took place very soon after I went to live with my old master, and under the following circumstances. Aunt Hester went out one night—where or for what I do not know—and happened to be absent when my master desired her presence. He had ordered her not to go out evenings, and warned her that she must never let him catch her in company with a young man, who was paying attention to her belonging to Colonel Lloyd. The young man's name was Ned Roberts, generally called Lloyd's Ned. Why master was so careful of her, may be safely left to conjecture. She was a woman of noble form, and of graceful proportions, having very few equals, and fewer superiors, in personal appearance, among the colored or white women of our neighborhood.

Aunt Hester had not only disobeyed his orders in going out, but had been found in company with Lloyd's Ned; which circumstance, I found, from what he said while whipping her, was the chief offence. Had he been a man of pure morals himself, he might have been thought interested in protecting the innocence of my aunt; but those who knew him will not suspect him of any such virtue. Before he commenced whipping Aunt Hester, he took her into the kitchen, and stripped her from neck to waist, leaving her neck, shoulders, and back, entirely naked. He then told her to cross her hands, calling her at the same time a d——d b——h. After crossing her hands, he tied them with a strong rope, and led her to a stool under a large hook in the joist, put in for the purpose. He made her get upon the stool, and tied her hands to the hook. She now stood fair for his infernal purpose. Her arms were stretched up at their full length, so that she stood upon the ends of her toes. He then said to her, “Now, you d—d b—h, I’ll learn you how to disobey my orders!” and after rolling up his sleeves, he commenced to lay on the heavy cowskin, and soon the warm, red blood (amid heart-rending shrieks from her, and horrid oaths from him) came dripping to the floor. I was so terrified and horror-stricken at the sight, that I hid myself in a closet, and dared not venture out till long after the bloody transaction was over. I expected it would be my turn next. It was all new to me. I had never seen anything like it before. I had always lived with my grandmother on the outskirts of the plantation, where she was put to raise the children of the younger women. I had therefore been, until now, out of the way of the bloody scenes that often occurred on the plantation.

II

My master's family consisted of two sons, Andrew and Richard; one daughter, Lucretia, and her husband, Captain Thomas Auld. They lived in one house, upon the home plantation of Colonel Edward Lloyd. My master was Colonel Lloyd's clerk and superintendent. He was what might be called the overseer of the overseers. I spent two years of childhood on this plantation in my old master's family. It was here that I witnessed the bloody transaction recorded in the first chapter; and as I received my first impressions of slavery on this plantation, I will give some description of it, and of slavery as it there existed. The plantation is about twelve miles north of Easton, in Talbot County, and is situated on the border of Miles River. The principal products raised upon it were tobacco, corn, and wheat. These were raised in great abundance; so that, with the products of this and the other farms belonging to him, he was able to keep in almost constant employment a large sloop, in carrying them to market at Baltimore. This sloop was named Sally Lloyd, in honor of one of the colonel's daughters. My master's son-in-law, Captain Auld, was master of the vessel; she was otherwise manned by the colonel's own slaves. Their names were Peter, Isaac, Rich, and Jake. These were esteemed very highly by the other slaves, and looked upon as the privileged ones of the plantation; for it was no small affair, in the eyes of the slaves, to be allowed to see Baltimore.

Colonel Lloyd kept from three to four hundred slaves on his home plantation, and owned a large number more on the neighboring farms belonging to him. The names of the farms nearest to the home plantation were Wye Town and New Design. Wye Town was under the overseership of a man named Noah Willis. New Design was under the overseership of a Mr. Townsend. The overseers of these, and all the rest of the farms, numbering over twenty, received advice and direction from the managers of the home plantation. This was the great business place. It was the seat of government for the whole twenty farms. All disputes among the overseers were settled here. If a slave was convicted of any high misdemeanor, became unmanageable, or evinced a determination to run away, he was brought immediately here, severely whipped, put on board the sloop, carried to Baltimore, and sold to Austin Woolfolk, or some other slave-trader, as a warning to the slaves remaining.

Here, too, the slaves of all the other farms received their monthly allowance of food, and their yearly clothing. The men and women slaves received, as their monthly allowance of food, eight pounds of pork, or its equivalent in fish, and one bushel of corn meal. Their yearly clothing consisted of two coarse linen shirts, one pair of linen trousers, like the shirts, one jacket, one pair of trousers for winter, made of coarse negro cloth, one pair of stockings, and one pair of shoes; the whole of which could not have cost more than seven dollars. The allowance of the slave children was given to their mothers, or the old women having the care of them. The children unable to work in the field had neither shoes, stockings, jackets, nor trousers, given to them; their clothing consisted of two coarse linen shirts per year. When these failed them, they went naked until the next allowance-day. Children from seven to ten years old, of both sexes, almost naked, might be seen at all seasons of the year.

There were no beds given the slaves, unless one coarse blanket be considered such, and none but the men and women had these. This, however, is not considered a very great privation. They find less difficulty from the want of beds, than from the want of time to sleep; for when their day's work in the field is done, the most of them having their washing, mending, and cooking to do, and having few or none of the ordinary facilities for doing either of these, very many of their sleeping hours are consumed in preparing for the field the coming day; and when this is done, old and young, male and female, married and single, drop down side by side, on one common bed—the cold, damp floor—each covering himself or herself with their miserable blankets; and here they sleep till they are summoned to the field by the driver's horn. At the sound of this, all must rise, and be off to the field. There must be no halting; everyone must be at his or her post; and woe betides them who hear not this morning summons to the field; for if they are not awakened by the sense of hearing, they are by the sense of feeling: no age nor sex finds any favor. Mr. Severe, the overseer, used to stand by the door of the quarter, armed with a large hickory stick and heavy cowskin, ready to whip anyone who was so unfortunate as not to hear, or, from any other cause, was prevented from being ready to start for the field at the sound of the horn.

Mr. Severe was rightly named: he was a cruel man. I have seen him whip a woman, causing the blood to run half an hour at the time; and this, too, in the midst of her crying children, pleading for their mother's release. He seemed to take pleasure in manifesting his fiendish barbarity. Added to his cruelty, he was a profane swearer. It was enough to chill the blood and stiffen the hair of an ordinary man to hear him talk. Scarce a sentence escaped him but that was commenced or concluded by some horrid oath. The field was the place to witness his cruelty and profanity. His presence made it both the field of blood and of blasphemy. From the rising till the going down of the sun, he was cursing, raving, cutting, and slashing among the slaves of the field, in the most frightful manner. His career was short. He died very soon after I went to Colonel Lloyd's; and he died as he lived, uttering, with his dying groans, bitter curses and horrid oaths. His death was regarded by the slaves as the result of a merciful Providence.

Mr. Severe's place was filled by a Mr. Hopkins. He was a very different man. He was less cruel, less profane, and made less noise, than Mr. Severe. His course was characterized by no extraordinary demonstrations of cruelty. He whipped, but seemed to take no pleasure in it. He was called by the slaves a good overseer.

The home plantation of Colonel Lloyd wore the appearance of a country village. All the mechanical operations for all the farms were performed here. The shoemaking and mending, the blacksmithing, cartwrighting, coopering, weaving, and grain-grinding, were all performed by the slaves on the home plantation. The whole place wore a business-like aspect very unlike the neighboring farms. The number of houses, too, conspired to give it advantage over the neighboring farms. It was called by the slaves the *Great House Farm.* Few privileges were esteemed higher, by the slaves of the out-farms, than that of being selected to do errands at the Great House Farm. It was associated in their minds with greatness. A representative could not be prouder of his election to a seat in the American Congress, than a slave on one of the out-farms would be of his election to do errands at the Great House Farm. They regarded it as evidence of great confidence reposed in them by their overseers; and it was on this account, as well as a constant desire to be out of the field from under the driver's lash, that they esteemed it a high privilege, one worth careful living for. He was called the smartest and most trusty fellow, who had this honor conferred upon him the most frequently. The competitors for this office sought as diligently to please their overseers, as the office-seekers in the political parties seek to please and deceive the people. The same traits of character might be seen in Colonel Lloyd's slaves, as are seen in the slaves of the political parties.

The slaves selected to go to the Great House Farm, for the monthly allowance for themselves and their fellow-slaves, were peculiarly enthusiastic. While on their way, they would make the dense old woods, for miles around, reverberate with their wild songs, revealing at once the highest joy and the deepest sadness. They would compose and sing as they went along, consulting neither time nor tune. The thought that came up, came out—if not in the word, in the sound—and as frequently in the one as in the other. They would sometimes sing the most pathetic sentiment in the most rapturous tone, and the most rapturous sentiment in the most pathetic tone. Into all of their songs they would manage to weave something of the Great House Farm. Especially would they do this, when leaving home. They would then sing most exultingly the following words:

> I am going away to the Great House Farm!
>   O, yea! O, yea! O!

This they would sing, as a chorus, to words which to many would seem unmeaning jargon, but which, nevertheless, were full of meaning to themselves. I have sometimes thought that the mere hearing of those songs would do more to impress some minds with the horrible character of slavery, than the reading of whole volumes of philosophy on the subject could do.

I did not, when a slave, understand the deep meaning of those rude and apparently incoherent songs. I was myself within the circle; so that I neither saw nor heard as those without might see and hear. They told a tale of woe which was then altogether beyond my feeble comprehension; they were tones loud, long, and deep; they breathed the prayer and complaint of souls boiling over with the bitterest anguish. Every tone was a testimony against slavery, and a prayer to God for deliverance from chains. The hearing of those wild notes always depressed my spirit, and filled me with ineffable sadness. I have frequently found myself in tears while hearing them. The mere recurrence to those songs, even now, afflicts me; and while I am writing these lines, an expression of feeling has already found its way down my cheek. To those songs I trace my first glimmering conception of the dehumanizing character of slavery. I can never get rid of that conception. Those songs still follow me, to deepen my hatred of slavery, and quicken my sympathies for my brethren in bonds. If anyone wishes to be impressed with the soul-killing effects of slavery, let him go to Colonel Lloyd's plantation, and, on allowance-day, place himself in the deep pine woods, and there let him, in silence, analyze the sounds that shall pass through the chambers of his soul—and if he is not thus impressed, it will only be because "there is no flesh in his obdurate heart."

I have often been utterly astonished, since I came to the north, to find persons who could speak of the singing, among slaves, as evidence of their contentment and happiness. It is impossible to conceive of a greater mistake. Slaves sing most when they are most unhappy. The songs of the slave represent the sorrows of his heart; and he is relieved by them, only as an aching heart is relieved by its tears. At least, such is my experience. I have often sung to drown my sorrow, but seldom to express my happiness. Crying for joy, and singing for joy, were alike uncommon to me while in the jaws of slavery. The singing of a man cast away upon a desolate island might be as appropriately considered as evidence of contentment and happiness, as the singing of a slave; the songs of the one and of the other are prompted by the same emotion.

III

Colonel Lloyd kept a large and finely cultivated garden, which afforded almost constant employment for four men, besides the chief gardener, (Mr. M'Durmond). This garden was probably the greatest attraction of the place. During the summer months, people came from far and near—from Baltimore, Easton, and Annapolis—to see it. It abounded in fruits of almost every description, from the hardy apple of the north to the delicate orange of the south. This garden was not the least source of trouble on the plantation. Its excellent fruit was quite a temptation to the hungry swarms of boys, as well as the older slaves, belonging to the colonel, few of whom had the virtue or the vice to resist it. Scarcely a day passed, during the summer, but that some slave had to take the lash for stealing fruit. The colonel had to resort to all kinds of stratagems to keep his slaves out of the garden. The last and most successful one was that of tarring his fence all around; after which, if a slave was caught with any tar upon his person, it was deemed sufficient proof that he had either been into the garden, or had tried to get in. In either case, he was severely whipped by the chief gardener. This plan worked well; the slaves became as fearful of tar as of the lash. They seemed to realize the impossibility of touching *tar* without being defiled.

The colonel also kept a splendid riding equipage. His stable and carriage-house presented the appearance of some of our large city livery establishments. His horses were of the finest form and noblest blood. His carriage-house contained three splendid coaches, three or four gigs, besides dearborns and barouches of the most fashionable style.

This establishment was under the care of two slaves—old Barney and young Barney—father and son. To attend to this establishment was their sole work. But it was by no means an easy employment; for in nothing was Colonel Lloyd more particular than in the management of his horses. The slightest inattention to these was unpardonable, and was visited upon those, under whose care they were placed, with the severest punishment; no excuse could shield them, if the colonel only suspected any want of attention to his horses—a supposition which he frequently indulged, and one which, of course, made the office of old and young Barney a very trying one. They never knew when they were safe from punishment. They were frequently whipped when least deserving, and escaped whipping when most deserving it. Everything depended upon the looks of the horses, and the state of Colonel Lloyd's own mind when his horses were brought to him for use. If a horse did not move fast enough, or hold his head high enough, it was owing to some fault of his keepers. It was painful to stand near the stable-door, and hear the various complaints against the keepers when a horse was taken out for use. "This horse has not had proper attention. He has not been sufficiently rubbed and curried, or he has not been properly fed; his food was too wet or too dry; he got it too soon or too late; he was too hot or too cold; he had too much hay, and not enough of grain; or he had too much grain, and not enough of hay; instead of old Barney's attending to the horse, he had very improperly left it to his son." To all these complaints, no matter how unjust, the slave must answer never a word. Colonel Lloyd could not brook any contradiction from a slave. When he spoke, a slave must stand, listen, and tremble; and such was literally the case. I have seen Colonel Lloyd make old Barney, a man between fifty and sixty years of age, uncover his bald head, kneel down upon the cold, damp ground, and receive upon his naked and toil-worn shoulders more than thirty lashes at the time. Colonel Lloyd had three sons—Edward, Murray, and Daniel—and three sons-in-law, Mr. Winder, Mr. Nicholson, and Mr. Lowndes. All of these lived at the Great House Farm, and enjoyed the luxury of whipping the servants when they pleased, from old Barney down to William Wilkes, the coach-driver. I have seen Winder make one of the house-servants stand off from him a suitable distance to be touched with the end of his whip, and at every stroke raise great ridges upon his back.

To describe the wealth of Colonel Lloyd would be almost equal to describing the riches of Job. He kept from ten to fifteen house-servants. He was said to own a thousand slaves, and I think this estimate quite within the truth. Colonel Lloyd owned so many that he did not know them when he saw them; nor did all the slaves of the out-farms know him. It is reported of him, that, while riding along the road one day, he met a colored man, and addressed him in the usual manner of speaking to colored people on the public highways of the south: "Well, boy, whom do you belong to?" "To Colonel Lloyd," replied the slave. "Well, does the colonel treat you well?" "No, sir," was the ready reply. "What, does he work you too hard?" "Yes, sir." "Well, don't he give you enough to eat?" "Yes, sir, he gives me enough, such as it is."

The colonel, after ascertaining where the slave belonged, rode on; the man also went on about his business, not dreaming that he had been conversing with his master. He thought, said, and heard nothing more of the matter, until two or three weeks afterwards. The poor man was then informed by his overseer that, for having found fault with his master, he was now to be sold to a Georgia trader. He was immediately chained and handcuffed; and thus, without a moment's warning, he was snatched away, and forever sundered, from his family and friends, by a hand more unrelenting than death. This is the penalty of telling the truth, of telling the simple truth, in answer to a series of plain questions.

It is partly in consequence of such facts, that slaves, when inquired of as to their condition and the character of their masters, almost universally say they are contented, and that their masters are kind. The slaveholders have been known to send in spies among their slaves, to ascertain their views and feelings in regard to their condition. The frequency of this has had the effect to establish among the slaves the maxim, that a still tongue makes a wise head. They suppress the truth rather than take the consequences of telling it, and in so doing prove themselves a part of the human family. If they have anything to say of their masters, it is generally in their masters' favor, especially when speaking to an untried man. I have been frequently asked, when a slave, if I had a kind master, and do not remember ever to have given a negative answer; nor did I, in pursuing this course, consider myself as uttering what was absolutely false; for I always measured the kindness of my master by the standard of kindness set up among slaveholders around us. Moreover, slaves are like other people, and imbibe prejudices quite common to others. They think their own better than that of others. Many, under the influence of this prejudice, think their own masters are better than the masters of other slaves; and this, too, in some cases, when the very reverse is true. Indeed, it is not uncommon for slaves even to fall out and quarrel among themselves about the relative goodness of their masters, each contending for the superior goodness of his own over that of the others. At the very same time, they mutually execrate their masters when viewed separately. It was so on our plantation. When Colonel Lloyd's slaves met the slaves of Jacob Jepson, they seldom parted without a quarrel about their masters; Colonel Lloyd's slaves contending that he was the richest, and Mr. Jepson's slaves that he was the smartest, and most of a man. Colonel Lloyd's slaves would boast his ability to buy and sell Jacob Jepson. Mr. Jepson's slaves would boast his ability to whip Colonel Lloyd. These quarrels would almost always end in a fight between the parties, and those that whipped were supposed to have gained the point at issue. They seemed to think that the greatness of their masters was transferable to themselves. It was considered as being bad enough to be a slave; but to be a poor man's slave was deemed a disgrace indeed!

IV

Mr. Hopkins remained but a short time in the office of overseer. Why his career was so short, I do not know, but suppose he lacked the necessary severity to suit Colonel Lloyd. Mr. Hopkins was succeeded by Mr. Austin Gore, a man possessing, in an eminent degree, all those traits of character in dispensable to what is called a first-rate overseer. Mr. Gore had served Colonel Lloyd, in the capacity of overseer, upon one of the out-farms, and had shown himself worthy of the high station of overseer upon the home of Great House Farm.

Mr. Gore was proud, ambitious, and persevering. He was artful, cruel, and obdurate. He was just the man for such a place, and it was just the place for such a man. It afforded scope for the full exercise of all his powers, and he seemed to be perfectly at home in it. He was one of those who could torture the slightest look, word, or gesture, on the part of the slave, into impudence, and would treat it accordingly. There must be no answering back to him; no explanation was allowed a slave, showing himself to have been wrongfully accused. Mr. Gore acted fully up to the maxim laid down by slaveholders—"It is better that a dozen slaves should suffer under the lash, than that the overseer should be convicted, in the presence of the slaves, of having been at fault." No matter how innocent a slave might be—it availed him nothing, when accused by Mr. Gore of any misdemeanor. To be accused was to be convicted, and to be convicted was to be punished; the one always following the other with immutable certainty. To escape punishment was to escape accusation; and few slaves had the fortune to do either, under the overseership of Mr. Gore. He was just proud enough to demand the most debasing homage of the slave, and quite servile enough to crouch, himself, at the feet of the master. He was ambitious enough to be contented with nothing short of the highest rank of overseers, and persevering enough to reach the height of his ambition. He was cruel enough to inflict the severest punishment, artful enough to descend to the lowest trickery, and obdurate enough to be insensible to the voice of a reproving conscience. He was, of all the overseers, the most dreaded by the slaves. His presence was painful; his eye flashed confusion; and seldom was his sharp, shrill voice heard, without producing horror and trembling in their ranks.

Mr. Gore was a grave man, and, though a young man, he indulged in no jokes, said no funny words, seldom smiled. His words were in perfect keeping with his looks, and his looks were in perfect keeping with his words. Overseers will sometimes indulge in a witty word, even with the slaves; not so with Mr. Gore. He spoke but to command, and commanded but to be obeyed; he dealt sparingly with his words, and bountifully with his whip, never using the former where the latter would answer as well. When he whipped, he seemed to do so from a sense of duty, and feared no consequences. He did nothing reluctantly, no matter how disagreeable; always at his post, never inconsistent. He never promised but to fulfill. He was, in a word, a man of the most inflexible firmness and stone-like coolness.

His savage barbarity was equalled only by the consummate coolness with which he committed the grossest and most savage deeds upon the slaves under his charge. Mr. Gore once undertook to whip one of Colonel Lloyd's slaves, by the name of Demby. He had given Demby but few stripes, when, to get rid of the scourging, he ran and plunged himself into a creek, and stood there at the depth of his shoulders, refusing to come out. Mr. Gore told him that he would give him three calls, and that, if he did not come out at the third call, he would shoot him. The first call was given. Demby made no response, but stood his ground. The second and third calls were given with the same result. Mr. Gore then, without consultation or deliberation with anyone, not even giving Demby an additional call, raised his musket to his face, taking deadly aim at his standing victim, and in an instant poor Demby was no more. His mangled body sank out of sight, and blood and brains marked the water where he had stood.

A thrill of horror flashed through every soul upon the plantation, excepting Mr. Gore. He alone seemed cool and collected. He was asked by Colonel Lloyd and my old master, why he resorted to this extraordinary expedient. His reply was (as well as I can remember), that Demby had become unmanageable. He was setting a dangerous example to the other slaves—one which, if suffered to pass without some such demonstration on his part, would finally lead to the total subversion of all rule and order upon the plantation. He argued that if one slave refused to be corrected, and escaped with his life, the other slaves would soon copy the example; the result of which would be, the freedom of the slaves, and the enslavement of the whites. Mr. Gore's defence was satisfactory. He was continued in his station as overseer upon the home plantation. His fame as an overseer went abroad. His horrid crime was not even submitted to judicial investigation. It was committed in the presence of slaves, and they of course could neither institute a suit, nor testify against him; and thus the guilty perpetrator of one of the bloodiest and most foul murders goes unwhipped of justice, and uncensured by the community in which he lives. Mr. Gore lived in St. Michael's, Talbot County, Maryland, when I left there; and if he is still alive, he very probably lives there now; and if so, he is now, as he was then, as highly esteemed and as much respected as though his guilty soul had not been stained with his brother's blood.

I speak advisedly when I say this—that killing a slave, or any colored person, in Talbot County, Maryland, is not treated as a crime, either by the courts or the community. Mr. Thomas Lanman, of St. Michael's, killed two slaves, one of whom he killed with a hatchet, by knocking his brains out. He used to boast of the commission of the awful and bloody deed. I have heard him do so laughingly, saying, among other things, that he was the only benefactor of his country in the company, and that when others would do as much as he had done, we should be relieved of "the d——d niggers."

The wife of Mr. Giles Hicks, living but a short distance from where I used to live, murdered my wife's cousin, a young girl between fifteen and sixteen years of age, mangling her person in the most horrible manner, breaking her nose and breastbone with a stick, so that the poor girl expired in a few hours afterward. She was immediately buried, but had not been in her untimely grave but a few hours before she was taken up and examined by the coroner, who decided that she had come to her death by severe beating. The offence for which this girl was thus murdered was this—She had been set that night to mind Mrs. Hicks's baby, and during the night she fell asleep, and the baby cried. She, having lost her rest for several nights previous, did not hear the crying. They were both in the room with Mrs. Hicks. Mrs. Hicks, finding the girl slow to move, jumped from her bed, seized an oak stick of wood by the fireplace, and with it broke the girl's nose and breastbone, and thus ended her life. I will not say that this most horrid murder produced no sensation in the community. It did produce sensation, but not enough to bring the murderess to punishment. There was a warrant issued for her arrest, but it was never served. Thus she escaped not only punishment, but even the pain of being arraigned before a court for her horrid crime.

Whilst I am detailing bloody deeds which took place during my stay on Colonel Lloyd's plantation, I will briefly narrate another, which occurred about the same time as the murder of Demby by Mr. Gore.

Colonel Lloyd's slaves were in the habit of spending a part of their nights and Sundays in fishing for oysters, and in this way made up the deficiency of their scanty allowance. An old man belonging to Colonel Lloyd, while thus engaged, happened to get beyond the limits of Colonel Lloyd's, and on the premises of Mr. Beal Bondly. At this trespass, Mr. Bondly took offence, and with his musket came down to the shore, and blew its deadly contents into the poor old man.

Mr. Bondly came over to see Colonel Lloyd the next day, whether to pay him for his property, or to justify himself in what he had done, I know not. At any rate, this whole fiendish transaction was soon hushed up. There was very little said about it at all, and nothing done. It was a common saying, even among little white boys, that it was worth a half-cent to kill a "nigger," and a half-cent to bury one.

V

As to my own treatment while I lived on Colonel Lloyd's plantation, it was very similar to that of the other slave children. I was not old enough to work in the field, and there being little else than field work to do, I had a great deal of leisure time. The most I had to do was to drive up the cows at evening, keep the fowls out of the garden, keep the front yard clean, and run of errands for my old master's daughter, Mrs. Lucretia Auld. The most of my leisure time I spent in helping Master Daniel Lloyd in finding his birds, after he had shot them. My connection with Master Daniel was of some advantage to me. He became quite attached to me, and was a sort of protector of me. He would not allow the older boys to impose upon me, and would divide his cakes with me.

I was seldom whipped by my old master, and suffered little from anything else than hunger and cold. I suffered much from hunger, but much more from cold. In hottest summer and coldest winter, I was kept almost naked—no shoes, no stockings, no jacket, no trousers, nothing on but a coarse tow linen shirt, reaching only to my knees. I had no bed. I must have perished with cold, but that, the coldest nights, I used to steal a bag which was used for carrying corn to the mill. I would crawl into this bag, and there sleep on the cold, damp, clay floor, with my head in and feet out. My feet have been so cracked with the frost, that the pen with which I am writing might be laid in the gashes.

We were not regularly allowanced. Our food was coarse corn meal boiled. This was called *mush*. It was put into a large wooden tray or trough, and set down upon the ground. The children were then called, like so many pigs, and like so many pigs they would come and devour the mush; some with oyster shells, others with pieces of shingle, some with naked hands, and none with spoons. He that ate fastest got most; he that was strongest secured the best place; and few left the trough satisfied.

I was probably between seven and eight years old when I left Colonel Lloyd's plantation. I left it with joy. I shall never forget the ecstasy with which I received the intelligence that my old master (Anthony) had determined to let me go to Baltimore, to live with Mr. Hugh Auld, brother to my old master's son-in-law, Captain Thomas Auld. I received this information about three days before my departure. They were three of the happiest days I ever enjoyed. I spent the most part of all these three days in the creek, washing off the plantation scurf, and preparing myself for my departure.

The pride of appearance which this would indicate was not my own. I spent the time in washing, not so much because I wished to, but because Mrs. Lucretia had told me I must get all the dead skin off my feet and knees before I could go to Baltimore; for the people in Baltimore were very cleanly, and would laugh at me if I looked dirty. Besides, she was going to give me a pair of trousers, which I should not put on unless I got all the dirt off me. The thought of owning a pair of trousers was great indeed! It was almost a sufficient motive, not only to make me take off what would be called by pig drovers the mange, but the skin itself. I went at it in good earnest, working for the first time with the hope of reward.

The ties that ordinarily bind children to their homes were all suspended in my case. I found no severe trial in my departure. My home was charmless; it was not home to me; on parting from it, I could not feel that I was leaving anything which I could have enjoyed by staying. My mother was dead, my grandmother lived far off, so that I seldom saw her. I had two sisters and one brother, that lived in the same house with me; but the early separation of us from our mother had well nigh blotted the fact of our relationship from our memories. I looked for home elsewhere, and was confident of finding none which I should relish less than the one which I was leaving. If, however, I found in my new home hardship, hunger, whipping, and nakedness, I had the consolation that I should not have escaped any one of them by staying. Having already had more than a taste of them in the house of my old master, and having endured them there, I very naturally inferred my ability to endure them elsewhere, and especially at Baltimore; for I had something of the feeling about Baltimore that is expressed in the proverb, that "being hanged in England is preferable to dying a natural death in Ireland." I had the strongest desire to see Baltimore. Cousin Tom, though not fluent in speech, had inspired me with that desire by his eloquent description of the place. I could never point out anything at the Great House, no matter how beautiful or powerful, but that he had seen something at Baltimore far exceeding, both in beauty and strength, the object which I pointed out to him. Even the Great House itself, with all its pictures, was far inferior to many buildings in Baltimore. So strong was my desire, that I thought a gratification of it would fully compensate for whatever loss of comforts I should sustain by the exchange. I left without a regret, and with the highest hopes of future happiness.

We sailed out of Miles River for Baltimore on a Saturday morning. I remember only the day of the week, for at that time I had no knowledge of the days of the month, nor the months of the year. On setting sail, I walked aft, and gave to Colonel Lloyd's plantation what I hoped would be the last look. I then placed myself in the bows of the sloop, and there spent the remainder of the day in looking ahead, interesting myself in what was in the distance rather than in things nearby or behind.

In the afternoon of that day, we reached Annapolis, the capital of the State. We stopped but a few moments, so that I had no time to go on shore. It was the first large town that I had ever seen, and though it would look small compared with some of our New England factory villages, I thought it a wonderful place for its size—more imposing even than the Great House Farm!

We arrived at Baltimore early on Sunday morning, landing at Smith's Wharf, not far from Bowley's Wharf. We had on board the sloop a large flock of sheep; and after aiding in driving them to the slaughterhouse of Mr. Curtis on Louden Slater's Hill, I was conducted by Rich, one of the hands belonging on board of the sloop, to my new home in Alliciana Street, near Mr. Gardner's ship-yard, on Fells Point.

Mr. and Mrs. Auld were both at home, and met me at the door with their little son Thomas, to take care of whom I had been given. And here I saw what I had never seen before; it was a white face beaming with the most kindly emotions; it was the face of my new mistress, Sophia Auld. I wish I could describe the rapture that flashed through my soul as I beheld it. It was a new and strange sight to me, brightening up my pathway with the light of happiness. Little Thomas was told, there was his Freddy—and I was told to take care of little Thomas; and thus I entered upon the duties of my new home with the most cheering prospect ahead.

I look upon my departure from Colonel Lloyd's plantation as one of the most interesting events of my life. It is possible, and even quite probable, that but for the mere circumstance of being removed from that plantation to Baltimore, I should have today, instead of being here seated by my own table, in the enjoyment of freedom and the happiness of home, writing this Narrative, been confined in the galling chains of slavery. Going to live at Baltimore laid the foundation, and opened the gateway, to all my subsequent prosperity. I have ever regarded it as the first plain manifestation of that kind providence which has ever since attended me, and marked my life with so many favors. I regarded the selection of myself as being somewhat remarkable. There were a number of slave children that might have been sent from the plantation to Baltimore. There were those younger, those older, and those of the same age. I was chosen from among them all, and was the first, last, and only choice.

I may be deemed superstitious, and even egotistical, in regarding this event as a special interposition of divine Providence in my favor. But I should be false to the earliest sentiments of my soul, if I suppressed the opinion. I prefer to be true to myself, even at the hazard of incurring the ridicule of others, rather than to be false, and incur my own abhorrence. From my earliest recollection, I date the entertainment of a deep conviction that slavery would not always be able to hold me within its foul embrace; and in the darkest hours of my career in slavery, this living word of faith and spirit of hope departed not from me, but remained like ministering angels to cheer me through the gloom. This good spirit was from God, and to him I offer thanksgiving and praise.

VI

My new mistress proved to be all she appeared when I first met her at the door—a woman of the kindest heart and finest feelings. She had never had a slave under her control previously to myself, and prior to her marriage she had been dependent upon her own industry for a living. She was by trade a weaver; and by constant application to her business, she had been in a good degree preserved from the blighting and dehumanizing effects of slavery. I was utterly astonished at her goodness. I scarcely knew how to behave towards her. She was entirely unlike any other white woman I had ever seen. I could not approach her as I was accustomed to approach other white ladies. My early instruction was all out of place. The crouching servility, usually so acceptable a quality in a slave, did not answer when manifested toward her. Her favor was not gained by it; she seemed to be disturbed by it. She did not deem it impudent or unmannerly for a slave to look her in the face. The meanest slave was put fully at ease in her presence, and none left without feeling better for having seen her. Her face was made of heavenly smiles, and her voice of tranquil music.

But, alas! this kind heart had but a short time to remain such. The fatal poison of irresponsible power was already in her hands, and soon commenced its infernal work. That cheerful eye, under the influence of slavery, soon became red with rage; that voice, made all of sweet accord, changed to one of harsh and horrid discord; and that angelic face gave place to that of a demon.

Very soon after I went to live with Mr. and Mrs. Auld, she very kindly commenced to teach me the A, B, C. After I had learned this, she assisted me in learning to spell words of three or four letters. Just at this point of my progress, Mr. Auld found out what was going on, and at once forbade Mrs. Auld to instruct me further, telling her, among other things, that it was unlawful, as well as unsafe, to teach a slave to read. To use his own words, further, he said, "If you give a nigger an inch, he will take an ell. A nigger should know nothing but to obey his master—to do as he is told to do. Learning would *spoil* the best nigger in the world. Now," said he, "if you teach that nigger (speaking of myself) how to read, there would be no keeping him. It would forever unfit him to be a slave. He would at once become unmanageable, and of no value to his master. As to himself, it could do him no good, but a great deal of harm. It would make him discontented and unhappy." These words sank deep into my heart, stirred up sentiments within that lay slumbering, and called into existence an entirely new train of thought. It was a new and special revelation, explaining dark and mysterious things, with which my youthful understanding had struggled, but struggled in vain. I now understood what had been to me a most perplexing difficulty—to wit, the white man's power to enslave the black man. It was a grand achievement, and I prized it highly. From that moment, I understood the pathway from slavery to freedom. It was just what I wanted, and I got it at a time when I the least expected it. Whilst I was saddened by the thought of losing the aid of my kind mistress, I was gladdened by the invaluable instruction which, by the merest accident, I had gained from my master. Though conscious of the difficulty of learning without a teacher, I set out with high hope, and a fixed purpose, at whatever cost of trouble, to learn how to read. The very decided manner with which he spoke, and strove to impress his wife with the evil consequences of giving me instruction, served to convince me that he was deeply sensible of the truths he was uttering. It gave me the best assurance that I might rely with the utmost confidence on the results which, he said, would flow from teaching me to read. What he most dreaded, that I most desired. What he most loved, that I most hated. That which to him was a great evil, to be carefully shunned, was to me a great good, to be diligently sought; and the argument which he so warmly urged, against my learning to read, only served to inspire me with a desire and determination to learn. In learning to read, I owe almost as much to the bitter opposition of my master, as to the kindly aid of my mistress. I acknowledge the benefit of both.

I had resided but a short time in Baltimore before I observed a marked difference, in the treatment of slaves, from that which I had witnessed in the country. A city slave is almost a freeman, compared with a slave on the plantation. He is much better fed and clothed, and enjoys privileges altogether unknown to the slave on the plantation. There is a vestige of decency, a sense of shame, that does much to curb and check those outbreaks of atrocious cruelty so commonly enacted upon the plantation. He is a desperate slaveholder, who will shock the humanity of his nonslaveholding neighbors with the cries of his lacerated slave. Few are willing to incur the odium attaching to the reputation of being a cruel master; and above all things, they would not be known as not giving a slave enough to eat. Every city slaveholder is anxious to have it known of him, that he feeds his slaves well; and it is due to them to say, that most of them do give their slaves enough to eat. There are, however, some painful exceptions to this rule. Directly opposite to us, on Philpot Street, lived Mr. Thomas Hamilton. He owned two slaves. Their names were Henrietta and Mary. Henrietta was about twenty-two years of age, Mary was about fourteen; and of all the mangled and emaciated creatures I ever looked upon, these two were the most so. His heart must be harder than stone, that could look upon these unmoved. The head, neck, and shoulders of Mary were literally cut to pieces. I have frequently felt her head, and found it nearly covered with festering sores, caused by the lash of her cruel mistress. I do not know that her master ever whipped her, but I have been an eye-witness to the cruelty of Mrs. Hamilton. I used to be in Mr. Hamilton's house nearly every day. Mrs. Hamilton used to sit in a large chair in the middle of the room, with a heavy cowskin always by her side, and scarce an hour passed during the day but was marked by the blood of one of these slaves. The girls seldom passed her without her saying, "Move faster, you *black gip!*" at the same time giving them a blow with the cowskin over the head or shoulders, often drawing the blood. She would then say, "Take that, you *black gip!*"—continuing, "If you don't move faster, I'll move you!" Added to the cruel lashings to which these slaves were subjected, they were kept nearly half-starved. They seldom knew what it was to eat a full meal. I have seen Mary contending with the pigs for the offal thrown into the street. So much was Mary kicked and cut to pieces, that she was oftener called "*pecked*" than by her name.

VII

I lived in Master Hugh's family about seven years. During this time, I succeeded in learning to read and write. In accomplishing this, I was compelled to resort to various stratagems. I had no regular teacher. My mistress, who had kindly commenced to instruct me, had, in compliance with the advice and direction of her husband, not only ceased to instruct, but had set her face against my being instructed by anyone else. It is due, however, to my mistress to say of her, that she did not adopt this course of treatment immediately. She at first lacked the depravity indispensable to shutting me up in mental darkness. It was at least necessary for her to have some training in the exercise of irresponsible power, to make her equal to the task of treating me as though I were a brute.

My mistress was, as I have said, a kind and tender hearted woman; and in the simplicity of her soul she commenced, when I first went to live with her, to treat me as she supposed one human being ought to treat another. In entering upon the duties of a slaveholder, she did not seem to perceive that I sustained to her the relation of a mere chattel, and that for her to treat me as a human being was not only wrong, but dangerously so. Slavery proved as injurious to her as it did to me. When I went there, she was a pious, warm, and tender hearted woman. There was no sorrow or suffering for which she had not a tear. She had bread for the hungry, clothes for the naked, and comfort for every mourner that came within her reach. Slavery soon proved its ability to divest her of these heavenly qualities. Under its influence, the tender heart became stone, and the lamblike disposition gave way to one of tiger-like fierceness. The first step in her downward course was in her ceasing to instruct me. She now commenced to practise her husband's precepts. She finally became even more violent in her opposition than her husband himself. She was not satisfied with simply doing as well as he had commanded; she seemed anxious to do better. Nothing seemed to make her more angry than to see me with a newspaper. She seemed to think that here lay the danger. I have had her rush at me with a face made all up of fury, and snatch from me a newspaper, in a manner that fully revealed her apprehension. She was an apt woman; and a little experience soon demonstrated, to her satisfaction, that education and slavery were incompatible with each other.

From this time I was most narrowly watched. If I was in a separate room any considerable length of time, I was sure to be suspected of having a book, and was at once called to give an account of myself. All this, however, was too late. The first step had been taken. Mistress, in teaching me the alphabet, had given me the *inch*, and no precaution could prevent me from taking the *ell*.

The plan which I adopted, and the one by which I was most successful, was that of making friends of all the little white boys whom I met in the street. As many of these as I could, I converted into teachers. With their kindly aid, obtained at different times and in different places, I finally succeeded in learning to read. When I was sent on errands, I always took my book with me, and by doing one part of my errand quickly, I found time to get a lesson before my return. I used also to carry bread with me, enough of which was always in the house, and to which I was always welcome; for I was much better off in this regard than many of the poor white children in our neighborhood. This bread I used to bestow upon the hungry little urchins, who, in return, would give me that more valuable bread of knowledge. I am strongly tempted to give the names of two or three of those little boys, as a testimonial of the gratitude and affection I bear them; but prudence forbids—not that it would injure me, but it might embarrass them; for it is almost an unpardonable offence to teach slaves to read in this Christian country. It is enough to say of the dear little fellows, that they lived on Philpot Street, very near Durgin and Bailey's shipyard. I used to talk this matter of slavery over with them. I would sometimes say to them, I wished I could be as free as they would be when they got to be men. "You will be free as soon as you are twenty-one, *but I am a slave for life!* Have not I as good a right to be free as you have?" These words used to trouble them; they would express for me the liveliest sympathy, and console me with the hope that something would occur by which I might be free.

I was now about twelve years old, and the thought of being *a slave for life* began to bear heavily upon my heart. Just about this time, I got hold of a book entitled "The Columbian Orator." Every opportunity I got, I used to read this book. Among much of other interesting matter, I found in it a dialogue between a master and his slave. The slave was represented as having run away from his master three times. The dialogue represented the conversation which took place between them, when the slave was retaken the third time. In this dialogue, the whole argument in behalf of slavery was brought forward by the master, all of which was disposed of by the slave. The slave was made to say some very smart as well as impressive things in reply to his master—things which had the desired though unexpected effect; for the conversation resulted in the voluntary emancipation of the slave on the part of the master.

In the same book, I met with one of Sheridan's mighty speeches on and in behalf of Catholic emancipation. These were choice documents to me. I read them over and over again with unabated interest. They gave tongue to interesting thoughts of my own soul, which had frequently flashed through my mind, and died away for want of utterance. The moral which I gained from the dialogue was the power of truth over the conscience of even a slaveholder. What I got from Sheridan was a bold denunciation of slavery, and a powerful vindication of human rights. The reading of these documents enabled me to utter my thoughts, and to meet the arguments brought forward to sustain slavery; but while they relieved me of one difficulty, they brought on another even more painful than the one of which I was relieved. The more I read, the more I was led to abhor and detest my enslavers. I could regard them in no other light than a band of successful robbers, who had left their homes, and gone to Africa, and stolen us from our homes, and in a strange land reduced us to slavery. I loathed them as being the meanest as well as the most wicked of men. As I read and contemplated the subject, behold! that very discontentment which Master Hugh had predicted would follow my learning to read had already come, to torment and sting my soul to unutterable anguish. As I writhed under it, I would at times feel that learning to read had been a curse rather than a blessing. It had given me a view of my wretched condition, without the remedy. It opened my eyes to the horrible pit, but to no ladder upon which to get out. In moments of agony, I envied my fellow-slaves for their stupidity. I have often wished myself a beast. I preferred the condition of the meanest reptile to my own. Anything, no matter what, to get rid of thinking! It was this everlasting thinking of my condition that tormented me. There was no getting rid of it. It was pressed upon me by every object within sight or hearing, animate or inanimate. The silver trump of freedom had roused my soul to eternal wakefulness. Freedom now appeared, to disappear no more forever. It was heard in every sound, and seen in everything. It was ever present to torment me with a sense of my wretched condition. I saw nothing without seeing it, I heard nothing without hearing it, and felt nothing without feeling it. It looked from every star, it smiled in every calm, breathed in every wind, and moved in every storm.

I often found myself regretting my own existence, and wishing myself dead; and but for the hope of being free, I have no doubt but that I should have killed myself, or done something for which I should have been killed. While in this state of mind, I was eager to hear anyone speak of slavery. I was a ready listener. Every little while, I could hear something about the abolitionists. It was some time before I found what the word meant. It was always used in such connections as to make it an interesting word to me. If a slave ran away and succeeded in getting clear, or if a slave killed his master, set fire to a barn, or did anything very wrong in the mind of a slaveholder, it was spoken of as the fruit of *abolition*. Hearing the word in this connection very often, I set about learning what it meant. The dictionary afforded me little or no help. I found it was "the act of abolishing"; but then I did not know what was to be abolished. Here I was perplexed. I did not dare to ask anyone about its meaning, for I was satisfied that it was something they wanted me to know very little about. After a patient waiting, I got one of our city papers, containing an account of the number of petitions from the north, praying for the abolition of slavery in the District of Columbia, and of the slave trade between the States. From this time I understood the words *abolition* and *abolitionist*, and always drew near when that word was spoken, expecting to hear something of importance to myself and fellow-slaves. The light broke in upon me by degrees. I went one day down on the wharf of Mr. Waters; and seeing two Irishmen unloading a scow of stone, I went, unasked, and helped them. When we had finished, one of them came to me and asked me if I were a slave. I told him I was. He asked, "Are ye a slave for life?" I told him that I was. The good Irishman seemed to be deeply affected by the statement. He said to the other that it was a pity so fine a little fellow as myself should be a slave for life. He said it was a shame to hold me. They both advised me to run away to the north; that I should find friends there, and that I should be free. I pretended not to be interested in what they said, and treated them as if I did not understand them; for I feared they might be treacherous. White men have been known to encourage slaves to escape, and then, to get the reward, catch them and return them to their masters. I was afraid that these seemingly good men might use me so; but I nevertheless remembered their advice, and from that time I resolved to run away. I looked forward to a time at which it would be safe for me to escape. I was too young to think of doing so immediately; besides, I wished to learn how to write, as I might have occasion to write my own pass. I consoled myself with the hope that I should one day find a good chance. Meanwhile, I would learn to write.

The idea as to how I might learn to write was suggested to me by being in Durgin and Bailey's ship-yard, and frequently seeing the ship carpenters, after hewing, and getting a piece of timber ready for use, write on the timber the name of that part of the ship for which it was intended. When a piece of timber was intended for the larboard side, it would be marked thus—"L." When a piece was for the starboard side, it would be marked thus—"S." A piece for the larboard side forward, would be marked thus—"L. F." When a piece was for starboard side forward, it would be marked thus—"S. F." For larboard aft, it would be marked thus—"L. A." For starboard aft, it would be marked thus—"S. A." I soon learned the names of these letters, and for what they were intended when placed upon a piece of timber in the ship-yard. I immediately commenced copying them, and in a short time was able to make the four letters named. After that, when I met with any boy who I knew could write, I would tell him I could write as well as he. The next word would be, "I don't believe you. Let me see you try it." I would then make the letters which I had been so fortunate as to learn, and ask him to beat that. In this way I got a good many lessons in writing, which it is quite possible I should never have gotten in any other way. During this time, my copy-book was the board fence, brick wall, and pavement; my pen and ink was a lump of chalk. With these, I learned mainly how to write. I then commenced and continued copying the Italics in Webster's Spelling Book, until I could make them all without looking on the book. By this time, my little Master Thomas had gone to school, and learned how to write, and had written over a number of copy-books. These had been brought home, and shown to some of our near neighbors, and then laid aside. My mistress used to go to class meeting at the Wilk Street meeting-house every Monday afternoon, and leave me to take care of the house.

When left thus, I used to spend the time in writing in the spaces left in Master Thomas's copy-book, copying what he had written. I continued to do this until I could write a hand very similar to that of Master Thomas. Thus, after a long, tedious effort for years, I finally succeeded in learning how to write.

VIII

In a very short time after I went to live at Baltimore, my old master's youngest son Richard died; and in about three years and six months after his death, my old master, Captain Anthony, died, leaving only his son, Andrew, and daughter, Lucretia, to share his estate. He died while on a visit to see his daughter at Hillsborough. Cut off thus unexpectedly, he left no will as to the disposal of his property. It was therefore necessary to have a valuation of the property, that it might be equally divided between Mrs. Lucretia and Master Andrew. I was immediately sent for, to be valued with the other property. Here again my feelings rose up in detestation of slavery. I had now a new conception of my degraded condition. Prior to this, I had become, if not insensible to my lot, at least partly so. I left Baltimore with a young heart overborne with sadness, and a soul full of apprehension. I took passage with Captain Rowe, in the schooner Wild Cat, and, after a sail of about twenty-four hours, I found myself near the place of my birth. I had now been absent from it almost, if not quite, five years. I, however, remembered the place very well. I was only about five years old when I left it, to go and live with my old master on Colonel Lloyd's plantation; so that I was now between ten and eleven years old.

We were all ranked together at the valuation. Men and women, old and young, married and single, were ranked with horses, sheep, and swine. There were horses and men, cattle and women, pigs and children, all holding the same rank in the scale of being, and were all subjected to the same narrow examination. Silvery-headed age and sprightly youth, maids and matrons, had to undergo the same indelicate inspection. At this moment, I saw more clearly than ever the brutalizing effects of slavery upon both slave and slaveholder.

After the valuation, then came the division. I have no language to express the high excitement and deep anxiety which were felt among us poor slaves during this time. Our fate for life was now to be decided; we had no more voice in that decision than the brutes among whom we were ranked. A single word from the white men was enough—against all our wishes, prayers, and entreaties—to sunder forever the dearest friends, dearest kindred, and strongest ties known to human beings. In addition to the pain of separation, there was the horrid dread of falling into the hands of Master Andrew. He was known to us all as being a most cruel wretch—a common drunkard, who had, by his reckless mismanagement and profligate dissipation, already wasted a large portion of his father's property. We all felt that we might as well be sold at once to the Georgia traders, as to pass into his hands; for we knew that that would be our inevitable condition—a condition held by us all in the utmost horror and dread.

I suffered more anxiety than most of my fellow slaves. I had known what it was to be kindly treated; they had known nothing of the kind. They had seen little or nothing of the world. They were in very deed men and women of sorrow, and acquainted with grief. Their backs had been made familiar with the bloody lash, so that they had become callous; mine was yet tender; for while at Baltimore I got few whippings, and few slaves could boast of a kinder master and mistress than myself; and the thought of passing out of their hands into those of Master Andrew a man who, but a few days before, to give me a sample of his bloody disposition, took my little brother by the throat, threw him on the ground, and with the heel of his boot stamped upon his head till the blood gushed from his nose and ears—was well calculated to make me anxious as to my fate. After he had committed this savage outrage upon my brother, he turned to me, and said that was the way he meant to serve me one of these days—meaning, I suppose, when I came into his possession.

Thanks to a kind Providence, I fell to the portion of Mrs. Lucretia, and was sent immediately back to Baltimore, to live again in the family of Master Hugh. Their joy at my return equalled their sorrow at my departure. It was a glad day to me. I had escaped a worse than lion's jaws. I was absent from Baltimore, for the purpose of valuation and division, just about one month, and it seemed to have been six.

Very soon after my return to Baltimore, my mistress, Lucretia, died, leaving her husband and one child, Amanda; and in a very short time after her death, Master Andrew died. Now all the property of my old master, slaves included, was in the hands of strangers—strangers who had had nothing to do with accumulating it. Not a slave was left free. All remained slaves, from the youngest to the oldest. If any one thing in my experience, more than another, served to deepen my conviction of the infernal character of slavery, and to fill me with unutterable loathing of slaveholders, it was their base ingratitude to my poor old grandmother. She had served my old master faithfully from youth to old age. She had been the source of all his wealth; she had peopled his plantation with slaves; she had become a great grandmother in his service. She had rocked him in infancy, attended him in childhood, served him through life, and at his death wiped from his icy brow the cold death-sweat, and closed his eyes forever. She was nevertheless left a slave—a slave for life—a slave in the hands of strangers; and in their hands she saw her children, her grandchildren, and her great-grandchildren, divided, like so many sheep, without being gratified with the small privilege of a single word, as to their or her own destiny. And, to cap the climax of their base ingratitude and fiendish barbarity, my grandmother, who was now very old, having outlived my old master and all his children, having seen the beginning and end of all of them, and her present owners finding she was of but little value, her frame already racked with the pains of old age, and complete helplessness fast stealing over her once active limbs, they took her to the woods, built her a little hut, put up a little mud-chimney, and then made her welcome to the privilege of supporting herself there in perfect loneliness; thus virtually turning her out to die! If my poor old grandmother now lives, she lives to suffer in utter loneliness; she lives to remember and mourn over the loss of children, the loss of grandchildren, and the loss of great grandchildren. They are, in the language of the slave's poet, Whittier—

> Gone, gone, sold and gone
> To the rice swamp dank and lone,
> Where the slave-whip ceaseless swings,
> Where the noisome insect stings,
> Where the fever-demon strews
> Poison with the falling dews,
> Where the sickly sunbeams glare
> Through the hot and misty air—
>   Gone, gone, sold and gone
>   To the rice swamp dank and lone,
>   From Virginia hills and waters—
>   Woe is me, my stolen daughters!

The hearth is desolate. The children, the unconscious children, who once sang and danced in her presence, are gone. She gropes her way, in the darkness of age, for a drink of water. Instead of the voices of her children, she hears by day the moans of the dove, and by night the screams of the hideous owl. All is gloom. The grave is at the door. And now, when weighed down by the pains and aches of old age, when the head inclines to the feet, when the beginning and ending of human existence meet, and helpless infancy and painful old age combine together—at this time, this most needful time, the time for the exercise of that tenderness and affection which children only can exercise towards a declining parent—my poor old grandmother, the devoted mother of twelve children, is left all alone, in yonder little hut, before a few dim embers. She stands—she sits—she staggers—she falls—she groans—she dies—and there are none of her children or grandchildren present, to wipe from her wrinkled brow the cold sweat of death, or to place beneath the sod her fallen remains. Will not a righteous God visit for these things?

In about two years after the death of Mrs. Lucretia, Master Thomas married his second wife. Her name was Rowena Hamilton. She was the eldest daughter of Mr. William Hamilton. Master now lived in St. Michael's. Not long after his marriage, a misunderstanding took place between himself and Master Hugh; and as a means of punishing his brother, he took me from him to live with himself at St. Michael's. Here I underwent another most painful separation. It, however, was not so severe as the one I dreaded at the division of property; for, during this interval, a great change had taken place in Master Hugh and his once kind and affectionate wife. The influence of brandy upon him, and of slavery upon her, had effected a disastrous change in the characters of both; so that, as far as they were concerned, I thought I had little to lose by the change. But it was not to them that I was attached. It was to those little Baltimore boys that I felt the strongest attachment. I had received many good lessons from them, and was still receiving them, and the thought of leaving them was painful indeed. I was leaving, too, without the hope of ever being allowed to return. Master Thomas had said he would never let me return again. The barrier betwixt himself and brother he considered impassable.

I then had to regret that I did not at least make the attempt to carry out my resolution to run away; for the chances of success are tenfold greater from the city than from the country.

I sailed from Baltimore for St. Michael's in the sloop Amanda, Captain Edward Dodson. On my passage, I paid particular attention to the direction which the steamboats took to go to Philadelphia. I found, instead of going down, on reaching North Point they went up the bay, in a north-easterly direction. I deemed this knowledge of the utmost importance. My determination to run away was again revived. I resolved to wait only so long as the offering of a favorable opportunity. When that came, I was determined to be off.

IX

I have now reached a period of my life when I can give dates. I left Baltimore, and went to live with Master Thomas Auld, at St. Michael's, in March, 1832. It was now more than seven years since I lived with him in the family of my old master, on Colonel Lloyd's plantation. We of course were now almost entire strangers to each other. He was to me a new master, and I to him a new slave. I was ignorant of his temper and disposition; he was equally so of mine. A very short time, however, brought us into full acquaintance with each other. I was made acquainted with his wife not less than with himself. They were well matched, being equally mean and cruel. I was now, for the first time during a space of more than seven years, made to feel the painful gnawings of hunger—a something which I had not experienced before since I left Colonel Lloyd's plantation. It went hard enough with me then, when I could look back to no period at which I had enjoyed a sufficiency. It was tenfold harder after living in Master Hugh's family, where I had always had enough to eat, and of that which was good. I have said Master Thomas was a mean man. He was so. Not to give a slave enough to eat, is regarded as the most aggravated development of meanness even among slaveholders. The rule is, no matter how coarse the food, only let there be enough of it. This is the theory; and in the part of Maryland from which I came, it is the general practice—though there are many exceptions. Master Thomas gave us enough of neither coarse nor fine food. There were four slaves of us in the kitchen—my sister Eliza, my aunt Priscilla, Henny, and myself; and we were allowed less than a half of a bushel of corn-meal per week, and very little else, either in the shape of meat or vegetables. It was not enough for us to subsist upon. We were therefore reduced to the wretched necessity of living at the expense of our neighbors. This we did by begging and stealing, whichever came handy in the time of need, the one being considered as legitimate as the other. A great many times have we poor creatures been nearly perishing with hunger, when food in abundance lay mouldering in the safe and smokehouse, and our pious mistress was aware of the fact; and yet that mistress and her husband would kneel every morning, and pray that God would bless them in basket and store!

Bad as all slaveholders are, we seldom meet one destitute of every element of character commanding respect. My master was one of this rare sort. I do not know of one single noble act ever performed by him. The leading trait in his character was meanness; and if there were any other element in his nature, it was made subject to this. He was mean; and, like most other mean men, he lacked the ability to conceal his meanness. Captain Auld was not born a slaveholder. He had been a poor man, master only of a Bay craft. He came into possession of all his slaves by marriage; and of all men, adopted slaveholders are the worst. He was cruel, but cowardly. He commanded without firmness. In the enforcement of his rules, he was at times rigid, and at times lax. At times, he spoke to his slaves with the firmness of Napoleon and the fury of a demon; at other times, he might well be mistaken for an inquirer who had lost his way. He did nothing of himself. He might have passed for a lion, but for his ears. In all things noble which he attempted, his own meanness shone most conspicuous. His airs, words, and actions, were the airs, words, and actions of born slaveholders, and, being assumed, were awkward enough. He was not even a good imitator. He possessed all the disposition to deceive, but wanted the power. Having no resources within himself, he was compelled to be the copyist of many, and being such, he was forever the victim of inconsistency; and of consequence he was an object of contempt, and was held as such even by his slaves. The luxury of having slaves of his own to wait upon him was something new and unprepared for. He was a slaveholder without the ability to hold slaves. He found himself incapable of managing his slaves either by force, fear, or fraud. We seldom called him "master"; we generally called him "Captain Auld," and were hardly disposed to title him at all. I doubt not that our conduct had much to do with making him appear awkward, and of consequence fretful. Our want of reverence for him must have perplexed him greatly. He wished to have us call him master, but lacked the firmness necessary to command us to do so. His wife used to insist upon our calling him so, but to no purpose. In August, 1832, my master attended a Methodist camp-meeting held in the Bay-side, Talbot County, and there experienced religion. I indulged a faint hope that his conversion would lead him to emancipate his slaves, and that, if he did not do this, it would, at any rate, make him more kind and humane. I was disappointed in both these respects. It neither made him to be humane to his slaves, nor to emancipate them. If it had any effect on his character, it made him more cruel and hateful in all his ways; for I believe him to have been a much worse man after his conversion than before. Prior to his conversion, he relied upon his own depravity to shield and sustain him in his savage barbarity; but after his conversion, he found religious sanction and support for his slaveholding cruelty. He made the greatest pretensions to piety. His house was the house of prayer. He prayed morning, noon, and night. He very soon distinguished himself among his brethren, and was soon made a class-leader and exhorter. His activity in revivals was great, and he proved himself an instrument in the hands of the church in converting many souls. His house was the preachers' home. They used to take great pleasure in coming there to put up; for while he starved us, he stuffed them. We have had three or four preachers there at a time. The names of those who used to come most frequently while I lived there, were Mr. Storks, Mr. Ewery, Mr. Humphry, and Mr. Hickey. I have also seen Mr. George Cookman at our house. We slaves loved Mr. Cookman. We believed him to be a good man. We thought him instrumental in getting Mr. Samuel Harrison, a very rich slaveholder, to emancipate his slaves; and by some means got the impression that he was laboring to effect the emancipation of all the slaves. When he was at our house, we were sure to be called in to prayers. When the others were there, we were sometimes called in and sometimes not. Mr. Cookman took more notice of us than either of the other ministers. He could not come among us without betraying his sympathy for us, and, stupid as we were, we had the sagacity to see it.

While I lived with my master in St. Michael's, there was a white young man, a Mr. Wilson, who proposed to keep a Sabbath school for the instruction of such slaves as might be disposed to learn to read the New Testament. We met but three times, when Mr. West and Mr. Fairbanks, both class-leaders, with many others, came upon us with sticks and other missiles, drove us off, and forbade us to meet again. Thus ended our little Sabbath school in the pious town of St. Michael's.

I have said my master found religious sanction for his cruelty. As an example, I will state one of many facts going to prove the charge. I have seen him tie up a lame young woman, and whip her with a heavy cowskin upon her naked shoulders, causing the warm red blood to drip; and, in justification of the bloody deed, he would quote this passage of Scripture—"He that knoweth his master's will, and doeth it not, shall be beaten with many stripes."

Master would keep this lacerated young woman tied up in this horrid situation four or five hours at a time. I have known him to tie her up early in the morning, and whip her before breakfast; leave her, go to his store, return at dinner, and whip her again, cutting her in the places already made raw with his cruel lash. The secret of master's cruelty toward "Henny" is found in the fact of her being almost helpless. When quite a child, she fell into the fire, and burned herself horribly. Her hands were so burnt that she never got the use of them. She could do very little but bear heavy burdens. She was to master a bill of expense; and as he was a mean man, she was a constant offence to him. He seemed desirous of getting the poor girl out of existence. He gave her away once to his sister; but, being a poor gift, she was not disposed to keep her. Finally, my benevolent master, to use his own words, "set her adrift to take care of herself." Here was a recently-converted man, holding on upon the mother, and at the same time turning out her helpless child, to starve and die! Master Thomas was one of the many pious slaveholders who hold slaves for the very charitable purpose of taking care of them.

My master and myself had quite a number of differences. He found me unsuitable to his purpose. My city life, he said, had had a very pernicious effect upon me. It had almost ruined me for every good purpose, and fitted me for everything which was bad. One of my greatest faults was that of letting his horse run away, and go down to his father-in law's farm, which was about five miles from St. Michael's. I would then have to go after it. My reason for this kind of carelessness, or carefulness, was, that I could always get something to eat when I went there. Master William Hamilton, my master's father-in-law, always gave his slaves enough to eat. I never left there hungry, no matter how great the need of my speedy return. Master Thomas at length said he would stand it no longer. I had lived with him nine months, during which time he had given me a number of severe whippings, all to no good purpose. He resolved to put me out, as he said, to be broken; and, for this purpose, he let me for one year to a man named Edward Covey. Mr. Covey was a poor man, a farm-renter. He rented the place upon which he lived, as also the hands with which he tilled it. Mr. Covey had acquired a very high reputation for breaking young slaves, and this reputation was of immense value to him. It enabled him to get his farm tilled with much less expense to himself than he could have had it done without such a reputation. Some slaveholders thought it not much loss to allow Mr. Covey to have their slaves one year, for the sake of the training to which they were subjected, without any other compensation. He could hire young help with great ease, in consequence of this reputation. Added to the natural good qualities of Mr. Covey, he was a professor of religion—a pious soul—a member and a class-leader in the Methodist church. All of this added weight to his reputation as a "nigger-breaker." I was aware of all the facts, having been made acquainted with them by a young man who had lived there. I nevertheless made the change gladly; for I was sure of getting enough to eat, which is not the smallest consideration to a hungry man.

X

I had left Master Thomas's house, and went to live with Mr. Covey, on the 1st of January, 1833. I was now, for the first time in my life, a field hand. In my new employment, I found myself even more awkward than a country boy appeared to be in a large city. I had been at my new home but one week before Mr. Covey gave me a very severe whipping, cutting my back, causing the blood to run, and raising ridges on my flesh as large as my little finger. The details of this affair are as follows: Mr. Covey sent me, very early in the morning of one of our coldest days in the month of January, to the woods, to get a load of wood. He gave me a team of unbroken oxen. He told me which was the in-hand ox, and which the off-hand one. He then tied the end of a large rope around the horns of the in-hand ox, and gave me the other end of it, and told me, if the oxen started to run, that I must hold on upon the rope. I had never driven oxen before, and of course I was very awkward. I, however, succeeded in getting to the edge of the woods with little difficulty; but I had got a very few rods into the woods, when the oxen took fright, and started full tilt, carrying the cart against trees, and over stumps, in the most frightful manner. I expected every moment that my brains would be dashed out against the trees. After running thus for a considerable distance, they finally upset the cart, dashing it with great force against a tree, and threw themselves into a dense thicket. How I escaped death, I do not know. There I was, entirely alone, in a thick wood, in a place new to me. My cart was upset and shattered, my oxen were entangled among the young trees, and there was none to help me. After a long spell of effort, I succeeded in getting my cart righted, my oxen disentangled, and again yoked to the cart. I now proceeded with my team to the place where I had, the day before, been chopping wood, and loaded my cart pretty heavily, thinking in this way to tame my oxen. I then proceeded on my way home. I had now consumed one half of the day. I got out of the woods safely, and now felt out of danger. I stopped my oxen to open the woods gate; and just as I did so, before I could get hold of my ox-rope, the oxen again started, rushed through the gate, catching it between the wheel and the body of the cart, tearing it to pieces, and coming within a few inches of crushing me against the gate-post. Thus twice, in one short day, I escaped death by the merest chance. On my return, I told Mr. Covey what had happened, and how it happened. He ordered me to return to the woods again immediately. I did so, and he followed on after me. Just as I got into the woods, he came up and told me to stop my cart, and that he would teach me how to trifle away my time, and break gates. He then went to a large gum-tree, and with his axe cut three large switches, and, after trimming them up neatly with his pocket knife, he ordered me to take off my clothes. I made him no answer, but stood with my clothes on. He repeated his order. I still made him no answer, nor did I move to strip myself. Upon this he rushed at me with the fierceness of a tiger, tore off my clothes, and lashed me till he had worn out his switches, cutting me so savagely as to leave the marks visible for a long time after. This whipping was the first of a number just like it, and for similar offences.

I lived with Mr. Covey one year. During the first six months, of that year, scarce a week passed without his whipping me. I was seldom free from a sore back. My awkwardness was almost always his excuse for whipping me. We were worked fully up to the point of endurance. Long before day we were up, our horses fed, and by the first approach of day we were off to the field with our hoes and ploughing teams. Mr. Covey gave us enough to eat, but scarce time to eat it. We were often less than five minutes taking our meals. We were often in the field from the first approach of day till its last lingering ray had left us; and at saving-fodder time, midnight often caught us in the field binding blades.

Covey would be out with us. The way he used to stand it, was this. He would spend the most of his afternoons in bed. He would then come out fresh in the evening, ready to urge us on with his words, example, and frequently with the whip. Mr. Covey was one of the few slaveholders who could and did work with his hands. He was a hard-working man. He knew by himself just what a man or a boy could do. There was no deceiving him. His work went on in his absence almost as well as in his presence; and he had the faculty of making us feel that he was ever present with us. This he did by surprising us. He seldom approached the spot where we were at work openly, if he could do it secretly. He always aimed at taking us by surprise. Such was his cunning, that we used to call him, among ourselves, "the snake." When we were at work in the cornfield, he would sometimes crawl on his hands and knees to avoid detection, and all at once he would rise nearly in our midst, and scream out, "Ha, ha! Come, come! Dash on, dash on!" This being his mode of attack, it was never safe to stop a single minute. His comings were like a thief in the night. He appeared to us as being ever at hand. He was under every tree, behind every stump, in every bush, and at every window, on the plantation. He would sometimes mount his horse, as if bound to St. Michael's, a distance of seven miles, and in half an hour afterwards you would see him coiled up in the corner of the wood-fence, watching every motion of the slaves. He would, for this purpose, leave his horse tied up in the woods. Again, he would sometimes walk up to us, and give us orders as though he was upon the point of starting on a long journey, turn his back upon us, and make as though he was going to the house to get ready; and, before he would get half way thither, he would turn short and crawl into a fence-corner, or behind some tree, and there watch us till the going down of the sun.

Mr. Covey's *forte* consisted in his power to deceive. His life was devoted to planning and perpetrating the grossest deceptions. Everything he possessed in the shape of learning or religion, he made conform to his disposition to deceive. He seemed to think himself equal to deceiving the Almighty. He would make a short prayer in the morning, and a long prayer at night; and, strange as it may seem, few men would at times appear more devotional than he. The exercises of his family devotions were always commenced with singing; and, as he was a very poor singer himself, the duty of raising the hymn generally came upon me. He would read his hymn, and nod at me to commence. I would at times do so; at others, I would not. My non-compliance would almost always produce much confusion. To show himself independent of me, he would start and stagger through with his hymn in the most discordant manner. In this state of mind, he prayed with more than ordinary spirit. Poor man! such was his disposition, and success at deceiving, I do verily believe that he sometimes deceived himself into the solemn belief, that he was a sincere worshipper of the most high God; and this, too, at a time when he may be said to have been guilty of compelling his woman slave to commit the sin of adultery. The facts in the case are these: Mr. Covey was a poor man; he was just commencing in life; he was only able to buy one slave; and, shocking as is the fact, he bought her, as he said, for a *breeder*. This woman was named Caroline. Mr. Covey bought her from Mr. Thomas Lowe, about six miles from St. Michael's. She was a large, able-bodied woman, about twenty years old. She had already given birth to one child, which proved her to be just what he wanted. After buying her, he hired a married man of Mr. Samuel Harrison, to live with him one year; and him he used to fasten up with her every night! The result was, that, at the end of the year, the miserable woman gave birth to twins. At this result Mr. Covey seemed to be highly pleased, both with the man and the wretched woman. Such was his joy, and that of his wife, that nothing they could do for Caroline during her confinement was too good, or too hard, to be done. The children were regarded as being quite an addition to his wealth.

If at any one time of my life more than another, I was made to drink the bitterest dregs of slavery, that time was during the first six months of my stay with Mr. Covey. We were worked in all weathers. It was never too hot or too cold; it could never rain, blow, hail, or snow, too hard for us to work in the field. Work, work, work, was scarcely more the order of the day than of the night. The longest days were too short for him, and the shortest nights too long for him. I was somewhat unmanageable when I first went there, but a few months of this discipline tamed me. Mr. Covey succeeded in breaking me. I was broken in body, soul, and spirit. My natural elasticity was crushed, my intellect languished, the disposition to read departed, the cheerful spark that lingered about my eye died; the dark night of slavery closed in upon me; and behold a man transformed into a brute!

Sunday was my only leisure time. I spent this in a sort of beast-like stupor, between sleep and wake, under some large tree. At times I would rise up, a flash of energetic freedom would dart through my soul, accompanied with a faint beam of hope, that flickered for a moment, and then vanished. I sank down again, mourning over my wretched condition. I was sometimes prompted to take my life, and that of Covey, but was prevented by a combination of hope and fear. My sufferings on this plantation seem now like a dream rather than a stern reality.

Our house stood within a few rods of the Chesapeake Bay, whose broad bosom was ever white with sails from every quarter of the habitable globe. Those beautiful vessels, robed in purest white, so delightful to the eye of freemen, were to me so many shrouded ghosts, to terrify and torment me with thoughts of my wretched condition. I have of ten, in the deep stillness of a summer's Sabbath, stood all alone upon the lofty banks of that noble bay, and traced, with saddened heart and tearful eye, the countless number of sails moving off to the mighty ocean. The sight of these always affected me powerfully. My thoughts would compel utterance; and there, with no audience but the Almighty, I would pour out my soul's complaint, in my rude way, with an apostrophe to the moving multitude of ships:

"You are loosed from your moorings, and are free; I am fast in my chains, and am a slave! You move merrily before the gentle gale, and I sadly before the bloody whip! You are freedom's swift-winged angels, that fly round the world; I am confined in bands of iron! O that I were free! O, that I were on one of your gallant decks, and under your protecting wing! Alas! betwixt me and you, the turbid waters roll. Go on, go on. O that I could also go! Could I but swim! If I could fly! O, why was I born a man, of whom to make a brute! The glad ship is gone; she hides in the dim distance. I am left in the hottest hell of unending slavery. O God, save me! God, deliver me! Let me be free! Is there any God? Why am I a slave? I will run away. I will not stand it. Get caught, or get clear, I'll try it. I had as well die with ague as the fever. I have only one life to lose. I had as well be killed running as die standing. Only think of it; one hundred miles straight north, and I am free! Try it? Yes! God helping me, I will. It cannot be that I shall live and die a slave. I will take to the water. This very bay shall yet bear me into freedom. The steamboats steered in a north-east course from North Point. I will do the same; and when I get to the head of the bay, I will turn my canoe adrift, and walk straight through Delaware into Pennsylvania. When I get there, I shall not be required to have a pass; I can travel without being disturbed. Let but the first opportunity offer, and, come what will, I am off. Meanwhile, I will try to bear up under the yoke. I am not the only slave in the world. Why should I fret? I can bear as much as any of them. Besides, I am but a boy, and all boys are bound to someone. It may be that my misery in slavery will only increase my happiness when I get free. There is a better day coming."

Thus I used to think, and thus I used to speak to myself; goaded almost to madness at one moment, and at the next reconciling myself to my wretched lot.

I have already intimated that my condition was much worse, during the first six months of my stay at Mr. Covey's, than in the last six. The circumstances leading to the change in Mr. Covey's course toward me form an epoch in my humble history. You have seen how a man was made a slave; you shall see how a slave was made a man. On one of the hottest days of the month of August, 1833, Bill Smith, William Hughes, a slave named Eli, and myself, were engaged in fanning wheat. Hughes was clearing the fanned wheat from before the fan. Eli was turning, Smith was feeding, and I was carrying wheat to the fan. The work was simple, requiring strength rather than intellect; yet, to one entirely unused to such work, it came very hard. About three o'clock of that day, I broke down; my strength failed me; I was seized with a violent aching of the head, attended with extreme dizziness; I trembled in every limb. Finding what was coming, I nerved myself up, feeling it would never do to stop work. I stood as long as I could stagger to the hopper with grain. When I could stand no longer, I fell, and felt as if held down by an immense weight. The fan of course stopped; everyone had his own work to do; and no one could do the work of the other, and have his own go on at the same time.

Mr. Covey was at the house, about one hundred yards from the treading-yard where we were fanning. On hearing the fan stop, he left immediately, and came to the spot where we were. He hastily inquired what the matter was. Bill answered that I was sick, and there was no one to bring wheat to the fan. I had by this time crawled away under the side of the post and rail-fence by which the yard was enclosed, hoping to find relief by getting out of the sun. He then asked where I was. He was told by one of the hands. He came to the spot, and, after looking at me awhile, asked me what was the matter. I told him as well as I could, for I scarce had strength to speak. He then gave me a savage kick in the side, and told me to get up. I tried to do so, but fell back in the attempt. He gave me another kick, and again told me to rise. I again tried, and succeeded in gaining my feet; but, stooping to get the tub with which I was feeding the fan, I again staggered and fell. While down in this situation, Mr. Covey took up the hickory slat with which Hughes had been striking off the half-bushel measure, and with it gave me a heavy blow upon the head, making a large wound, and the blood ran freely; and with this again told me to get up. I made no effort to comply, having now made up my mind to let him do his worst. In a short time after receiving this blow, my head grew better. Mr. Covey had now left me to my fate. At this moment I resolved, for the first time, to go to my master, enter a complaint, and ask his protection. In order to do this, I must that afternoon walk seven miles; and this, under the circumstances, was truly a severe undertaking. I was exceedingly feeble; made so as much by the kicks and blows which I received, as by the severe fit of sickness to which I had been subjected. I, however, watched my chance, while Covey was looking in an opposite direction, and started for St. Michael's. I succeeded in getting a considerable distance on my way to the woods, when Covey discovered me, and called after me to come back, threatening what he would do if I did not come. I disregarded both his calls and his threats, and made my way to the woods as fast as my feeble state would allow; and thinking I might be overhauled by him if I kept the road, I walked through the woods, keeping far enough from the road to avoid detection, and near enough to prevent losing my way. I had not gone far before my little strength again failed me. I could go no farther. I fell down, and lay for a considerable time. The blood was yet oozing from the wound on my head. For a time I thought I should bleed to death; and think now that I should have done so, but that the blood so matted my hair as to stop the wound. After lying there about three quarters of an hour, I nerved myself up again, and started on my way, through bogs and briers, barefooted and bareheaded, tearing my feet sometimes at nearly every step; and after a journey of about seven miles, occupying some five hours to perform it, I arrived at master's store. I then presented an appearance enough to affect any but a heart of iron. From the crown of my head to my feet, I was covered with blood. My hair was all clotted with dust and blood; my shirt was stiff with blood. I suppose I looked like a man who had escaped a den of wild beasts, and barely escaped them. In this state I appeared before my master, humbly entreating him to interpose his authority for my protection. I told him all the circumstances as well as I could, and it seemed, as I spoke, at times to affect him. He would then walk the floor, and seek to justify Covey by saying he expected I deserved it. He asked me what I wanted. I told him, to let me get a new home; that as sure as I lived with Mr. Covey again, I should live with but to die with him; that Covey would surely kill me; he was in a fair way for it. Master Thomas ridiculed the idea that there was any danger of Mr. Covey's killing me, and said that he knew Mr. Covey; that he was a good man, and that he could not think of taking me from him; that, should he do so, he would lose the whole year's wages; that I belonged to Mr. Covey for one year, and that I must go back to him, come what might; and that I must not trouble him with any more stories, or that he would himself *get hold of me.* After threatening me thus, he gave me a very large dose of salts, telling me that I might remain in St. Michael's that night (it being quite late), but that I must be off back to Mr. Covey's early in the morning; and that if I did not, he would *get hold of me*, which meant that he would whip me. I remained all night, and, according to his orders, I started off to Covey's in the morning (Saturday morning), wearied in body and broken in spirit. I got no supper that night, or breakfast that morning. I reached Covey's about nine o'clock; and just as I was getting over the fence that divided Mrs. Kemp's fields from ours, out ran Covey with his cowskin, to give me another whipping. Before he could reach me, I succeeded in getting to the cornfield; and as the corn was very high, it afforded me the means of hiding. He seemed very angry, and searched for me a long time. My behavior was altogether unaccountable. He finally gave up the chase, thinking, I suppose, that I must come home for something to eat; he would give himself no further trouble in looking for me. I spent that day mostly in the woods, having the alternative before me—to go home and be whipped to death, or stay in the woods and be starved to death. That night, I fell in with Sandy Jenkins, a slave with whom I was somewhat acquainted. Sandy had a free wife who lived about four miles from Mr. Covey's; and it being Saturday, he was on his way to see her. I told him my circumstances, and he very kindly invited me to go home with him. I went home with him, and talked this whole matter over, and got his advice as to what course it was best for me to pursue. I found Sandy an old adviser. He told me, with great solemnity, I must go back to Covey; but that before I went, I must go with him into another part of the woods, where there was a certain *root*, which, if I would take some of it with me, carrying it *always on my right side*, would render it impossible for Mr. Covey, or any other white man, to whip me. He said he had carried it for years; and since he had done so, he had never received a blow, and never expected to while he carried it. I at first rejected the idea, that the simple carrying of a root in my pocket would have any such effect as he had said, and was not disposed to take it; but Sandy impressed the necessity with much earnestness, telling me it could do no harm, if it did no good. To please him, I at length took the root, and, according to his direction, carried it upon my right side. This was Sunday morning. I immediately started for home; and upon entering the yard gate, out came Mr. Covey on his way to meeting. He spoke to me very kindly, bade me drive the pigs from a lot nearby, and passed on towards the church. Now, this singular conduct of Mr. Covey really made me begin to think that there was something in the *root* which Sandy had given me; and had it been on any other day than Sunday, I could have attributed the conduct to no other cause than the influence of that root; and as it was, I was half inclined to think the *root* to be something more than I at first had taken it to be. All went well till Monday morning. On this morning, the virtue of the *root* was fully tested. Long before daylight, I was called to go and rub, curry, and feed, the horses. I obeyed, and was glad to obey. But whilst thus engaged, whilst in the act of throwing down some blades from the loft, Mr. Covey entered the stable with a long rope; and just as I was half out of the loft, he caught hold of my legs, and was about tying me. As soon as I found what he was up to, I gave a sudden spring, and as I did so, he holding to my legs, I was brought sprawling on the stable floor. Mr. Covey seemed now to think he had me, and could do what he pleased; but at this moment—from whence came the spirit I don't know—I resolved to fight; and, suiting my action to the resolution, I seized Covey hard by the throat; and as I did so, I rose. He held on to me, and I to him. My resistance was so entirely unexpected that Covey seemed taken all aback. He trembled like a leaf. This gave me assurance, and I held him uneasy, causing the blood to run where I touched him with the ends of my fingers. Mr. Covey soon called out to Hughes for help. Hughes came, and, while Covey held me, attempted to tie my right hand. While he was in the act of doing so, I watched my chance, and gave him a heavy kick close under the ribs. This kick fairly sickened Hughes, so that he left me in the hands of Mr. Covey. This kick had the effect of not only weakening Hughes, but Covey also. When he saw Hughes bending over with pain, his courage quailed. He asked me if I meant to persist in my resistance. I told him I did, come what might; that he had used me like a brute for six months, and that I was determined to be used so no longer. With that, he strove to drag me to a stick that was lying just out of the stable door. He meant to knock me down. But just as he was leaning over to get the stick, I seized him with both hands by his collar, and brought him by a sudden snatch to the ground. By this time, Bill came. Covey called upon him for assistance. Bill wanted to know what he could do. Covey said, "Take hold of him, take hold of him!" Bill said his master hired him out to work, and not to help to whip me; so he left Covey and myself to fight our own battle out. We were at it for nearly two hours. Covey at length let me go, puffing and blowing at a great rate, saying that if I had not resisted, he would not have whipped me half so much. The truth was, that he had not whipped me at all. I considered him as getting entirely the worst end of the bargain; for he had drawn no blood from me, but I had from him. The whole six months afterwards, that I spent with Mr. Covey, he never laid the weight of his finger upon me in anger. He would occasionally say, he didn't want to get hold of me again. "No," thought I, "you need not; for you will come off worse than you did before."

This battle with Mr. Covey was the turning point in my career as a slave. It rekindled the few expiring embers of freedom, and revived within me a sense of my own manhood. It recalled the departed self-confidence, and inspired me again with a determination to be free. The gratification afforded by the triumph was a full compensation for whatever else might follow, even death itself. He only can understand the deep satisfaction which I experienced, who has himself repelled by force the bloody arm of slavery. I felt as I never felt before. It was a glorious resurrection, from the tomb of slavery, to the heaven of freedom. My long-crushed spirit rose, cowardice departed, bold defiance took its place; and I now resolved that, however long I might remain a slave in form, the day had passed forever when I could be a slave in fact. I did not hesitate to let it be known of me, that the white man who expected to succeed in whipping, must also succeed in killing me.

From this time I was never again what might be called fairly whipped, though I remained a slave four years afterwards. I had several fights, but was never whipped.

It was for a long time a matter of surprise to me why Mr. Covey did not immediately have me taken by the constable to the whipping-post, and there regularly whipped for the crime of raising my hand against a white man in defence of myself. And the only explanation I can now think of does not entirely satisfy me; but such as it is, I will give it. Mr. Covey enjoyed the most unbounded reputation for being a first-rate overseer and negro-breaker. It was of considerable importance to him. That reputation was at stake; and had he sent me—a boy about sixteen years old—to the public whipping-post, his reputation would have been lost; so, to save his reputation, he suffered me to go unpunished.

My term of actual service to Mr. Edward Covey ended on Christmas day, 1833. The days between Christmas and New Year's day are allowed as holidays; and, accordingly, we were not required to perform any labor, more than to feed and take care of the stock. This time we regarded as our own, by the grace of our masters; and we therefore used or abused it nearly as we pleased. Those of us who had families at a distance, were generally allowed to spend the whole six days in their society. This time, however, was spent in various ways. The staid, sober, thinking and industrious ones of our number would employ themselves in making corn-brooms, mats, horse-collars, and baskets; and another class of us would spend the time in hunting opossums, hares, and coons. But by far the larger part engaged in such sports and merriments as playing ball, wrestling, running foot-races, fiddling, dancing, and drinking whisky; and this latter mode of spending the time was by far the most agreeable to the feelings of our masters. A slave who would work during the holidays was considered by our masters as scarcely deserving them. He was regarded as one who rejected the favor of his master. It was deemed a disgrace not to get drunk at Christmas; and he was regarded as lazy indeed, who had not provided himself with the necessary means, during the year, to get whisky enough to last him through Christmas.

From what I know of the effect of these holidays upon the slave, I believe them to be among the most effective means in the hands of the slaveholder in keeping down the spirit of insurrection. Were the slaveholders at once to abandon this practice, I have not the slightest doubt it would lead to an immediate insurrection among the slaves. These holidays serve as conductors, or safety-valves, to carry off the rebellious spirit of enslaved humanity. But for these, the slave would be forced up to the wildest desperation; and woe betide the slaveholder, the day he ventures to remove or hinder the operation of those conductors! I warn him that, in such an event, a spirit will go forth in their midst, more to be dreaded than the most appalling earthquake.

The holidays are part and parcel of the gross fraud, wrong, and inhumanity of slavery. They are professedly a custom established by the benevolence of the slaveholders; but I undertake to say, it is the result of selfishness, and one of the grossest frauds committed upon the down-trodden slave. They do not give the slaves this time because they would not like to have their work during its continuance, but because they know it would be unsafe to deprive them of it. This will be seen by the fact, that the slaveholders like to have their slaves spend those days just in such a manner as to make them as glad of their ending as of their beginning. Their object seems to be, to disgust their slaves with freedom, by plunging them into the lowest depths of dissipation. For instance, the slaveholders not only like to see the slave drink of his own accord, but will adopt various plans to make him drunk. One plan is, to make bets on their slaves, as to who can drink the most whisky without getting drunk; and in this way they succeed in getting whole multitudes to drink to excess. Thus, when the slave asks for virtuous freedom, the cunning slaveholder, knowing his ignorance, cheats him with a dose of vicious dissipation, artfully labelled with the name of liberty. The most of us used to drink it down, and the result was just what might be supposed; many of us were led to think that there was little to choose between liberty and slavery. We felt, and very properly too, that we had almost as well be slaves to man as to rum. So, when the holidays ended, we staggered up from the filth of our wallowing, took a long breath, and marched to the field—feeling, upon the whole, rather glad to go, from what our master had deceived us into a belief was freedom, back to the arms of slavery.

I have said that this mode of treatment is a part of the whole system of fraud and inhumanity of slavery. It is so. The mode here adopted to disgust the slave with freedom, by allowing him to see only the abuse of it, is carried out in other things. For instance, a slave loves molasses; he steals some. His master, in many cases, goes off to town, and buys a large quantity; he returns, takes his whip, and commands the slave to eat the molasses, until the poor fellow is made sick at the very mention of it. The same mode is sometimes adopted to make the slaves refrain from asking for more food than their regular allowance. A slave runs through his allowance, and applies for more. His master is enraged at him; but, not willing to send him off without food, gives him more than is necessary, and compels him to eat it within a given time. Then, if he complains that he cannot eat it, he is said to be satisfied neither full nor fasting, and is whipped for being hard to please! I have an abundance of such illustrations of the same principle, drawn from my own observation, but think the cases I have cited sufficient. The practice is a very common one.

On the first of January, 1834, I left Mr. Covey, and went to live with Mr. William Freeland, who lived about three miles from St. Michael's. I soon found Mr. Freeland a very different man from Mr. Covey. Though not rich, he was what would be called an educated southern gentleman. Mr. Covey, as I have shown, was a well-trained negro-breaker and slave-driver. The former (slaveholder though he was) seemed to possess some regard for honor, some reverence for justice, and some respect for humanity. The latter seemed totally insensible to all such sentiments. Mr. Freeland had many of the faults peculiar to slaveholders, such as being very passionate and fretful; but I must do him the justice to say, that he was exceedingly free from those degrading vices to which Mr. Covey was constantly addicted. The one was open and frank, and we always knew where to find him. The other was a most artful deceiver, and could be understood only by such as were skilful enough to detect his cunningly-devised frauds. Another advantage I gained in my new master was, he made no pretensions to, or profession of, religion; and this, in my opinion, was truly a great advantage. I assert most unhesitatingly, that the religion of the south is a mere covering for the most horrid crimes—a justifier of the most appalling barbarity—a sanctifier of the most hateful frauds—and a dark shelter under, which the darkest, foulest, grossest, and most infernal deeds of slaveholders find the strongest protection. Were I to be again reduced to the chains of slavery, next to that enslavement, I should regard being the slave of a religious master the greatest calamity that could befall me. For of all slaveholders with whom I have ever met, religious slaveholders are the worst. I have ever found them the meanest and basest, the most cruel and cowardly, of all others. It was my unhappy lot not only to belong to a religious slaveholder, but to live in a community of such religionists. Very near Mr. Freeland lived the Rev. Daniel Weeden, and in the same neighborhood lived the Rev. Rigby Hopkins. These were members and ministers in the Reformed Methodist Church. Mr. Weeden owned, among others, a woman slave, whose name I have forgotten. This woman's back, for weeks, was kept literally raw, made so by the lash of this merciless, *religious* wretch. He used to hire hands. His maxim was, Behave well or behave ill, it is the duty of a master occasionally to whip a slave, to remind him of his master's authority. Such was his theory, and such his practice.

Mr. Hopkins was even worse than Mr. Weeden. His chief boast was his ability to manage slaves. The peculiar feature of his government was that of whipping slaves in advance of deserving it. He always managed to have one or more of his slaves to whip every Monday morning. He did this to alarm their fears, and strike terror into those who escaped. His plan was to whip for the smallest offences, to prevent the commission of large ones. Mr. Hopkins could always find some excuse for whipping a slave. It would astonish one, unaccustomed to a slaveholding life, to see with what wonderful ease a slaveholder can find things, of which to make occasion to whip a slave. A mere look, word, or motion—a mistake, accident, or want of power—are all matters for which a slave may be whipped at any time. Does a slave look dissatisfied? It is said, he has the devil in him, and it must be whipped out. Does he speak loudly when spoken to by his master? Then he is getting high-minded, and should be taken down a button-hole lower. Does he forget to pull off his hat at the approach of a white person? Then he is wanting in reverence, and should be whipped for it. Does he ever venture to vindicate his conduct, when censured for it? Then he is guilty of impudence—one of the greatest crimes of which a slave can be guilty. Does he ever venture to suggest a different mode of doing things from that pointed out by his master? He is indeed presumptuous, and getting above himself; and nothing less than a flogging will do for him. Does he, while ploughing, break a plough—or, while hoeing, break a hoe? It is owing to his carelessness, and for it a slave must always be whipped. Mr. Hopkins could always find something of this sort to justify the use of the lash, and he seldom failed to embrace such opportunities. There was not a man in the whole county, with whom the slaves who had the getting their own home, would not prefer to live, rather than with this Rev. Mr. Hopkins. And yet there was not a man anywhere round, who made higher professions of religion, or was more active in revivals—more attentive to the class, love-feast, prayer and preaching meetings, or more devotional in his family—that prayed earlier, later, louder, and longer—than this same reverend slave-driver, Rigby Hopkins.

But to return to Mr. Freeland, and to my experience while in his employment. He, like Mr. Covey, gave us enough to eat; but, unlike Mr. Covey, he also gave us sufficient time to take our meals. He worked us hard, but always between sunrise and sunset. He required a good deal of work to be done, but gave us good tools with which to work. His farm was large, but he employed hands enough to work it, and with ease, compared with many of his neighbors. My treatment, while in his employment, was heavenly, compared with what I experienced at the hands of Mr. Edward Covey.

Mr. Freeland was himself the owner of but two slaves. Their names were Henry Harris and John Harris. The rest of his hands he hired. These consisted of myself, Sandy Jenkins,* and Handy Caldwell. Henry and John were quite intelligent, and in a very little while after I went

*This is the same man who gave me the roots to prevent my being whipped by Mr. Covey. He was "a clever soul." We used frequently to talk about the fight with Covey, and as often as we did so, he would claim my success as the result of the roots which he gave me. This superstition is very common among the more ignorant slaves. A slave seldom dies but that his death is attributed to trickery.

there, I succeeded in creating in them a strong desire to learn how to read. This desire soon sprang up in the others also. They very soon mustered up some old spelling-books, and nothing would do but that I must keep a Sabbath school. I agreed to do so, and accordingly devoted my Sundays to teaching these my loved fellow-slaves how to read. Neither of them knew his letters when I went there. Some of the slaves of the neighboring farms found what was going on, and also availed themselves of this little opportunity to learn to read. It was understood, among all who came, that there must be as little display about it as possible. It was necessary to keep our religious masters at St. Michael's unacquainted with the fact, that, instead of spending the Sabbath in wrestling, boxing, and drinking whisky, we were trying to learn how to read the will of God; for they had much rather see us engaged in those degrading sports, than to see us behaving like intellectual, moral, and accountable beings. My blood boils as I think of the bloody manner in which Messrs. Wright Fairbanks and Garrison West, both class-leaders, in connection with many others, rushed in upon us with sticks and stones, and broke up our virtuous little Sabbath school, at St. Michael's—all calling themselves Christians! humble followers of the Lord Jesus Christ! But I am again digressing.

I held my Sabbath school at the house of a free colored man, whose name I deem it imprudent to mention; for should it be known, it might embarrass him greatly, though the crime of holding the school was committed ten years ago. I had at one time over forty scholars, and those of the right sort, ardently desiring to learn. They were of all ages, though mostly men and women. I look back to those Sundays with an amount of pleasure not to be expressed. They were great days to my soul. The work of instructing my dear fellow-slaves was the sweetest engagement with which I was ever blessed. We loved each other, and to leave them at the close of the Sabbath was a severe cross indeed. When I think that these precious souls are today shut up in the prison-house of slavery, my feelings overcome me, and I am almost ready to ask, "Does a righteous God govern the universe? and for what does he hold the thunders in his right hand, if not to smite the oppressor, and deliver the spoiled out of the hand of the spoiler?" These dear souls came not to Sabbath school because it was popular to do so, nor did I teach them because it was reputable to be thus engaged. Every moment they spent in that school, they were liable to be taken up, and given thirty-nine lashes. They came because they wished to learn. Their minds had been starved by their cruel masters.

They had been shut up in mental darkness. I taught them, because it was the delight of my soul to be doing something that looked like bettering the condition of my race. I kept up my school nearly the whole year I lived with Mr. Freeland; and, beside my Sabbath school, I devoted three evenings in the week, during the winter, to teaching the slaves at home. And I have the happiness to know, that several of those who came to Sabbath school learned how to read; and that one, at least, is now free through my agency.

The year passed off smoothly. It seemed only about half as long as the year which preceded it. I went through it without receiving a single blow. I will give Mr. Freeland the credit of being the best master I ever had, *till I became my own master*. For the ease with which I passed the year, I was, however, somewhat indebted to the society of my fellow-slaves. They were noble souls; they not only possessed loving hearts, but brave ones. We were linked and interlinked with each other. I loved them with a love stronger than anything I have experienced since. It is sometimes said that we slaves do not love and confide in each other. In answer to this assertion, I can say, I never loved any or confided in any people more than my fellow slaves, and especially those with whom I lived at Mr. Freeland's. I believe we would have died for each other. We never undertook to do anything, of any importance, without a mutual consultation. We never moved separately. We were one; and as much so by our tempers and dispositions, as by the mutual hardships to which we were necessarily subjected by our condition as slaves.

At the close of the year 1834, Mr. Freeland again hired me of my master, for the year 1835. But, by this time, I began to want to live *upon free land* as well as *with Freeland*; and I was no longer content, therefore, to live with him or any other slaveholder. I began, with the commencement of the year, to prepare myself for a final struggle, which should decide my fate one way or the other. My tendency was upward. I was fast approaching manhood, and year after year had passed, and I was still a slave. These thoughts roused me—I must do something. I therefore resolved that 1835 should not pass without witnessing an attempt, on my part, to secure my liberty. But I was not willing to cherish this determination alone. My fellow-slaves were dear to me. I was anxious to have them participate with me in this, my life-giving determination. I therefore, though with great prudence, commenced early to ascertain their views and feelings in regard to their condition, and to imbue their minds with thoughts of freedom. I bent myself to devising ways and means for our escape, and meanwhile strove, on all fitting occasions, to impress them with the gross fraud and inhumanity of slavery. I went first to Henry, next to John, then to the others. I found, in them all, warm hearts and noble spirits. They were ready to hear, and ready to act when a feasible plan should be proposed. This was what I wanted. I talked to them of our want of manhood, if we submitted to our enslavement without at least one noble effort to be free. We met often, and consulted frequently, and told our hopes and fears, recounted the difficulties, real and imagined, which we should be called on to meet. At times we were almost disposed to give up, and try to content ourselves with our wretched lot; at others, we were firm and unbending in our determination to go. Whenever we suggested any plan, there was shrinking—the odds were fearful. Our path was beset with the greatest obstacles; and if we succeeded in gaining the end of it, our right to be free was yet questionable—we were yet liable to be returned to bondage. We could see no spot, this side of the ocean, where we could be free. We knew nothing about Canada. Our knowledge of the north did not extend farther than New York; and to go there, and be forever harassed with the frightful liability of being returned to slavery—with the certainty of being treated tenfold worse than before—the thought was truly a horrible one, and one which it was not easy to overcome. The case sometimes stood thus: At every gate through which we were to pass, we saw a watchman—at every ferry a guard—on every bridge a sentinel—and in every wood a patrol. We were hemmed in upon every side. Here were the difficulties, real or imagined—the good to be sought, and the evil to be shunned. On the one hand, there stood slavery, a stern reality, glaring frightfully upon us—its robes already crimsoned with the blood of millions, and even now feasting itself greedily upon our own flesh. On the other hand, away back in the dim distance, under the flickering light of the north star, behind some craggy hill or snow-covered mountain, stood a doubtful freedom—half frozen—beckoning us to come and share its hospitality. This in itself was sometimes enough to stagger us; but when we permitted ourselves to survey the road, we were frequently appalled. Upon either side we saw grim death, assuming the most horrid shapes. Now it was starvation, causing us to eat our own flesh—now we were contending with the waves, and were drowned—now we were overtaken, and torn to pieces by the fangs of the terrible bloodhound. We were stung by scorpions, chased by wild beasts, bitten by snakes, and finally, after having nearly reached the desired spot—after swimming rivers, encountering wild beasts, sleeping in the woods, suffering hunger and nakedness—we were overtaken by our pursuers, and, in our resistance, we were shot dead upon the spot! I say, this picture sometimes appalled us, and made us "rather bear those ills we had, than fly to others, that we knew not of."

In coming to a fixed determination to run away, we did more than Patrick Henry, when he resolved upon liberty or death. With us it was a doubtful liberty at most, and almost certain death if we failed. For my part, I should prefer death to hopeless bondage.

Sandy, one of our number, gave up the notion, but still encouraged us. Our company then consisted of Henry Harris, John Harris, Henry Bailey, Charles Roberts, and myself. Henry Bailey was my uncle, and belonged to my master. Charles married my aunt: he belonged to my master's father-in-law, Mr. William Hamilton.

The plan we finally concluded upon was, to get a large canoe belonging to Mr. Hamilton, and upon the Saturday night previous to Easter holidays, paddle directly up the Chesapeake Bay. On our arrival at the head of the bay, a distance of seventy or eighty miles from where we lived, it was our purpose to turn our canoe adrift, and follow the guidance of the north star till we got beyond the limits of Maryland. Our reason for taking the water route was, that we were less liable to be suspected as runaways; we hoped to be regarded as fishermen; whereas, if we should take the land route, we should be subjected to interruptions of almost every kind. Anyone having a white face, and being so disposed, could stop us, and subject us to examination.

The week before our intended start, I wrote several protections, one for each of us. As well as I can remember, they were in the following words, to wit:

> This is to certify that I, the undersigned, have given the bearer, my servant, full liberty to go to Baltimore, and spend the Easter holidays. Written with mine own hand, &c., 1835.
>
> WILLIAM HAMILTON,
> Near St. Michael's, in Talbot County, Maryland

We were not going to Baltimore; but, in going up the bay, we went toward Baltimore, and these protections were only intended to protect us while on the bay.

As the time drew near for our departure, our anxiety became more and more intense. It was truly a matter of life and death with us. The strength of our determination was about to be fully tested. At this time, I was very active in explaining every difficulty, removing every doubt, dispelling every fear, and inspiring all with the firmness indispensable to success in our undertaking; assuring them that half was gained the instant we made the move; we had talked long enough; we were now ready to move; if not now, we never should be; and if we did not intend to move now, we had as well fold our arms, sit down, and acknowledge ourselves fit only to be slaves. This, none of us were prepared to acknowledge. Every man stood firm; and at our last meeting, we pledged ourselves afresh, in the most solemn manner, that, at the time appointed, we would certainly start in pursuit of freedom. This was in the middle of the week, at the end of which we were to be off. We went, as usual, to our several fields of labor, but with bosoms highly agitated with thoughts of our truly hazardous undertaking. We tried to conceal our feelings as much as possible; and I think we succeeded very well.

After a painful waiting, the Saturday morning, whose night was to witness our departure, came. I hailed it with joy, bring what of sadness it might. Friday night was a sleepless one for me. I probably felt more anxious than the rest, because I was, by common consent, at the head of the whole affair. The responsibility of success or failure lay heavily upon me. The glory of the one, and the confusion of the other, were alike mine. The first two hours of that morning were such as I never experienced before, and hope never to again. Early in the morning, we went, as usual, to the field. We were spreading manure; and all at once, while thus engaged, I was overwhelmed with an indescribable feeling, in the fulness of which I turned to Sandy, who was nearby, and said, "We are betrayed!" "Well," said he, "that thought has this moment struck me." We said no more. I was never more certain of anything.

The horn was blown as usual, and we went up from the field to the house for breakfast. I went for the form, more than for want of anything to eat that morning. Just as I got to the house, in looking out at the lane gate, I saw four white men, with two colored men. The white men were on horseback, and the colored ones were walking behind, as if tied. I watched them a few moments till they got up to our lane gate. Here they halted, and tied the colored men to the gate-post. I was not yet certain as to what the matter was. In a few moments, in rode Mr. Hamilton, with a speed betokening great excitement. He came to the door, and inquired if Master William was in. He was told he was at the barn. Mr. Hamilton, without dismounting, rode up to the barn with extraordinary speed. In a few moments, he and Mr. Freeland returned to the house. By this time, the three constables rode up, and in great haste dismounted, tied their horses, and met Master William and Mr. Hamilton returning from the barn; and after talking awhile, they all walked up to the kitchen door. There was no one in the kitchen but myself and John. Henry and Sandy were up at the barn. Mr. Freeland put his head in at the door, and called me by name, saying, there were some gentlemen at the door who wished to see me. I stepped to the door, and inquired what they wanted. They at once seized me, and, without giving me any satisfaction, tied me—lashing my hands closely together. I insisted upon knowing what the matter was. They at length said, that they had learned I had been in a "scrape," and that I was to be examined before my master; and if their information proved false, I should not be hurt.

In a few moments, they succeeded in tying John. They then turned to Henry, who had by this time returned, and commanded him to cross his hands. "I won't!" said Henry, in a firm tone, indicating his readiness to meet the consequences of his refusal. "Won't you?" said Tom Graham, the constable. "No, I won't!" said Henry, in a still stronger tone. With this, two of the constables pulled out their shining pistols, and swore, by their Creator, that they would make him cross his hands or kill him. Each cocked his pistol, and, with fingers on the trigger, walked up to Henry, saying, at the same time, if he did not cross his hands, they would blow his damned heart out. "Shoot me, shoot me!" said Henry; "you can't kill me but once. Shoot, shoot—and be damned! *I won't be tied!*" This he said in a tone of loud defiance; and at the same time, with a motion as quick as lightning, he with one single stroke dashed the pistols from the hand of each constable. As he did this, all hands fell upon him, and, after beating him some time, they finally overpowered him, and got him tied.

During the scuffle, I managed, I know not how, to get my pass out, and, without being discovered, put it into the fire. We were all now tied; and just as we were to leave for Easton jail, Betsy Freeland, mother of William Freeland, came to the door with her hands full of biscuits, and divided them between Henry and John. She then delivered herself of a speech, to the following effect—addressing herself to me, she said, "*You devil! You yellow devil!* it was you that put it into the heads of Henry and John to run away. But for you, you long-legged mulatto devil! Henry nor John would never have thought of such a thing." I made no reply, and was immediately hurried off towards St. Michael's. Just a moment previous to the scuffle with Henry, Mr. Hamilton suggested the propriety of making a search for the protections which he had understood Frederick had written for himself and the rest. But, just at the moment he was about carrying his proposal into effect, his aid was needed in helping to tie Henry; and the excitement attending the scuffle caused them either to forget, or to deem it unsafe, under the circumstances, to search. So we were not yet convicted of the intention to run away.

When we got about half way to St. Michael's, while the constables having us in charge were looking ahead, Henry inquired of me what he should do with his pass. I told him to eat it with his biscuit, and own nothing; and we passed the word around, "*Own nothing*"; and "*Own nothing!*" said we all. Our confidence in each other was unshaken. We were resolved to succeed or fail together, after the calamity had befallen us as much as before. We were now prepared for anything. We were to be dragged that morning fifteen miles behind horses, and then to be placed in the Easton jail. When we reached St. Michael's, we underwent a sort of examination. We all denied that we ever intended to run away. We did this more to bring out the evidence against us, than from any hope of getting clear of being sold; for, as I have said, we were ready for that. The fact was, we cared but little where we went, so we went together. Our greatest concern was about separation. We dreaded that more than any thing this side of death. We found the evidence against us to be the testimony of one person; our master would not tell who it was; but we came to a unanimous decision among ourselves as to who their informant was. We were sent off to the jail at Easton. When we got there, we were delivered up to the sheriff, Mr. Joseph Graham, and by him placed in jail. Henry, John, and myself, were placed in one room together—Charles, and Henry Bailey, in another. Their object in separating us was to hinder concert.

We had been in jail scarcely twenty minutes, when a swarm of slave traders, and agents for slave traders, flocked into jail to look at us, and to as certain if we were for sale. Such a set of beings I never saw before! I felt myself surrounded by so many fiends from perdition. A band of pirates never looked more like their father, the devil. They laughed and grinned over us, saying, "Ah, my boys! we have got you, haven't we?" And after taunting us in various ways, they one by one went into an examination of us, with intent to ascertain our value. They would impudently ask us if we would not like to have them for our masters. We would make them no answer, and leave them to find out as best they could. Then they would curse and swear at us, telling us that they could take the devil out of us in a very little while, if we were only in their hands.

While in jail, we found ourselves in much more comfortable quarters than we expected when we went there. We did not get much to eat, nor that which was very good; but we had a good clean room, from the windows of which we could see what was going on in the street, which was very much better than though we had been placed in one of the dark, damp cells. Upon the whole, we got along very well, so far as the jail and its keeper were concerned. Immediately after the holidays were over, contrary to all our expectations, Mr. Hamilton and Mr. Freeland came up to Easton, and took Charles, the two Henrys, and John, out of jail, and carried them home, leaving me alone. I regarded this separation as a final one. It caused me more pain than anything else in the whole transaction. I was ready for any thing rather than separation. I supposed that they had consulted together, and had decided that, as I was the whole cause of the intention of the others to run away, it was hard to make the innocent suffer with the guilty; and that they had, therefore, concluded to take the others home, and sell me, as a warning to the others that remained. It is due to the noble Henry to say, he seemed almost as reluctant at leaving the prison as at leaving home to come to the prison. But we knew we should, in all probability, be separated, if we were sold; and since he was in their hands, he concluded to go peaceably home.

I was now left to my fate. I was all alone, and within the walls of a stone prison. But a few days before, and I was full of hope. I expected to have been safe in a land of freedom; but now I was covered with gloom, sunk down to the utmost despair. I thought the possibility of freedom was gone. I was kept in this way about one week, at the end of which, Captain Auld, my master, to my surprise and utter astonishment, came up, and took me out, with the intention of sending me, with a gentleman of his acquaintance, into Alabama. But, from some cause or other, he did not send me to Alabama, but concluded to send me back to Baltimore, to live again with his brother Hugh, and to learn a trade.

Thus, after an absence of three years and one month, I was once more permitted to return to my old home at Baltimore. My master sent me away, because there existed against me a very great prejudice in the community, and he feared I might be killed.

In a few weeks after I went to Baltimore, Master Hugh hired me to Mr. William Gardner, an extensive ship-builder, on Fell's Point. I was put there to learn how to calk. It, however, proved a very unfavorable place for the accomplishment of this object. Mr. Gardner was engaged that spring in building two large man-of-war brigs, professedly for the Mexican government. The vessels were to be launched in the July of that year, and in failure thereof, Mr. Gardner was to lose a considerable sum; so that when I entered, all was hurry. There was no time to learn anything. Every man had to do that which he knew how to do. In entering the ship-yard, my orders from Mr. Gardner were, to do whatever the carpenters commanded me to do. This was placing me at the beck and call of about seventy-five men. I was to regard all these as masters. Their word was to be my law. My situation was a most trying one. At times I needed a dozen pair of hands. I was called a dozen ways in the space of a single minute. Three or four voices would strike my ear at the same moment. It was—"Fred, come help me to cant this timber here."—"Fred, come carry this timber yonder."—"Fred, bring that roller here."—"Fred, go get a fresh can of water."—"Fred, come help saw off the end of this timber."—"Fred, go quick, and get the crowbar."—"Fred, hold on the end of this fall."—"Fred, go to the blacksmith's shop, and get a new punch."—"Hurra, Fred! run and bring me a cold chisel."—"I say, Fred, bear a hand, and get up a fire as quick as lightning under that steam-box."—"Halloo, nigger! come, turn this grindstone."—"Come, come! move, move! and *bowse* this timber forward."—"I say, darky, blast your eyes, why don't you heat up some pitch?"—"Halloo! halloo! halloo!" (Three voices at the same time.) "Come here!—Go there!—Hold on where you are! Damn you, if you move, I'll knock your brains out!"

This was my school for eight months; and I might have remained there longer, but for a most horrid fight I had with four of the white apprentices, in which my left eye was nearly knocked out, and I was horribly mangled in other respects. The facts in the case were these: Until a very little while after I went there, white and black ship-carpenters worked side by side, and no one seemed to see any impropriety in it. All hands seemed to be very well satisfied. Many of the black carpenters were freemen. Things seemed to be going on very well. All at once, the white carpenters knocked off, and said they would not work with free colored workmen. Their reason for this, as alleged, was, that if free colored carpenters were encouraged, they would soon take the trade into their own hands, and poor white men would be thrown out of employment. They therefore felt called upon at once to put a stop to it. And, taking advantage of Mr. Gardner's necessities, they broke off, swearing they would work no longer, unless he would discharge his black carpenters. Now, though this did not extend to me in form, it did reach me in fact. My fellow-apprentices very soon began to feel it degrading to them to work with me. They began to put on airs, and talk about the "niggers" taking the country, saying we all ought to be killed; and, being encouraged by the journeymen, they commenced making my condition as hard as they could, by hectoring me around, and sometimes striking me. I, of course, kept the vow I made after the fight with Mr. Covey, and struck back again, regardless of consequences; and while I kept them from combining, I succeeded very well; for I could whip the whole of them, taking them separately. They, however, at length combined, and came upon me, armed with sticks, stones, and heavy handspikes. One came in front with a half brick. There was one at each side of me, and one behind me. While I was attending to those in front, and on either side, the one behind ran up with the hand-spike, and struck me a heavy blow upon the head. It stunned me. I fell, and with this they all ran upon me, and fell to beating me with their fists. I let them lay on for a while, gathering strength. In an instant, I gave a sudden surge, and rose to my hands and knees. Just as I did that, one of their number gave me, with his heavy boot, a powerful kick in the left eye. My eyeball seemed to have burst. When they saw my eye closed, and badly swollen, they left me. With this I seized the hand-spike, and for a time pursued them. But here the carpenters interfered, and I thought I might as well give it up. It was impossible to stand my hand against so many. All this took place in sight of not less than fifty white ship-carpenters, and not one interposed a friendly word; but some cried, "Kill the damned nigger! Kill him! kill him! He struck a white person." I found my only chance for life was in flight. I succeeded in getting away without an additional blow, and barely so; for to strike a white man is death by Lynch law—and that was the law in Mr. Gardner's ship-yard; nor is there much of any other out of Mr. Gardner's ship-yard.

I went directly home, and told the story of my wrongs to Master Hugh; and I am happy to say of him, irreligious as he was, his conduct was heavenly, compared with that of his brother Thomas under similar circumstances. He listened attentively to my narration of the circumstances leading to the savage outrage, and gave many proofs of his strong indignation at it. The heart of my once over-kind mistress was again melted into pity. My puffed-out eye and blood-covered face moved her to tears. She took a chair by me, washed the blood from my face, and, with a mother's tenderness, bound up my head, covering the wounded eye with a lean piece of fresh beef. It was almost compensation for my suffering to witness, once more, a manifestation of kindness from this, my once affectionate old mistress. Master Hugh was very much enraged. He gave expression to his feelings by pouring out curses upon the heads of those who did the deed. As soon as I got a little the better of my bruises, he took me with him to Esquire Watson's, on Bond Street, to see what could be done about the matter. Mr. Watson inquired who saw the assault committed. Master Hugh told him it was done in Mr. Gardner's ship-yard at midday, where there were a large company of men at work. "As to that," he said, "the deed was done, and there was no question as to who did it." His answer was, he could do nothing in the case, unless some white man would come forward and testify. He could issue no warrant on my word. If I had been killed in the presence of a thousand colored people, their testimony combined would have been insufficient to have arrested one of the murderers. Master Hugh, for once, was compelled to say this state of things was too bad. Of course, it was impossible to get any white man to volunteer his testimony in my behalf, and against the white young men. Even those who may have sympathized with me were not prepared to do this. It required a degree of courage unknown to them to do so; for just at that time, the slightest manifestation of humanity toward a colored person was denounced as abolitionism, and that name subjected its bearer to frightful liabilities. The watch words of the bloody-minded in that region, and in those days, were, "Damn the abolitionists!" and "Damn the niggers!" There was nothing done, and probably nothing would have been done if I had been killed. Such was, and such remains, the state of things in the Christian city of Baltimore.

Master Hugh, finding he could get no redress, refused to let me go back again to Mr. Gardner. He kept me himself, and his wife dressed my wound till I was again restored to health. He then took me into the ship-yard of which he was foreman, in the employment of Mr. Walter Price. There I was immediately set to calking, and very soon learned the art of using my mallet and irons. In the course of one year from the time I left Mr. Gardner's, I was able to command the highest wages given to the most experienced calkers. I was now of some importance to my master. I was bringing him from six to seven dollars per week. I sometimes brought him nine dollars per week: my wages were a dollar and a half a day. After learning how to calk, I sought my own employment, made my own contracts, and collected the money, which I earned. My pathway became much more smooth than before; my condition was now much more comfortable. When I could get no calking to do, I did nothing. During these leisure times, those old notions about freedom would steal over me again. When in Mr. Gardner's employment, I was kept in such a perpetual whirl of excitement, I could think of nothing, scarcely, but my life; and in thinking of my life, I almost forgot my liberty. I have observed this in my experience of slavery—that whenever my condition was improved, instead of its increasing my contentment, it only increased my desire to be free, and set me to thinking of plans to gain my freedom. I have found that, to make a contented slave, it is necessary to make a thoughtless one. It is necessary to darken his moral and mental vision, and, as far as possible, to annihilate the power of reason. He must be able to detect no inconsistencies in slavery; he must be made to feel that slavery is right; and he can be brought to that only when he ceases to be a man.

I was now getting, as I have said, one dollar and fifty cents per day. I contracted for it; I earned it; it was paid to me; it was rightfully my own; yet, upon each returning Saturday night, I was compelled to deliver every cent of that money to Master Hugh. And why? Not because he earned it—not because he had any hand in earning it—not because I owed it to him—nor because he possessed the slightest shadow of a right to it; but solely because he had the power to compel me to give it up. The right of the grim visaged pirate upon the high seas is exactly the same.

XI

I now come to that part of my life during which I planned, and finally succeeded in making, my escape from slavery. But before narrating any of the peculiar circumstances, I deem it proper to make known my intention not to state all the facts connected with the transaction. My reasons for pursuing this course may be understood from the following: First, were I to give a minute statement of all the facts, it is not only possible, but quite probable, that others would thereby be involved in the most embarrassing difficulties. Secondly, such a statement would most undoubtedly induce greater vigilance on the part of slaveholders than has existed heretofore among them; which would, of course, be the means of guarding a door whereby some dear brother bondman might escape his galling chains. I deeply regret the necessity that impels me to suppress any thing of importance connected with my experience in slavery. It would afford me great pleasure indeed, as well as materially add to the interest of my narrative, were I at liberty to gratify a curiosity, which I know exists in the minds of many, by an accurate statement of all the facts pertaining to my most fortunate escape. But I must deprive myself of this pleasure, and the curious of the gratification, which such a statement would afford. I would allow myself to suffer under the greatest imputations which evil-minded men might suggest, rather than exculpate myself, and thereby run the hazard of closing the slightest avenue by which a brother slave might clear himself of the chains and fetters of slavery.

I have never approved of the very public manner in which some of our western friends have conducted what they call the *underground railroad*, but which I think, by their open declarations, has been made most emphatically the *upperground railroad.* I honor those good men and women for their noble daring, and applaud them for willingly subjecting themselves to bloody persecution, by openly avowing their participation in the escape of slaves. I, however, can see very little good resulting from such a course, either to themselves or the slaves escaping; while, upon the other hand, I see and feel assured that those open declarations are a positive evil to the slaves remaining, who are seeking to escape. They do nothing towards enlightening the slave, whilst they do much towards enlightening the master. They stimulate him to greater watchfulness, and enhance his power to capture his slave. We owe something to the slave south of the line as well as to those north of it; and in aiding the latter on their way to freedom, we should be careful to do nothing which would be likely to hinder the former from escaping from slavery. I would keep the merciless slaveholder profoundly ignorant of the means of flight adopted by the slave. I would leave him to imagine himself surrounded by myriads of invisible tormentors, ever ready to snatch from his infernal grasp his trembling prey. Let him be left to feel his way in the dark; let darkness commensurate with his crime hover over him; and let him feel that at every step he takes, in pursuit of the flying bondman, he is running the frightful risk of having his hot brains dashed out by an invisible agency. Let us render the tyrant no aid; let us not hold the light by which he can trace the footprints of our flying brother. But enough of this. I will now proceed to the statement of those facts, connected with my escape, for which I am alone responsible, and for which no one can be made to suffer but myself.

In the early part of the year 1838, I became quite restless. I could see no reason why I should, at the end of each week, pour the reward of my toil into the purse of my master. When I carried to him my weekly wages, he would, after counting the money, look me in the face with a robber-like fierceness, and ask, "Is this all?" He was satisfied with nothing less than the last cent. He would, however, when I made him six dollars, sometimes give me six cents, to encourage me. It had the opposite effect. I regarded it as a sort of admission of my right to the whole. The fact that he gave me any part of my wages was proof, to my mind, that he believed me entitled to the whole of them. I always felt worse for having received anything; for I feared that the giving me a few cents would ease his conscience, and make him feel himself to be a pretty honorable sort of robber. My discontent grew upon me. I was ever on the look-out for means of escape; and, finding no direct means, I determined to try to hire my time, with a view of getting money with which to make my escape. In the spring of 1838, when Master Thomas came to Baltimore to purchase his spring goods, I got an opportunity, and applied to him to allow me to hire my time.

He unhesitatingly refused my request, and told me this was another stratagem by which to escape. He told me I could go nowhere but that he could get me; and that, in the event of my running away, he should spare no pains in his efforts to catch me. He exhorted me to content myself, and be obedient. He told me, if I would be happy, I must lay out no plans for the future. He said, if I behaved myself properly, he would take care of me. Indeed, he advised me to complete thoughtlessness of the future, and taught me to depend solely upon him for happiness. He seemed to see fully the pressing necessity of setting aside my intellectual nature, in order to contentment in slavery. But in spite of him, and even in spite of myself, I continued to think, and to think about the injustice of my enslavement, and the means of escape.

About two months after this, I applied to Master Hugh for the privilege of hiring my time. He was not acquainted with the fact that I had applied to Master Thomas, and had been refused. He too, at first, seemed disposed to refuse; but, after some reflection, he granted me the privilege, and proposed the following terms: I was to be allowed all my time, make all contracts with those for whom I worked, and find my own employment; and, in return for this liberty, I was to pay him three dollars at the end of each week; find myself in calking tools, and in board and clothing. My board was two dollars and a half per week. This, with the wear and tear of clothing and calking tools, made my regular expenses about six dollars per week. This amount I was compelled to make up, or relinquish the privilege of hiring my time. Rain or shine, work or no work, at the end of each week the money must be forthcoming, or I must give up my privilege. This arrangement, it will be perceived, was decidedly in my master's favor. It relieved him of all need of looking after me. His money was sure. He received all the benefits of slaveholding without its evils; while I endured all the evils of a slave, and suffered all the care and anxiety of a freeman. I found it a hard bargain. But, hard as it was, I thought it better than the old mode of getting along. It was a step towards freedom to be allowed to bear the responsibilities of a freeman, and I was determined to hold on upon it. I bent myself to the work of making money. I was ready to work at night as well as day, and by the most untiring perseverance and industry, I made enough to meet my expenses, and lay up a little money every week. I went on thus from May till August. Master Hugh then refused to allow me to hire my time longer. The ground for his refusal was a failure on my part, one Saturday night, to pay him for my week's time. This failure was occasioned by my attending a camp meeting about ten miles from Baltimore. During the week, I had entered into an engagement with a number of young friends to start from Baltimore to the camp-ground early Saturday evening; and being detained by my employer, I was unable to get down to Master Hugh's without disappointing the company. I knew that Master Hugh was in no special need of the money that night. I therefore decided to go to camp meeting, and upon my return pay him the three dollars. I staid at the camp meeting one day longer than I intended when I left. But as soon as I returned, I called upon him to pay him what he considered his due. I found him very angry; he could scarce restrain his wrath. He said he had a great mind to give me a severe whipping. He wished to know how I dared go out of the city without asking his permission. I told him I hired my time and while I paid him the price, which he asked for it, I did not know that I was bound to ask him when and where I should go. This reply troubled him; and, after reflecting a few moments, he turned to me, and said I should hire my time no longer; that the next thing he should know of, I would be running away. Upon the same plea, he told me to bring my tools and clothing home forthwith. I did so; but instead of seeking work, as I had been accustomed to do previously to hiring my time, I spent the whole week without the performance of a single stroke of work. I did this in retaliation. Saturday night, he called upon me as usual for my week's wages. I told him I had no wages; I had done no work that week. Here we were upon the point of coming to blows. He raved, and swore his determination to get hold of me. I did not allow myself a single word; but was resolved, if he laid the weight of his hand upon me, it should be blow for blow. He did not strike me, but told me that he would find me in constant employment in future. I thought the matter over during the next day, Sunday, and finally resolved upon the third day of September, as the day upon which I would make a second attempt to secure my freedom. I now had three weeks during which to prepare for my journey. Early on Monday morning, before Master Hugh had time to make any engagement for me, I went out and got employment of Mr. Butler, at his ship-yard near the drawbridge, upon what is called the City Block, thus making it unnecessary for him to seek employment for me. At the end of the week, I brought him between eight and nine dollars. He seemed very well pleased, and asked why I did not do the same the week before. He little knew what my plans were. My object in working steadily was to remove any suspicion he might entertain of my intent to run away; and in this I succeeded admirably. I suppose he thought I was never better satisfied with my condition than at the very time during which I was planning my escape. The second week passed, and again I carried him my full wages; and so well pleased was he, that he gave me twenty-five cents (quite a large sum for a slaveholder to give a slave), and bade me to make a good use of it. I told him I would.

Things went on without very smoothly indeed, but within there was trouble. It is impossible for me to describe my feelings as the time of my contemplated start drew near. I had a number of warm-hearted friends in Baltimore—friends that I loved almost as I did my life—and the thought of being separated from them forever was painful beyond expression. It is my opinion that thousands would escape from slavery, who now remain, but for the strong cords of affection that bind them to their friends. The thought of leaving my friends was decidedly the most painful thought with which I had to contend. The love of them was my tender point, and shook my decision more than all things else. Besides the pain of separation, the dread and apprehension of a failure exceeded what I had experienced at my first attempt. The appalling defeat I then sustained returned to torment me. I felt assured that, if I failed in this attempt, my case would be a hopeless one—it would seal my fate as a slave forever. I could not hope to get off with anything less than the severest punishment, and being placed beyond the means of escape. It required no very vivid imagination to depict the most frightful scenes through which I should have to pass, in case I failed. The wretchedness of slavery, and the blessedness of freedom, were perpetually before me. It was life and death with me. But I remained firm, and, according to my resolution, on the third day of September 1838, I left my chains, and succeeded in reaching New York without the slightest interruption of any kind. How I did so—what means I adopted—what direction I travelled, and by what mode of conveyance—I must leave unexplained, for the reasons before mentioned.

I have been frequently asked how I felt when I found myself in a free State. I have never been able to answer the question with any satisfaction to myself. It was a moment of the highest excitement I ever experienced. I suppose I felt as one may imagine the unarmed mariner to feel when he is rescued by a friendly man-of-war from the pursuit of a pirate. In writing to a dear friend, immediately after my arrival at New York, I said I felt like one who had escaped a den of hungry lions. This state of mind, however, very soon subsided; and I was again seized with a feeling of great insecurity and loneliness. I was yet liable to be taken back, and subjected to all the tortures of slavery. This in itself was enough to damp the ardor of my enthusiasm. But the loneliness overcame me. There I was in the midst of thousands, and yet a perfect stranger; without home and without friends, in the midst of thousands of my own brethren—children of a common Father, and yet I dared not to unfold to any one of them my sad condition. I was afraid to speak to anyone for fear of speaking to the wrong one, and thereby falling into the hands of money-loving kidnappers, whose business it was to lie in wait for the panting fugitive, as the ferocious beasts of the forest lie in wait for their prey. The motto which I adopted when I started from slavery was this—"Trust no man!" I saw in every white man an enemy, and in almost every colored man cause for distrust. It was a most painful situation; and, to understand it, one must needs experience it, or imagine himself in similar circumstances. Let him be a fugitive slave in a strange land—a land given up to be the hunting ground for slaveholders—whose inhabitants are legalized kidnappers—where he is every moment subjected to the terrible liability of being seized upon by his fellowmen, as the hideous crocodile seizes upon his prey!—I say, let him place himself in my situation—without home or friends—without money or credit—wanting shelter, and no one to give it—wanting bread, and no money to buy it—and at the same time let him feel that he is pursued by merciless men-hunters, and in total darkness as to what to do, where to go, or where to stay—perfectly helpless both as to the means of defence and means of escape—in the midst of plenty, yet suffering the terrible gnawings of hunger—in the midst of houses, yet having no home—among fellow-men, yet feeling as if in the midst of wild beasts, whose greediness to swallow up the trembling and half-famished fugitive is only equalled by that with which the monsters of the deep swallow up the helpless fish upon which they subsist—I say, let him be placed in this most trying situation—the situation in which I was placed—then, and not till then, will he fully appreciate the hardships of, and know how to sympathize with, the toil-worn and whip-scarred fugitive slave.

Thank Heaven, I remained but a short time in this distressed situation. I was relieved from it by the humane hand of Mr. David Ruggles, whose vigilance, kindness, and perseverance, I shall never forget. I am glad of an opportunity to express, as far as words can, the love and gratitude I bear him. Mr. Ruggles is now afflicted with blindness, and is himself in need of the same kind offices which he was once so forward in the performance of toward others. I had been in New York but a few days, when Mr. Ruggles sought me out, and very kindly took me to his boarding-house at the corner of Church and Lespenard Streets. Mr. Ruggles was then very deeply engaged in the memorable *Darg* case, as well as at tending to a number of other fugitive slaves, devising ways and means for their successful escape; and, though watched and hemmed in on almost every side, he seemed to be more than a match for his enemies.

Very soon after I went to Mr. Ruggles, he wished to know of me where I wanted to go; as he deemed it unsafe for me to remain in New York. I told him I was a calker, and should like to go where I could get work. I thought of going to Canada; but he decided against it, and in favor of my going to New Bedford, thinking I should be able to get work there at my trade. At this time, Anna,[†] my intended wife, came on; for I wrote to her immediately after my arrival at New York (notwithstanding my homeless, houseless, and helpless condition), informing her of my successful flight, and wishing her to come on forthwith. In a few days after her arrival, Mr. Ruggles called in the Rev. J. W. C. Pennington, who, in the presence of Mr. Ruggles, Mrs. Michaels, and two or three others, performed the marriage ceremony, and gave us a certificate, of which the following is an exact copy:

> This may certify, that I joined together in holy matrimony Frederick Johnson[‡] and Anna Murray, as man and wife, in the presence of Mr. David Ruggles and Mrs. Michaels.
>
> JAMES W. C. PENNINGTON
> New York, Sept. 15, 1838

Upon receiving this certificate, and a five-dollar bill from Mr. Ruggles, I shouldered one part of our baggage, and Anna took up the other, and we set out forthwith to take passage on board of the steamboat John W. Richmond for Newport, on our way to New Bedford. Mr. Ruggles gave me a letter to a Mr. Shaw in Newport, and told me, in case my money did not serve me to New Bedford, to stop in Newport and obtain further assistance; but upon our arrival at Newport, we were so anxious to get to a place of safety, that, notwithstanding we

[†]She was free.
[‡]I had changed my name from Frederick Bailey to that of Johnson.

lacked the necessary money to pay our fare, we decided to take seats in the stage, and promise to pay when we got to New Bedford. We were encouraged to do this by two excellent gentlemen, residents of New Bedford, whose names I afterward ascertained to be Joseph Ricketson and William C. Taber. They seemed at once to understand our circumstances, and gave us such assurance of their friendliness as put us fully at ease in their presence. It was good indeed to meet with such friends, at such a time. Upon reaching New Bedford, we were directed to the house of Mr. Nathan Johnson, by whom we were kindly received, and hospitably provided for. Both Mr. and Mrs. Johnson took a deep and lively interest in our welfare. They proved themselves quite worthy of the name of abolitionists. When the stage-driver found us unable to pay our fare, he held on upon our baggage as security for the debt. I had but to mention the fact to Mr. Johnson, and he forthwith advanced the money.

We now began to feel a degree of safety, and to prepare ourselves for the duties and responsibilities of a life of freedom. On the morning after our arrival at New Bedford, while at the breakfast-table, the question arose as to what name I should be called by. The name given me by my mother was, "Frederick Augustus Washington Bailey." I, however, had dispensed with the two middle names long before I left Maryland so that I was generally known by the name of "Frederick Bailey." I started from Baltimore bearing the name of "Stanley." When I got to New York, I again changed my name to "Frederick Johnson," and thought that would be the last change. But when I got to New Bedford, I found it necessary again to change my name. The reason of this necessity was, that there were so many Johnsons in New Bedford, it was already quite difficult to distinguish between them. I gave Mr. Johnson the privilege of choosing me a name, but told him he must not take from me the name of "Frederick." I must hold on to that, to preserve a sense of my identity. Mr. Johnson had just been reading the "Lady of the Lake," and at once suggested that my name be "Douglass." From that time until now I have been called "Frederick Douglass"; and as I am more widely known by that name than by either of the others, I shall continue to use it as my own.

I was quite disappointed at the general appearance of things in New Bedford. The impression, which I had received respecting the character and condition of the people of the north, I found to be singularly erroneous. I had very strangely supposed, while in slavery, that few of the comforts, and scarcely any of the luxuries, of life were enjoyed at the north, compared with what were enjoyed by the slaveholders of the south. I probably came to this conclusion from the fact that northern people owned no slaves. I supposed that they were about upon a level with the non-slaveholding population of the south. I knew *they* were exceedingly poor, and I had been accustomed to regard their poverty as the necessary consequence of their being non-slaveholders. I had somehow imbibed the opinion that, in the absence of slaves, there could be no wealth, and very little refinement. And upon coming to the north, I expected to meet with a rough, hard-handed, and uncultivated population, living in the most Spartan like simplicity, knowing nothing of the ease, luxury, pomp, and grandeur of southern slaveholders. Such being my conjectures, anyone acquainted with the appearance of New Bedford may very readily infer how palpably I must have seen my mistake.

In the afternoon of the day when I reached New Bedford, I visited the wharves, to take a view of the shipping. Here I found myself surrounded with the strongest proofs of wealth. Lying at the wharves, and riding in the stream, I saw many ships of the finest model, in the best order, and of the largest size. Upon the right and left, I was walled in by granite warehouses of the widest dimensions, stowed to their utmost capacity with the necessaries and comforts of life. Added to this, almost everybody seemed to be at work, but noiselessly so, compared with what I had been accustomed to in Baltimore. There were no loud songs heard from those engaged in loading and unloading ships. I heard no deep oaths or horrid curses on the laborer. I saw no whipping of men; but all seemed to go smoothly on. Every man appeared to understand his work, and went at it with a sober, yet cheerful earnestness, which betokened the deep interest, which he felt in what he was doing, as well as a sense of his own dignity as a man. To me this looked exceedingly strange. From the wharves I strolled around and over the town, gazing with wonder and admiration at the splendid churches, beautiful dwellings, and finely-cultivated gardens; evincing an amount of wealth, comfort, taste, and refinement, such as I had never seen in any part of slaveholding Maryland.

Everything looked clean, new, and beautiful. I saw few or no dilapidated houses, with poverty stricken inmates; no half-naked children and bare footed women, such as I had been accustomed to see in Hillsborough, Easton, St. Michael's, and Baltimore. The people looked more able, stronger, healthier, and happier, than those of Maryland. I was for once made glad by a view of extreme wealth, without being saddened by seeing extreme poverty. But the most astonishing as well as the most interesting thing to me was the condition of the colored people, a great many of whom, like myself, had escaped thither as a refuge from the hunters of men. I found many, who had not been seven years out of their chains, living in finer houses, and evidently enjoying more of the comforts of life, than the average of slaveholders in Maryland. I will venture to assert, that my friend Mr. Nathan Johnson (of whom I can say with a grateful heart, "I was hungry, and he gave me meat; I was thirsty, and he gave me drink; I was a stranger, and he took me in") lived in a neater house; dined at a better table; took, paid for, and read, more newspapers; better understood the moral, religious, and political character of the nation—than nine tenths of the slaveholders in Talbot County Maryland. Yet Mr. Johnson was a working man. His hands were hardened by toil, and not his alone, but those also of Mrs. Johnson. I found the colored people much more spirited than I had supposed they would be. I found among them a determination to protect each other from the blood-thirsty kidnapper, at all hazards. Soon after my arrival, I was told of a circumstance which illustrated their spirit. A colored man and a fugitive slave were on unfriendly terms. The former was heard to threaten the latter with informing his master of his where abouts. Straightway a meeting was called among the colored people, under the stereotyped notice, "Business of importance!" The betrayer was invited to attend. The people came at the appointed hour, and organized the meeting by appointing a very religious old gentleman as president, who, I believe, made a prayer, after which he addressed the meeting as follows:

> Friends, we have got him here, and I would recommend that you young men just take him outside the door, and kill him!

With this, a number of them bolted at him; but they were intercepted by some more timid than themselves, and the betrayer escaped their vengeance, and has not been seen in New Bedford since. I believe there have been no more such threats, and should there be hereafter, I doubt not that death would be the consequence.

I found employment, the third day after my arrival, in stowing a sloop with a load of oil. It was new, dirty, and hard work for me; but I went at it with a glad heart and a willing hand. I was now my own master. It was a happy moment, the rapture of which can be understood only by those who have been slaves. It was the first work, the reward of which was to be entirely my own. There was no Master Hugh standing ready, the moment I earned the money, to rob me of it. I worked that day with a pleasure I had never before experienced. I was at work for myself and newly-married wife. It was to me the starting-point of a new existence. When I got through with that job, I went in pursuit of a job of calking; but such was the strength of prejudice against color, among the white calkers, that they refused to work with me, and of course I could get no employment.[§] Finding my trade of no immediate benefit, I threw off my calking habiliments, and prepared myself to do any kind of work I could get to do. Mr. Johnson kindly let me have his wood-horse and saw, and I very soon found myself a plenty of work. There was no work too hard—none too dirty. I was ready to saw wood, shovel coal, carry wood, sweep the chimney, or roll oil casks—all of which I did for nearly three years in New Bedford, before I became known to the anti-slavery world.

In about four months after I went to New Bedford, there came a young man to me, and inquired if I did not wish to take the "Liberator." I told him I did; but, just having made my escape from slavery, I remarked that I was unable to pay for it then. I, however, finally became a subscriber to it. The paper came, and I read it from week to week with such feelings as it would be quite idle for me to attempt to describe. The paper became my meat and my drink. My soul was set all on fire. Its sympathy for my brethren in bonds—its scathing denunciations of slaveholders—its faithful exposures of slavery—and its powerful attacks upon the upholders of the institution—sent a thrill of joy through my soul, such as I had never felt before!

I had not long been a reader of the "Liberator," before I got a pretty correct idea of the principles, measures and spirit of the anti-slavery reform. I took right hold of the cause. I could do but little; but what I could, I did with a joyful heart, and never felt happier than when in an anti-slavery meeting. I seldom had much to say at the meetings, because what I wanted to say was said so much better by others. But, while attending an anti-slavery convention at Nantucket, on the 11th of August, 1841, I felt strongly moved to speak, and was at the same time much urged to do so by Mr. William C. Coffin, a gentleman who had heard me speak in the colored people's meeting at New Bedford. It was a severe cross, and I took it up reluctantly. The

[§] I am told that colored persons can now get employment at calking in New Bedford—a result of anti-slavery effort.

truth was, I felt myself a slave, and the idea of speaking to white people weighed me down. I spoke but a few moments, when I felt a degree of freedom, and said what I desired with considerable ease. From that time until now, I have been engaged in pleading the cause of my brethren—with what success, and with what devotion, I leave those acquainted with my labors to decide.

Appendix

I find, since reading over the foregoing Narrative, that I have, in several instances, spoken in such a tone and manner, respecting religion, as may possibly lead those unacquainted with my religious views to suppose me an opponent of all religion. To remove the liability of such misapprehension, I deem it proper to append the following brief explanation. What I have said respecting and against religion, I mean strictly to apply to the *slaveholding religion* of this land, and with no possible reference to Christianity proper; for, between the Christianity of this land, and the Christianity of Christ, I recognize the widest possible difference—so wide, that to receive the one as good, pure, and holy, is of necessity to reject the other as bad, corrupt, and wicked. To be the friend of the one, is of necessity to be the enemy of the other. I love the pure, peaceable, and impartial Christianity of Christ: I therefore hate the corrupt, slaveholding, women-whipping, cradle-plundering, partial and hypocritical Christianity of this land. Indeed, I can see no reason, but the most deceitful one, for calling the religion of this land Christianity. I look upon it as the climax of all misnomers, the boldest of all frauds, and the grossest of all libels. Never was there a clearer case of "stealing the livery of the court of heaven to serve the devil in." I am filled with unutterable loathing when I contemplate the religious pomp and show, together with the horrible inconsistencies, which everywhere surround me. We have men-stealers for ministers, women-whippers for missionaries, and cradle-plunderers for church members. The man who wields the blood-clotted cowskin during the week fills the pulpit on Sunday, and claims to be a minister of the meek and lowly Jesus. The man who robs me of my earnings at the end of each week meets me as a class-leader on Sunday morning, to show me the way of life, and the path of salvation. He who sells my sister, for purposes of prostitution, stands forth as the pious advocate of purity. He who proclaims it a religious duty to read the Bible denies me the right of learning to read the name of the God who made me. He who is the religious advocate of marriage robs whole millions of its sacred influence, and leaves them to the ravages of wholesale pollution. The warm defender of the sacredness of the family relation is the same that scatters whole families—sundering husbands and wives, parents and children, sisters and brothers—leaving the hut vacant, and the hearth desolate. We see the thief preaching against theft, and the adulterer against adultery. We have men sold to build churches, women sold to support the gospel, and babes sold to purchase Bibles for the *poor heathen! all for the glory of God and the good of souls*! The slave auctioneer's bell and the church-going bell chime in with each other, and the bitter cries of the heart-broken slave are drowned in the religious shouts of his pious master. Revivals of religion and revivals in the slave-trade go hand in hand together. The slave prison and the church stand near each other. The clanking of fetters and the rattling of chains in the prison, and the pious psalm and solemn prayer in the church, may be heard at the same time. The dealers in the bodies and souls of men erect their stand in the presence of the pulpit, and they mutually help each other. The dealer gives his blood-stained gold to support the pulpit, and the pulpit, in return, covers his infernal business with the garb of Christianity. Here we have religion and robbery the allies of each other—devils dressed in angels' robes, and hell presenting the semblance of paradise.

Just God! and these are they,
   Who minister at thine altar, God of right!
Men who their hands, with prayer and blessing, lay
   On Israel's ark of light.

What! preach, and kidnap men?
   Give thanks, and rob thy own afflicted poor?
Talk of thy glorious liberty, and then
   Bolt hard the captive's door?

What! servants of thy own
   Merciful Son, who came to seek and save
The homeless and the outcast, fettering down
   The tasked and plundered slave!

Pilate and Herod friends!
   Chief priests and rulers, as of old, combine!
Just God and holy! is that church which lends
   Strength to the spoiler thine?

The Christianity of America is a Christianity, of whose votaries it may be as truly said, as it was of the ancient scribes and Pharisees, "They bind heavy burdens, and grievous to be borne, and lay them on men's shoulders, but they themselves will not move them with one of their fingers. All their works they do for to be seen of men. They love the upper most rooms at feasts, and the chief seats in the synagogues, . . . and to be called of men, Rabbi, Rabbi. But woe unto you, scribes and Pharisees, hypocrites! for ye shut up the kingdom of heaven against men; for ye neither go in yourselves, neither suffer ye them that are entering to go in. Ye devour widows' houses, and for a pretence make long prayers; therefore ye shall receive the greater damnation. Ye compass sea and land to make one proselyte, and when he is made, ye make him twofold more the child of hell than yourselves. Woe unto you, scribes and Pharisees, hypocrites! for ye pay tithe of mint, and anise, and cumin, and have omitted the weightier matters of the law, judgment, mercy, and faith; these ought ye to have done, and not to leave the other undone. Ye blind guides! which strain at a gnat, and swallow a camel. Woe unto you, scribes and Pharisees, hypocrites! for ye make clean the outside of the cup and of the platter; but within, they are full of extortion and excess. Woe unto you, scribes and Pharisees, hypocrites! for ye are like unto whited sepulchres, which indeed appear beautiful outward, but are within full of dead men's bones, and of all uncleanness. Even so ye also outwardly appear righteous unto men, but within ye are full of hypocrisy and iniquity."

Dark and terrible as is this picture, I hold it to be strictly true of the overwhelming mass of professed Christians in America. They strain at a gnat, and swallow a camel. Could anything be more true of our churches? They would be shocked at the proposition of fellowshipping a *sheep*-stealer; and at the same time they hug to their communion a *man*-stealer, and brand me with being an infidel, if I find fault with them for it. They attend with Pharisaical strictness to the outward forms of religion, and at the same time neglect the weightier matters of the law, judgment, mercy, and faith. They are always ready to sacrifice, but seldom to show mercy. They are they who are represented as professing to love God whom they have not seen, whilst they hate their brother whom they have seen. They love the heathen on the other side of the globe. They can pray for him, pay money to have the Bible put into his hand, and missionaries to instruct him; while they despise and totally neglect the heathen at their own doors.

Such is, very briefly, my view of the religion of this land; and to avoid any misunderstanding, growing out of the use of general terms, I mean, by the religion of this land, that which is revealed in the words, deeds, and actions, of those bodies, north and south, calling themselves Christian churches, and yet in union with slaveholders. It is against religion, as presented by these bodies, that I have felt it my duty to testify.

I conclude these remarks by copying the following portrait of the religion of the south (which is, by communion and fellowship, the religion of the north), which I soberly affirm is "true to the life," and without caricature or the slightest exaggeration. It is said to have been drawn, several years before the present anti-slavery agitation began, by a northern Methodist preacher, who, while residing at the south, had an opportunity to see slaveholding morals, manners, and piety, with his own eyes. "Shall I not visit for these things? saith the Lord. Shall not my soul be avenged on such a nation as this?"

A Parody

Come, saints and sinners, hear me tell
How pious priests whip Jack and Nell,
And women buy and children sell,
And preach all sinners down to hell,
   And sing of heavenly union.

They'll bleat and baa, dona like goats,
Gorge down black sheep, and strain at motes,
Array their backs in fine black coats,
Then seize their negroes by their throats,
   And choke, for heavenly union.

They'll church you if you sip a dram,
And damn you if you steal a lamb;
Yet rob old Tony, Doll, and Sam,
Of human rights, and bread and ham;
   Kidnapper's heavenly union.

They'll loudly talk of Christ's reward,
And bind his image with a cord,
And scold, and swing the lash abhorred,
And sell their brother in the Lord
   To handcuffed heavenly union.

They'll read and sing a sacred song,
And make a prayer both loud and long,
And teach the right and do the wrong,
Hailing the brother, sister throng,
With words of heavenly union.

We wonder how such saints can sing,
Or praise the Lord upon the wing,
Who roar, and scold, and whip, and sting,
And to their slaves and mammon cling,
In guilty conscience union.

They'll raise tobacco, corn, and rye,
And drive, and thieve, and cheat, and lie,
And lay up treasures in the sky,
By making switch and cowskin fly,
In hope of heavenly union.

They'll crack old Tony on the skull,
And preach and roar like Bashan bull,
Or braying ass, of mischief full,
Then seize old Jacob by the wool,
And pull for heavenly union.

A roaring, ranting, sleek man-thief,
Who lived on mutton, veal, and beef,
Yet never would afford relief
To needy, sable sons of grief,
Was big with heavenly union.

"Love not the world," the preacher said,
And winked his eye, and shook his head;
He seized on Tom, and Dick, and Ned,
Cut short their meat, and clothes, and bread,
Yet still loved heavenly union.

Another preacher whining spoke
Of One whose heart for sinners broke:
He tied old Nanny to an oak,
And drew the blood at every stroke,
And prayed for heavenly union.

Two others oped their iron jaws,
And waved their children-stealing paws;
There sat their children in gewgaws;
By stinting negroes' backs and maws,
They kept up heavenly union.

All good from Jack another takes,
And entertains their flirts and rakes,
Who dress as sleek as glossy snakes,
And cram their mouths with sweetened cakes;
And this goes down for union.

Sincerely and earnestly hoping that this little book may do something toward throwing light on the American slave system, and hastening the glad day of deliverance to the millions of my brethren in bonds—faithfully relying upon the power of truth, love, and justice, for success in my humble efforts—and solemnly pledging my self anew to the sacred cause—I subscribe myself,

FREDERICK DOUGLASS

Lynn, Mass., April 28, 1845

THE HEROIC SLAVE

I

Oh! child of grief, why weepest thou?
   Why droops thy sad and mournful brow?
Why is thy look so like despair?
   What deep, sad sorrow lingers there?

The State of Virginia is famous in American annals for the multitudinous array of her statesmen and heroes. She has been dignified by some the mother of statesmen. History has not been sparing in recording their names, or in blazoning their deeds. Her high position in this respect, has given her an enviable distinction among her sister States. With Virginia for his birth-place, even a man of ordinary parts, on account of the general partiality for her sons, easily rises to eminent stations. Men, not great enough to attract special attention in their native States, have, like a certain distinguished citizen in the State of New York, sighed and repined that they were not born in Virginia. Yet not all the great ones of the Old Dominion have, by the fact of their birth-place, escaped undeserved obscurity. By some strange neglect, *one* of the truest, manliest, and bravest of her children—one who, in after years, will, I think, command the pen of genius to set his merits forth, holds now no higher place in the records of that grand old Commonwealth than is held by a horse or an ox. Let those account for it who can, but there stands the fact, that a man who loved liberty as well as did Patrick Henry—who deserved it as much as Thomas Jefferson—and who fought for it with a valor as high, an arm as strong, and against odds as great, as he who led all the armies of the American colonies through the great war for freedom and independence, lives now only in the chattel records of his native State.

Glimpses of this great character are all that can now be presented. He is brought to view only by a few transient incidents, and these afford but partial satisfaction. Like a guiding star on a stormy night, he is seen through the parted clouds and the howling tempests; or, like the gray peak of a menacing rock on a perilous coast, he is seen by the quivering flash of angry lightning, and he again disappears covered with mystery.

Curiously, earnestly, anxiously we peer into the dark, and wish even for the blinding flash, or the light of northern skies to reveal him. But alas! he is still enveloped in darkness, and we return from the pursuit like a wearied and disheartened mother (after a tedious and unsuccessful search for a lost child), who returns weighed down with disappointment and sorrow. Speaking of marks, traces, possibles, and probabilities, we come before our readers.

In the spring of 1835, on a Sabbath morning, within hearing of the solemn peals of the church bells at a distant village a Northern traveller through the State of Virginia drew up his horse to drink at a sparkling brook, near the edge of a dark pine forest. While his weary and thirsty steed drew in the grateful water, the rider caught the sound of a human voice, apparently engaged in earnest conversation.

Following the direction of the sound, he descried, among the tall pines, the man whose voice had arrested his attention. "To whom can he be speaking?" thought the traveller. "He seems to be alone." The circumstance interested him much, and he became intensely curious to know what thoughts and feelings, or, it might be, high aspirations, guided those rich and mellow accents. Tying his horse at a short distance from the brook, he stealthily drew near the solitary speaker; and, concealing himself by the side of a huge fallen tree, he distinctly heard the following soliloquy:

"What, then, is life to me? it is aimless and worthless, and worse than worthless. Those birds, perched on yon swinging boughs, in friendly conclave, sounding forth their merry notes in seeming worship of the rising sun, though liable to the sportsman's fowling-piece, are still my superiors. They *live free*, though they may die slaves. They fly where they list by day, and retire in freedom at night. But what is freedom to me, or I to it? I am a *slave*—born a slave, an abject slave—even before I was made part of this breathing world, the scourge was plated for my back; the fetters were forged for my limbs. How mean a thing am I. That accursed and crawling snake, that miserable reptile, that has just glided into its slimy home, is freer and better off than I. He escaped my blow, and is safe. But here am I, a man—yes, *a man*!—with thoughts and wishes, with powers and faculties as far as angel's flight above that hated reptile—yet he is my superior, and scorns to own me as his master, or to stop to take my blows. When he saw my uplifted arm, he darted beyond my reach, and turned to give me battle.

I dare not do as much as that. I neither run nor fight, but do meanly stand, answering each heavy blow of a cruel master with doleful wails and piteous cries. I am galled with irons; but even these are more tolerable than the consciousness, the *galling* consciousness of cowardice and indecision. Can it be that I *dare* not run away? *Perish the thought*, I *dare* do anything which may be done by another. When that young man struggled with the waves *for life*, and others stood back appalled in helpless horror, did I not plunge in, forgetful of life, to save his? The raging bull from whom all others fled, pale with fright, did I not keep at bay with a single pitchfork? Could a coward do that? No—*no*—I wrong myself—I am no coward. *Liberty* I will have, or die in the attempt to gain it. This working that others may live in idleness! This cringing submission to insolence and curses! This living under the constant dread and apprehension of being sold and transferred, like a mere brute, is *too* much for me. I will stand it no longer. What others have done, I will do. These trusty legs, or these sinewy arms shall place me among the free. Tom escaped; so can I. The North Star will not be less kind to me than to him. I will follow it. I will at least make the trial. I have nothing to lose. If I am caught, I shall only be a slave. If I am shot, I shall only lose a life which is a burden and a curse. If I get clear (as something tells me I shall), liberty, the inalienable birthright of every man, precious and priceless, will be mine. My resolution is fixed. *I shall be free*."

At these words the traveller raised his head cautiously and noiselessly, and caught, from his hiding-place, a full view of the unsuspecting speaker. Madison (for that was the name of our hero) was standing erect, a smile of satisfaction rippled upon his expressive countenance, like that which plays upon the face of one who has but just solved a difficult problem, or vanquished a malignant foe; for at that moment he was free, at least in spirit. The future gleamed brightly before him, and his fetters lay broken at his feet. His air was triumphant.

Madison was of manly form. Tall, symmetrical, round, and strong. In his movements he seemed to combine, with the strength of the lion, a lion's elasticity. His torn sleeves disclosed arms like polished iron. His face was "black, but comely." His eye, lit with emotion, kept guard under a brow as dark and as glossy as the raven's wing. His whole appearance betokened Herculean strength; yet there was nothing savage or forbidding in his aspect. A child might play in his arms, or dance on his shoulders. A giant's strength but not a giant's heart was in him. His broad mouth and nose spoke only of good nature and kindness. But his voice, that unfailing index of the soul, though full and melodious, had that in it which could terrify as well as charm. He was just the man you would choose when hardships were to be endured, or danger to be encountered—intelligent and brave. He had the head to conceive, and the hand to execute. In a word, he was one to be sought as a friend, but to be dreaded as an enemy.

As our traveller gazed upon him, he almost trembled at the thought of his dangerous intrusion. Still he could not quit the place. He had long desired to sound the mysterious depths of the thoughts and feelings of a slave. He was not, therefore, disposed to allow so providential an opportunity to pass unimproved. He resolved to hear more; so he listened again for those mellow and mournful accents which, he says, made such an impression upon him as can never be erased. He did not have to wait long. There came another gush from the same full fountain; now bitter, and now sweet. Scathing denunciations of the cruelty and injustice of slavery; heart-touching narrations of his own personal suffering, intermingled with prayers to the God of the oppressed for help and deliverance, were followed by presentations of the dangers and difficulties of escape, and formed the burden of his eloquent utterances; but his high resolution clung to him—for he ended each speech by an emphatic declaration of his purpose to be free. It seemed that the very repetition of this imparted a glow to his countenance. The hope of freedom seemed to sweeten, for a season, the bitter cup of slavery, and to make it, for a time, tolerable; for when in the very whirlwind of anguish—when his heart's cord seemed screwed up to snapping tension, hope sprung up and soothed his troubled spirit. Fitfully he would exclaim, "How can I leave her? Poor thing! what can she do when I am gone? Oh! oh! 'tis impossible that I can leave poor Susan!"

A brief pause intervened. Our traveller raised his head, and saw again the sorrow-smitten slave. His eye was fixed upon the ground. The strong man staggered under a heavy load. Recovering himself, he argued thus aloud: "All is uncertain here. Tomorrow's sun may not rise before I am sold, and separated from her I love. What, then, could I do for her? I should be in more hopeless slavery, and she no nearer to liberty—whereas if I were free—my arms my own—I might devise the means to rescue her."

This said, Madison cast around a searching glance, as if the thought of being overheard had flashed across his mind. He said no more, but, with measured steps, walked away, and was lost to the eye of our traveller amidst the wildering woods.

Long after Madison had left the ground, Mr. Listwell (our traveller) remained in motionless silence, meditating on the extraordinary revelations to which he had listened. He seemed fastened to the spot, and stood half hoping, half fearing the return of the sable preacher to his solitary temple. The speech of Madison rung through the chambers of his soul, and vibrated through his entire frame. "Here is indeed a man," thought he, "of rare endowments, a child of God—guilty of no crime but the color of his skin—hiding away from the face of humanity, and pouring out his thoughts and feelings, his hopes and resolutions to the lonely woods; to him those distant church bells have no grateful music. He shuns the church, the altar, and the great congregation of Christian worshippers, and wanders away to the gloomy forest, to utter in the vacant air complaints and griefs, which the religion of his times and his country can neither console nor relieve. Goaded almost to madness by the sense of the injustice done him, he resorts hither to give vent to his pent up feelings, and to debate with himself the feasibility of plans, plans of his own invention, for his own deliverance. From this hour I am an abolitionist. I have seen enough and heard enough, and I shall go to my home in Ohio resolved to atone for my past indifference to this ill-starred race, by making such exertions as I shall be able to do, for the speedy emancipation of every slave in the land."

II

The gaudy, blabbling, and remorseful day
Is crept into the bosom of the sea;
And now loud-howling wolves arouse the jades
That drag the tragic melancholy night;
Who, with their drowsy, slow, and flagging wings
Clip dead men's graves, and from their misty jaws
Breathe foul contagious-darkness in the air.
—Shakespeare

Five years after the foregoing singular occurrence, in the winter of 1840, Mr. and Mrs. Listwell sat together by the fireside of their own happy home, in the State of Ohio. The children were all gone to bed. A single lamp burnt brightly on the centre-table. All was still and comfortable within; but the night was cold and dark; a heavy wind sighed and moaned sorrowfully around the house and barn, occasionally bringing against the clattering windows a stray leaf from the large oak trees that embowered their dwelling. It was a night for strange noises and for strange fancies. A whole wilderness of thought might pass through one's mind during such an evening. The smouldering embers, partaking of the spirit of the restless night, became fruitful of varied and fantastic pictures, and revived many bygone scenes and old impressions. The happy pair seemed to sit in silent fascination, gazing on the fire. Suddenly this *reverie* was interrupted by a heavy growl. Ordinarily such an occurrence would have scarcely provoked a single word, or excited the least apprehension. But there are certain seasons when the slightest sound sends a jar through all the subtle chambers of the mind; and such a season was this. The happy pair started up, as if some sudden danger had come upon them. The growl was from their trusty watch-dog.

"What can it mean? Certainly no one can be out on such a night as this," said Mrs. Listwell.

"The wind has deceived the dog, my dear; he has mistaken the noise of falling branches, brought down by the wind, for that of the footsteps of persons coming to the house. I have several times tonight thought that I heard the sound of footsteps. I am sure, however, that it was but the wind. Friends would not be likely to come out at such an hour, or such a night; and thieves are too lazy and self-indulgent to expose themselves to this biting frost; but should there be anyone about, our brave old Monte, who is on the look-out, will not be slow in sounding the alarm."

Saying this they quietly left the window, whither they had gone to learn the cause of the menacing growl, and re-seated themselves by the fire, as if reluctant to leave the slowly expiring embers, although the hour was late. A few minutes only intervened after resuming their seats, when again their sober meditations were disturbed. Their faithful dog now growled and barked furiously, as if assailed by an advancing foe. Simultaneously the good couple arose, and stood in mute expectation. The contest without seemed fierce and violent. It was, however, soon over—the barking ceased, for, with true canine instinct, Monte quickly discovered that a friend, not an enemy of the family, was coming to the house, and instead of rushing to repel the supposed intruder, he was now at the door, whimpering and dancing for the admission of himself and his newly made friend.

Mr. Listwell knew by this movement that all was well; he advanced and opened the door, and saw by the light that streamed out into the darkness, a tall man advancing slowly towards the house, with a stick in one hand, and a small bundle in the other. "It is a traveller," thought he, "who has missed his way, and is coming to inquire the road. I am glad we did not go to bed earlier—I have felt all the evening as if somebody would be here tonight."

The man had now halted a short distance from the door, and looked prepared alike for flight or battle. "Come in, sir, don't be alarmed, you have probably lost your way."

Slightly hesitating, the traveller walked in; not, however, without regarding his host with a scrutinizing glance. "No, sir," said he, "I have come to ask you a greater favor."

Instantly Mr. Listwell exclaimed (as the recollection of the Virginia forest scene flashed upon him), "Oh, sir, I know not your name, but I have seen your face, and heard your voice before. I am glad to see you. *I know all*. You are flying for your liberty—be seated—banish all fear. You are safe under my roof."

This recognition, so unexpected, rather disconcerted and disquieted the noble fugitive. The timidity and suspicion of persons escaping from slavery are easily awakened, and often what is intended to dispel the one, and to allay the other, has precisely the opposite effect. It was so in this case. Quickly observing the unhappy impression made by his words and action, Mr. Listwell assumed a more quiet and inquiring aspect, and finally succeeded in removing the apprehensions which his very natural and generous salutation had aroused.

Thus assured, the stranger said, "Sir, you have rightly guessed, I am, indeed, a fugitive from slavery. My name is Madison—Madison Washington my mother used to call me. I am on my way to Canada, where I learn that persons of my color are protected in all the rights of men; and my object in calling upon you was, to beg the privilege of resting my weary limbs for the night in your barn. It was my purpose to have continued my journey till morning; but the piercing cold, and the frowning darkness compelled me to seek shelter; and, seeing a light through the lattice of your window, I was encouraged to come here to beg the privilege named. You will do me a great favor by affording me shelter for the night."

"A resting-place, indeed, sir, you shall have; not, however, in my barn, but in the best room of my house. Consider yourself, if you please, under the roof of a friend; for such I am to you, and to all your deeply injured race."

While this introductory conversation was going on, the kind lady had revived the fire, and was diligently preparing supper; for she, not less than her husband, felt for the sorrows of the oppressed and hunted ones of earth, and was always glad of an opportunity to do them a service. A bountiful repast was quickly prepared, and the hungry and toil-worn bondman was cordially invited to partake thereof. Gratefully he acknowledged the favor of his benevolent benefactress; but appeared scarcely to understand what such hospitality could mean. It was the first time in his life that he had met so humane and friendly a greeting at the hands of persons whose color was unlike his own; yet it was impossible for him to doubt the charitableness of his new friends, or the genuineness of the welcome so freely given; and he therefore, with many thanks, took his seat at the table with Mr. and Mrs. Listwell, who, desirous to make him feel at home, took a cup of tea themselves, while urging upon Madison the best that the house could afford.

Supper over, all doubts and apprehensions banished, the three drew around the blazing fire, and a conversation commenced which lasted till long after midnight.

"Now," said Madison to Mr. Listwell, "I was a little surprised and alarmed when I came in, by what you said; do tell me, sir, *why* you thought you had seen my face before, and by what you knew me to be a fugitive from slavery; for I am sure that I never was before in this neighborhood, and I certainly sought to conceal what I supposed to be the manner of a fugitive slave."

Mr. Listwell at once frankly disclosed the secret; describing the place where he first saw him; rehearsing the language which he (Madison) had used; referring to the effect which his manner and speech had made upon him; declaring the resolution he there formed to be an abolitionist; telling how often he had spoken of the circumstance, and the deep concern he had ever since felt to know what had become of him; and whether he had carried out the purpose to make his escape, as in the woods he declared he would do.

"Ever since that morning," said Mr. Listwell, "you have seldom been absent from my mind, and though now I did not dare to hope that I should ever see you again, I have often wished that such might be my fortune; for, from that hour, your face seemed to be daguerreotyped on my memory."

Madison looked quite astonished, and felt amazed at the narration to which he had listened. After recovering himself he said, "I well remember that morning, and the bitter anguish that wrung my heart; I will state the occasion of it. I had, on the previous Saturday, suffered a cruel lashing; had been tied up to the limb of a tree, with my feet chained together, and a heavy iron bar placed between my ankles. Thus suspended, I received on my naked back forty stripes, and was kept in this distressing position three or four hours, and was then let down, only to have my torture increased; for my bleeding back, gashed by the cow-skin, was washed by the overseer with old brine, partly to augment my suffering, and partly, as he said, to prevent inflammation. My crime was that I had stayed longer at the mill, the day previous, than it was thought I ought to have done, which, I assured my master and the overseer, was no fault of mine; but no excuses were allowed. 'Hold your tongue, you impudent rascal,' met my every explanation. Slaveholders are so imperious when their passions are excited, as to construe every word of the slave into insolence. I could do nothing but submit to the agonizing infliction. Smarting still from the wounds, as well as from the consciousness of being whipt for no cause, I took advantage of the absence of my master, who had gone to church, to spend the time in the woods, and brood over my wretched lot. Oh, sir, I remember it well—and can never forget it."

"But this was five years ago; where have you been since?"

"I will try to tell you," said Madison. "Just four weeks after that Sabbath morning, I gathered up the few rags of clothing I had, and started, as I supposed, for the North and for freedom. I must not stop to describe my feelings on taking this step. It seemed like taking a leap into the dark. The thought of leaving my poor wife and two little children caused me indescribable anguish; but consoling myself with the reflection that once free, I could, possibly, devise ways and means to gain their freedom also, I nerved myself up to make the attempt. I started, but ill-luck attended me; for after being out a whole week, strange to say, I still found myself on my master's grounds; the third night after being out, a season of clouds and rain set in, wholly preventing me from seeing the North Star, which I had trusted as my guide, not dreaming that clouds might intervene between us.

"This circumstance was fatal to my project, for in losing my star, I lost my way; so when I supposed I was far towards the North, and had almost gained my freedom, I discovered myself at the very point from which I had started. It was a severe trial, for I arrived at home in great destitution; my feet were sore, and in travelling in the dark, I had dashed my foot against a stump, and started a nail, and lamed myself. I was wet and cold; one week had exhausted all my stores; and when I landed on my master's plantation, with all my work to do over again—hungry, tired, lame, and bewildered—I almost cursed the day that I was born. In this extremity I approached the quarters. I did so stealthily, although in my desperation I hardly cared whether I was discovered or not. Peeping through the rents of the quarters, I saw my fellow-slaves seated by a warm fire, merrily passing away the time, as though their hearts knew no sorrow. Although I envied their seeming contentment, all wretched as I was, I despised the cowardly acquiescence in their own degradation which it implied, and felt a kind of pride and glory in my own desperate lot. I dared not enter the quarters—for where there is seeming contentment with slavery, there is certain treachery to freedom. I proceeded towards the great-house, in the hope of catching a glimpse of my poor wife, whom I knew might be trusted with my secrets even on the scaffold. Just as I reached the fence which divided the field from the garden, I saw a woman in the yard, who in the darkness I took to be my wife; but a nearer approach told me it was not she. I was about to speak; had I done so, I would not have been here this night; for an alarm would have been sounded, and the hunters been put on my track. Here were hunger, cold, thirst, disappointment, and chagrin, confronted only by the dim hope of liberty. I tremble to think of that dreadful hour. To face the deadly cannon's mouth in warm blood unterrified, is, I think, a small achievement, compared with a conflict like this with gaunt starvation. The gnawings of hunger conquers by degrees, till all that a man has he would give in exchange for a single crust of bread. Thank God, I was not quite reduced to this extremity.

"Happily for me, before the fatal moment of utter despair, my good wife made her appearance in the yard. It was she; I knew her step. All was well now. I was, however, afraid to speak, lest I should frighten her. Yet speak I did; and, to my great joy, my voice was known. Our meeting can be more easily imagined than described. For a time hunger, thirst, weariness, and lameness were forgotten. But it was soon necessary for her to return to the house. She being a house-servant, her absence from the kitchen, if discovered, might have excited suspicion. Our parting was like tearing the flesh from my bones; yet it was the part of wisdom for her to go. She left me with the purpose of meeting me at midnight in the very forest where you last saw me. She knew the place well, as one of my melancholy resorts, and could easily find it, though the night was dark.

"I hastened away, therefore, and concealed myself, to await the arrival of my good angel. As I lay there among the leaves, I was strongly tempted to return again to the house of my master and give myself up; but remembering my solemn pledge on that memorable Sunday morning, I was able to linger out the two long hours between ten and midnight. I may well call them long hours. I have endured much hardship; I have encountered many perils; but the anxiety of those two hours, was the bitterest I ever experienced. True to her word, my wife came laden with provisions, and we sat down on the side of a log, at that dark and lonesome hour of the night. I cannot say we talked; our feelings were too great for that; yet we came to an understanding that I should make the woods my home, for if I gave myself up, I should be whipped and sold away; and if I started for the North, I should leave a wife doubly dear to me. We mutually determined, therefore, that I should remain in the vicinity. In the dismal swamps I lived, sir, five long years—a cave for my home during the day. I wandered about at night with the wolf and the bear—sustained by the promise that my good Susan would meet me in the pine woods at least once a week. This promise was redeemed, I assure you, to the letter, greatly to my relief. I had partly become contented with my mode of life, and had made up my mind to spend my days there; but the wilderness that sheltered me thus long took fire, and refused longer to be my hiding-place.

"I will not harrow up your feelings by portraying the terrific scene of this awful conflagration. There is nothing to which I can liken it. It was horribly and indescribably grand. The whole world seemed on fire, and it appeared to me that the day of judgment had come; that the burning bowels of the earth had burst forth, and that the end of all things was at hand. Bears and wolves scorched from their mysterious hiding-places in the earth, and all the wild inhabitants of the untrodden forest, filled with a common dismay, ran forth, yelling, howling, bewildered amidst the smoke and flame. The very heavens seemed to rain down fire through the towering trees; it was by the merest chance that I escaped the devouring element. Running before it, and stopping occasionally to take breath, I looked back to behold its frightful ravages, and to drink in its savage magnificence. It was awful, thrilling, solemn, beyond compare. When aided by the fitful wind, the merciless tempest of fire swept on, sparkling, creaking, cracking, curling, roaring, out-doing in its dreadful splendor a thousand thunderstorms at once. From tree to tree it leaped, swallowing them up in its lurid, baleful glare; and leaving them leafless, limbless, charred, and lifeless behind. The scene was overwhelming, stunning—nothing was spared—cattle, tame and wild, herds of swine and of deer, wild beasts of every name and kind—huge night-birds, bats, and owls, that had retired to their homes in lofty tree-tops to rest, perished in that fiery storm. The long-winged buzzard and croaking raven mingled their dismal cries with those of the countless myriads of small birds that rose up to the skies, and were lost to the sight in clouds of smoke and flame. Oh, I shudder when I think of it! Many a poor wandering fugitive, who, like myself, had sought among wild beasts the mercy denied by our fellow men, saw, in helpless consternation, his dwelling-place and city of refuge reduced to ashes forever. It was this grand conflagration that drove me hither; I ran alike from fire and from slavery."

After a slight pause (for both speaker and hearers were deeply moved by the above recital), Mr. Listwell, addressing Madison, said, "If it does not weary you too much, do tell us something of your journeyings since this disastrous burning—we are deeply interested in everything which can throw light on the hardships of persons escaping from slavery; we could hear you talk all night; are there no incidents that you could relate of your travels hither? or are they such that you do not like to mention them?"

"For the most part, sir, my course has been uninterrupted; and, considering the circumstances, at times even pleasant. I have suffered little for want of food; but I need not tell you how I got it. Your moral code may differ from mine, as your customs and usages are different. The fact is, sir, during my flight, I felt myself robbed by society of all my just rights; that I was in an enemy's land, who sought both my life and my liberty. They had transformed me into a brute; made merchandise of my body, and, for all the purposes of my flight, turned day into night—and guided by my own necessities, and in contempt of their conventionalities, I did not scruple to take bread where I could get it."

"And just there you were right," said Mr. Listwell; "I once had doubts on this point myself, but a conversation with Gerrit Smith (a man, by the way, that I wish you could see, for he is a devoted friend of your race, and I know he would receive you gladly), put an end to all my doubts on this point. But do not let me interrupt you."

"I had but one narrow escape during my whole journey," said Madison.

"Do let us hear of it," said Mr. Listwell.

"Two weeks ago," continued Madison, "after travelling all night, I was overtaken by daybreak, in what seemed to me an almost interminable wood. I deemed it unsafe to go farther, and, as usual, I looked around for a suitable tree in which to spend the day. I liked one with a bushy top, and found one just to my mind. Up I climbed, and hiding myself as well as I could, I, with this strap (pulling one out of his old coat-pocket), lashed myself to a bough, and flattered myself that I should get a *good night's* sleep that day; but in this I was soon disappointed. I had scarcely got fastened to my natural hammock, when I heard the voices of a number of persons, apparently approaching the part of the woods where I was. Upon my word, sir, I dreaded more these human voices than I should have done those of wild beasts. I was at a loss to know what to do. If I descended, I should probably be discovered by the men; and if they had dogs I should, doubtless, be '*treed*.' It was an anxious moment, but hardships and dangers have been the accompaniments of my life; and have, perhaps, imparted to me a certain hardness of character, which, to some extent, adapts me to them. In my present predicament, I decided to hold my place in the tree-top, and abide the consequences. But here I must disappoint you; for the men, who were all colored, halted at least a hundred yards from me, and began with their axes, in right good earnest, to attack the trees. The sound of their laughing axes was like the report of as many well-charged pistols. By and by there came down at least a dozen trees with a terrible crash. They leaped upon the fallen trees with an air of victory. I could see no dog with them, and felt myself comparatively safe, though I could not forget the possibility that some freak or fancy might bring the axe a little nearer my dwelling than comported with my safety.

"There was no sleep for me that day, and I wished for night. You may imagine that the thought of having the tree attacked under me was far from agreeable, and that it very easily kept me on the look-out. The day was not without diversion. The men at work seemed to be a gay set; and they would often make the woods resound with that uncontrolled laughter for which we, as a race, are remarkable. I held my place in the tree till sunset—saw the men put on their jackets to be off. I observed that all left the ground except one, whom I saw sitting on the side of a stump, with his head bowed, and his eyes apparently fixed on the ground. I became interested in him. After sitting in the position to which I have alluded ten or fifteen minutes, he left the stump, walked directly towards the tree in which I was secreted, and halted almost under the same. He stood for a moment and looked around, deliberately and reverently took off his hat, by which I saw that he was a man in the evening of life, slightly bald and quite gray. After laying down his hat carefully, he knelt and prayed aloud, and such a prayer, the most fervent, earnest, and solemn, to which I think I ever listened. After reverently addressing the Almighty, as the all-wise, all-good, and the common Father of all mankind, he besought God for grace, for strength, to bear up under, and to endure, as a good soldier, all the hardships and trials which beset the journey of life, and to enable him to live in a manner which accorded with the gospel of Christ. His soul now broke out in humble supplication for deliverance from bondage. 'O thou,' said he, 'that hearest the raven's cry, take pity on poor me! O deliver me! O deliver me! in mercy, O God, deliver me from the chains and manifold hardships of slavery! With thee, O Father, all things are possible. Thou canst stand and measure the earth. Thou hast beheld and drove asunder the nations—all power is in thy hand—thou didst say of old, "I have seen the affliction of my people, and am come to deliver them"—O look down upon our afflictions, and have mercy upon us.' But I cannot repeat his prayer, nor can I give you an idea of its deep pathos. I had given but little attention to religion, and had but little faith in it; yet, as the old man prayed, I felt almost like coming down and kneeling by his side, and mingling my broken complaint with his.

"He had already gained my confidence; as how could it be otherwise? I knew enough of religion to know that the man who prays in secret is far more likely to be sincere than he who loves to pray standing in the street, or in the great congregation. When he arose from his knees, like another Zacheus, I came down from the tree. He seemed a little alarmed at first, but I told him my story, and the good man embraced me in his arms, and assured me of his sympathy.

"I was now about out of provisions, and thought I might safely ask him to help me replenish my store. He said he had no money; but if he had, he would freely give it me. I told him I had *one dollar*; it was all the money I had in the world. I gave it to him, and asked him to purchase some crackers and cheese, and to kindly bring me the balance; that I would remain in or near that place, and would come to him on his return, if he would whistle. He was gone only about an hour. Meanwhile, from some cause or other, I know not what (but as you shall see very wisely), I changed my place. On his return I started to meet him; but it seemed as if the shadow of approaching danger fell upon my spirit, and checked my progress. In a very few minutes, closely on the heels of the old man, I distinctly saw *fourteen men*, with something like guns in their hands."

"Oh! the old wretch!" exclaimed Mrs. Listwell "he had betrayed you, had he?"

"I think not," said Madison, "I cannot believe that the old man was to blame. He probably went into a store, asked for the articles for which I sent, and presented the bill I gave him; and it is so unusual for slaves in the country to have money, that fact, doubtless, excited suspicion, and gave rise to inquiry, I can easily believe that the truthfulness of the old man's character compelled him to disclose the facts;

and thus were these blood-thirsty men put on my track. Of course I did not present myself; but hugged my hiding-place securely. If discovered and attacked, I resolved to sell my life as dearly as possible.

"After searching about the woods silently for a time, the whole company gathered around the old man; one charged him with lying, and called him an old villain; said he was a thief; charged him with stealing money; said if he did not instantly tell where he got it, they would take the shirt from his old back, and give him thirty-nine lashes.

"'I did *not* steal the money,' said the old man, 'it was given me, as I told you at the store; and if the man who gave it me is not here, it is not my fault.'

"'Hush! you lying old rascal; we'll make you smart for it. You shall not leave this spot until you have told where you got that money.'

"They now took hold of him, and began to strip him; while others went to get sticks with which to beat him. I felt, at the moment, like rushing out in the midst of them; but considering that the old man would be whipped the more for having aided a fugitive slave, and that, perhaps, in the *melee* he might be killed outright, I disobeyed this impulse. They tied him to a tree, and began to whip him. My own flesh crept at every blow, and I seem to hear the old man's piteous cries even now. They laid thirty-nine lashes on his bare back, and were going to repeat that number, when one of the company besought his comrades to desist. 'You'll kill the d——d old scoundrel! You've already whipt a dollar's worth out of him, even if he stole it!' 'O yes,' said another, 'let him down. He'll never tell us another lie, I'll warrant ye!' With this, one of the company untied the old man, and bid him go about his business.

"The old man left, but the company remained as much as an hour, scouring the woods. Round and round they went, turning up the underbrush, and peering about like so many bloodhounds. Two or three times they came within six feet of where I lay. I tell you I held my stick with a firmer grasp than I did in coming up to your house tonight. I expected to level one of them at least. Fortunately, however, I eluded their pursuit, and they left me alone in the woods.

"My last dollar was now gone, and you may well suppose I felt the loss of it; but the thought of being once again free to pursue my journey, prevented that depression which a sense of destitution causes; so swinging my little bundle on my back, I caught a glimpse of the *Great Bear* (which ever points the way to my beloved star), and I started again on my journey. What I lost in money I made up at a hen-roost that same night, upon which I fortunately came."

"But you didn't eat your food raw? How did you cook it?" said Mrs. Listwell.

"O no, Madam," said Madison, turning to his little bundle—"I had the means of cooking." Here he took out of his bundle an old-fashioned tinder-box, and taking up a piece of a file, which he brought with him, he struck it with a heavy flint, and brought out at least a dozen sparks at once. "I have had this old box," said he, "more than five years. It is the *only* property saved from the fire in the dismal swamp. It has done me good service. It has given me the means of broiling many a chicken!"

It seemed quite a relief to Mrs. Listwell to know that Madison had, at least, lived upon cooked food. Women have a perfect horror of eating uncooked food.

By this time thoughts of what was best to be done about getting Madison to Canada, began to trouble Mr. Listwell; for the laws of Ohio were very stringent against anyone who should aid, or who were found aiding a slave to escape through that State. A citizen, for the simple act of taking a fugitive slave in his carriage, had just been stripped of all his property, and thrown penniless upon the world. Notwithstanding this, Mr. Listwell was determined to see Madison safely on his way to Canada. "Give yourself no uneasiness," said he to Madison, "for if it cost my farm, I shall see you safely out of the States, and on your way to a land of liberty. Thank God that there is *such* a land so near us! You will spend tomorrow with us, and tomorrow night I will take you in my carriage to the lake. Once upon that, and you are safe."

"Thank you! thank you," said the fugitive; "I will commit myself to your care."

For the *first* time during *five* years, Madison enjoyed the luxury of resting his limbs on a comfortable bed, and inside a human habitation. Looking at the white sheets, he said to Mr. Listwell, "What, sir! you don't mean that I shall sleep in that bed?"

"Oh yes, oh yes."

After Mr. Listwell left the room, Madison said he really hesitated whether or not he should lie on the floor; for that was *far* more comfortable and inviting than any bed to which he had been used.

We pass over the thoughts and feelings, the hopes and fears, the plan and purposes, that revolved in the mind of Madison during the day that he was secreted at the house of Mr. Listwell. The reader will be content to know that nothing occurred to endanger his liberty, or to excite alarm. Many were the little attentions bestowed upon him in his quiet retreat and hiding-place. In the evening, Mr. Listwell, after treating Madison to a new suit of winter clothes, and replenishing his exhausted purse with five dollars, all in silver, brought out his two-horse wagon, well provided with buffaloes, and silently started off with him to Cleveland. They arrived there without interruption, a few minutes before sunrise the next morning. Fortunately the steamer Admiral lay at the wharf, and was to start for Canada at nine o'clock. Here the last anticipated danger was surmounted. It was feared that just at this point the hunters of men might be on the look-out, and, possibly, pounce upon their victim. Mr. Listwell saw the captain of the boat; cautiously sounded him on the matter of carrying liberty-loving passengers, before he introduced his precious charge. This done, Madison was conducted on board. With usual generosity this true subject of the emancipating queen welcomed Madison in and assured him that he should be safely landed in Canada, free of charge. Madison now felt himself no more a piece of merchandise, but a passenger, and, like any other passenger, going about his business, carrying with him what belonged to him, and nothing which rightfully belonged to anybody else.

Wrapped in his new winter suit, snug and comfortable, a pocket full of silver, safe from his pursuers, embarked for a free country, Madison gave every sign of sincere gratitude, and bade his kind benefactor farewell, with such a grip of the hand as bespoke a heart full of honest manliness, and a soul that knew how to appreciate kindness. It need scarcely be said that Mr. Listwell was deeply moved by the gratitude and friendship he had excited in a nature so noble as that of the fugitive. He went to his home that day with a joy and gratification which knew no bounds. He had done something "to deliver the spoiled out of the hands of the spoiler," he had given bread to the hungry, and clothes to the naked; he had befriended a man to whom the laws of his country forbade all friendship—and in proportion to the odds against his righteous deed, was the delightful satisfaction that gladdened his heart. On reaching home, he exclaimed, "*He is safe—he is safe—he is safe,*"—and the cup of his joy was shared by his excellent lady. The following letter was received from Madison a few days after.

Windsor, Canada *West*, Dec. 16, 1840

My dear Friend—for such you truly are:

Madison is out of the woods at last; I nestle in the mane of the British lion, protected by the mighty paw from the talons and the beak of the American eagle. I AM FREE, and breathe an atmosphere too pure for *slaves*, slave-hunters, or slaveholders. My heart is full. As many thanks to you, sir, and to your kind lady, as there are pebbles on the shores of lake Erie; and may the blessing of God rest upon you both. You will never be forgotten by your profoundly grateful friend,

MADISON WASHINGTON

III

His head was with his heart,
And that was far away!
—Childe Harold

Just upon the edge of the great road from Petersburg, Virginia, to Richmond, and only about fifteen miles from the latter place, there stands a somewhat ancient and famous public tavern, quite notorious in its better days, as being the grand resort for most of the leading gamblers, horse-racers, cock-fighters, and slave-traders from all the country round about. This old rookery, the nucleus of all sorts of birds, mostly those of ill omen, has, like everything else peculiar to Virginia, lost much of its ancient consequence and splendor; yet it keeps up some appearance of gaiety and high life, and is still frequented, even by respectable travellers, who are unacquainted with its past history and present condition. Its fine old portico looks well at a distance, and gives the building an air of grandeur. A nearer view, however, does little to sustain this pretension. The house is large, and its style imposing, but time and dissipation, unfailing in their results, have made ineffaceable marks upon it, and it must, in the common course of events, soon be numbered with things that were. The gloomy mantle of ruin is, already, outspread to envelop it, and its remains, even but now remind one of a human skull, after the flesh has mingled with the earth. Old hats and rags fill the places in the upper windows once occupied by large panes of glass, and the molding boards along the roofing have dropped off from their places, leaving holes and crevices in the rented wall for bats and swallows to build their nests in. The platform of the portico, which fronts the highway is a rickety affair, its planks are loose, and in some places entirely gone, leaving effective mantraps in their stead for nocturnal ramblers. The wooden pillars, which once supported it, but which now hang as encumbrances, are all rotten, and tremble with the touch. A part of the stable, a fine old structure in its day, which has given comfortable shelter to hundreds of the noblest steeds of "the Old Dominion" at once, was blown down many years ago, and never has been, and probably never will be, rebuilt. The doors of the barn are in wretched condition; they will shut with a little human strength to help their worn out hinges, but not otherwise. The side of the great building seen from the road is much discolored in sundry places by slops poured from the upper windows, rendering it unsightly and offensive in other respects. Three or four great dogs, looking as dull and gloomy as the mansion itself, lie stretched out along the door-sills under the portico; and double the number of loafers, some of them completely rum-ripe, and others ripening, dispose themselves like so many sentinels about the front of the house. These latter understand the science of scraping acquaintance to perfection. They know everybody, and almost everybody knows them. Of course, as their title implies, they have no regular employment. They are (to use an expressive phrase) *hangers on*, or still better, they are what sailors would denominate *holders-on to the slack, in everybody's mess, and in nobody's watch.* They are, however, as good as the newspaper for the events of the day, and they sell their knowledge almost as cheap. Money they seldom have; yet they always have capital the most reliable. They make their way with a succeeding traveller by intelligence gained from a preceding one. All the great names of Virginia they know by heart, and have seen their owners often. The history of the house is folded in their lips, and they rattle off stories in connection with it, equal to the guides at Dryburgh Abbey. He must be a shrewd man, and well skilled in the art of evasion, who gets out of the hands of these fellows without being at the expense of a treat.

It was at this old tavern while on a second visit to the State of Virginia in1841, that Mr. Listwell, unacquainted with the fame of the place, turned aside, about sunset, to pass the night. Riding up to the house, he had scarcely dismounted, when one of the half dozen barroom fraternity met and addressed him in a manner exceedingly bland and accommodating.

"Fine evening, sir."

"Very fine," said Mr. Listwell. "This is a tavern, I believe?"

"O yes, sir, yes; although you may think it looks a little the worse for wear, it was once as good a house as any in Virginy. I make no doubt if ye spend the night here, you'll think it a good house yet; for there aint a more accommodating man in the country than you'll find the landlord."

Listwell: "The most I want is a good bed for myself, and a full manger for my horse. If I get these, I shall be quite satisfied."

Loafer: "Well, I alloys like to hear a gentleman talk for his horse; and just because the horse can't talk for itself. A man that don't care about his beast, and don't look arter it when he's travelling, aint much in my eye anyhow. Now, sir, I likes a horse, and I'll guarantee your horse will be taken good care on here. That old stable, for all you see it looks so shabby now, once sheltered the great *Eclipse*, when he run here agin *Batchelor* and *Jumping Jemmy*. Them was fast horses, but he beat 'em both."

Listwell: "Indeed."

Loafer: "Well I rather reckon you've travelled a right smart distance today, from the look of your horse?"

Listwell: "Forty miles only."

Loafer: "Well! I'll be damed if that aint a pretty good *only*. Mister, that beast of yours is a singed cat, I warrant you. I never see'd a creature like that that wasn't good on the road. You've come about forty miles, then?"

Listwell: "Yes, yes, and a pretty good pace at that."

Loafer: "You're somewhat in a hurry, then, I make no doubt? I reckon I could guess if I would, what you're going to Richmond for? It wouldn't be much of a guess either; for it's rumored hereabouts, that there's to be the greatest sale of niggers at Richmond tomorrow that has taken place there in a long time; and I'll be bound you're a going there to have a hand in it."

Listwell: "Why, you must think, then, that there's money to be made at that business?"

Loafer: "Well, 'pon my honor, sir, I never made any that way myself; but it stands to reason that it's a money making business; for almost all other business in Virginia is dropped to engage in this. One thing is sartain, I never see'd a nigger-buyer yet that hadn't a plenty of money, and he wasn't as free with it as water. I has known one on em to treat as high as twenty times in a night; and, ginerally speaking, they's men of edication, and knows all about the government. The fact is, sir, I alloys like to hear 'em talk, bekase I alloys can learn something from them."

Listwell: "What may I call your name, sir?"

Loafer: "Well, now, they calls me Wilkes. I'm known all around by the gentlemen that comes here. They all knows old Wilkes."

Listwell: "Well, Wilkes, you seem to be acquainted here, and I see you have a strong liking for a horse. Be so good as to speak a kind word for mine to the hostler tonight, and you'll not lose anything by it."

Loafer: "Well, sir, I see you don't say much, but you've got an insight into things. It's alloys wise to get the good will of them that's acquainted about a tavern; for a man don't know when he goes into a house what may happen, or how much he may need a friend."

Here the loafer gave Mr. Listwell a significant grin, which expressed a sort of triumphant pleasure at having, as he supposed, by his tact succeeded in placing so fine appearing a gentleman under obligations to him.

The pleasure, however, was not mutual; for there was something so insinuating in the glance of this loquacious customer, that Mr. Listwell was very glad to get quit of him, and to do so more successfully, he ordered his supper to be brought to him in his private room, private to the eye, but not to the ear. This room was directly over the bar, and the plastering being off, nothing but pine boards and naked laths separated him from the disagreeable company below—he could easily hear what was said in the bar-room, and was rather glad of the advantage it afforded, for, as you shall see, it furnished him important hints as to the manner and deportment he should assume during his stay at that tavern.

Mr. Listwell says he had got into his room but a few moments, when he heard the officious Wilkes below, in a tone of disappointment, exclaim, "Whar's that gentleman?" Wilkes was evidently expecting to meet with his friend at the bar-room, on his return, and had no doubt of his doing the handsome thing. "He has gone to his room," answered the landlord, "and has ordered his supper to be brought to him."

Here someone shouted out, "Who is he, Wilkes? Where's he going?"

"Well, now, I'll be hanged if I know; but I'm willing to make any man a bet of this old hat agin a five dollar bill, that that gent is as full of money as a dog is of fleas. He's going down to Richmond to buy niggers, I make no doubt. He's no fool, I warrant ye."

"Well, he acts d—d strange," said another, "anyhow. I likes to see a man, when he comes up to a tavern, to come straight into the bar-room, and show that he's a man among men. Nobody was going to bite him."

"Now, I don't blame him a bit for not coming in here. That man knows his business, and means to take care on his money," answered Wilkes.

"Wilkes, you're a fool. You only say that, because you hope to get a few coppers out on him."

"You only measure my corn by your half-bushel, I won't say that you're only mad bekase I got the chance of speaking to him first."

"O Wilkes! you're known here. You'll praise up anybody that will give you a copper; besides, 't is my opinion that that fellow who took his long slab-sides up stairs, for all the world just like a half-scared woman, afraid to look honest men in the face, is a *Northerner*, and as mean as dish-water."

"Now what will you bet of that," said Wilkes.

The speaker said, "I make no bets with you, 'kase you can get that fellow upstairs there to say anything."

"Well," said Wilkes, "I am willing to bet any man in the company that *that* gentleman is a *nigger*-buyer. He didn't tell me so right down, but I reckon I knows enough about men to give a pretty clean guess as to what they are arter."

The dispute as to *who* Mr. Listwell was, what his business, where he was going, etc., was kept up with much animation for some time, and more than once threatened a serious disturbance of the peace. Wilkes had his friends as well as his opponents. After this sharp debate, the company amused them selves by drinking whiskey, and telling stories. The latter consisting of quarrels, fights, *recontres*, and duels, in which distinguished persons of that neighborhood, and frequenters of that house, had been actors. Some of these stories were frightful enough, and were told, too, with a relish which bespoke the pleasure of the parties with the horrid scenes they portrayed. It would not be proper here to give the reader any idea of the vulgarity and dark profanity which rolled, as "a sweet morsel," under these corrupt tongues. A more brutal set of creatures, perhaps, never congregated.

Disgusted, and a little alarmed withal, Mr. Listwell, who was not accustomed to such entertainment, at length retired, but not to sleep. He was *too* much wrought upon by what he had heard to rest quietly, and what snatches of sleep he got, were interrupted by dreams which were anything than pleasant. At eleven o'clock, there seemed to be several hundreds of persons crowding into the house. A loud and confused clamor, cursing and cracking of whips, and the noise of chains startled him from his bed; for a moment he would have given the half of his farm in Ohio to have been at home. This uproar was kept up with undulating course, till near morning. There was loud laughing—loud singing—loud cursing—and yet there seemed to be weeping and mourning in the midst of all. Mr. Listwell said he had heard enough during the forepart of the night to convince him that a buyer of men and women stood the best chance of being respected. And he, therefore, thought it best to say nothing which might undo the favorable opinion that had been formed of him in the bar-room by at least one of the fraternity that swarmed about it. While he would not avow himself a purchaser of slaves, he deemed it not prudent to disavow it. He felt that he might, properly, refuse to cast such a pearl before parties which, to him, were worse than swine. To reveal himself, and to impart a knowledge of his real character and sentiments would, to say the least, be imparting intelligence with the certainty of seeing it and himself both abused. Mr. Listwell confesses, that this reasoning did not altogether satisfy his conscience, for, hating slavery as he did, and regarding it to be the immediate duty of every man to cry out against it, "without compromise and without concealment," it was hard for him to admit to himself the possibility of circumstances wherein a man might, properly, hold his tongue on the subject. Having as little of the spirit of a martyr as Erasmus, he concluded, like the latter, that it was wiser to trust the mercy of God for his soul, than the humanity of slave-traders for his body. Bodily fear, not conscientious scruples, prevailed.

In this spirit he rose early in the morning, manifesting no surprise at what he had heard during the night. His quondam friend was soon at his elbow, boring him with all sorts of questions. All, however, directed to find out his character, business, residence, purposes, and destination. With the most perfect appearance of good nature and carelessness, Mr. Listwell evaded these meddlesome inquiries, and turned conversation to general topics, leaving himself and all that specially pertained to him, out of discussion. Disengaging himself from their troublesome companionship, he made his way towards an old bowling-alley, which was connected with the house, and which, like all the rest, was in very bad repair.

On reaching the alley Mr. Listwell saw, for the first time in his life, a slave-gang on their way to market. A sad sight truly. Here were one hundred and thirty human beings—children of a common Creator—guilty of no crime—men and women, with hearts, minds, and deathless spirits, chained and fettered, and bound for the market, in a Christian country—in a country boasting of its liberty, independence, and high civilization! Humanity converted into merchandise, and linked in iron bands, with no regard to decency or humanity! All sizes, ages, and sexes, mothers, fathers, daughters, brothers, sisters—all huddled together, on their way to market to be sold and separated from home, and from each other *forever*. And all to fill the pockets of men too lazy to work for an honest living, and who gain their fortune by plundering the helpless, and trafficking in the souls and sinews of men. As he gazed upon this revolting and heart-rending scene, our informant said he almost doubted the existence of a God of justice! And he stood wondering that the earth did not open and swallow up such wickedness.

In the midst of these recollections, and while running his eye up and down the fettered ranks, he met the glance of one whose face he thought he had seen before. To be resolved, he moved towards the spot. It was *Madison Washington!* Here was a scene for the pencil! Had Mr. Listwell been confronted by one risen from the dead, he could not have been more appalled. He was completely stunned. A thunderbolt could not have struck him more dumb. He stood, for a few moments as motionless as one petrified; collecting himself, he at length exclaimed, "*Madison, is that you?*"

The noble fugitive, but little less astonished than himself, answered cheerily, "O yes, sir, they've got me again."

Thoughtless of consequences for the moment, Mr. Listwell ran up to his old friend, placing his hands upon his shoulders, and looked him in the face! Speechless they stood gazing at each other as if to be doubly resolved that there was no mistake about the matter, till Madison motioned his friend away, intimating a fear lest the keepers should find him there, and suspect him of tampering with the slaves.

"They will soon be out to look after us. You can come when they go to breakfast, and I will tell you all."

Pleased with this arrangement, Mr. Listwell passed out of the alley; but only just in time to save himself, for, while near the door, he observed three men making their way to the alley. The thought occurred to him to await their arrival, as the best means of diverting the ever ready suspicions of the guilty.

While the scene between Mr. Listwell and his friend Madison was going on, the other slaves stood as mute spectators—at a loss to know what all this could mean. As he left, he heard the man chained to Madison ask, "Who is that gentleman?"

"He is a friend of mine. I cannot tell you now. Suffice it to say he is a friend. You shall hear more of him before long, but mark me! whatever shall pass between that gentleman and me, in your hearing, I pray you will say nothing about it. We are chained here together—ours is a common lot; and that gentleman is not less *your* friend than *mine*." At these words, all mysterious as they were, the unhappy company gave signs of satisfaction and hope. It seems that Madison, by that mesmeric power which is the invariable accompaniment of genius, had already won the confidence of the gang, and was a sort of general-in-chief among them.

By this time the keepers arrived. A horrid trio, well fitted for their demoniacal work. Their uncombed hair came down over foreheads *"villainously low,"* and with eyes, mouths, and noses to match. "Hallo! hallo!" they growled out as they entered. "Are you all there!"

"All here," said Madison.

"Well, well, that's right! your journey will soon be over. You'll be in Richmond by eleven today, and then you'll have an easy time of it."

"I say, gal, what in the devil are you crying about?" said one of them. "I'll give you something to cry about, if you don't mind." This was said to a girl, apparently not more than twelve years old, who had been weeping bitterly. She had, probably, left behind her a loving mother, affectionate sisters, brothers, and friends, and her tears were but the natural expression of her sorrow, and the only solace. But the dealers in human flesh have *no* respect for such sorrow. They look upon it as a protest against their cruel injustice, and they are prompt to punish it.

This is a puzzle not easily solved. *How* came he here? what can I do for him? may I not even now be in some way compromised in this affair? were thoughts that troubled Mr. Listwell, and made him eager for the promised opportunity of speaking to Madison.

The bell now sounded for breakfast, and keepers and drivers, with pistols and bowie-knives gleaming from their belts, hurried in, as if to get the best places.

Taking the chance now afforded, Mr. Listwell hastened back to the bowling-alley. Reaching Madison, he said, "Now do tell me all about the matter. Do you know me?"

"Oh, yes," said Madison, "I know you well, and shall never forget you nor that cold and dreary night you gave me shelter. I must be short," he continued, "for they'll soon be out again. This, then, is the story in brief. On reaching Canada, and getting over the excitement of making my escape, sir, my thoughts turned to my poor wife, who had well deserved my love by her virtuous fidelity and undying affection for me. I could not bear the thought of leaving her in the cruel jaws of slavery, without making an effort to rescue her. First, I tried to get money to her; but oh! the process was *too slow*. I despaired of accomplishing it. She was in all my thoughts by day, and my dreams by night. At times I could almost hear her voice, saying, 'O Madison! Madison! will you then leave me here? can you leave me here to die? No! no! you will come! you will come!' I was wretched. I lost my appetite. I could neither work, eat, nor sleep, till I resolved to hazard my own liberty, to gain that of my wife! But I must be short. Six weeks ago I reached my old master's place. I laid about the neighborhood nearly a week, watching my chance, and, finally, I ventured upon the desperate attempt to reach my poor wife's room by means of a ladder. I reached the window, but the noise in raising it frightened my wife, and she screamed and fainted. I took her in my arms, and was descending the ladder, when the dogs began to bark furiously, and before I could get to the woods the white folks were roused. The cool night air soon restored my wife, and she readily recognized me. We made the best of our way to the woods, but it was now too late—the dogs were after us as though they would have torn us to pieces. It was all over with me now! My old master and his two sons ran out with loaded rifles, and before we were out of gunshot, our ears were assailed with '*Stop! stop! or be shot down.*' Nevertheless we ran on. Seeing that we gave no heed to their calls, they fired, and my poor wife fell by my side dead, while I received but a slight flesh wound. I now became desperate, and stood my ground, and awaited their attack over her dead body. They rushed upon me, with their rifles in hand. I parried their blows, and fought them 'till I was knocked down and overpowered."

"Oh! it was madness to have returned," said Mr. Listwell.

"Sir, I could not be free with the galling thought that my poor wife was still a slave. With her in slavery, my body, not my spirit, was free. I was taken to the house—chained to a ring-bolt—my wounds dressed. I was kept there three days. All the slaves, for miles around, were brought to see me. Many slaveholders came with their slaves, using me as proof of the completeness of their power, and of the impossibility of slaves getting away. I was taunted, jeered at, and berated by them, in a manner that pierced me to the soul. Thank God, I was able to smother my rage, and to bear it all with seeming composure. After my wounds were nearly healed, I was taken to a tree and stripped, and I received sixty lashes on my naked back. A few days after, I was sold to a slave-trader, and placed in this gang for the New Orleans market."

"Do you think your master would sell you to me?"

"O no, sir! I was sold on condition of my being taken South. Their motive is revenge."

"Then, then," said Mr. Listwell, "I fear I can do nothing for you. Put your trust in God, and bear your sad lot with the manly fortitude which becomes a man. I shall see you at Richmond, but don't recognize me." Saying this, Mr. Listwell handed Madison ten dollars; said a few words to the other slaves; received their hearty "God bless you," and made his way to the house.

Fearful of exciting suspicion by too long delay, our friend went to the breakfast table, with the air of one who half reproved the greediness of those who rushed in at the sound of the bell. A cup of coffee was all that he could manage. His feelings were too bitter and excited, and his heart was too full with the fate of poor Madison (whom he loved as well as admired) to relish his breakfast; and although he sat long after the company had left the table, he really did little more than change the position of his knife and fork. The strangeness of meeting again one whom he had met on two several occasions before, under extraordinary circumstances, was well calculated to suggest the idea that a supernatural power, a wakeful providence, or an inexorable fate, had linked their destiny together; and that no efforts of his could disentangle him from the mysterious web of circumstances which enfolded him.

On leaving the table, Mr. Listwell nerved himself up and walked firmly into the bar-room. He was at once greeted again by that talkative chatter-box, Mr. Wilkes.

"Them's a likely set of niggers in the alley there," said Wilkes.

"Yes, they're fine looking fellows, one of them I should like to purchase, and for him I would be willing to give a handsome sum."

Turning to one of his comrades, and with a grin of victory, Wilkes said, "Aha, Bill, did you hear that? I told you I know'd that gentleman wanted to buy niggers, and would bid as high as any purchaser in the market."

"Come, come," said Listwell, "don't be too loud in your praise, you are old enough to know that prices rise when purchasers are plenty."

"That's a fact," said Wilkes, "I see you knows the rope—and there's not a man in old Virginy whom I'd rather help to make a good bargain than you, sir."

Mr. Listwell here threw a dollar at Wilkes (which the latter caught with a dexterous hand), saying, "Take that for your kind good will." Wilkes held up the dollar to his right eye, with a grin of victory, and turned to the morose grumbler in the corner who had questioned the liberality of a man of whom he knew nothing.

Mr. Listwell now stood as well with the company as any other occupant of the bar-room.

We pass over the hurry and bustle, the brutal vociferations of the slave-drivers in getting their unhappy gang in motion for Richmond; and we need not narrate every application of the lash to those who faltered in the journey. Mr. Listwell followed the train at a long distance, with a sad heart; and on reaching Richmond, left his horse at a hotel, and made his way to the wharf in the direction of which he saw the slave-coffle driven. He was just in time to see the whole company embark for New Orleans. The thought struck him that, while mixing with the multitude, he might do his friend Madison one last service, and he stept into a hardware store and purchased three strong *files*. These he took with him, and standing near the small boat, which lay in waiting to bear the company by parcels to the side of the brig that lay in the stream, he managed, as Madison passed him, to slip the files into his pocket, and at once darted back among the crowd.

All the company now on board, the imperious voice of the captain sounded, and instantly a dozen hardy seamen were in the rigging, hurrying aloft to unfurl the broad canvas of our Baltimore built American Slaver. The sailors hung about the ropes, like so many black cats, now in the round-tops, now in the cross-trees, now on the yard-arms, all was bluster and activity. Soon the broad fore topsail, the royal and top gallant sail were spread to the breeze. Round went the heavy windlass, clank, clank went the fall-bit—the anchors weighed—jibs, mainsails, and topsails hauled to the wind, and the long, low, black slaver, with her cargo of human flesh, careened and moved forward to the sea.

Mr. Listwell stood on the shore, and watched the slaver till the last speck of her upper sails faded from sight, and announced the limit of human vision. "Farewell! farewell! brave and true man! God grant that brighter skies may smile upon your future than have yet looked down upon your thorny pathway."

Saying this to himself, our friend lost no time in completing his business, and in making his way homewards, gladly shaking off from his feet the dust of Old Virginia.

IV

Oh, where's the slave so lowly
  Condemn'd to chains unholy,
Who could he burst
  His bonds at first
Would pine beneath them slowly?
—Moore

Know ye not
Who would be free *themselves* must strike the blow.
—Childe Harold

What a world of inconsistency, as well as of wickedness, is suggested by the smooth and gliding phrase, *American Slave Trade*; and how strange and perverse is that moral sentiment which loathes, execrates, and brands as piracy and as deserving of death the carrying away into captivity men, women, and children from the *African coast*; but which is neither shocked nor disturbed by a similar traffic, carried on with the same motives and purposes, and characterized by even *more* odious peculiarities on the coast of our *Model Republic*. We execrate and hang the wretch guilty of this crime on the coast of Guinea, while we respect and applaud the guilty participators in this murderous business on the enlightened shores of the Chesapeake. The inconsistency is so flagrant and glaring, that it would seem to cast a doubt on the doctrine of the innate moral sense of mankind.

Just two months after the sailing of the Virginia slave brig, which the reader has seen move off to sea so proudly with her human cargo for the New Orleans market, there chanced to meet, in the Marine Coffee-house at Richmond, a company of *ocean birds*, when the following conversation, which throws some light on the subsequent history, not only of Madison Washington, but of the hundred and thirty human beings with whom we last saw him chained.

"I say, shipmate, you had rather rough weather on your late passage to Orleans?" said Jack Williams, a regular old salt, tauntingly, to a trim, compact, manly looking person, who proved to be the first mate of the slave brig in question.

"Foul play, as well as foul weather," replied the firmly knit personage, evidently but little inclined to enter upon a subject which terminated so ingloriously to the captain and officers of the American slaver.

"Well, betwixt you and me," said Williams, "that whole affair on board of the *Creole* was miserably and disgracefully managed. Those black rascals got the upper hand of ye altogether; and, in my opinion, the whole disaster was the result of ignorance of the real character of *darkies* in general. With half a dozen *resolute* white men, (I say it not boastingly) I could have had the rascals in irons in ten minutes, not because I'm so strong, but I know how to manage 'em. With my back against the *caboose*, I could, myself, have flogged a dozen of them; and had I been on board, by every monster of the deep, every black devil of 'em all would have had his neck stretched from the yard-arm. Ye made a mistake in yer manner of fighting 'em. All that is needed in dealing with a set of rebellious *darkies*, is to show that yer not afraid of 'em. For my own part, I would not honor a dozen niggers, by pointing a gun at one on 'em—a good stout whip, or a stiff rope's end, is better than all the guns at Old Point to quell a *nigger* insurrection. Why, sir, to take a gun to a *nigger* is the best way you can select to tell him you are afraid of him, and the best way of inviting his attack."

This speech made quite a sensation among the company, and a part of them indicated solicitude for the answer which might be made to it. Our first mate replied, "Mr. Williams, all that you've now said sounds very well *here* on shore, where, perhaps, you have studied negro character. I do not profess to understand the subject as well as yourself; but it strikes me, you apply the same rule in dissimilar cases. It is quite easy to talk of flogging niggers here on land, where you have the sympathy of the community, and the whole physical force of the government, State and national, at your command, and where, if a negro shall lift his hand against a white man, the whole community, with one accord, are ready to unite in shooting him down. I say, in such circumstances, it's easy to talk of flogging negroes and of negro cowardice; but, sir, I deny that the negro is, naturally, a coward, or that your theory of managing slaves will stand the test of *salt* water. It may do very well for an overseer, a contemptible hireling, to take advantage of fears already in existence, and which his presence has no power to inspire; to swagger about whip in hand, and discourse on the timidity and cowardice of negroes; for they have a smooth sea and a fair wind. It is one thing to manage a company of slaves on a Virginia plantation, and quite another thing to quell an insurrection on the lonely billows of the Atlantic, where every breeze speaks of courage and liberty. For the negro to act cowardly on shore, may be to act wisely; and I've some doubts whether *you*, Mr. Williams, would find it very convenient were you a slave in Algiers, to raise your hand against the bayonets of a whole government."

"By George, shipmate," said Williams, "you're coming rather *too* near. Either I've fallen very low in your estimation, or your notions of negro courage have got up a button-hole too high. Now I more than ever wish I'd been on board of that luckless craft. I'd have given ye practical evidence of the truth of my theory. I don't doubt there's some difference in being at sea. But a nigger's a nigger, on sea or land; and is a coward, find him where you will; a drop of blood from one on 'em will skeer a hundred. A knock on the nose, or a kick on the shin, will tame the wildest *'darkey'* you can fetch me. I say again, and will stand by it, I could, with half a dozen good men, put the whole nineteen on 'em in irons, and have carried them safe to New Orleans too. Mind, I don't blame you, but I do say, and every gentleman here will bear me out in it, that the fault was somewhere, or them niggers would never have got off as they have done. For my part I feel ashamed to have the idea go abroad, that a ship load of slaves can't be safely taken from Richmond to New Orleans. I should like, merely to redeem the character of Virginia sailors, to take charge of a ship load on 'em tomorrow."

Williams went on in this strain, occasionally casting an imploring glance at the company for applause for his wit, and sympathy for his contempt of negro courage. He had, evidently, however, waked up the wrong passenger; for besides being in the right, his opponent carried that in his eye which marked him a man not to be trifled with.

"Well, sir," said the sturdy mate, "you can select your own method for distinguishing yourself—the path of ambition in this direction is quite open to you in Virginia, and I've no doubt that you will be highly appreciated and compensated for all your valiant achievements in that line; but for myself, while I do not profess to be a giant, I have resolved never to set my foot on the deck of a slave ship, either as officer, or common sailor again; I have got enough of it."

"Indeed! indeed!" exclaimed Williams, derisively.

"Yes, *indeed*," echoed the mate; "but don't misunderstand me. It is not the high value that I set upon my life that makes me say what I have said; yet I'm resolved never to endanger my life again in a cause which my conscience does not approve. I dare say *here* what many men *feel*, but *dare not speak*, that this whole slave-trading business is a disgrace and scandal to Old Virginia."

"Hold! hold on! shipmate," said Williams, "I hardly thought you'd have shown your colors so soon—I'll be hanged if you're not as good an abolitionist as Garrison himself."

The mate now rose from his chair, manifesting some excitement. "What do you mean, sir," said he, in a commanding tone. "*That man does not live who shall offer me an insult with impunity.*"

The effect of these words was marked; and the company clustered around. Williams, in an apologetic tone, said, "Shipmate! keep your temper. I meant no insult. We all know that Tom Grant is no coward, and what I said about your being an abolitionist was simply this: you *might* have put down them black mutineers and murderers, but your conscience held you back."

"In that, too," said Grant, "you were mistaken. I did all that any man with equal strength and presence of mind could have done. The fact is, Mr. Williams, you underrate the courage as well as the skill of these negroes, and further, you do not seem to have been correctly informed about the case in hand at all."

"All I know about it is," said Williams, "that on the ninth day after you left Richmond, a dozen or two of the niggers ye had on board, came on deck and took the ship from you—had her steered into a British port, where, by the by, every woolly head of them went ashore and was free. Now I take this to be a discreditable piece of business, and one demanding explanation."

"There are a great many discreditable things in the world," said Grant. "For a ship to go down under a calm sky is, upon the first flush of it, disgraceful either to sailors or caulkers. But when we learn, that by some mysterious disturbance in nature, the waters parted beneath, and swallowed the ship up, we lose our indignation and disgust in lamentation of the disaster, and in awe of the Power which controls the elements."

"Very true, very true," said Williams, "I should be very glad to have an explanation which would relieve the affair of its present discreditable features. I have desired to see you ever since you got home, and to learn from you a full statement of the facts in the case. To me the whole thing seems unaccountable. I cannot see how a dozen or two of ignorant negroes, not one of whom had ever been to sea before, and all of them were closely ironed between decks, should be able to get their fetters off, rush out of the hatchway in open daylight, kill two white men, the one the captain and the other their master, and then carry the ship into a British port, where every '*darkey*' of them was set free. There must have been great carelessness, or cowardice somewhere!"

The company, which had listened in silence during most of this discussion, now became much excited. One said, I agree with Williams; and several said the thing looks black enough. After the temporary tumultuous exclamations had subsided—

"I see," said Grant, "how you regard this case, and how difficult it will be for me to render our ship's company blameless in your eyes. Nevertheless, I will state the facts precisely as they came under my own observation. Mr. Williams speaks of 'ignorant negroes,' and, as a general rule, they are ignorant; but had he been on board the *Creole* as I was, he would have seen cause to admit that there are exceptions to this general rule. The leader of the mutiny in question was just as shrewd a fellow as ever I met in my life, and was as well fitted to lead in a dangerous enterprise as any one white man in ten thousand. The name of this man, strange to say, (ominous of greatness) was *Madison Washington*. In the short time he had been on board, he had secured the confidence of every officer. The negroes fairly worshipped him. His manner and bearing were such, that no one could suspect him of a murderous purpose. The only feeling with which we regarded him was, that he was a powerful, good-disposed negro. He seldom spake to anyone, and when he did speak, it was with the utmost propriety. His words were well chosen, and his pronunciation equal to that of any schoolmaster. It was a mystery to us *where* he got his knowledge of language; but as little was said to him, none of us knew the extent of his intelligence and ability till it was too late. It seems he brought three files with him on board, and must have gone to work upon his fetters the first night out; and he must have worked well at that; for on the day of the rising, he got the irons *off eighteen* besides himself.

"The attack began just about twilight in the evening. Apprehending a squall, I had commanded the second mate to order all hands on deck, to take in sail. A few minutes before this I had seen Madison's head above the hatchway, looking out upon the white-capped waves at the leeward. I think I never saw him look more good-natured. I stood just about midship, on the larboard side. The captain was pacing the quarter-deck on the starboard side, in company with Mr. Jameson, the owner of most of the slaves on board. Both were armed. I had just told the men to lay aloft, and was looking to see my orders obeyed, when I heard the discharge of a pistol on the starboard side; and turning suddenly around, the very deck seemed covered with fiends from the pit. The nineteen negroes were all on deck, with their broken fetters in their hands, rushing in all directions. I put my hand quickly in my pocket to draw out my jack-knife; but before I could draw it, I was knocked senseless to the deck. When I came to myself (which I did in a few minutes, I suppose, for it was yet quite light), there was not a white man on deck. The sailors were all aloft in the rigging, and dared not come down. Captain Clarke and Mr. Jameson lay stretched on the quarter-deck, *both dying,* while Madison himself stood at the helm unhurt.

"I was completely weakened by the loss of blood, and had not recovered from the stunning blow which felled me to the deck; but it was a little too much for me, even in my prostrate condition, to see our good brig commanded by a *black murderer*. So I called out to the men to come down and take the ship, or die in the attempt. Suiting the action to the word, I started aft. 'You murderous villain,' said I, to the imp at the helm, and rushed upon him to deal him a blow, when he pushed me back with his strong, black arm, as though I had been a boy of twelve. I looked around for the men. They were still in the rigging. Not one had come down. I started towards Madison again. The rascal now told me to stand back. 'Sir,' said he, 'your life is in my hands. I could have killed you a dozen times over during this last half hour, and could kill you now. You call me a *black murderer*. I am not a murderer. God is my witness that LIBERTY, not *malice*, is the motive for this night's work. I have done no more to those dead men yonder, than they would have done to me in like circumstances. We have struck for our freedom, and if a true man's heart be in you, you win honor us for the deed. We have done that which you applaud your fathers for doing, and if we are murderers, *so were they*.'

"I felt little disposition to reply to this impudent speech. By heaven, it disarmed me. The fellow loomed up before me. I forgot his blackness in the dignity of his manner, and the eloquence of his speech. It seemed as if the *souls of both the great dead* (whose names he bore) had entered him. To the sailors in the rigging he said: 'Men! the battle is over—your captain is dead. I have complete command of this vessel. All resistance to my authority will be in vain. My men have won their liberty, with no other weapons but their *own broken fetters*. We are nineteen in number. We do not thirst for your blood, we demand only our rightful freedom. Do not flatter yourselves that I am ignorant of chart or compass. I know both. We are now only about sixty miles from Nassau. Come down, and do your duty. Land us in Nassau, and not a hair of your heads shall be hurt.'

"I shouted, '*Stay where you are, men,*'—when a sturdy black fellow ran at me with a handspike, and would have split my head open, but for the interference of Madison, who darted between me and the blow. 'I know what you are up to,' said the latter to me. 'You want to navigate this brig into a slave port, where you would have us all hanged; but you'll miss it; before this brig shall touch a slave-cursed shore while I am on board, I will myself put a match to the magazine, and blow her, and be blown with her, into a thousand fragments. Now I have saved your life twice within these last twenty minutes—for, when you lay helpless on deck, my men were about to kill you. I held them in check. And if you now (seeing I am your friend and not your enemy) persist in your resistance to my authority, I give you fair warning, *you shall die*.'

"Saying this to me, he cast a glance into the rigging where the terror-stricken sailors were clinging, like so many frightened monkeys, and commanded them to come down, in a tone from which there was no appeal; for four men stood by with muskets in hand, ready at the word of command to shoot them down.

"I now became satisfied that resistance was out of the question; that my best policy was to put the brig into Nassau, and secure the assistance of the American consul at the port. I felt sure that the authorities would enable us to secure the murderers, and bring them to trial.

"By this time the apprehended squall had burst upon us. The wind howled furiously—the ocean was white with foam, which, on account of the darkness, we could see only by the quick flashes of lightning that darted occasionally from the angry sky. All was alarm and confusion. Hideous cries came up from the slave women. Above the roaring billows a succession of heavy thunder rolled along, swelling the terrific din. Owing to the great darkness, and a sudden shift of the wind, we found ourselves in the trough of the sea. When shipping a heavy sea over the starboard bow, the bodies of the captain and Mr. Jameson were washed overboard. For awhile we had dearer interests to look after than slave property. A more savage thunder-gust never swept the ocean. Our brig rolled and creaked as if every bolt would be started, and every thread of oakum would be pressed out of the seams. 'To the pumps! to the pumps!' I cried, but not a sailor would quit his grasp. Fortunately this squall soon passed over, or we must have been food for sharks.

"During all the storm, Madison stood firmly at the helm—his keen eye fixed upon the binnacle. He was not indifferent to the dreadful hurricane; yet he met it with the equanimity of an old sailor. He was silent but not agitated. The first words he uttered after the storm had slightly subsided, were characteristic of the man. 'Mr. mate, you cannot write the bloody laws of slavery on those restless billows. The ocean, if not the land, is free.' I confess, gentlemen, I felt myself in the presence of a superior man; one who, had he been a white man, I would have followed willingly and gladly in any honorable enterprise. Our difference of color was the only ground for difference of action. It was not that his principles were wrong in the abstract; for they are the principles of 1776. But I could not bring myself to recognize their application to one whom I deemed my inferior.

"But to my story. What happened now is soon told. Two hours after the frightful tempest had spent itself, we were plump at the wharf in Nassau. I sent two of our men immediately to our consul with a statement of facts, requesting his interference in our behalf. What he did, or whether he did anything, I don't know; but, by order of the authorities, a company of *black* soldiers came on board, for the purpose, as they said, of protecting the property. These impudent rascals, when I called on them to assist me in keeping the slaves on board, sheltered themselves adroitly under their instructions only to protect property—and said they did not recognize *persons as property*. I told them that by the laws of Virginia and the laws of the United States, the slaves on board were as much property as the barrels of flour in the hold. At this the stupid blockheads showed their *ivory*, rolled up their white eyes in horror, as if the idea of putting men on a footing with merchandise were revolting to their humanity. When these instructions were understood among the negroes, it was impossible for us to keep them on board. They deliberately gathered up their baggage before our eyes, and, against our remonstrances, poured through the gangway—formed themselves into a procession on the wharf—bid farewell to all on board, and, uttering the wildest shouts of exultation, they marched, amidst the deafening cheers of a multitude of sympathizing spectators, under the triumphant leadership of their heroic chief and deliverer, *Madison Washington*."

(1853)

SPEECHES AND ESSAYS

The Church and Prejudice

At the South I was a member of the Methodist Church. When I came north, I thought one Sunday I would attend communion, at one of the churches of my denomination, in the town I was staying. The white people gathered round the altar, the blacks clustered by the door. After the good minister had served out the bread and wine to one portion of those near him, he said, "These may withdraw, and others come forward"; thus he proceeded till all the white members had been served. Then he took a long breath, and looking out towards the door, exclaimed, "Come up, colored friends, come up! for you know God is no respecter of persons!" I haven't been there to see the sacraments taken since.

At New Bedford, where I live, there was a great revival of religion not long ago—many were converted and "received" as they said, "into the kingdom of heaven." But it seems, the kingdom of heaven is like a net; at least so it was according to the practice of these pious Christians; and when the net was drawn ashore, they had to set down and cull out the fish. Well, it happened now that some of the fish had rather black scales; so these were sorted out and packed by themselves. But among those who experienced religion at this time was a colored girl; she was baptized in the same water as the rest; so she thought she might sit at the Lord's table and partake of the same sacramental elements with the others. The deacon handed round the cup, and when he came to the black girl, he could not pass her, for there was the minister looking right at him, and as he was a kind of abolitionist, the deacon was rather afraid of giving him offence; so he handed the girl the cup, and she tasted. Now it so happened that next to her sat a young lady who had been converted at the same time, baptized in the same water, and put her trust in the same blessed Saviour; yet when the cup containing the precious blood which had been shed for all, came to her, she rose in disdain, and walked out of the church. Such was the religion she had experienced!

Another young lady fell into a trance. When she awoke, she declared she had been to heaven. Her friends were all anxious to know what and whom she had seen there; so she told the whole story. But there was one good old lady whose curiosity went beyond that of all the others—and she inquired of the girl that had the vision, if she saw any black folks in heaven? After some hesitation, the reply was, *"Oh! I didn't go into the kitchen!"*

Thus you see, my hearers, this prejudice goes even into the church of God. And there are those who carry it so far that it is disagreeable to them even to think of going to heaven, if colored people are going there too. And whence comes it? The grand cause is slavery; but there are others less prominent; one of them is the way in which children in this part of the country are instructed to regard the blacks.

"Yes!" exclaimed an old gentleman, interrupting him—"when they behave wrong, they are told, 'black man come catch you.'"

Yet people in general will say they like colored men as well as any other, but in their proper place! They assign us that place; they don't let us do it for ourselves, nor will they allow us a voice in the decision. They will not allow that we have a head to think, and a heart to feel, and a soul to aspire. They treat us not as men, but as dogs—they cry "Stu-boy!" and expect us to run and do their bidding. That's the way we are liked. You degrade us, and then ask why we are degraded—you shut our mouths, and then ask why we don't speak—you close our colleges and seminaries against us, and then ask why we don't know more.

But all this prejudice sinks into insignificance in my mind, when compared with the enormous iniquity of the system which is its cause—the system that sold my four sisters and my brothers into bondage—and which calls in its priests to defend it even from the Bible! The slaveholding ministers preach up the divine right of the slaveholders to property in their fellow-men. The southern preachers say to the poor slave, "Oh! if you wish to be happy in time, happy in eternity, you must be obedient to your masters; their interest is yours. God made one portion of men to do the working, and another to do the thinking; how good God is! Now, you have no trouble or anxiety; but ah! you can't imagine how perplexing it is to your masters and mistresses to have so much thinking to do in your behalf! You cannot appreciate your blessings; you know not how happy a thing it is for you, that you were born of that portion of the human family which has the working, instead of the thinking to do! Oh! how grateful and obedient you ought to be to your masters! How beautiful are the arrangements of Providence! Look at your hard, horny hands—see how nicely they are adapted to the labor you have to perform! Look at our delicate fingers, so exactly fitted for our station, and see how manifest it is that God designed us to be His thinkers, and you the workers—Oh! the wisdom of God!"—I used to attend a Methodist church, in which my master was a class leader; he would talk most sanctimoniously about the dear Redeemer, who was sent "to preach deliverance to the captives, and set at liberty them that are bruised"—he could pray at morning, pray at noon, and pray at night; yet he could lash up my poor cousin by his two thumbs, and inflict stripes and blows upon his bare back, till the blood streamed to the ground! all the time quoting scripture, for his authority, and appealing to that passage of the Holy Bible which says, "He that knoweth his master's will, and doeth it not, shall be beaten with many stripes!" Such was the amount of this good Methodist's piety.

(1841)

We Have Decided to Stay

Mr. Chairman, and Ladies and Gentlemen:

It is with great hesitation that I consent to rise here to speak, after the able speech to which you have just listened. I had far rather remain a listener to others, than to become myself a speaker at this stage of the proceedings of this meeting. I do not hope to be able, in the few remarks I have to make, to say anything new or eloquent, for it will be time indeed to discuss new truths, when old ones shall have been recognized and adopted.

For seventeen years, Mr. Chairman, the Abolitionists of the United States have been encountering obloquy, scorn, and opposition of the most furious character, for uttering—what? Their conviction that a man is a man—that every man belongs to himself and to no one else. In propagating this idea, this simple proposition, we have met with all sorts of opposition, and with all sorts of arguments drawn from the Bible, from the Constitution, and from philosophy, till at length many have arrived at the sage conclusion that a man is something else than a man, and that he has not the rights of a man.

An event has just occurred in the District of Columbia, the Capitol of the country, known to you all, which furnishes the proof of this assertion. Some seventy-seven men, women, and children, took it into their heads, contrary to the Constitution, that they were men, not *three fifths of men*—that they would leave the refined avocation of blacking boots for nothing for members of Congress, and seek an asylum from oppression and tyranny in some of the Northern States, or under the protection of the British Lion in Canada. The sequel is well known; they were pursued by a band of armed men, overtaken, and brought back in chains, and the men who aided them in their flight are in a dungeon, and there they will probably end their lives.

Very little is thought about this affair—very little noise is made about it. It excites about as much remark, and about as much sympathy as if as many horses had broken away from the halters of their owners, and again been recovered.

Sir, we have, in this country, no adequate idea of humanity yet; the nation does not feel that these are men, it cannot see through the dark skin and curly hair of the black man, anything like humanity, or that has claims to human rights. Had they been white men and women, or were they regarded as human beings, this nation would have been agitated to its centre, and rocked as with an earthquake shock, and like the nations of the Old World, would have rung with the thunders of freedom against tyranny, at such an event as this.

We do not regard these men as formed in the image of God. We do not see that in the persons of these men and women whose rights have been stricken down, whose virtuous attempt to gain their freedom, has been defeated, the violation of the common rights of man.

Even the gallant Hale, of the Liberty party, does not dare to speak of the men who aided their escape, as having done a noble deed. To be sure, he can bring in a proposition for the better protection of *property* in the District of Columbia, but he makes no allusion whatever, to the rights of black men. This proposition in relation to the rights of property, is regarded by his adherents as a noble act; as a timely measure; as indicating great courage and heroism. Nor do I care to deny it. But what is the inference? If it be a noble act, a courageous act, to move in the Capitol of the nation, in the Senate of the United States, a bill to protect property from the assaults of a brutal and ferocious mob—if that be bold, of course it would be no less daring and fanatical to move in that District, that the rights of *man* be protected. [*Applause*]

I do not propose to make a lengthy speech, but I would like to say a few words about how these things look to others.

> O wad some power the giftie gie us
> To see oursels as others see us.

I would like to hold up to you a picture; not drawn by an American pen or pencil, but by a foreigner. I want to show you how you look abroad in the delectable business of kidnapping and slave-driving.

Sometimes since—I think it was in the December number of "Punch"—I saw an excellent pictorial description of America. What think you it was? It was entitled, "Brother Jonathan." It was a long, lean, gaunt, shrivelled looking creature, stretched out on two chairs, and his legs resting on the prostrate bust of Washington; projecting from behind was a cat o' nine tails knotted at the ends; around his person he wore a belt in which were stuck those truly American implements, a bowie knife, dirk, and revolving pistol; behind him was a whipping post, with a naked woman tied to it, and a strong-armed American citizen in the act of scourging her livid flesh with a cowskin. At his feet was another group—a sale going on, of human cattle, and around the auctioneer's table were gathered the *respectability*—the religion represented in the person of the clergy—of America, buying them for export to the goodly city of New Orleans. Little further on there was a scene of branding—a small group of slaves tied hand and foot, while their patriotic and philanthropic masters were burning their name into their quivering flesh. Further on, there was a drove of slaves, bound for New Orleans. Above these and several other scenes illustrative of the character of our institutions, waved the star spangled banner. Still further back in the distance was the picture of the achievements of our gallant army in Mexico, shooting, stabbing, hanging; destroying property, and massacreing the innocent with the innocent, not with the guilty, and over all this was a picture of the Devil himself, looking down with Satanic satisfaction on passing events. [*Laughter*]

Here I conceive to be a true picture of America, and I hesitate not to say that this description falls far short of the real facts, and of the aspect we bear to the world around us.

Sir, although we have heard conflicting views uttered here today, of hopeful and desponding aspects (if, indeed, we have any desponding aspects brought to us), still, I think much more may be said in behalf of the hopeful aspects. The signs of the times have been already alluded to; we have very properly gone beyond the limits of the United States.

I see some of the audience are going out, which makes me think I have spoken long enough; some plants thrive better by being cut off, and perhaps my speech may as well be cut off here; not because there is not more to be said, but because your energies have been taxed quite enough already. [*Cries of go on!*] Since, then, you wish me to proceed, and, as Henry Clay says, "I am always subject to the will of the people," there may yet be room for something of a speech.

As I was proceeding to remark concerning the hopeful aspects of the times, I wish to bring with more distinctness before your minds, the news which comes from abroad—the action of the Provisional

Government of France. We have been accustomed, in this country, to hear much talk about "Christian America, and Infidel France." I want to say in behalf of France, that I go for that infidelity—no matter how heinous it may be in the estimation of the American people—which strikes the chains from the limbs of our brethren; and against that Christianity which puts them on, [*Applause*]—for that infidelity, which, in the person of Cremieux, one of the members of the Provisional Government of France, speaks to the black and mulatto men, that come to congratulate them, and express their sentiments upon the immediate emancipation of their brethren in the French islands. I sympathize with that infidelity that speaks to them in language like this: *friends! brothers! men!* In France, the negro is a man, while you who are throwing up your caps, and waving your banners, and making beautiful speeches in behalf of liberty, deny us our humanity, and traffic in our flesh.

Sir, I would like to bring more vividly to before this audience, the wrongs of my down-trodden countrymen. I have no disposition to look at this matter in any sentimental light, but to bring before you stern facts, and keep forever before the American people the damning and disgraceful fact, that three millions of people are in chains today—that while we are here speaking in their behalf, saying noble words and doing noble deeds, they are under the yoke, smarting beneath the lash, sundered from each other, trafficked in and brutally treated; and that the American nation, to keep them in their present condition, stands ready with its ten thousand bayonets, to plunge them into their hearts. If they attempt to strike for their freedom, I want every man north of Mason and Dixon's line, whenever they attend an Anti-Slavery meeting, to remember that it is the Northern area that does this—that you are not only guilty of withholding your influence, but that you are the positive enemies of the slave, the positive holders of the slave, and that in your right arm rests the physical power that keeps him under the yoke. [*Applause*]

I want you to feel that I am addressing slaveholders; speaking to men who have entered into a solemn league and covenant with the slaveholders of the country, that in any emergency, if at any time the spirit of freedom finds a lodgment in the bosom of the American slave, and they shall be moved to throw up barricades against their tyrants, as the French did in the streets of Paris, that you, every man of you that swears to support the Constitution, is sworn to pour leaden death into their hearts. I am speaking to slaveholders, and if I speak plainly, set it not down to impudence, but to opposition to Slavery. For God's sake, let a man speak when he cannot do anything else; when fetters are on his limbs, let him have this small right of making his wrongs known; at least, let it be done in New York. I am glad to see there is a disposition to let it be done here—to allow him to tell what is in him, with regard to his own personal wrongs at any rate.

Sir, I have been frequently denounced because I have dared to speak against the American nation, against the Church—the Northern churches especially, charging them with being the slaveholders of the country. I desire to say here, as elsewhere, that I am not at all ambitious of the ill opinions of my countrymen, nor do I desire their hatred; but I must say, as I have said, that I want no man's friendship, no matter how high he may stand in Church or State, I want no man's sympathies or approbation who is not ready to strike the chains from the limbs of my brethren. I do not ask the esteem and friendship of any minister or any man, no matter how high his standing, nor do I wish to shake any man's hand, who stands indifferent to the wrongs of my brethren. Some have boasted that when Fred Douglass has been at their houses, he has been treated kindly, but as soon as he got into their pulpits he began to abuse them—that as soon as the advantage is given him, he takes it to stab those who befriend him. Friends, I wish to stab no man, but if you stand on the side of the slaveholder, and cry out "the Union as it is," "the Constitution as it is," "the Church as it is," you may expect that the heart that throbs beneath this bosom, will give utterance against you. I am bound to speak, and, whenever there is an opportunity to do so, I *will* speak against Slavery.

I meant to have said a word about Colonization, as I observed there was a *very dark-looking* individual here (Gov. Pinney, of Liberia), for whose special benefit I wished to say something on that subject. But as I do not see him here now, there is no necessity to discuss this subject for his benefit. When he was pointed out to me, I thought it remarkable, that so dark a man should be in favour of colonization; but there are some simple-minded men *even among coloured people.* [*Laughter*]. I will just say, however, that we have had some advice given us lately, from very high authority. I allude to Henry Clay, who in his last speech before the Colonization Society, at Washington, advised the free coloured people of the United States that they had better go to Africa.

He says he does not wish to coerce us, but thinks we had better go! [*Laughter and applause*] What right has he to tell us to go? We have as much right to stay here as he has. [*Laughter*] I don't care if you *did* throw up your caps for him when he came to this city—I don't care if he did give you "his heart on the outside of the city Hall and his hand on the inside"; I have as much right to stay here as he has! [*With great humor.*] And I want to say to our white friends, that we, coloured folks, have had the subject under consideration, and *have decided to stay!* [*Great laughter*] I want to say to any colonization friends here, that they may give their minds no further uneasiness on our account, for our minds are made up. [*Laughter*] I think this is about the best argument on that subject.

Now there is one thing more about us colored folks; it is this, that under all these most adverse circumstances, we live and move and have our being, and that too in peace, [*Laughter*] and are almost persuaded that there is a providence in our staying here. I do not know but the United States would rot in its tyranny, if there were not some negroes in this land—some to clink their chains in the care of listening humanity, and from whose prostrate forms the lessons of liberty can be taught to the whites. [*Applause*]

It is through us now that you are learning that your own rights are stricken down. At this time it is the Abolitionist that holds up the lamp that shows the political parties of the North their fetters and chains. A little while ago, and the Northern men were bound in the strange fanatic delusion, that they had something to do with making of Presidents of the United States: that is about given up now. No one now of common sense, or common reading, imagines for a moment that New York has anything to do with deciding who the President shall be. They are allowed to vote, but what is the amount of this privilege? It is to vote for the slaveholder, or whom the slaveholders select.

No men that are now accounted sane, think of any other than of a slaveholder or assassin, or both, who shall hold the destinies of the nation [*Laughter*]—and the reason is because the people are convinced that they belong—as they used to say to the coloured boys of the South, to the party. They used sometimes to ask me, "boy who do you belong to?" and I used to answer "to Captain Thomas Auld, of St. Michaels' a class-leader in the Methodist Episcopal church"; and now I would ask, "who do you belong to?" [*Laughter*] I will tell you.

You *belong* to the Democratic party, to the Whig party, and these parties belong to the slaveholder, and the slaveholder rules the country. As the boy said about ruling England: "I rule mamma, and mamma rules papa, and papa rules the people, and the people rule England." To be sure you have the right to vote, which is like what I heard once of a certain boy, who said he was going to live with his uncle Robert, and when I go there, said he, I am going to do just as I please—*if uncle Robert will let me!*

The Northern people are going to do just as they please if the slaveholders will let them. The little bit of opposition that has manifested itself in that little protuberance on American politics—the Wilmot proviso—which our friend Gay has fully described as a tempest in a teapot, has now quite flattened down. The Whigs, who said we will stand by it at all hazards, have fairly backed out; they did so last fall; they got afraid of the Union. In Ohio I heard men striking their fists together, saying they would stand by it at all hazards; and after a little while, the Ohio State Legislature come to the conclusion, after having carefully considered the matter, that "to press the question of no more slave territory must be disastrous to our American Union."—New York came out expressly in favour of the Proviso and it has since seen that the Union will be perilled by adherence to that principle. And all over the North there is this fainting away before that power which was before undefined, as has been so eloquently touched upon by my friend Phillips; for while men hold up their hands in favour of the Union and the Constitution, there is a moral conflict in their hearts, for, as was so beautifully expressed by Mr. Parker, of Boston, men cannot fight Slavery under the Constitution; the Constitution soils the armour about them; we cannot strike Slavery while we have it on us: there is no other way to throw it off.

I have no prepared speech, and I will not weary you any longer. I have sometimes thought since the late occurrences in France, that there may be an under current in men's hearts here as there was in Paris; Louis Philippe thought himself perfectly secure surrounded by his 300,000 soldiers, who, with fixed bayonets, were ready to support him in the suppression of the riots; but the troops were found to fraternize with the people; the soldier joined the civilian to assert and defend his rights. So I believe here, after all we have said against the American people, there is yet an under current pervading the mass of the people in this country, uniting Democrat and Whig, and men of no party, taking hold in quarters we know not of, which shall one day rise up in one glorious Fraternity for Freedom, uniting into one mighty phalanx of freemen to bring down the haughty citadel of Slavery with all its bloody towers and turrets.

There's a good time coming boys,
A good time coming,
Wait a little longer.
We may not live to see the day,
But earth shall glisten in the ray
Of the good time coming;
Cannon balls may aid the truth,
But thought's a weapon stronger,
We'll win our battle by its aid,
Wait a little longer.

(1848)

The Meaning of July Fourth for the Negro

Mr. President, Friends and Fellow Citizens:

He who could address this audience without a quailing sensation, has stronger nerves than I have. I do not remember ever to have appeared as a speaker before any assembly more shrinkingly, nor with greater distrust of my ability, than I do this day. A feeling has crept over me quite unfavorable to the exercise of my limited powers of speech. The task before me is one which requires much previous thought and study for its proper performance. I know that apologies of this sort are generally considered flat and unmeaning. I trust, however, that mine will not be so considered. Should I seem at ease, my appearance would much misrepresent me. The little experience I have had in addressing public meetings, in country school houses, avails me nothing on the present occasion.

The papers and placards say that I am to deliver a Fourth of July Oration. This certainly sounds large, and out of the common way, for me. It is true that I have often had the privilege to speak in this beautiful Hall, and to address many who now honor me with their presence. But neither their familiar faces, nor the perfect gage I think I have of Corinthian Hall seems to free me from embarrassment.

The fact is, ladies and gentlemen, the distance between this platform and the slave plantation, from which I escaped, is considerable—and the difficulties to he overcome in getting from the latter to the former are by no means slight. That I am here today is, to me, a matter of astonishment as well as of gratitude. You will not, therefore, be surprised, if in what I have to say I evince no elaborate preparation, nor grace my speech with any high sounding exordium. With little experience and with less learning, I have been able to throw my thoughts hastily and imperfectly together; and trusting to your patient and generous indulgence I will proceed to lay them before you.

This, for the purpose of this celebration, is the Fourth of July. It is the birthday of your National Independence, and of your political freedom. This, to you, as what the Passover was to the emancipated people of God. It carries your minds back to the day, and to the act of your great deliverance; and to the signs, and to the wonders, associated with that act, and that day. This celebration also marks the beginning of another year of your national life; and reminds you that the Republic of America is now 76 years old. I am glad, fellow citizens, that your nation is so young. Seventy-six years, though a good old age for a man, is but a mere speck in the life of a nation. Three score years and ten is the allotted time for individual men; but nations number their years by thousands. According to this fact, you are, even now, only in the beginning of your national career, still lingering in the period of childhood. I repeat, I am glad this is so. There is hope in the thought, and hope is much needed, under the dark clouds which lower above the horizon. The eye of the reformer is met with angry flashes, portending disastrous times; but his heart may well beat lighter at the thought that America is young, and that she is still in the impressible stage of her existence. May he not hope that high lessons of wisdom, of justice and of truth, will yet give direction to her destiny? Were the nation older, the patriot's heart might be sadder, and the reformer's brow heavier. Its future might be shrouded in gloom, and the hope of its prophets go out in sorrow. There is consolation in the thought that America is young. Great streams are not easily turned from channels, worn deep in the course of ages. They may sometimes rise in quiet and stately majesty, and inundate the land, refreshing and fertilizing the earth with their mysterious properties. They may also rise in wrath and fury, and bear away, on their angry waves, the accumulated wealth of years of toil and hardship. They, however, gradually flow back to the same old channel, and flow on as serenely as ever. But, while the river may not be turned aside, it may dry up, and leave nothing behind but the withered branch, and the unsightly rock, to howl in the abyss-sweeping wind, the sad tale of departed glory. As with rivers so with nations.

Fellow citizens, I shall not presume to dwell at length on the associations that cluster about this day. The simple story of it is, that, 76 years ago, the people of this country were British subjects. The style and title of your "sovereign people" (in which you now glory) was not then born. You were under the British Crown. Your fathers esteemed the English Government as the home government; and England as the fatherland. This home government, you know, although a considerable distance from your home, did, in the exercise of its parental prerogatives, impose upon its colonial children, such restraints, burdens and limitations, as, in its mature judgment, it deemed wise, right and proper.

But your fathers, who had not adopted the fashionable idea of this day, of the infallibility of government, and the absolute character of its acts, presumed to differ from the home government in respect to the wisdom and the justice of some of those burdens and restraints. They went so far in their excitement as to pronounce the measures of government unjust, unreasonable, and oppressive, and altogether such as ought not to be quietly submitted to. I scarcely need say, fellow citizens, that my opinion of those measures fully accords with that of your fathers. Such a declaration of agreement on my part would not be worth much to anybody. It would certainly prove nothing as to what part I might have taken had I lived during the great controversy of 1776. To say now that America was right, and England wrong, is exceedingly easy. Everybody can say it; the dastard, not less than the noble brave, can flippantly discant on the tyranny of England towards the American Colonies. It is fashionable to do so; but there was a time when, to pronounce against England, and in favor of the cause of the colonies, tried men's souls. They who did so were accounted in their day plotters of mischief, agitators and rebels, dangerous men. To side with the right against the wrong, with the weak against the strong, and with the oppressed against the oppressor! here lies the merit, and the one which, of all others, seems unfashionable in our day. The cause of liberty may be stabbed by the men who glory in the deeds of your fathers. But, to proceed.

Feeling themselves harshly and unjustly treated, by the home government, your fathers, like men of honesty, and men of spirit, earnestly sought redress. They petitioned and remonstrated; they did so in a decorous, respectful, and loyal manner. Their conduct was wholly unexceptionable. This, however, did not answer the purpose. They saw themselves treated with sovereign indifference, coldness and scorn. Yet they persevered. They were not the men to look back.

As the sheet anchor takes a firmer hold, when the ship is tossed by the storm, so did the cause of your fathers grow stronger as it breasted the chilling blasts of kingly displeasure. The greatest and best of British statesmen admitted its justice, and the loftiest eloquence of the British Senate came to its support. But, with that blindness which seems to be the unvarying characteristic of tyrants, since Pharaoh and his hosts were drowned in the Red Sea, the British Government persisted in the exactions complained of.

The madness of this course, we believe, is admitted now, even by England; but we fear the lesson is wholly lost on our present rulers.

Oppression makes a wise man mad. Your fathers were wise men, and if they did not go mad, they became restive under this treatment. They felt themselves the victims of grievous wrongs, wholly incurable in their colonial capacity. With brave men there is always a remedy for oppression. Just here, the idea of a total separation of the colonies from the crown was born! It was a startling idea, much more so than we, at this distance of time, regard it. The timid and the prudent (as has been intimated) of that day were, of course, shocked and alarmed by it.

Such people lived then, had lived before, and will, probably, ever have a place on this planet; and their course, in respect to any great change (no matter how great the good to be attained, or the wrong to be redressed by it), may be calculated with as much precision as can be the course of the stars. They hate all changes, but silver, gold and copper change! Of this sort of change they are always strongly in favor.

These people were called Tories in the days of your fathers; and the appellation, probably, conveyed the same idea that is meant by a more modern, though a somewhat less euphonious term, which we often find in our papers, applied to some of our old politicians.

Their opposition to the then dangerous thought was earnest and powerful; but, amid all their terror and affrighted vociferations against it, the alarming and revolutionary idea moved on, and the country with it.

On the 2nd of July, 1776, the old Continental Congress, to the dismay of the lovers of ease, and the worshipers of property, clothed that dreadful idea with all the authority of national sanction. They did so in the form of a resolution; and as we seldom hit upon resolutions, drawn up in our day, whose transparency is at all equal to this, it may refresh your minds and help my story if I read it.

> Resolved, That these united colonies are, and of right, ought to be free and Independent States; that they are absolved from all allegiance to the British Crown; and that all political connection between them and the State of Great Britain is, and ought to be, dissolved.

Citizens, your fathers made good that resolution. They succeeded; and today you reap the fruits of their success. The freedom gained is yours; and you, therefore, may properly celebrate this anniversary. The 4th of July is the first great fact in your nation's history—the very ring-bolt in the chain of your yet undeveloped destiny.

Pride and patriotism, not less than gratitude, prompt you to celebrate and to hold it in perpetual remembrance. I have said that the Declaration of Independence is the ringbolt to the chain of your nation's destiny; so, indeed, I regard it. The principles contained in that instrument are saving principles. Stand by those principles, be true to them on all occasions, in all places, against all foes, and at whatever cost.

From the round top of your ship of state, dark and threatening clouds may be seen. Heavy billows, like mountains in the distance, disclose to the leeward huge forms of flinty rocks! That bolt drawn, that chain broken, and all is lost. Cling to this day—cling to it, and to its principles, with the grasp of a storm-tossed mariner to a spar at midnight.

The coming into being of a nation, in any circumstances, is an interesting event. But, besides general considerations, there were peculiar circumstances which make the advent of this republic an event of special attractiveness.

The whole scene, as I look back to it, was simple, dignified and sublime. The population of the country, at the time, stood at the insignificant number of three millions. The country was poor in the munitions of war. The population was weak and scattered, and the country a wilderness unsubdued. There were then no means of concert and combination, such as exist now. Neither steam nor lightning had then been reduced to order and discipline. From the Potomac to the Delaware was a journey of many days. Under these, and innumerable other disadvantages, your fathers declared for liberty and independence and triumphed.

Fellow citizens, I am not wanting in respect for the fathers of this republic. The signers of the Declaration of Independence were brave men. They were great men, too—great enough to give frame to a great age. It does not often happen to a nation to raise, at one time, such a number of truly great men. The point from which I am compelled to view them is not, certainly, the most favorable; and yet I cannot contemplate their great deeds with less than admiration. They were statesmen, patriots and heroes, and for the good they did, and the principles they contended for, I will unite with you to honor their memory.

They loved their country better than their own private interests; and, though this is not the highest form of human excellence, all will concede that it is a rare virtue, and that when it is exhibited it ought to command respect. He who will, intelligently, lay down his life for his country is a man whom it is not in human nature to despise. Your fathers staked their lives, their fortunes, and their sacred honor, on the cause of their country. In their admiration of liberty, they lost sight of all other interests.

They were peace men; but they preferred revolution to peaceful submission to bondage. They were quiet men; but they did not shrink from agitating against oppression. They showed forbearance; but that they knew its limits. They believed in order; but not in the order of tyranny. With them, nothing was "settled" that was not right. With them, justice, liberty and humanity were "final"; not slavery and oppression. You may well cherish the memory of such men. They were great in their day and generation. Their solid manhood stands out the more as we contrast it with these degenerate times.

How circumspect, exact and proportionate were all their movements! How unlike the politicians of an hour! Their statesmanship looked beyond the passing moment, and stretched away in strength into the distant future. They seized upon eternal principles, and set a glorious example in their defence. Mark them! Fully appreciating the hardships to be encountered, firmly believing in the right of their cause, honorably inviting the scrutiny of an on-looking world, reverently appealing to heaven to attest their sincerity, soundly comprehending the solemn responsibility they were about to assume, wisely measuring the terrible odds against them, your fathers, the fathers of this republic, did, most deliberately, under the inspiration of a glorious patriotism, and with a sublime faith in the great principles of justice and freedom, lay deep, the corner-stone of the national superstructure, which has risen and still rises in grandeur around you.

Of this fundamental work, this day is the anniversary. Our eyes are met with demonstrations of joyous enthusiasm. Banners and pennants wave exultingly on the breeze. The din of business, too, is hushed. Even mammon seems to have quitted his grasp on this day. The ear-piercing fife and the stirring drum unite their accents with the ascending peal of a thousand church bells. Prayers are made, hymns are sung, and sermons are preached in honor of this day; while the quick martial tramp of a great and multitudinous nation, echoed back by all the hills, valleys and mountains of a vast continent, bespeak the occasion one of thrilling and universal interest—nation's jubilee.

Friends and citizens, I need not enter further into the causes which led to this anniversary. Many of you understand them better than I do. You could instruct me in regard to them. That is a branch of knowledge in which you feel, perhaps, a much deeper interest than your speaker. The causes which led to the separation of the colonies from the British crown have never lacked for a tongue. They have all been taught in your common schools, narrated at your firesides, unfolded from your pulpits, and thundered from your legislative halls, and are as familiar to you as household words. They form the staple of your national poetry and eloquence.

I remember, also, that, as a people, Americans are remarkably familiar with all facts which make in their own favor. This is esteemed by some as a national trait—perhaps a national weakness. It is a fact, that whatever makes for the wealth or for the reputation of Americans and can be had cheap! will be found by Americans. I shall not be charged with slandering Americans if I say I think the American side of any question may be safely left in American hands.

I leave, therefore, the great deeds of your fathers to other gentlemen whose claim to have been regularly descended will be less likely to be disputed than mine!

My business, if I have any here today, is with the present. The accepted time with God and His cause is the ever-living now.

> Trust no future, however pleasant,
> Let the dead past bury its dead;
> Act, act in the living present,
> Heart within, and God overhead.

We have to do with the past only as we can make it useful to the present and to the future. To all inspiring motives, to noble deeds which can be gained from the past, we are welcome. But now is the time, the important time. Your fathers have lived, died, and have done their work, and have done much of it well. You live and must die, and you must do your work. You have no right to enjoy a child's share in the labor of your fathers, unless your children are to be blest by your labors. You have no right to wear out and waste the hard-earned fame of your fathers to cover your indolence. Sydney Smith tells us that men seldom eulogize the wisdom and virtues of their fathers, but to excuse some folly or wickedness of their own. This truth is not a doubtful one. There are illustrations of it near and remote, ancient and modern. It was fashionable, hundreds of years ago, for the children of Jacob to boast, we have "Abraham to our father," when they had long lost Abraham's faith and spirit. That people contented themselves under the shadow of Abraham's great name, while they repudiated the deeds which made his name great. Need I remind you that a similar thing is being done all over this country today? Need I tell you that the Jews are not the only people who built the tombs of the prophets, and garnished the sepulchers of the righteous? Washington could not die till he had broken the chains of his slaves. Yet his monument is built up by the price of human blood, and the traders in the bodies and souls of men shout—" "We have Washington to our father"—Alas! that it should be so; yet it is.

> The evil, that men do, lives after them,
> The good is oft interred with their bones.

Fellow citizens, pardon me, allow me to ask, why am I called upon to speak here today? What have I, or those I represent, to do with your national independence? Are the great principles of political freedom and of natural justice, embodied in that Declaration of Independence, extended to us? and am I, therefore, called upon to bring our humble offering to the national altar, and to confess the benefits and express devout gratitude for the blessings resulting from your independence to us?

Would to God, both for your sakes and ours, that an affirmative answer could be truthfully returned to these questions! Then would my task be light, and my burden easy and delightful. For who is there so cold, that a nation's sympathy could not warm him? Who so obdurate and dead to the claims of gratitude, that would not thankfully acknowledge such priceless benefits? Who so stolid and selfish, that would not give his voice to swell the hallelujahs of a nation's jubilee, when the chains of servitude had been torn from his limbs? I am not that man. In a case like that, the dumb might eloquently speak, and the "lame man leap as an hart."

But such is not the state of the case. I say it with a sad sense of the disparity between us. I am not included within the pale of this glorious anniversary! Your high independence only reveals the immeasurable distance between us. The blessings in which you, this day, rejoice, are not enjoyed in common. The rich inheritance of justice, liberty, prosperity and independence, bequeathed by your fathers, is shared by you, not by me. The sunlight that brought light and healing to you, has brought stripes and death to me. This Fourth July is *yours*, not *mine*. *You* may rejoice, I must mourn. To drag a man in fetters into the grand illuminated temple of liberty, and call upon him to join you in joyous anthems, were inhuman mockery and sacrilegious irony. Do you mean, citizens, to mock me, by asking me to speak today? If so, there is a parallel to your conduct. And let me warn you that it is dangerous to copy the example of a nation whose crimes, towering up to heaven, were thrown down by the breath of the Almighty, burying that nation in irrevocable ruin! I can today take up the plaintive lament of a peeled and woe-smitten people!

"By the rivers of Babylon, there we sat down. Yea! we wept when we remembered Zion. We hanged our harps upon the willows in the midst thereof. For there, they that carried us away captive, required of us a song; and they who wasted us required of us mirth, saying, Sing us one of the songs of Zion. How can we sing the Lord's song in a strange land? If I forget thee, O Jerusalem, let my right hand forget her cunning. If I do not remember thee, let my tongue cleave to the roof of my mouth."

Fellow citizens, above your national, tumultuous joy, I hear the mournful wail of millions! whose chains, heavy and grievous yesterday, are, today, rendered more intolerable by the jubilee shouts that reach them. If I do forget, if I do not faithfully remember those bleeding children of sorrow this day, "may my right hand forget her cunning, and may my tongue cleave to the roof of my mouth!" To forget them, to pass lightly over their wrongs, and to chime in with the popular theme, would be treason most scandalous and shocking, and would make me a reproach before God and the world. My subject, then, fellow citizens, is American slavery. I shall see this day and its popular characteristics from the slave's point of view. Standing there identified with the American bondman, making his wrongs mine, I do not hesitate to declare, with all my soul, that the character and conduct of this nation never looked blacker to me than on this 4th of July! Whether we turn to the declarations of the past, or to the professions of the present, the conduct of the nation seems equally hideous and revolting. America is false to the past, false to the present, and solemnly binds herself to be false to the future. Standing with God and the crushed and bleeding slave on this occasion, I will, in the name of humanity which is outraged, in the name of liberty which is fettered, in the name of the constitution and the Bible which are disregarded and trampled upon, dare to call in question and to denounce, with all the emphasis I can command, everything that serves to perpetuate slavery—the great sin and shame of America! "I will not equivocate; I will not excuse"; I will use the severest language I can command; and yet not one word shall escape me that any man, whose judgment is not blinded by prejudice, or who is not at heart a slaveholder, shall not confess to be right and just.

But I fancy I hear someone of my audience say, "It is just in this circumstance that you and your brother abolitionists fail to make a favorable impression on the public mind. Would you argue more, and denounce less; would you persuade more, and rebuke less; your cause would be much more likely to succeed." But, I submit, where all is plain there is nothing to be argued. What point in the anti-slavery creed would you have me argue? On what branch of the subject do the people of this country need light? Must I undertake to prove that the slave is a man? That point is conceded already. Nobody doubts it. The slaveholders themselves acknowledge it in the enactment of laws for their government. They acknowledge it when they punish disobedience on the part of the slave. There are seventy-two crimes in the State of Virginia which, if committed by a black man (no matter how ignorant he be), subject him to the punishment of death; while only two of the same crimes will subject a white man to the like punishment. What is this but the acknowledgment that the slave is a moral, intellectual, and responsible being? The manhood of the slave is conceded. It is admitted in the fact that Southern statute books are covered with enactments forbidding, under severe fines and penalties, the teaching of the slave to read or to write. When you can point to any such laws in reference to the beasts of the field, then I may consent to argue the manhood of the slave. When the dogs in your streets, when the fowls of the air, when the cattle on your hills, when the fish of the sea, and the reptiles that crawl, shall be unable to distinguish the slave from a brute, then will I argue with you that the slave is a man!

For the present, it is enough to affirm the equal manhood of the Negro race. Is it not astonishing that, while we are ploughing, planting, and reaping, using all kinds of mechanical tools, erecting houses, constructing bridges, building ships, working in metals of brass, iron, copper, silver and gold; that, while we are reading, writing and ciphering, acting as clerks, merchants and secretaries, having among us lawyers, doctors, ministers, poets, authors, editors, orators and teachers; that, while we are engaged in all manner of enterprises common to other men, digging gold in California, capturing the whale in the Pacific, feeding sheep and cattle on the hill-side, living, moving, acting, thinking, planning, living in families as husbands, wives and children, and, above all, confessing and worshipping the Christian's God, and looking hopefully for life and immortality beyond the grave, we are called upon to prove that we are men!

Would you have me argue that man is entitled to liberty? that he is the rightful owner of his own body? You have already declared it. Must I argue the wrongfulness of slavery? Is that a question for Republicans? Is it to be settled by the rules of logic and argumentation, as a matter beset with great difficulty, involving a doubtful application of the principle of justice, hard to be understood? How should I look today, in the presence of Americans, dividing, and subdividing a discourse, to show that men have a natural right to freedom? speaking of it relatively and positively, negatively and affirmatively. To do so, would be to make myself ridiculous, and to offer an insult to your understanding. There is not a man beneath the canopy of heaven that does not know that slavery is wrong *for him.*

What, am I to argue that it is wrong to make men brutes, to rob them of their liberty, to work them without wages, to keep them ignorant of their relations to their fellow men, to beat them with sticks, to flay their flesh with the lash, to load their limbs with irons, to hunt them with dogs, to sell them at auction, to sunder their families, to knock out their teeth, to burn their flesh, to starve them into obedience and submission to their masters? Must I argue that a system thus marked with blood, and stained with pollution, is *wrong*? No! I will not. I have better employment for my time and strength than such arguments would imply.

What, then, remains to be argued? Is it that slavery is not divine; that God did not establish it; that our doctors of divinity are mistaken? There is blasphemy in the thought. That which is inhuman, cannot be divine! Who can reason on such a proposition? They that can, may; I cannot. The time for such argument is passed.

At a time like this, scorching irony, not convincing argument, is needed. O! had I the ability, and could reach the nation's ear, I would, today, pour out a fiery stream of biting ridicule, blasting reproach, withering sarcasm, and stern rebuke. For it is not light that is needed, but fire; it is not the gentle shower, but thunder. We need the storm, the whirlwind, and the earthquake. The feeling of the nation must be quickened; the conscience of the nation must be roused; the propriety of the nation must be startled; the hypocrisy of the nation must be exposed; and its crimes against God and man must be proclaimed and denounced.

What, to the American slave, is your 4th of July? I answer; a day that reveals to him, more than all other days in the year, the gross injustice and cruelty to which he is the constant victim. To him, your celebration is a sham; your boasted liberty, an unholy license; your national greatness, swelling vanity; your sounds of rejoicing are empty and heartless; your denunciation of tyrants, brass fronted impudence; your shouts of liberty and equality, hollow mockery; your prayers and hymns, your sermons and thanksgivings, with all your religious parade and solemnity, are, to Him, mere bombast, fraud, deception, impiety, and hypocrisy—a thin veil to cover up crimes which would disgrace a nation of savages. There is not a nation on the earth guilty of practices more shocking and bloody than are the people of the United States, at this very hour.

Go where you may, search where you will, roam through all the monarchies and despotisms of the Old World, travel through South America, search out every abuse, and when you have found the last, lay your facts by the side of the everyday practices of this nation, and you will say with me, that, for revolting barbarity and shameless hypocrisy, America reigns without a rival.

Take the American slave-trade, which we are told by the papers, is especially prosperous just now. Ex-Senator Benton tells us that the price of men was never higher than now. He mentions the fact to show that slavery is in no danger. This trade is one of the peculiarities of American institutions. It is carried on in all the large towns and cities in one-half of this confederacy; and millions are pocketed every year by dealers in this horrid traffic. In several states this trade is a chief source of wealth. It is called (in contradistinction to the foreign slave-trade) "the internal slave-trade." It is, probably, called so, too, in order to divert from it the horror with which the foreign slave-trade is contemplated. That trade has long since been denounced by this government as piracy. It has been denounced with burning words from the high places of the nation as an execrable traffic. To arrest it, to put an end to it, this nation keeps a squadron, at immense cost, on the coast of Africa. Everywhere, in this country, it is safe to speak of this foreign slave-trade as a most inhuman traffic, opposed alike to the Jaws of God and of man. The duty to extirpate and destroy it, is admitted even by our doctors of divinity. In order to put an end to it, some of these last have consented that their colored brethren (nominally free) should leave this country, and establish themselves on the western coast of Africa! It is, however, a notable fact that, while so much execration is poured out by Americans upon all those engaged in the foreign slave-trade, the men engaged in the slave-trade between the states pass without condemnation, and their business is deemed honorable.

Behold the practical operation of this internal slave-trade, the American slave-trade, sustained by American politics and American religion. Here you will see men and women reared like swine for the market. You know what is a swine-drover? I will show you a man-drover. They inhabit all our Southern States. They perambulate the country, and crowd the highways of the nation, with droves of human stock. You will see one of these human flesh jobbers, armed with pistol, whip, and bowie-knife, driving a company of a hundred men, women, and children, from the Potomac to the slave market at New Orleans. These wretched people are to be sold singly, or in lots, to suit purchasers. They are food for the cotton-field and the deadly sugar-mill. Mark the sad procession, as it moves wearily along, and the inhuman wretch who drives them. Hear his savage yells and his blood-curdling oaths, as he hurries on his affrighted captives! There, see the old man with locks thinned and gray. Cast one glance, if you please, upon that young mother, whose shoulders are bare to the scorching sun, her briny tears falling on the brow of the babe in her arms. See, too, that girl of thirteen, weeping, yes! weeping, as she thinks of the mother from whom she has been torn! The drove moves tardily. Heat and sorrow have nearly consumed their strength; suddenly you hear a quick snap, like the discharge of a rifle; the fetters clank, and the chain rattles simultaneously; your ears are saluted with a scream, that seems to have torn its way to the centre of your soul The crack you heard was the sound of the slave-whip; the scream you heard was from the woman you saw with the babe. Her speed had faltered under the weight of her child and her chains! that gash on her shoulder tells her to move on. Follow this drove to New Orleans. Attend the auction; see men examined like horses; see the forms of women rudely and brutally exposed to the shocking gaze of American slave-buyers. See this drove sold and separated forever; and never forget the deep, sad sobs that arose from that scattered multitude. Tell me, citizens, where, under the sun, you can witness a spectacle more fiendish and shocking. Yet this is but a glance at the American slave-trade, as it exists, at this moment, in the ruling part of the United States.

I was born amid such sights and scenes. To me the American slave-trade is a terrible reality. When a child, my soul was often pierced with a sense of its horrors. I lived on Philpot Street, Fell's Point, Baltimore, and have watched from the wharves the slave ships in the Basin, anchored from the shore, with their cargoes of human flesh, waiting for favorable winds to waft them down the Chesapeake. There was, at that time, a grand slave mart kept at the head of Pratt Street, by Austin Woldfolk. His agents were sent into every town and county in Maryland, announcing their arrival, through the papers, and on flaming "hand-bills," headed cash for Negroes. These men were generally well dressed men, and very captivating in their manners; ever ready to drink, to treat, and to gamble. The fate of many a slave has depended upon the turn of a single card; and many a child has been snatched from the arms of its mother by bargains arranged in a state of brutal drunkenness.

The flesh-mongers gather up their victims by dozens, and drive them, chained, to the general depot at Baltimore. When a sufficient number has been collected here, a ship is chartered for the purpose of conveying the forlorn crew to Mobile, or to New Orleans. From the slave prison to the ship, they are usually driven in the darkness of night; for since the anti-slavery agitation, a certain caution is observed.

In the deep, still darkness of midnight, I have been often aroused by the dead, heavy footsteps, and the piteous cries of the chained gangs that passed our door. The anguish of my boyish heart was intense; and I was often consoled, when speaking to my mistress in the morning, to hear her say that the custom was very wicked; that she hated to hear the rattle of the chains and the heart-rending cries. I was glad to find one who sympathized with me in my horror.

Fellow citizens, this murderous traffic is, today, in active operation in this boasted republic. In the solitude of my spirit I see clouds of dust raised on the highways of the South; I see the bleeding footsteps; I hear the doleful wail of fettered humanity on the way to the slave-markets, where the victims are to be sold like horses, sheep, and swine, knocked off to the highest bidder. There I see the tenderest ties ruthlessly broken, to gratify the lust, caprice and rapacity of the buyers and sellers of men. My soul sickens at the sight.

> Is this the land your Fathers loved,
> The freedom which they toiled to win?
> Is this the earth whereon they moved?
> Are these the graves they slumber in?

But a still more inhuman, disgraceful, and scandalous state of things remains to be presented. By an act of the American Congress, not yet two years old, slavery has been nationalized in its most horrible and revolting form. By that act, Mason and Dixon's line has been obliterated; New York has become as Virginia; and the power to hold, hunt, and sell men, women and children, as slaves, remains no longer a mere state institution, but is now an institution of the whole United States. The power is co-extensive with the star-spangled banner, and American Christianity. Where these go, may also go the merciless slave-hunter. Where these are, man is not sacred. He is a bird for the sportsman's gun. By that most foul and fiendish of all human decrees, the liberty and person of every man are put in peril. Your broad republican domain is hunting ground for *men*. Not for thieves and robbers, enemies of society, merely, but for men guilty of no crime. Your law-makers have commanded all good citizens to engage in this hellish sport. Your President, your Secretary of State, your *lords*, *nobles*, and ecclesiastics enforce, as a duty you owe to your free and glorious country, and to your God, that you do this accursed thing. Not fewer than forty Americans have, within the past two years, been hunted down and, without a moment's warning, hurried away in chains, and consigned to slavery and excruciating torture. Some of these have had wives and children, dependent on them for bread; but of this, no account was made. The right of the hunter to his prey stands superior to the right of marriage, and to *all* rights in this republic, the rights of God included! For black men there is neither law nor justice, humanity nor religion. The Fugitive Slave *Law* makes mercy to them a crime; and bribes the judge who tries them. An American judge gets ten dollars for every victim he consigns to slavery, and five, when he fails to do so. The oath of any two villains is sufficient, under this hell-black enactment, to send the most pious and exemplary black man into the remorseless jaws of slavery! His own testimony is nothing. He can bring no witnesses for himself. The minister of American justice is bound by the law to hear but *one* side; and *that* side is the side of the oppressor. Let this damning fact be perpetually told. Let it be thundered around the world that in tyrant-killing, king-hating, people-loving, democratic, Christian America the seats of justice are filled with judges who hold their offices under an open and palpable *bribe*, and are bound, in deciding the case of a man's liberty, *to hear only his accusers*!

In glaring violation of justice, in shameless disregard of the forms of administering law, in cunning arrangement to entrap the defenceless, and in diabolical intent this Fugitive Slave Law stands alone in the annals of tyrannical legislation. I doubt if there be another nation on the globe having the brass and the baseness to put such a law on the statute-book. If any man in this assembly thinks differently from me in this matter, and feels able to disprove my statements, I will gladly confront him at any suitable time and place he may select.

I take this law to be one of the grossest infringements of Christian Liberty, and, if the churches and ministers of our country were nor stupidly blind, or most wickedly indifferent, they, too, would so regard it.

At the very moment that they are thanking God for the enjoyment of civil and religious liberty, and for the right to worship God according to the dictates of their own consciences, they are utterly silent in respect to a law which robs religion of its chief significance and makes it utterly worthless to a world lying in wickedness. Did this law concern the "mint, anise, and cummin"—abridge the right to sing psalms, to partake of the sacrament, or to engage in any of the ceremonies of religion, it would be smitten by the thunder of a thousand pulpits. A general shout would go up from the church demanding *repeal, repeal, instant repeal!*—And it would go hard with that politician who presumed to solicit the votes of the people without inscribing this motto on his banner. Further, if this demand were not complied with, another Scotland would be added to the history of religious liberty, and the stern old covenanters would be thrown into the shade. A John Knox would be seen at every church door and heard from every pulpit, and Fillmore would have no more quarter than was shown by Knox to the beautiful, but treacherous, Queen Mary of Scotland. The fact that the church of our country (with fractional exceptions) does not esteem "the Fugitive Slave Law" as a declaration of war against religious liberty, implies that that church regards religion simply as a form of worship, an empty ceremony, and not a vital principle, requiring active benevolence, justice, love, and good will towards man. It esteems sacrifice above mercy; psalm-singing above right doing; solemn meetings above practical righteousness. A worship that can be conducted by persons who refuse to give shelter to the houseless, to give bread to the hungry, clothing to the naked, and who enjoin obedience to a law forbidding these acts of mercy is a curse, not a blessing to mankind. The Bible addresses all such persons as "scribes, pharisees, hypocrites, who pay tithe of *mint*, *anise*, and *cummin*, and have omitted the weightier matters of the law, judgment, mercy, and faith."

But the church of this country is not only indifferent to the wrongs of the slave, it actually takes sides with the oppressors. It has made itself the bulwark of American slavery, and the shield of American slave-hunters. Many of its most eloquent Divines, who stand as the very lights of the church, have shamelessly given the sanction of religion and the Bible to the whole slave system. They have taught that man may, properly, be a slave; that the relation of master and slave is ordained of God; that to send back an escaped bondman to his master is clearly the duty of all the followers of the Lord Jesus Christ; and this horrible blasphemy is palmed off upon the world for Christianity.

For my part, I would say, welcome infidelity! welcome atheism! welcome anything! in preference to the gospel, *as preached by those Divines*! They convert the very name of religion into an engine of tyranny and barbarous cruelty, and serve to confirm more infidels, in this age, than all the infidel writings of Thomas Paine, Voltaire, and Bolingbroke put together have done! These ministers make religion a cold and flinty-hearted thing, having neither principles of right action nor bowels of compassion. They strip the love of God of its beauty and leave the throne of religion a huge, horrible, repulsive form. It is a religion for oppressors, tyrants, man-stealers, and thugs. It is not that "*pure and undefiled religion*" which is from above, and which is "*first pure, then peaceable, easy to be entreated, full of mercy and good fruits, without partiality, and without hypocrisy.*" But a religion which favors the rich against the poor; which exalts the proud above the humble; which divides mankind into two classes, tyrants and slaves; which says to the man in chains, *stay there*; and to the oppressor, *oppress on*; it is a religion which may be professed and enjoyed by all the robbers and enslavers of mankind; it makes God a respecter of persons, denies his fatherhood of the race, and tramples in the dust the great truth of the brotherhood of man. All this we affirm to be true of the popular church, and the popular worship of our land and nation—a religion, a church, and a worship which, on the authority of inspired wisdom, we pronounce to be an abomination in the sight of God. In the language of Isaiah, the American church might be well addressed, "Bring no more vain oblations; incense is an abomination unto me: the new moons and Sabbaths, the calling of assemblies, I cannot away with; it is iniquity, even the solemn meeting. Your new moons, and your appointed feasts my soul hateth. They are a trouble to me; I am weary to bear them; and when ye spread forth your hands I will hide mine eyes from you.

"Yea' when ye make many prayers, I will not hear. Your hands are full of blood; cease to do evil, learn to do well; seek judgment; relieve the oppressed; judge for the fatherless; plead for the widow."

The American church is guilty, when viewed in connection with what it is doing to uphold slavery; but it is superlatively guilty when viewed in its connection with its ability to abolish slavery.

The sin of which it is guilty is one of omission as well as of commission. Albert Barnes but uttered what the common sense of every man at all observant of the actual state of the case will receive as truth, when he declared that "There is no power out of the church that could sustain slavery an hour, if it were not sustained in it."

Let the religious press, the pulpit, the Sunday School, the conference meeting, the great ecclesiastical, missionary, Bible and tract associations of the land array their immense powers against slavery, and slaveholding; and the whole system of crime and blood would be scattered to the winds, and that they do not do this involves them in the most awful responsibility of which the mind can conceive.

In prosecuting the anti-slavery enterprise, we have been asked to spare the church, to spare the ministry; but *how*, we ask, could such a thing be done? We are met on the threshold of our efforts for the redemption of the slave, by the church and ministry of the country, in battle arrayed against us; and we are compelled to fight or flee. From *what* quarter, I beg to know, has proceeded a fire so deadly upon our ranks, during the last two years, as from the Northern pulpit? As the champions of oppressors, the chosen men of American theology have appeared—men honored for their so-called piety, and their real learning. The Lords of Buffalo, the Springs of New York, the Lathrops of Auburn, the Coxes and Spencers of Brooklyn, the Gannets and Sharps of Boston, the Deweys of Washington, and other great religious lights of the land have, in utter denial of the authority of Him by whom they professed to be called to the ministry, deliberately taught us, against the example of the Hebrews, and against the remonstrance of the Apostles, *that we ought to obey man's law before the law of God.*

My spirit wearies of such blasphemy; and how such men can be supported, as the "standing types and representatives of Jesus Christ," is a mystery which I leave others to penetrate. In speaking of the American church, however, let it be distinctly understood that I mean the *great mass* of the religious organizations of our land. There are exceptions, and I thank God that there are. Noble men may be found, scattered all over these Northern States, of whom Henry Ward Beecher, of Brooklyn; Samuel J. May, of Syracuse; and my esteemed friend (Rev. R. R. Raymond) on the platform, are shining examples; and let me say further, that, upon these men lies the duty to inspire our ranks with high religious faith and zeal, and to cheer us on in the great mission of the slave's redemption from his chains.

One is struck with the difference between the attitude of the American church towards the anti-slavery movement, and that occupied by the churches in England towards a similar movement in that country. There, the church, true to its mission of ameliorating, elevating and improving the condition of mankind, came forward promptly, bound up the wounds of the West Indian slave, and restored him to his liberty. There, the question of emancipation was a high religious question. It was demanded in the name of humanity, and according to the law of the living God. The Sharps, the Clarksons, the Wilberforces, the Buxtons, the Burchells, and the Knibbs were alike famous for their piety and for their philanthropy. The anti-slavery movement there was not an anti-church movement, for the reason that the church took its full share in prosecuting that movement: and the anti-slavery movement in this country will cease to be an anti-church movement, when the church of this country shall assume a favorable instead of a hostile position towards that movement.

Americans! your republican politics, not less than your republican religion, are flagrantly inconsistent. You boast of your love of liberty, your superior civilization, and your pure Christianity, while the whole political power of the nation (as embodied in the two great political parties) is solemnly pledged to support and perpetuate the enslavement of three million of your countrymen. You hurl your anathemas at the crowned headed tyrants of Russia and Austria and pride yourselves on your Democratic institutions, while you yourselves consent to be the mere *tools* and *body-guards* of the tyrants of Virginia and Carolina. You invite to your shores fugitives of oppression from abroad, honor them with banquets, greet them with ovations, cheer them, toast them, salute them, protect them, and pour out your money to them like water; but the fugitives from oppression in your own land you advertise, hunt, arrest, shoot, and kill. You glory in your refinement and your universal education; yet you maintain a system as barbarous and dreadful as ever stained the character of a nation—a system begun in avarice, supported in pride, and perpetuated in cruelty. You shed tears over fallen Hungary, and make the sad story of her wrongs the theme of your poets, statesmen, and orators, till your gallant sons are ready to fly to arms to vindicate her cause against the oppressor; but, in regard to the ten thousand wrongs of the American slave, you would enforce the strictest silence, and would hail him as an enemy of the nation who dares to make those wrongs the subject of public discourse! You are all on fire at the mention of liberty for France or for Ireland; but are as cold as an iceberg at the thought of liberty for the enslaved of America. You discourse eloquently on the dignity of labor; yet, you sustain a system which, in its very essence, casts a stigma upon labor. You can bare your bosom to the storm of British artillery to throw off a three-penny tax on tea; and yet wring the last hard earned farthing from the grasp of the black laborers of your country. You profess to believe "that, of one blood, God made all nations of men to dwell on the face of all the earth," and hath commanded all men, everywhere, to love one another; yet you notoriously hate (and glory in your hatred) all men whose skins are not colored like your own. You declare before the world, and are understood by the world to declare that you "*hold these truths to be self-evident, that all men are created equal; and are endowed by their Creator with certain inalienable rights; and that among these are, life, liberty, and the pursuit of happiness*"; and yet, you hold securely, in a bondage which, according to your own Thomas Jefferson, "*is worse than ages of that which your fathers rose in rebellion to oppose,*" *a seventh part* of the inhabitants of your country.

Fellow citizens, I will not enlarge further on your national inconsistencies. The existence of slavery in this country brands your republicanism as a sham, your humanity as a base pretense, and your Christianity as a lie. It destroys your moral power abroad: it corrupts your politicians at home. It saps the foundation of religion; it makes your name a hissing and a bye-word to a mocking earth. It is the antagonistic force in your government, the only thing that seriously disturbs and endangers your Union. It fetters your progress; it is the enemy of improvement; the deadly foe of education; it fosters pride; it breeds insolence; it promotes vice; it shelters crime; it is a curse to the earth that supports it; and yet you cling to it as if it were the sheet anchor of all your hopes. Oh! be warned! be warned! a horrible reptile is coiled up in your nation's bosom; the venomous creature is nursing at the tender breast of your youthful republic; *for the love of God, tear away*, and fling from you the hideous monster, and *let the weight of twenty millions crush and destroy it forever!*

But it is answered in reply to all this, that precisely what I have now denounced is, in fact, guaranteed and sanctioned by the Constitution of the United States; that, the right to hold, and to hunt slaves is a part of that Constitution framed by the illustrious Fathers of this Republic.

Then, I dare to affirm, notwithstanding all I have said before, your fathers stooped, basely stooped

> To palter with us in a double sense:
> And keep the word of promise to the ear,
> But break it to the heart.

and instead of being the honest men I have before declared them to be, they were the veriest impostors that ever practised on mankind. This is the inevitable conclusion, and from it there is no escape; but I differ from those who charge this baseness on the framers of the Constitution of the United States. It is a slander upon their memory, at least, so I believe. There is not time now to argue the constitutional question at length; nor have I the ability to discuss it as it ought to be discussed. The subject has been handled with masterly power by Lysander Spooner, Esq. by William Goodell, by Samuel E. Sewall, Esq., and last, though not least, by Gerrit Smith, Esq. These gentlemen have, as I think, fully and clearly vindicated the Constitution from any design to support slavery for an hour.

Fellow citizens! there is no matter in respect to which the people of the North have allowed themselves to be so ruinously imposed upon as that of the pro-slavery character of the Constitution. In that instrument I hold there is neither warrant, license, nor sanction of the hateful thing; but interpreted, as it ought to be interpreted, the Constitution is a glorious liberty document. Read its preamble, consider its purposes. Is slavery among them? Is it at the gate way? or is it in the temple? it is neither. While I do not intend to argue this question on the present occasion, let me ask, if it be not somewhat singular that, if the Constitution were intended to be, by its framers and adopters, a slaveholding instrument, why neither slavery, slaveholding, nor slave can anywhere be found in it. What would be thought of an instrument, drawn up, legally drawn up, for the purpose of entitling the city of Rochester to a tract of land, in which no mention of land was made? Now, there are certain rules of interpretation for the proper understanding of all legal instruments. These rules are well established. They are plain, common sense rules, such as you and I, and all of us, can understand and apply, without having passed years in the study of law. I scout the idea that the question of the constitutionality, or unconstitutionality of slavery, is not a question for the people. I hold that every American citizen has a right to form an opinion of the constitution, and to propagate that opinion, and to use all honorable means to make his opinion the prevailing one. Without this right, the liberty of an American citizen would be as insecure as that of a Frenchman. Ex-Vice-President Dallas tells us that the constitution is an object to which no American mind can be too attentive, and no American heart too devoted. He further says, the Constitution, in its words, is plain and intelligible, and is meant for the home-bred, unsophisticated understandings of our fellow citizens. Senator Berrien tells us that the Constitution is the fundamental law, that which controls all others. The charter of our liberties, which every citizen has a personal interest in understanding thoroughly. The testimony of Senator Breese, Lewis Cass, and many others that might be named, who are everywhere esteemed as sound lawyers, so regard the constitution. I take it, therefore, that it is not presumption in a private citizen to form an opinion of that instrument.

Now, take the Constitution according to its plain reading, and I defy the presentation of a single pro-slavery clause in it. On the other hand, it will be found to contain principles and purposes, entirely hostile to the existence of slavery.

I have detained my audience entirely too long already. At some future period I will gladly avail myself of an opportunity to give this subject a full and fair discussion.

Allow me to say, in conclusion, notwithstanding the dark picture I have this day presented, of the state of the nation, I do not despair of this country. There are forces in operation which must inevitably work the downfall of slavery.

"The arm of the Lord is not shortened," and the doom of slavery is certain. I, therefore, leave off where I began, with hope. While drawing encouragement from "the Declaration of Independence," the great principles it contains, and the genius of American Institutions, my spirit is also cheered by the obvious tendencies of the age. Nations do not now stand in the same relation to each other that they did ages ago. No nation can now shut itself up from the surrounding world and trot round in the same old path of its fathers without interference. The time was when such could be done. Long established customs of hurtful character could formerly fence themselves in, and do their evil work with social impunity. Knowledge was then confined and enjoyed by the privileged few, and the multitude walked on in mental darkness. But a change has now come over the affairs of mankind. Walled cities and empires have become unfashionable. The arm of commerce has borne away the gates of the strong city. Intelligence is penetrating the darkest corners of the globe. It makes its pathway over and under the sea, as well as on the earth. Wind, steam, and lightning are its chartered agents. Oceans no longer divide, but link nations together. From Boston to London is now a holiday excursion. Space is comparatively annihilated. Thoughts expressed on one side of the Atlantic are distinctly heard on the other.

The far off and almost fabulous Pacific rolls in grandeur at our feet. The Celestial Empire, the mystery of ages, is being solved. The fiat of the Almighty, "Let there be Light," has not yet spent its force. No abuse, no outrage whether in taste, sport or avarice, can now hide itself from the all-pervading light. The iron shoe, and crippled foot of China must be seen in contrast with nature. Africa must rise and put on her yet unwoven garment. "Ethiopia shall stretch out her hand unto God." In the fervent aspirations of William Lloyd Garrison, I say, and let every heart join in saying it:

God speed the year of jubilee
The wide world o'er!
When from their galling chains set free,
Th' oppress'd shall vilely bend the knee,
And wear the yoke of tyranny
Like brutes no more.
That year will come, and freedom's reign.
To man his plundered rights again
Restore.
God speed the day when human blood
Shall cease to flow!
In every clime be understood,
The claims of human brotherhood,
And each return for evil, good, Not blow for blow;
That day will come all feuds to end,
And change into a faithful friend
Each foe. (1852)

Fighting Rebels with Only One Hand

What on earth is the matter with the American Government and people? Do they really covet the world's ridicule as well as their own social and political ruin? What are they thinking about, or don't they condescend to think at all? So, indeed, it would seem from their blindness in dealing with the tremendous issue now upon them. Was there ever anything like it before? They are sorely pressed on every hand by a vast army of slaveholding rebels, flushed with success, and infuriated by the darkest inspirations of a deadly hate, bound to rule or ruin. Washington, the seat of Government, after ten thousand assurances to the contrary, is now positively in danger of falling before the rebel army. Maryland, a little while ago considered safe for the Union, is now admitted to be studded with the materials for insurrection, and which may flame forth at any moment. Every resource of the nation, whether of men or money, whether of wisdom or strength, could be well employed to avert the impending ruin. Yet most evidently the demands of the hour are not comprehended by the Cabinet or the crowd. Our Presidents, Governors, Generals and Secretaries are calling, with almost frantic vehemance, for men. "Men! men! send us men!" they scream, or the cause of the Union is gone, the life of a great nation is ruthlessly sacrificed, and the hopes of a great nation go out in darkness; and yet these very officers, representing the people and Government, steadily and persistently refuse to receive the very class of men which have a deeper interest in the defeat and humiliation of the rebels, than all others. Men are wanted in Missouri—wanted in Western Virginia, to hold and defend what has been already gained; they are wanted in Texas, and all along the sea coast, and though the Government has at its command a class in the country deeply interested in suppressing the insurrection, it sternly refuses to summon from among the vast multitude a single man, and degrades and insults the whole class by refusing to allow any of their number to defend with their strong arms and brave hearts the national cause. What a spectacle of blind, unreasoning prejudice and pusillanimity is this! The national edifice is on fire. Every man who can carry a bucket of water, or remove a brick, is wanted; but those who have the care of the building, having a profound respect for the feeling of the national burglars who set the building on fire, are determined that the flames shall only be extinguished by Indo-Caucasian hands, and to have the building burnt rather than save it by means of any other. Such is the pride, the stupid prejudice and folly that rules the hour.

Why does the Government reject the Negro? Is he not a man? Can he not wield a sword, fire a gun, march and countermarch, and obey orders like any other? Is there the least reason to believe that a regiment of well-drilled Negroes would deport themselves less soldier-like on the battlefield than the raw troops gathered up generally from the towns and cities of the State of New York? We do believe that such soldiers, if allowed to take up arms in defence of the Government, and made to feel that they are hereafter to be recognized as persons having rights, would set the highest example of order and general good behavior to their fellow soldiers, and in every way add to the national power.

If persons so humble as we can be allowed to speak to the President of the United States, we should ask him if this dark and terrible hour of the nation's extremity is a time for consulting a mere vulgar and unnatural prejudice? We should ask him if national preservation and necessity were not better guides in this emergency than either the tastes of the rebels, or the pride and prejudices of the vulgar? We would tell him that General Jackson in a slave state fought side by side with Negroes at New Orleans, and like a true man, despising meanness, he bore testimony to their bravery at the close of the war. We would tell him that colored men in Rhode Island and Connecticut performed their full share in the war of the Revolution, and that men of the same color, such as the noble Shields Green, Nathaniel Turner and Denmark Vesey stand ready to peril everything at the command of the Government. We would tell him that this is no time to fight with one hand, when both are needed; that this is no time to fight only with your white hand, and allow your black hand to remain tied.

Whatever may be the folly and absurdity of the North, the South at least is true and wise. The Southern papers no longer indulge in the vulgar expression, "free niggers." That class of bipeds are now called "colored residents." The Charleston papers say:

> The colored residents of this city can challenge comparison with their class, in any city or town, in loyalty or devotion to the cause of the

> South. Many of them individually, and without ostentation, have been contributing liberally, and on Wednesday evening, the 7th inst., a very large meeting was held by them, and a committee appointed to provide for more efficient aid. The proceedings of the meeting will appear in results hereinafter to be reported.

It is now pretty well established, that there are at the present moment many colored men in the Confederate army doing duty not only as cooks, servants and laborers, but as real soldiers, having muskets on their shoulders, and bullets in their pockets, ready to shoot down loyal troops, and do all that soldiers may to destroy the Federal Government and build up that of the traitors and rebels. There were such soldiers at Manassas, and they are probably there still. There is a Negro in the army as well as in the fence, and our Government is likely to find it out before the war comes to an end. That the Negroes are numerous in the rebel army, and do for that army its heaviest work, is beyond question. They have been the chief laborers upon those temporary defences in which the rebels have been able to mow down our men. Negroes helped to build the batteries at Charleston. They relieve their gentlemanly and military masters from the stiffening drudgery of the camp, and devote them to the nimble and dexterous use of arms. Rising above vulgar prejudice, the slaveholding rebel accepts the aid of the black man as readily as that of any other. If a bad cause can do this, why should a good cause be less wisely conducted? We insist upon it, that one black regiment in such a war as this is, without being any more brave and orderly, would be worth to the Government more than two of any other; and that, while the Government continues to refuse the aid of colored men, thus alienating them from the national cause, and giving the rebels the advantage of them, it will not deserve better fortunes than it has thus far experienced. Men in earnest don't fight with one hand, when they might fight with two, and a man drowning would not refuse to be saved even by a colored hand.

(1861)

What the Black Man Wants

I came here, as I come always to the meetings in New England, as a listener, and not as a speaker; and one of the reasons why I have not been more frequently to the meetings of this society, has been because of the disposition on the part of some of my friends to call me out upon the platform, even when they knew that there was some difference of opinion and of feeling between those who rightfully belong to this platform and myself; and for fear of being misconstrued, as desiring to interrupt or disturb the proceedings of these meetings, I have usually kept away, and have thus been deprived of that educating influence, which I am always free to confess is of the highest order, descending from this platform. I have felt, since I have lived out West [Douglass means west of Boston, in Rochester, NY], that in going there I parted from a great deal that was valuable; and I feel, every time I come to these meetings, that I have lost a great deal by making my home west of Boston, west of Massachusetts; for, if anywhere in the country there is to be found the highest sense of justice, or the truest demands for my race, I look for it in the East, I look for it here. The ablest discussions of the whole question of our rights occur here, and to be deprived of the privilege of listening to those discussions is a great deprivation.

I do not know, from what has been said, that there is any difference of opinion as to the duty of abolitionists, at the present moment. How can we get up any difference at this point, or any point, where we are so united, so agreed? I went especially, however, with that word of Mr. Phillips, which is the criticism of Gen. Banks and Gen. Banks' policy. [Gen. Banks instituted a labor policy in Louisiana that was discriminatory of blacks, claiming that it was to help prepare them to better handle freedom. Wendell Phillips countered by saying, "If there is anything patent in the whole history of our thirty years' struggle, it is that the Negro no more needs to be prepared for liberty than the white man."] I hold that that policy is our chief danger at the present moment; that it practically enslaves the Negro, and makes the Proclamation [the Emancipation Proclamation] of 1863 a mockery and delusion. What is freedom? It is the right to choose one's own employment. Certainly it means that, if it means anything; and when any individual or combination of individuals undertakes to decide for any man when he shall work, where he shall work, at what he shall work, and for what he shall work, he or they practically reduce him to slavery. [*Applause*] He is a slave. That I understand Gen. Banks to do—to determine for the so-called freedman, when, and where, and at what, and for how much he shall work, when he shall be punished, and by whom punished. It is absolute slavery. It defeats the beneficent intention of the Government, if it has beneficent intentions, in regards to the freedom of our people.

I have had but one idea for the last three years to present to the American people, and the phraseology in which I clothe it is the old abolition phraseology. I am for the "immediate, unconditional, and universal" enfranchisement of the black man, in every State in the Union. [*Loud applause*] Without this, his liberty is a mockery; without this, you might as well almost retain the old name of slavery for his condition; for in fact, if he is not the slave of the individual master, he is the slave of society, and holds his liberty as a privilege, not as a right. He is at the mercy of the mob, and has no means of protecting himself.

It may be objected, however, that this pressing of the Negro's right to suffrage is premature. Let us have slavery abolished, it may be said, let us have labor organized, and then, in the natural course of events, the right of suffrage will be extended to the Negro. I do not agree with this. The constitution of the human mind is such, that if it once disregards the conviction forced upon it by a revelation of truth, it requires the exercise of a higher power to produce the same conviction afterwards. The American people are now in tears. The Shenandoah has run blood—the best blood of the North. All around Richmond, the blood of New England and of the North has been shed—of your sons, your brothers and your fathers. We all feel, in the existence of this Rebellion, that judgments terrible, wide-spread, far-reaching, overwhelming, are abroad in the land; and we feel, in view of these judgments, just now, a disposition to learn righteousness. This is the hour. Our streets are in mourning, tears are falling at every fireside, and under the chastisement of this Rebellion we have almost come up to the point of conceding this great, this all-important right of suffrage. I fear that if we fail to do it now, if abolitionists fail to press it now, we may not see, for centuries to come, the same disposition that exists at this moment. [*Applause*] Hence, I say, now is the time to press this right.

It may be asked, "Why do you want it? Some men have got along very well without it. Women have not this right." Shall we justify one wrong by another? This is the sufficient answer. Shall we at this moment justify the deprivation of the Negro of the right to vote, because someone else is deprived of that privilege? I hold that women, as well as men, have the right to vote [*Applause*], and my heart and voice go with the movement to extend suffrage to woman; but that question rests upon another basis than which our right rests. We may be asked, I say, why we want it. I will tell you why we want it. We want it because it is our right, first of all. No class of men can, without insulting their own nature, be content with any deprivation of their rights. We want it again, as a means for educating our race. Men are so constituted that they derive their conviction of their own possibilities largely by the estimate formed of them by others. If nothing is expected of a people, that people will find it difficult to contradict that expectation. By depriving us of suffrage, you affirm our incapacity to form an intelligent judgment respecting public men and public measures; you declare before the world that we are unfit to exercise the elective franchise, and by this means lead us to undervalue ourselves, to put a low estimate upon ourselves, and to feel that we have no possibilities like other men. Again, I want the elective franchise, for one, as a colored man, because ours is a peculiar government, based upon a peculiar idea, and that idea is universal suffrage. If I were in a monarchial government, or an autocratic or aristocratic government, where the few bore rule and the many were subject, there would be no special stigma resting upon me, because I did not exercise the elective franchise. It would do me no great violence. Mingling with the mass I should partake of the strength of the mass; I should be supported by the mass, and I should have the same incentives to endeavor with the mass of my fellow-men; it would be no particular burden, no particular deprivation; but here where universal suffrage is the rule, where that is the fundamental idea of the Government, to rule us out is to make us an exception, to brand us with the stigma of inferiority, and to invite to our heads the missiles of those about us; therefore, I want the franchise for the black man.

There are, however, other reasons, not derived from any consideration merely of our rights, but arising out of the conditions of the South, and of the country—considerations which have already been referred to by Mr. Phillips—considerations which must arrest the attention of statesmen. I believe that when the tall heads of this Rebellion shall have been swept down, as they will be swept down, when the Davises and Toombses and Stephenses, and others who are leading this Rebellion shall have been blotted out, there will be this rank undergrowth of treason, to which reference has been made, growing up there, and interfering with, and thwarting the quiet operation of the Federal Government in those states. You will see those traitors, handing down, from sire to son, the same malignant spirit which they have manifested and which they are now exhibiting, with malicious hearts, broad blades, and bloody hands in the field, against our sons and brothers. That spirit will still remain; and whoever sees the Federal Government extended over those Southern States will see that Government in a strange land, and not only in a strange land, but in an enemy's land. A post-master of the United States in the South will find himself surrounded by a hostile spirit; a collector in a Southern port will find himself surrounded by a hostile spirit; a United States marshal or United States judge will be surrounded there by a hostile element. That enmity will not die out in a year, will not die out in an age. The Federal Government will be looked upon in those States precisely as the Governments of Austria and France are looked upon in Italy at the present moment. They will endeavor to circumvent, they will endeavor to destroy, the peaceful operation of this Government. Now, where will you find the strength to counterbalance this spirit, if you do not find it in the Negroes of the South? They are your friends, and have always been your friends. They were your friends even when the Government did not regard them as such. They comprehended the genius of this war before you did. It is a significant fact, it is a marvellous fact, it seems almost to imply a direct interposition of Providence, that this war, which began in the interest of slavery on both sides, bids fair to end in the interest of liberty on both sides. [*Applause*] It was begun, I say, in the interest of slavery on both sides. The South was fighting to take slavery out of the Union, and the North was fighting to keep it in the Union; the South fighting to get it beyond the limits of the United States Constitution, and the North fighting to retain it within those limits; the South fighting for new guarantees, and the North fighting for the old guarantees—both despising the Negro, both insulting the Negro. Yet, the Negro, apparently endowed with wisdom from on high, saw more clearly the end from the beginning than we did. When Seward said the status of no man in the country would be changed by the war, the Negro did not believe him. [*Applause*] When our generals sent their underlings in shoulder-straps to hunt the flying Negro back from our lines into the jaws of slavery, from which he had escaped, the Negroes thought that a mistake had been made, and that the intentions of the Government had not been rightly understood by our officers in shoulder-straps, and they continued to come into our lines, threading their way through bogs and fens, over briers and thorns, fording streams, swimming rivers, bringing us tidings as to the safe path to march, and pointing out the dangers that threatened us. They are our only friends in the South, and we should be true to them in this their trial hour, and see to it that they have the elective franchise.

I know that we are inferior to you in some things—virtually inferior. We walk about you like dwarfs among giants. Our heads are scarcely seen above the great sea of humanity. The Germans are superior to us; the Irish are superior to us; the Yankees are superior to us [*Laughter*]; they can do what we cannot, that is, what we have not hitherto been allowed to do. But while I make this admission, I utterly deny, that we are originally, or naturally, or practically, or in any way, or in any important sense, inferior to anybody on this globe. [*Loud applause*] This charge of inferiority is an old dodge. It has been made available for oppression on many occasions. It is only about six centuries since the blue-eyed and fair-haired Anglo-Saxons were considered inferior by the haughty Normans, who once trampled upon them. If you read the history of the Norman Conquest, you will find that this proud Anglo-Saxon was once looked upon as of coarser clay than his Norman master, and might be found in the highways and byways of Old England laboring with a brass collar on his neck, and the name of his master marked upon it. You were down then! [*Laughter and applause*] You are up now. I am glad you are up, and I want you to be glad to help us up also. [*Applause*]

The story of our inferiority is an old dodge, as I have said; for wherever men oppress their fellows, wherever they enslave them, they will endeavor to find the needed apology for such enslavement and oppression in the character of the people oppressed and enslaved. When we wanted, a few years ago, a slice of Mexico, it was hinted that the Mexicans were an inferior race, that the old Castilian blood had become so weak that it would scarcely run down hill, and that Mexico needed the long, strong and beneficent arm of the Anglo-Saxon care extended over it. We said that it was necessary to its salvation, and a part of the "manifest destiny" of this Republic, to extend our arm over that dilapidated government. So, too, when Russia wanted to take possession of a part of the Ottoman Empire, the Turks were an "inferior race." So, too, when England wants to set the heel of her power more firmly in the quivering heart of old Ireland, the Celts are an "inferior race." So, too, the Negro, when he is to be robbed of any right which is justly his, is an "inferior man." It is said that we are ignorant; I admit it. But if we know enough to be hung, we know enough to vote. If the Negro knows enough to pay taxes to support the government, he knows enough to vote; taxation and representation should go together. If he knows enough to shoulder a musket and fight for the flag, fight for the government, he knows enough to vote. If he knows as much when he is sober as an Irishman knows when drunk, he knows enough to vote, on good American principles. [*Laughter and applause*]

But I was saying that you needed a counterpoise in the persons of the slaves to the enmity that would exist at the South after the Rebellion is put down. I hold that the American people are bound, not only in self-defence, to extend this right to the freedmen of the South, but they are bound by their love of country, and by all their regard for the future safety of those Southern States, to do this—to do it as a measure essential to the preservation of peace there. But I will not dwell upon this. I put it to the American sense of honor. The honor of a nation is an important thing. It is said in the Scriptures, "What doth it profit a man if he gain the whole world, and lose his own soul?" It may be said, also, What doth it profit a nation if it gain the whole world, but lose its honor? I hold that the American government has taken upon itself a solemn obligation of honor, to see that this war—let it be long or short, let it cost much or let it cost little—that this war shall not cease until every freedman at the South has the right to vote. [*Applause*] It has bound itself to it. What have you asked the black men of the South, the black men of the whole country to do? Why, you have asked them to incure the enmity of their masters, in order to befriend you and to befriend this Government. You have asked us to call down, not only upon ourselves, but upon our children's children, the deadly hate of the entire Southern people. You have called upon us to turn our backs upon our masters, to abandon their cause and espouse yours; to turn against the South and in favor of the North; to shoot down the Confederacy and uphold the flag—the American flag. You have called upon us to expose ourselves to all the subtle machinations of their malignity for all time. And now, what do you propose to do when you come to make peace? To reward your enemies, and trample in the dust your friends? Do you intend to sacrifice the very men who have come to the rescue of your banner in the South, and incurred the lasting displeasure of their masters thereby? Do you intend to sacrifice them and reward your enemies? Do you mean to give your enemies the right to vote, and take it away from your friends? Is that wise policy? Is that honorable? Could American honor withstand such a blow? I do not believe you will do it. I think you will see to it that we have the right to vote. There is something too mean in looking upon the Negro, when you are in trouble, as a citizen, and when you are free from trouble, as an alien. When this nation was in trouble, in its early struggles, it looked upon the Negro as a citizen. In 1776 he was a citizen. At the time of the formation of the Constitution the Negro had the right to vote in eleven States out of the old thirteen. In your trouble you have made us citizens. In 1812 Gen. Jackson addressed us as citizens—"fellow citizens." He wanted us to fight. We were citizens then! And now, when you come to frame a conscription bill, the Negro is a citizen again. He has been a citizen just three times in the history of this government, and it has always been in time of trouble. In time of trouble we are citizens. Shall we be citizens in war, and aliens in peace? Would that be just?

I ask my friends who are apologizing for not insisting upon this right, where can the black man look, in this country, for the assertion of his right, if he may not look to the Massachusetts Anti-Slavery Society? Where under the whole heavens can he look for sympathy, in asserting this right, if he may not look to this platform? Have you lifted us up to a certain height to see that we are men, and then are any disposed to leave us there, without seeing that we are put in possession of all our rights? We look naturally to this platform for the assertion of all our rights, and for this one especially. I understand the anti-slavery societies of this country to be based on two principles—first, the freedom of the blacks of this country; and, second, the elevation of them. Let me not be misunderstood here. I am not asking for sympathy at the hands of abolitionists, sympathy at the hands of any. I think the American people are disposed often to be generous rather than just. I look over this country at the present time, and I see Educational Societies, Sanitary Commissions, Freedmen's Associations, and the like—all very good: but in regard to the colored people there is always more that is benevolent, I perceive, than just, manifested towards us. What I ask for the Negro is not benevolence, not pity, not sympathy, but simply justice. [*Applause*] The American people have always been anxious to know what they shall do with us. Gen. Banks was distressed with solicitude as to what he should do with the Negro. Everybody has asked the question, and they learned to ask it early of the abolitionists, "What shall we do with the Negro?" I have had but one answer from the beginning. Do nothing with us! Your doing with us has already played the mischief with us. Do nothing with us! If the apples will not remain on the tree of their own strength, if they are wormeaten at the core, if they are early ripe and disposed to fall, let them fall! I am not for tying or fastening them on the tree in any way, except by nature's plan, and if they will not stay there, let them fall. And if the Negro cannot stand on his own legs, let him fall also. All I ask is, give him a chance to stand on his own legs! Let him alone! If you see him on his way to school, let him alone, don't disturb him! If you see him going to the dinner table at a hotel, let him go! If you see him going to the ballot-box, let him alone, don't disturb him! [*Applause*] If you see him going into a work-shop, just let him alone—your interference is doing him a positive injury. Gen. Banks' "preparation" is of a piece with this attempt to prop up the Negro. Let him fall if he cannot stand alone! If the Negro cannot live by the line of eternal justice, so beautifully pictured to you in the illustration used by Mr. Phillips, the fault will not be yours, it will be his who made the Negro, and established that line for his government. [*Applause*] Let him live or die by that. If you will only untie his hands, and give him a chance, I think he will live. He will work as readily for himself as the white man. A great many delusions have been swept away by this war. One was, that the Negro would not work; he has proved his ability to work. Another was, that the Negro would not fight; that he possessed only the most sheepish attributes of humanity; was a perfect lamb, or an "Uncle Tom"; disposed to take off his coat whenever required, fold his hands, and be whipped by anybody who wanted to whip him. But the war has proved that there is a great deal of human nature in the Negro, and that "he will fight," as Mr. Quincy, our President, said, in earlier days than these, "when there is reasonable probability of his whipping anybody." [*Laughter and applause*]

(1865)

An Appeal to Congress for Impartial Suffrage

A very limited statement of the argument for impartial suffrage, and for including the negro in the body politic, would require more space than can be reasonably asked here. It is supported by reasons as broad as the nature of man, and as numerous as the wants of society. Man is the only government-making animal in the world. His right to a participation in the production and operation of government is an inference from his nature, as direct and self-evident as is his right to acquire property or education. It is no less a crime against the manhood of a man, to declare that he shall not share in the making and directing of the government under which he lives, than to say that he shall not acquire property and education. The fundamental and unanswerable argument in favor of the enfranchisement of the negro is found in the undisputed fact of his manhood. He is a man, and by every fact and argument by which any man can sustain his right to vote, the negro can sustain his right equally. It is plain that, if the right belongs to any, it belongs to all. The doctrine that some men have no rights that others are bound to respect, is a doctrine which we must banish as we have banished slavery, from which it emanated. If black men have no rights in the eyes of white men, of course the whites can have none in the eyes of the blacks. The result is a war of races, and the annihilation of all proper human relations.

But suffrage for the negro, while easily sustained upon abstract principles, demands consideration upon what are recognized as the urgent necessities of the case. It is a measure of relief—a shield to break the force of a blow already descending with violence, and render it harmless. The work of destruction has already been set in motion all over the South. Peace to the country has literally meant war to the loyal men of the South, white and black; and negro suffrage is the measure to arrest and put an end to that dreadful strife.

Something then, not by way of argument (for that has been done by Charles Sumner, Thaddeus Stevens, Wendell Phillips, Gerrit Smith, and other able men), but rather of statement and appeal.

For better or for worse (as in some of the old marriage ceremonies), the negroes are evidently a permanent part of the American population. They are too numerous and useful to be colonized, and too enduring and self-perpetuating to disappear by natural causes. Here they are, four millions of them, and, for weal or for woe, here they must remain. Their history is parallel to that of the country; but while the history of the latter has been cheerful and bright with blessings, theirs has been heavy and dark with agonies and curses. What O'Connell said of the history of Ireland may with greater truth be said of the negroes. It may be "traced like a wounded man through a crowd, by the blood." Yet the negroes have marvellously survived all the exterminating forces of slavery, and have emerged at the end of two hundred and fifty years of bondage, not morose, misanthropic, and revengeful, but cheerful, hopeful, and forgiving. They now stand before Congress and the country, not complaining of the past, but simply asking for a better future. The spectacle of these dusky millions thus imploring, not demanding, is touching; and if American statesmen could be moved by a simple appeal to the nobler elements of human nature, if they had not fallen, seemingly, into the incurable habit of weighing and measuring every proposition of reform by some standard of profit and loss, doing wrong from choice, and right only from necessity or some urgent demand of human selfishness, it would be enough to plead for the negroes on the score of past services and sufferings. But no such appeal shall be relied on here. Hardships, services, sufferings, and sacrifices are all waived. It is true that they came to the relief of the country at the hour of its extremest need. It is true that, in many of the rebellious States, they were almost the only reliable friends the nation had throughout the whole tremendous war. It is true that, notwithstanding their alleged ignorance, they were wiser than their masters, and knew enough to be loyal, while those masters only knew enough to be rebels and traitors. It is true that they fought side by side in the loyal cause with our gallant and patriotic white soldiers, and that, but for their help—divided as the loyal States were—the Rebels might have succeeded in breaking up the Union, thereby entailing border wars and troubles of unknown duration and incalculable calamity. All this and more is true of these loyal negroes. Many daring exploits will be told to their credit. Impartial history will paint them as men who deserved well of their country. It will tell how they forded and swam rivers, with what consummate address they evaded the sharp-eyed Rebel pickets, how they toiled in the darkness of night through the tangled marshes of briers and thorns, barefooted and weary, running the risk of losing their lives, to warn our generals of Rebel schemes to surprise and destroy our loyal army. It will tell how these poor people, whose rights we still despised, behaved to our wounded soldiers, when found cold, hungry, and bleeding on the deserted battle-field; how they assisted our escaping prisoners from Andersonville, Belle Isle, Castle Thunder, and elsewhere, sharing with them their wretched crusts, and otherwise affording them aid and comfort; how they promptly responded to the trumpet call for their services, fighting against a foe that denied them the rights of civilized warfare, and for a government which was without the courage to assert those rights and avenge their violation in their behalf; with what gallantry they flung themselves upon Rebel fortifications, meeting death as fearlessly as any other troops in the service. But upon none of these things is reliance placed. These facts speak to the better dispositions of the human heart; but they seem of little weight with the opponents of impartial suffrage.

It is true that a strong plea for equal suffrage might be addressed to the national sense of honor. Something, too, might be said of national gratitude. A nation might well hesitate before the temptation to betray its allies. There is something immeasurably mean, to say nothing of the cruelty, in placing the loyal negroes of the South under the political power of their Rebel masters. To make peace with our enemies is all well enough; but to prefer our enemies and sacrifice our friends—to exalt our enemies and cast down our friends—to clothe our enemies, who sought the destruction of the government, with all political power, and leave our friends powerless in their hands—is an act which need not be characterized here. We asked the negroes to espouse our cause, to be our friends, to fight for us, and against their masters; and now, after they have done all that we asked them to do—helped us to conquer their masters, and thereby directed toward themselves the furious hate of the vanquished—it is proposed in some quarters to turn them over to the political control of the common enemy of the government and of the negro. But of this let nothing be said in this place. Waiving humanity, national honor, the claims of gratitude, the precious satisfaction arising from deeds of charity and justice to the weak and defenceless—the appeal for impartial suffrage addresses itself with great pertinency to the darkest, coldest, and flintiest side of the human heart, and would wring righteousness from the unfeeling calculations of human selfishness.

For in respect to this grand measure it is the good fortune of the negro that enlightened selfishness, not less than justice, fights on his side. National interest and national duty, if elsewhere separated, are firmly united here. The American people can, perhaps, afford to brave the censure of surrounding nations for the manifest injustice and meanness of excluding its faithful black soldiers from the ballot-box, but it cannot afford to allow the moral and mental energies of rapidly increasing millions to be consigned to hopeless degradation.

Strong as we are, we need the energy that slumbers in the black man's arm to make us stronger. We want no longer any heavy-footed, melancholy service from the negro. We want the cheerful activity of the quickened manhood of these sable millions. Nor can we afford to endure the moral blight which the existence of a degraded and hated class must necessarily inflict upon any people among whom such a class may exist. Exclude the negroes as a class from political rights—teach them that the high and manly privilege of suffrage is to be enjoyed by white citizens only—that they may bear the burdens of the state, but that they are to have no part in its direction or its honors—and you at once deprive them of one of the main incentives to manly character and patriotic devotion to the interests of the government; in a word, you stamp them as a degraded caste—you teach them to despise themselves, and all others to despise them. Men are so constituted that they largely derive their ideas of their abilities and their possibilities from the settled judgments of their fellow-men, and especially from such as they read in the institutions under which they live. If these bless them, they are blest indeed; but if these blast them, they are blasted indeed. Give the negro the elective franchise, and you give him at once a powerful motive for all noble exertion, and make him a man among men. A character is demanded of him, and here as elsewhere demand favors supply. It is nothing against this reasoning that all men who vote are not good men or good citizens. It is enough that the possession and exercise of the elective franchise is in itself an appeal to the nobler elements of manhood, and imposes education as essential to the safety of society.

To appreciate the full force of this argument, it must be observed, that disfranchisement in a republican government based upon the idea of human equality and universal suffrage, is a very different thing from disfranchisement in governments based upon the idea of the divine right of kings, or the entire subjugation of the masses. Masses of men can take care of themselves. Besides, the disabilities imposed upon all are necessarily without that bitter and stinging element of invidiousness which attaches to disfranchisement in a republic. What is common to all works no special sense of degradation to any. But in a country like ours, where men of all nations, kindred, and tongues are freely enfranchised, and allowed to vote, to say to the negro, You shall not vote, is to deal his manhood a staggering blow, and to burn into his soul a bitter and goading sense of wrong, or else work in him a stupid indifference to all the elements of a manly character. As a nation, we cannot afford to have amongst us either this indifference and stupidity, or that burning sense of wrong. These sable millions are too powerful to be allowed to remain either indifferent or discontented. Enfranchise them, and they become self-respecting and country-loving citizens. Disfranchise them, and the mark of Cain is set upon them less mercifully than upon the first murderer, for no man was to hurt him. But this mark of inferiority—all the more palpable because of a difference of color—not only dooms the negro to be a vagabond, but makes him the prey of insult and outrage everywhere. While nothing may be urged here as to the past services of the negro, it is quite within the line of this appeal to remind the nation of the possibility that a time may come when the services of the negro may be a second time required. History is said to repeat itself, and, if so, having wanted the negro once, we may want him again. Can that statesmanship be wise which would leave the negro good ground to hesitate, when the exigencies of the country required his prompt assistance? Can that be sound statesmanship which leaves millions of men in gloomy discontent, and possibly in a state of alienation in the day of national trouble? Was not the nation stronger when two hundred thousand sable soldiers were hurled against the Rebel fortifications, than it would have been without them? Arming the negro was an urgent military necessity three years ago—are we sure that another quite as pressing may not await us? Casting aside all thought of justice and magnanimity, is it wise to impose upon the negro all the burdens involved in sustaining government against foes within and foes without, to make him equal sharer in all sacrifices for the public good, to tax him in peace and conscript him in war, and then coldly exclude him from the ballot-box?

Look across the sea. Is Ireland, in her present condition, fretful, discontented, compelled to support an establishment in which she does not believe, and which the vast majority of her people abhor, a source of power or of weakness to Great Britain? Is not Austria wise in removing all ground of complaint against her on the part of Hungary? And does not the Emperor of Russia act wisely, as well as generously, when he not only breaks up the bondage of the serf, but extends him all the advantages of Russian citizenship? Is the present movement in England in favor of manhood suffrage—for the purpose of bringing four millions of British subjects into full sympathy and co-operation with the British government—a wise and humane movement, or otherwise? Is the existence of a rebellious element in our borders—which New Orleans, Memphis, and Texas show to be only disarmed, but at heart as malignant as ever, only waiting for an opportunity to reassert itself with fire and sword—a reason for leaving four millions of the nation's truest friends with just cause of complaint against the Federal government? If the doctrine that taxation should go hand in hand with representation can be appealed to in behalf of recent traitors and rebels, may it not properly be asserted in behalf of a people who have ever been loyal and faithful to the government? The answers to these questions are too obvious to require statement. Disguise it as we may, we are still a divided nation. The Rebel States have still an anti-national policy. Massachusetts and South Carolina may draw tears from the eyes of our tender hearted President by walking arm in arm into his Philadelphia Convention, but a citizen of Massachusetts is still an alien in the Palmetto State. There is that, all over the South, which frightens Yankee industry, capital, and skill from its borders. We have crushed the Rebellion, but not its hopes or its malign purposes. The South fought for perfect and permanent control over the Southern laborer. It was a war of the rich against the poor. They who waged it had no objection to the government, while they could use it as a means of confirming their power over the laborer. They fought the government, not because they hated the government as such, but because they found it, as they thought, in the way between them and their one grand purpose of rendering permanent and indestructible their authority and power over the Southern laborer. Though the battle is for the present lost, the hope of gaining this object still exists, and pervades the whole South with a feverish excitement. We have thus far only gained a Union without unity, marriage without love, victory without peace. The hope of gaining by politics what they lost by the sword, is the secret of all this Southern unrest; and that hope must be extinguished before national ideas and objects can take full possession of the Southern mind. There is but one safe and constitutional way to banish that mischievous hope from the South, and that is by lifting the laborer beyond the unfriendly political designs of his former master. Give the negro the elective franchise, and you at once destroy the purely sectional policy, and wheel the Southern States into line with national interests and national objects. The last and shrewdest turn of Southern politics is a recognition of the necessity of getting into Congress immediately, and at any price. The South will comply with any conditions but suffrage for the negro. It will swallow all the unconstitutional test oaths, repeal all the ordinances of Secession, repudiate the Rebel debt, promise to pay the debt incurred in conquering its people, pass all the constitutional amendments, if only it can have the negro left under its political control. The proposition is as modest as that made on the mountain: "All these things will I give unto thee if thou wilt fall down and worship me."

But why are the Southerners so willing to make these sacrifices? The answer plainly is, they see in this policy the only hope of saving something of their old sectional peculiarities and power. Once firmly seated in Congress, their alliance with Northern Democrats re-established, their States restored to their former position inside the Union, they can easily find means of keeping the Federal government entirely too busy with other important matters to pay much attention to the local affairs of the Southern States. Under the potent shield of State Rights, the game would be in their own hands. Does any sane man doubt for a moment that the men who followed Jefferson Davis through the late terrible Rebellion, often marching barefooted and hungry, naked and penniless, and who now only profess an enforced loyalty, would plunge this country into a foreign war today, if they could thereby gain their coveted independence, and their still more coveted mastery over the negroes? Plainly enough, the peace not less than the prosperity of this country is involved in the great measure of impartial suffrage. King Cotton is deposed, but only deposed, and is ready today to reassert all his ancient pretensions upon the first favorable opportunity. Foreign countries abound with his agents. They are able, vigilant, devoted. The young men of the South burn with the desire to regain what they call the lost cause; the women are noisily malignant towards the Federal government. In fact, all the elements of treason and rebellion are there under the thinnest disguise which necessity can impose.

What, then, is the work before Congress? It is to save the people of the South from themselves, and the nation from detriment on their account. Congress must supplant the evident sectional tendencies of the South by national dispositions and tendencies. It must cause national ideas and objects to take the lead and control the politics of those States. It must cease to recognize the old slave-masters as the only competent persons to rule the South. In a word, it must enfranchise the negro, and by means of the loyal negroes and the loyal white men of the South build up a national party there, and in time bridge the chasm between North and South, so that our country may have a common liberty and a common civilization. The new wine must be put into new bottles. The lamb may not be trusted with the wolf. Loyalty is hardly safe with traitors.

Statesmen of America! beware what you do. The ploughshare of rebellion has gone through the land beam-deep. The soil is in readiness, and the seed-time has come. Nations, not less than individuals, reap as they sow. The dreadful calamities of the past few years came not by accident, nor unbidden, from the ground. You shudder today at the harvest of blood sown in the spring-time of the Republic by your patriot fathers. The principle of slavery, which they tolerated under the erroneous impression that it would soon die out, became at last the dominant principle and power at the South. It early mastered the Constitution, became superior to the Union, and enthroned itself above the law.

Freedom of speech and of the press it slowly but successfully banished from the South, dictated its own code of honor and manners to the nation, brandished the bludgeon and the bowie-knife over Congressional debate, sapped the foundations of loyalty, dried up the springs of patriotism, blotted out the testimonies of the fathers against oppression, padlocked the pulpit, expelled liberty from its literature, invented nonsensical theories about master-races and slave-races of men, and in due season produced a Rebellion fierce, foul, and bloody.

This evil principle again seeks admission into our body politic. It comes now in shape of a denial of political rights to four million loyal colored people. The South does not now ask for slavery. It only asks for a large degraded caste, which shall have no political rights. This ends the case. Statesmen, beware what you do. The destiny of unborn and unnumbered generations is in your hands. Will you repeat the mistake of your fathers, who sinned ignorantly? or will you profit by the blood-bought wisdom all round you, and forever expel every vestige of the old abomination from our national borders? As you members of the Thirty-ninth Congress decide, will the country be peaceful, united, and happy, or troubled, divided, and miserable.

(1867)

The Color Line

Few evils are less accessible to the force of reason, or more tenacious of life and power, than a long-standing prejudice. It is a moral disorder, which creates the conditions necessary to its own existence, and fortifies itself by refusing all contradiction. It paints a hateful picture according to its own diseased imagination, and distorts the features of the fancied original to suit the portrait. As those who believe in the visibility of ghosts can easily see them, so it is always easy to see repulsive qualities in those we despise and hate.

Prejudice of race has at some time in their history afflicted all nations. "I am more holy than thou" is the boast of races, as well as that of the Pharisee. Long after the Norman invasion and the decline of Norman power, long after the sturdy Saxon had shaken off the dust of his humiliation and was grandly asserting his great qualities in all directions, the descendants of the invaders continued to regard their Saxon brothers as made of coarser clay than themselves, and were not well pleased when one of the former subject race came between the sun and their nobility. Having seen the Saxon a menial, a hostler, and a common drudge, oppressed and dejected for centuries, it was easy to invest him with all sorts of odious peculiarities, and to deny him all manly predicates. Though eight hundred years have passed away since Norman power entered England, and the Saxon has for centuries been giving his learning, his literature, his language, and his laws to the world more successfully than any other people on the globe, men in that country still boast their Norman origin and Norman perfections. This superstition of former greatness serves to fill out the shriveled sides of a meaningless race-pride which holds over after its power has vanished. With a very different lesson from the one this paper is designed to impress, the great Daniel Webster once told the people of Massachusetts (whose prejudices in the particular instance referred to were right) that they "had conquered the sea, and had conquered the land," but that "it remained for them to conquer their prejudices." At one time we are told that the people in some of the towns of Yorkshire cherished a prejudice so strong and violent against strangers and foreigners that one who ventured to pass through their streets would be pelted with stones.

Of all the races and varieties of men which have suffered from this feeling, the colored people of this country have endured most. They can resort to no disguises which will enable them to escape its deadly aim. They carry in front the evidence which marks them for persecution. They stand at the extreme point of difference from the Caucasian race, and their African origin can be instantly recognized, though they may be several removes from the typical African race. They may remonstrate like Shylock—"Hath not a Jew eyes? hath not a Jew hands, organs, dimensions, senses, affections, passions? fed with the same food, hurt with the same weapons, subject to the same diseases, healed by the same means, warmed and cooled by the same summer and winter, as a Christian is?"—but such eloquence is unavailing. They are negroes—and that is enough, in the eye of this unreasoning prejudice, to justify indignity and violence. In nearly every department of American life they are confronted by this insidious influence. It fills the air. It meets them at the workshop and factory, when they apply for work. It meets them at the church, at the hotel, at the ballot-box, and worst of all, it meets them in the jury-box. Without crime or offence against law or gospel, the colored man is the Jean Valjean of American society. He has escaped from the galleys, and hence all presumptions are against him. The workshop denies him work, and the inn denies him shelter; the ballot-box a fair vote, and the jury-box a fair trial. He has ceased to be the slave of society. He may not now be bought and sold like a beast in the market, but he is the trammeled victim of a prejudice, well calculated to repress his manly ambition, paralyze his energies, and make him a dejected and spiritless man, if not a sullen enemy to society, fit to prey upon life and property and to make trouble generally.

When this evil spirit is judge, jury, and prosecutor, nothing less than overwhelming evidence is sufficient to overcome the force of unfavorable presumptions.

Everything against the person with the hated color is promptly taken for granted; while everything in his favor is received with suspicion and doubt.

A boy of this color is found in his bed tied, mutilated, and bleeding, when forthwith all ordinary experience is set aside, and he is presumed to have been guilty of the outrage upon himself; weeks and months he is kept on trial for the offence, and every effort is made to entangle the poor fellow in the confused meshes of expert testimony (the least trustworthy of all evidence). This same spirit, which promptly assumes everything against us, just as readily denies or explains away everything in our favor. We are not, as a race, even permitted to appropriate the virtues and achievements of our individual representatives. Manliness, capacity, learning, laudable ambition, heroic service, by any of our number, are easily placed to the credit of the superior race. One drop of Teutonic blood is enough to account for all good and great qualities occasionally coupled with a colored skin; and on the other hand, one drop of negro blood, though in the veins of a man of Teutonic whiteness, is enough of which to predicate all offensive and ignoble qualities. In presence of this spirit, if a crime is committed, and the criminal is not positively known, a suspicious-looking colored man is sure to have been seen in the neighborhood. If an unarmed colored man is shot down and dies in his tracks, a jury, under the influence of this spirit, does not hesitate to find the murdered man the real criminal, and the murderer innocent.

Now let us examine this subject a little more closely. It is claimed that this wonder-working prejudice—this moral magic that can change virtue into vice, and innocence to crime; which makes the dead man the murderer, and holds the living homicide harmless—is a natural, instinctive, and invincible attribute of the white race, and one that cannot be eradicated; that even evolution itself cannot carry us beyond or above it. Alas for this poor suffering world (for four-fifths of mankind are colored), if this claim be true! In that case men are forever doomed to injustice, oppression, hate, and strife; and the religious sentiment of the world, with its grand idea of human brotherhood, its "peace on earth and good-will to men," and its golden rule, must be voted a dream, a delusion, and a snare.

But is this color prejudice the natural and inevitable thing it claims to be? If it is so, then it is utterly idle to write against it, preach, pray, or legislate against it, or pass constitutional amendments against it. Nature will have her course, and one might as well preach and pray to a horse against running, to a fish against swimming, or to a bird against flying. Fortunately, however, there is good ground for calling in question this high pretension of a vulgar and wicked prepossession.

If I could talk with all my white fellow-countrymen on this subject, I would say to them, in the language of Scripture: "Come and let us reason together." Now, without being too elementary and formal, it may be stated here that there are at least seven points which candid men will be likely to admit, but which, if admitted, will prove fatal to the popular thought and practice of the times.

First: If what we call prejudice against color be natural, i.e., a part of human nature itself, it follows that it must be co-extensive with human nature, and will and must manifest itself whenever and wherever the two races are brought into contact. It would not vary with either latitude, longitude, or altitude; but like fire and gunpowder, whenever brought together, there would be an explosion of contempt, aversion, and hatred.

Secondly: If it can be shown that there is anywhere on the globe any considerable country where the contact of the African and Caucasian is not distinguished by this explosion of race-wrath, there is reason to doubt that the prejudice is an ineradicable part of human nature.

Thirdly: If this so-called natural, instinctive prejudice can be satisfactorily accounted for by facts and considerations wholly apart from the color features of the respective races, thus placing it among the things subject to human volition and control, we may venture to deny the claim set up for it in the name of human nature.

Fourthly: If any considerable number of white people have overcome this prejudice in themselves, have cast it out as an unworthy sentiment, and have survived the operation, the fact shows that this prejudice is not at any rate a vital part of human nature, and may be eliminated from the race without harm.

Fifthly: If this prejudice shall, after all, prove to be, in its essence and in its natural manifestation, simply a prejudice against condition, and not against race or color, and that it disappears when this or that condition is absent, then the argument drawn from the nature of the Caucasian race falls to the ground.

Sixthly: If prejudice of race and color is only natural in the sense that ignorance, superstition, bigotry, and vice are natural, then it has no better defence than they, and should be despised and put away from human relations as an enemy to the peace, good order, and happiness of human society.

Seventhly: If, still further, this aversion to the negro arises out of the fact that he is as we see him, poor, spiritless, ignorant, and degraded, then whatever is humane, noble, and superior, in the mind of the superior and more fortunate race, will desire that all arbitrary barriers against his manhood, intelligence, and elevation shall be removed, and a fair chance in the race of life be given him.

The first of these propositions does not require discussion. It commends itself to the understanding at once. Natural qualities are common and universal, and do not change essentially on the mountain or in the valley. I come therefore to the second point—the existence of countries where this malignant prejudice, as we know it in America, does not prevail; where character, not color, is the passport to consideration; where the right of the black man to be a man, and a man among men, is not questioned; where he may, without offence, even presume to be a gentleman. That there are such countries in the world there is ample evidence. Intelligent and observing travelers, having no theory to support, men whose testimony would be received without question in respect of any other matter, and should not be questioned in this, tell us that they find no color prejudice in Europe, except among Americans who reside there. In England and on the Continent, the colored man is no more an object of hate than any other person. He mingles with the multitude unquestioned, without offence given or received. During the two years which the writer spent abroad, though he was much in society, and was sometimes in the company of lords and ladies, he does not remember one word, look, or gesture that indicated the slightest aversion to him on account of color. His experience was not in this respect exceptional or singular. Messrs. Remond, Ward, Garnet, Brown, Pennington, Crummell, and Bruce, all of them colored, and some of them black, bear the same testimony. If what these gentleman say (and it can be corroborated by a thousand witnesses) is true there is no prejudice against color in England, save as it is carried there by Americans—carried there as a moral disease from an infected country. It is American, not European; local, not general; limited, not universal, and must be ascribed to artificial conditions, and not to any fixed and universal law of nature.

The third point is: Can this prejudice against color, as it is called, be accounted for by circumstances outside and independent of race or color? If it can be thus explained, an incubus may be removed from the breasts of both the white and the black people of this country, as well as from that large intermediate population which has sprung up between these alleged irreconcilable extremes. It will help us to see that it is not necessary that the Ethiopian shall change his skin, nor needful that the white man shall change the essential elements of his nature, in order that mutual respect and consideration may exist between the two races.

Now it is easy to explain the conditions outside of race or color from which may spring feelings akin to those which we call prejudice. A man without the ability or the disposition to pay a just debt does not feel at ease in the presence of his creditor. He does not want to meet him on the street, or in the market-place. Such meeting makes him uncomfortable. He would rather find fault with the bill than pay the debt, and the creditor himself will soon develop in the eyes of the debtor qualities not altogether to his taste.

Someone has well said, we may easily forgive those who injure us, but it is hard to forgive those whom we injure. The greatest injury this side of death, which one human being can inflict on another, is to enslave him, to blot out his personality, degrade his manhood, and sink him to the condition of a beast of burden; and just this has been done here during more than two centuries. No other people under heaven, of whatever type or endowments, could have been so enslaved without falling into contempt and scorn on the part of those enslaving them. Their slavery would itself stamp them with odious features, and give their oppressors arguments in favor of oppression. Besides the long years of wrong and injury inflicted upon the colored race in this country, and the effect of these wrongs upon that race, morally, intellectually, and physically, corrupting their morals, darkening their minds, and twisting their bodies and limbs out of all approach to symmetry, there has been a mountain of gold—uncounted millions of dollars—resting upon them with crushing weight. During all the years of their bondage, the slave master had a direct interest in discrediting the personality of those he held as property. Every man who had a thousand dollars so invested had a thousand reasons for painting the black man as fit only for slavery. Having made him the companion of horses and mules, he naturally sought to justify himself by assuming that the negro was not much better than a mule. The holders of twenty hundred million dollars' worth of property in human chattels procured the means of influencing press, pulpit, and politician, and through these instrumentalities they belittled our virtues and magnified our vices, and have made us odious in the eyes of the world. Slavery had the power at one time to make and unmake Presidents, to construe the law, dictate the policy, set the fashion in national manners and customs, interpret the Bible, and control the church; and, naturally enough, the old masters set themselves up as much too high as they set the manhood of the negro too low. Out of the depths of slavery has come this prejudice and this color line. It is broad enough and black enough to explain all the malign influences which assail the newly emancipated millions today. In reply to this argument it will perhaps be said that the negro has no slavery now to contend with, and that having been free during the last sixteen years, he ought by this time to have contradicted the degrading qualities which slavery formerly ascribed to him. All very true as to the letter, but utterly false as to the spirit. Slavery is indeed gone, but its shadow still lingers over the country and poisons more or less the moral atmosphere of all sections of the republic. The money motive for assailing the negro which slavery represented is indeed absent, but love of power and dominion, strengthened by two centuries of irresponsible power, still remains.

Having now shown how slavery created and sustained this prejudice against race and color, and the powerful motive for its creation, the other four points made against it need not be discussed in detail and at length, but may only be referred to in a general way.

If what is called the instinctive aversion of the white race for the colored, when analyzed, is seen to be the same as that which men feel or have felt toward other objects wholly apart from color; if it should be the same as that sometimes exhibited by the haughty and rich to the humble and poor, the same as the Brahmin feels toward the lower caste, the same as the Norman felt toward the Saxon, the same as that cherished by the Turk against Christians, the same as Christians have felt toward the Jews, the same as that which murders a Christian in Wallachia, calls him a "dog" in Constantinople, oppresses and persecutes a Jew in Berlin, hunts down a socialist in St. Petersburg, drives a Hebrew from an hotel at Saratoga, that scorns the Irishman in London, the same as Catholics once felt for Protestants, the same as that which insults, abuses, and kills the Chinaman on the Pacific slope—then may we well enough affirm that this prejudice really has nothing whatever to do with race or color, and that it has its motive and mainspring in some other source with which the mere facts of color and race have nothing to do.

After all, some very well informed and very well meaning people will read what I have now said, and what seems to me so just and reasonable, and will still insist that the color of the negro has something to do with the feeling entertained toward him; that the white man naturally shudders at the thought of contact with one who is black—that the impulse is one which he can neither resist nor control. Let us see if this conclusion is a sound one. An argument is unsound when it proves too little or too much, or when it proves nothing. If color is an offence, it is so, entirely apart from the manhood it envelops. There must be something in color of itself to kindle rage and inflame hate, and render the white man generally uncomfortable. If the white man were really so constituted that color were, in itself, a torment to him, this grand old earth of ours would be no place for him. Colored objects confront him here at every point of the compass. If he should shrink and shudder every time he sees anything dark, he would have little time for anything else. He would require a colorless world to live in—a world where flowers, fields, and floods should all be of snowy whiteness; where rivers, lakes, and oceans should all be white; where all the men, and women, and children should be white; where all the fish of the sea, all the birds of the air, all the "cattle upon a thousand hills," should be white; where the heavens above and the earth beneath should be white, and where day and night should not be divided by light and darkness, but the world should be one eternal scene of light. In such a white world, the entrance of a black man would be hailed with joy by the inhabitants. Anybody or anything would be welcome that would break the oppressive and tormenting monotony of the all-prevailing white.

In the abstract, there is no prejudice against color. No man shrinks from another because he is clothed in a suit of black, nor offended with his boots because they are black. We are told by those who have resided there that a white man in Africa comes to think that ebony is about the proper color for man. Good old Thomas Whitson—a noble old Quaker—a man of rather odd appearance—used to say that even he would be handsome if he could change public opinion.

Aside from the curious contrast to himself, the white child feels nothing on the first sight of a colored man. Curiosity is the only feeling. The office of color in the color line is a very plain and subordinate one. It simply advertises the objects of oppression, insult, and persecution. It is not the maddening liquor, but the black letters on the sign telling the world where it may be had. It is not the hated Quaker, but the broad brim and the plain coat. It is not the hateful Cain, but the mark by which he is known. The color is innocent enough, but things with which it is coupled make it hated. Slavery, ignorance, stupidity, servility, poverty, dependence, are undesirable conditions. When these shall cease to be coupled with color, there will be no color line drawn. It may help in this direction to observe a few of the inconsistencies of the color-line feeling, for it is neither uniform in its operations nor consistent in its principles. Its contradictions in the latter respect would be amusing if the feeling itself were not so deserving of unqualified abhorrence. Our Californian brothers, of Hibernian descent, hate the Chinaman, and kill him, and when asked why they do so, their answer is that a Chinaman is so industrious he will do all the work, and can live by wages upon which other people would starve. When the same people and others are asked why they hate the colored people, the answer is that they are indolent and wasteful, and cannot take care of themselves. Statesmen of the South will tell you that the negro is too ignorant and stupid properly to exercise the elective franchise, and yet his greatest offence is that he acts with the only party intelligent enough in the eyes of the nation to legislate for the country. In one breath they tell us that the negro is so weak in intellect, and so destitute of manhood, that he is but the echo of designing white men, and yet in another they will virtually tell you that the negro is so clear in his moral perceptions, so firm in purpose, so steadfast in his convictions, that he cannot be persuaded by arguments or intimidated by threats, and that nothing but the shot-gun can restrain him from voting for the men and measures he approves. They shrink back in horror from contact with the negro as a man and a gentleman, but like him very well as a barber, waiter, coachman, or cook. As a slave, he could ride anywhere, side by side with his white master, but as a freeman, he must be thrust into the smoking-car. As a slave, he could go into the first cabin; as a freeman, he was not allowed abaft the wheel. Formerly it was said he was incapable of learning, and at the same time it was a crime against the State for any man to teach him to read. Today he is said to be originally and permanently inferior to the white race, and yet wild apprehensions are expressed lest six millions of this inferior race will somehow or other manage to rule over thirty-five millions of the superior race. If inconsistency can prove the hollowness of anything, certainly the emptiness of this pretense that color has any terrors is easily shown. The trouble is that most men, and especially mean men, want to have something under them. The rich man would have the poor man, the white would have the black, the Irish would have the negro, and the negro must have a dog, if he can get nothing higher in the scale of intelligence to dominate. This feeling is one of the vanities which enlightenment will dispel. A good but simple-minded Abolitionist said to me that he was not ashamed to walk with me down Broadway arm-in-arm, in open daylight, and evidently thought he was saying something that must be very pleasing to my self-importance, but it occurred to me, at the moment, this man does not dream of any reason why I might be ashamed to walk arm-in-arm with him through Broadway in open daylight. Riding in a stage-coach from Concord, New Hampshire, to Vergennes, Vermont, many years ago, I found myself on very pleasant terms with all the passengers through the night, but the morning light came to me as it comes to the stars; I was as Dr. Beecher says he was at the first fire he witnessed, when a bucket of cold water was poured down his back—"the fire was not put out, but he was." The fact is, the higher the colored man rises in the scale of society, the less prejudice does he meet.

The writer has met and mingled freely with the leading great men of his time—at home and abroad, in public halls and private houses, on the platform and at the fireside—and can remember no instance when among such men has he been made to feel himself an object of aversion. Men who are really great are too great to be small. This was gloriously true of the late Abraham Lincoln, William H. Seward, Salmon P. Chase, Henry Wilson, John P. Hale, Lewis Tappan, Edmund Quincy, Joshua R. Giddings, Gerrit Smith, and Charles Sumner, and many others among the dead. Good taste will not permit me now to speak of the living, except to say that the number of those who rise superior to prejudice is great and increasing. Let those who wish to see what is to be the future of America, as relates to races and race relations, attend, as I have attended, during the administration of President Hayes, the grand diplomatic receptions at the executive mansion, and see there, as I have seen, in its splendid east room, the wealth, culture, refinement, and beauty of the nation assembled, and with it the eminent representatives of other nations—the swarthy Turk with his "fez," the Englishman shining with gold, the German, the Frenchman, the Spaniard, the Japanese, the Chinaman, the Caucasian, the Mongolian, the Sandwich Islander, and the negro—all moving about freely, each respecting the rights and dignity of the other, and neither receiving nor giving offence.

Then let us pray that come it may,
As come it will for a' that,
That sense and worth, o'er a' the earth,
May bear the gree, and a' that;
That man to man the world o'er,
Shall brothers be for a' that.

(1881)

John Brown

Not to fan the flame of sectional animosity now happily in the process of rapid and I hope permanent extinction; not to revive and keep alive a sense of shame and remorse for a great national crime, which has brought own punishment, in loss of treasure, tears and blood; not to recount the long list of wrongs, inflicted on my race during more than two hundred years of merciless bondage; nor yet to draw, from the labyrinths of far-off centuries, incidents and achievements wherewith to rouse your passions, and enkindle your enthusiasm, but to pay a just debt long due, to vindicate in some degree a great historical character, of our own time and country, one with whom I was myself well acquainted, and whose friendship and confidence it was my good fortune to share, and to give you such recollections, impressions and facts, as I can, of a grand, brave and good old man, and especially to promote a better understanding of the raid upon Harper's Ferry of which he was the chief, is the object of this address.

In all the thirty years' conflict with slavery, if we except the late tremendous war, there is no subject which in its interest and importance will be remembered longer, or will form a more thrilling chapter in American history than this strange, wild, bloody and mournful drama. The story of it is still fresh in the minds of many who now hear me, but for the sake of those who may have forgotten its details, and in order to have our subject in its entire range more fully and clearly before us at the outset, I will briefly state the facts in that extraordinary transaction.

On the night of the 16th of October, 1859, there appeared near the confluence of the Potomac and Shenandoah rivers, a party of nineteen men—fourteen white and five colored. They were not only armed themselves, but had brought with them a large supply of arms for such persons as might join them. These men invaded Harper's Ferry, disarmed the watchman, took possession of the arsenal, rifle-factory, armory and other government property at that place, arrested and made prisoners nearly all the prominent citizens of the neighborhood, collected about fifty slaves, put bayonets into the hands of such as were able and willing to fight for their liberty, killed three men, proclaimed general emancipation, held the ground more than thirty hours, were subsequently overpowered and nearly all killed, wounded or captured, by a body of United States, troops, under command of Colonel Robert E. Lee, since famous as the rebel Gen. Lee. Three out of the nineteen invaders were captured whilst fighting, and one of these was Captain John Brown, the man who originated, planned and commanded the expedition. At the time of his capture Capt. Brown was supposed to be mortally wounded as he had several ugly gashes and bayonet wounds on his head and body; and apprehending that he might speedily die, or that he might be rescued by his friends, and thus the opportunity of making him a signal example of slave-holding vengeance would be lost, his captors hurried him to Charlestown two miles further within the border of Virginia, placed him in prison strongly guarded by troops, and before his wounds were healed he was brought into court, subjected to a nominal trial, convicted of high treason and inciting slaves to insurrection, and was executed. His corpse was given to his woe-stricken widow, and she, assisted by Anti-slavery friends, caused it to be borne to North Elba, Essex County, N.Y., and there his dust now reposes amid the silent, solemn and snowy grandeur of the Adirondacks.

Such is the story; with no line softened or hardened to my inclining. It certainly is not a story to please, but to pain. It is not a story to increase our sense of social safety and security, but to fill the imagination with wild and troubled fancies of doubt and danger. It was a sudden and startling surprise to the people of Harper's Ferry, and it is not easy to conceive of a situation more abundant in all the elements of horror and consternation. They had retired as usual to rest, with no suspicion that an enemy lurked in the surrounding darkness. They had quietly and trustingly given themselves up to "tired Nature's sweet restorer, balmy sleep," and while thus all unconscious of danger, they were roused from their peaceful slumbers by the sharp crack of the invader's rifle, and felt the keen-edged sword of war at their throats, three of their numbers being already slain.

Every feeling of the human heart was naturally outraged at this occurrence, and hence at the moment the air was full of denunciation and execration. So intense was this feeling, that few ventured to whisper a word of apology. But happily reason has her voice as well as feeling, and though slower in deciding, her judgments are broader, deeper, clearer and more enduring. It is not easy to reconcile human feeling to the shedding of blood for any purpose, unless indeed in the excitement which the shedding of blood itself occasions. The knife is to feeling always an offence. Even when in the hands of a skillful surgeon, it refuses consent to the operation long after reason has demonstrated its necessity. It even pleads the cause of the known murderer on the day of his execution, and calls society half criminal when, in cold blood, it takes life as a protection of itself from crime. Let no word be said against this holy feeling; more than to law and government are we indebted to this tender sentiment of regard for human life for the safety with which we walk the streets by day and sleep secure in our beds at night. It is nature's grand police, vigilant and faithful, sentineled in the soul, guarding against violence to peace and life. But whilst so much is freely accorded to feeling in the economy of human welfare, something more than feeling is necessary to grapple with a fact so grim and significant as was this raid. Viewed apart and alone, as a transaction separate and distinct from its antecedents and bearings, it takes rank with the most cold-blooded and atrocious wrongs ever perpetrated; but just here is the trouble—this raid on Harper's Ferry, no more than Sherman's march to the sea can consent to be thus viewed alone.

There is, in the world's government, a force which has in all ages been recognized, sometimes as Nemesis, sometimes as the judgment of God and sometimes as retributive justice; but under whatever name, all history attests the wisdom and beneficence of its chastisements, and men become reconciled to the agents through whom it operates, and have extolled them as heroes, benefactors and demigods.

To the broad vision of a true philosophy, nothing in this world stands alone. Everything is a necessary part of everything else. The margin of chance is narrowed by every extension of reason and knowledge, and nothing comes unbidden to the feast of human experience. The universe, of which we are a part, is continually proving itself a stupendous whole, a system of law and order, eternal and perfect. Every seed bears fruit after its kind, and nothing is reaped which was not sowed. The distance between seed time and harvest, in the moral world, may not be quite so well defined or as clearly intelligible as in the physical, but there is a seed time, and there is a harvest time, and though ages may intervene, and neither he who ploughed nor he who sowed may reap in person, yet the harvest nevertheless will surely come; and as in the physical world there are century plants, so it may be in the moral world, and their fruitage is as certain in the one as in the other. The bloody harvest of Harper's Ferry was ripened by the heat and moisture of merciless bondage of more than two hundred years. That startling cry of alarm on the bank of the Potomac was but the answering back of the avenging angel to the midnight invasions of Christian slave-traders on the sleeping hamlets of Africa. The history of the African slave-trade furnishes many illustrations far more cruel and bloody.

Viewed thus broadly our subject is worthy of thoughtful and dispassionate consideration. It invites the study of the poet, scholar, philosopher and statesman. What the masters in natural science have done for man in the physical world, the masters of social science may yet do for him in the moral world. Science now tells us when storms are in the sky, and when and where their violence will be most felt. Why may we not yet know with equal certainty when storms are in the moral sky, and how to avoid their desolating force? But I can invite you to no such profound discussions. I am not the man, nor is this the occasion for such philosophical enquiry. Mine is the word of grateful memory to an old friend; to tell you what I knew of him—what I knew of his inner life—of what he did and what he attempted, and thus if possible to make the mainspring of his actions manifest and thereby give you a clearer view of his character and services.

It is said that next in value to the performance of great deeds ourselves, is the capacity to appreciate such when performed by others; to more than this I do not presume. Allow me one other personal word before I proceed. In the minds of some of the American people I was myself credited with an important agency in the John Brown raid. Governor Henry A. Wise was manifestly of that opinion. He was at the pains of having Mr. Buchanan send his Marshals to Rochester to invite me to accompany them to Virginia. Fortunately I left town several hours previous to their arrival.

What ground there was for this distinguished consideration shall duly appear in the natural course of this lecture. I wish however to say just here that there was no foundation whatever for the charge that I in any wise urged or instigated John Brown to his dangerous work. I rejoice that it is my good fortune to have seen, not only the end of slavery, but to see the day when the whole truth can be told about this matter without prejudice to either the living or the dead. I shall however allow myself little prominence in these disclosures. Your interests, like mine, are in the all-commanding figure of the story, and to him I consecrate the hour. His zeal in the cause of my race was far greater than mine—it was as the burning sun to my taper light—mine was bounded by time, his stretched away to the boundless shores of eternity. I could live for the slave, but he could die for him. The crown of martyrdom is high, far beyond the reach of ordinary mortals, and yet happily no special greatness or superior moral excellence is necessary to discern and in some measure appreciate a truly great soul. Cold, calculating and unspiritual as most of us are, we are not wholly insensible to real greatness; and when we are brought in contact with a man of commanding mold, towering high and alone above the millions, free from all conventional fetters, true to his own moral convictions, a "law unto himself," ready to suffer misconstruction, ignoring torture and death for what he believes to be right, we are compelled to do him homage.

In the stately shadow, in the sublime presence of such a soul I find myself standing tonight; and how to do it reverence, how to do it justice, how to honor the dead with due regard to the living, has been a matter of anxious solicitude.

Much has been said of John Brown, much that is wise and beautiful, but in looking over what may be called the John Brown literature, I have been little assisted with material, and even less encouraged with any hope of success in treating the subject. Scholarship, genius and devotion have hastened with poetry and eloquence, story and song to this simple altar of human virtue, and have retired dissatisfied and distressed with the thinness and poverty of their offerings, as I shall with mine.

The difficulty in doing justice to the life and character of such a man is not altogether due to the quality of the zeal, or of the ability brought to the work, nor yet to any imperfections in the qualities of the man himself; the state of the moral atmosphere about us has much to do with it. The fault is not in our eyes, nor yet in the object, if under a murky sky we fail to discover the object. Wonderfully tenacious is the taint of a great wrong. The evil, as well as "the good that men do, lives after them." Slavery is indeed gone; but its long, black shadow yet falls broad and large over the face of the whole country. It is the old truth oft repeated, and never more fitly than now, "a prophet is without honor in his own country and among his own people." Though more than twenty years have rolled between us and the Harper's Ferry raid, though since then the armies of the nation have found it necessary to do on a large scale what John Brown attempted to do on small one, and the great captain who fought his way through slavery has filled with honor the Presidential chair, we yet stand too near the days of slavery, and the life and times of John Brown, to see clearly the true martyr and hero that he was and rightly to estimate the value of the man and his works. Like the great and good of all ages—the men born in advance of their times, the men whose bleeding footprints attest the immense cost of reform, and show us the long and dreary spaces, between the luminous points in the progress of mankind—this our noblest American hero must wait the polishing wheels of after-coming centuries to make his glory more manifest, and his worth more generally acknowledged. Such instances are abundant and familiar. If we go back four and twenty centuries, to the stately city of Athens, and search among her architectural splendor and her miracles of art for the Socrates of today, and as he stands in history, we shall find Ourselves perplexed and disappointed. In Jerusalem Jesus himself was only the "carpenter's son"—a young man wonderfully destitute of worldly prudence —pestilent fellow, "inexcusably and perpetually interfering in the world's business,"—"upsetting the tables of the money-changers"—preaching sedition, opposing the good old religion—"making himself greater than Abraham," and at the same time "keeping company" with very low people; but behold the change! He was a great miracle-worker, in his day, but time has worked for him a greater miracle than all his miracles, for now his name stands for all that is desirable in government, noble in life, orderly and beautiful in society. That which time has done for other great men of his class, that will time certainly do for John Brown. The brightest gems shine at first with subdued light, and the strongest characters are subject to the same limitations. Under the influence of adverse education and hereditary bias, few things are more difficult than to render impartial justice. Men hold up their hands to Heaven, and swear they will do justice, but what oaths against prejudice and against inclination! In the face of high-sounding professions and affirmations we know well how hard it is for a Turk to do justice to a Christian, or for a Christian to do justice to a Jew. How hard for an Englishman to do justice to an Irishman, for an Irishman to do justice to an Englishman, harder still for an American tainted by slavery to do justice to the Negro or the Negro's friends. "John Brown," said the late Wm. H. Seward, "was justly hanged." "John Brown," said the late John A. Andrew, "was right." It is easy to perceive the sources of these two opposite judgments: the one was the verdict of slaveholding and panic-stricken Virginia, the other was the verdict of the best heart and brain of free old

Massachusetts. One was the heated judgment of the passing and passionate hour, and the other was the calm, clear, unimpeachable judgment of the broad, illimitable future.

There is, however, one aspect of the present subject quite worthy of notice, for it makes the hero of Harper's Ferry in some degree an exception to the general rules to which I have just now adverted. Despite the hold which slavery had at time on the country, despite the popular prejudice against the Negro, despite the shock which the first alarm occasioned, almost from the first John Brown received a large measure of sympathy and appreciation. New England recognized in him the spirit which brought the pilgrims to Plymouth rock and hailed him as a martyr and saint. True he had broken the law, true he had struck for a despised people, true he had crept upon his foe stealthily, like a wolf upon the fold, and had dealt his blow in the dark whilst his enemy slept, but with all this and more to disturb the moral sense, men discerned in him the greatest and best qualities known to human nature, and pronounced him "good." Many consented to his death, and then went home and taught their children to sing his praise as one whose "soul is marching on" through the realms of endless bliss. One element in explanation of this somewhat anomalous circumstance will probably be found in the troubled times which immediately succeeded, for "when judgments are abroad in the world, men learn righteousness."

The country had before this learned the value of Brown's heroic character. He had shown boundless courage and skill in dealing with the enemies of liberty in Kansas. With men so few, and means so small, and odds against him so great, no captain ever surpassed him in achievements, some of which seem almost beyond belief. With only eight men in that bitter war, he met, fought and captured Henry Clay Pate, with twenty-five well armed and mounted men. In this memorable encounter, he selected his ground so wisely, handled his men so skillfully, and attacked the enemy so vigorously, that they could neither run nor fight, and were therefore compelled to surrender to a force less than one-third their own. With just thirty men on another important occasion during the same border war, he met and vanquished four hundred Missourians under the command of Gen. Read. These men had come into the territory under an oath never to return to their homes till they had stamped out the last vestige of free State spirit in Kansas; but a brush with old Brown took this high conceit out of them, and they were glad to get off upon any terms, without stopping to stipulate. With less than one hundred men to defend the town of Lawrence, he offered to lead them and give battle to fourteen hundred men on the banks of the Waukerusia river, and was much vexed when his offer was refused by Gen. Jim Lane and others to whom the defence of the town was confided. Before leaving Kansas, he went into the border of Missouri, and liberated a dozen slaves in a single night, and, in spite of slave laws and marshals, he brought these people through a half dozen States, and landed them safely in Canada. With eighteen men this man shook the whole social fabric of Virginia. With eighteen men he overpowered a town of nearly three thousand souls. With these eighteen men he held that large community firmly in his grasp for thirty long hours. With these eighteen men he rallied in a single night fifty slaves to his standard, and made prisoners of an equal number of the slaveholding class. With these eighteen men he defied the power and bravery of a dozen of the best militia companies that Virginia could send against him. Now, when slavery struck, as it certainly did strike, at the life of the country, it was not the fault of John Brown that our rulers did not at first know how to deal with it. He had already shown us the weak side of the rebellion, had shown us where to strike and how. It was not from lack of native courage that Virginia submitted for thirty long hours and at last was relieved only by Federal troops; but because the attack was made on the side of her conscience and thus armed her against herself. She beheld at her side the sullen brow of a black Ireland. When John Brown proclaimed emancipation to the slaves of Maryland and Virginia he added to his war power the force of a moral earthquake. Virginia felt all her strong-ribbed mountains to shake under the heavy tread of armed insurgents. Of his army of nineteen her conscience made an army of nineteen hundred.

Another feature of the times, worthy of notice, was the effect of this blow upon the country at large. At the first moment we were stunned and bewildered. Slavery had so benumbed the moral sense of the nation, that it never suspected the possibility of an explosion like this, and it was difficult for Captain Brown to get himself taken for what he really was. Few could seem to comprehend that freedom to the slaves was his only object. If you will go back with me to that time you will find that the most curious and contradictory versions of the affair were industriously circulated, and those which were the least rational and true seemed to command the readiest belief. In the view of some, it assumed tremendous proportions. To such it was nothing less than a wide-sweeping rebellion to overthrow the existing government, and construct another upon its ruins, with Brown for its President and Commander-in-Chief; the proof of this was found in the old man's carpet-bag in the shape of a constitution for a new Republic, an instrument which in reality had been executed to govern the conduct of his men in the mountains. Smaller and meaner natures saw in it nothing higher than a purpose to plunder. To them John Brown and his men were a gang of desperate robbers, who had learned by some means that government had sent a large sum of money to Harper's Ferry to pay off the workmen in its employ there, and they had gone thence to fill their pockets from this money. The fact is, that outside of a few friends, scattered in different parts of the country, and the slaveholders of Virginia, few persons understood the significance of the hour. That a man might do something very audacious and desperate for money, power or fame, was to the general apprehension quite possible; but, in face of plainly-written law, in face of constitutional guarantees protecting each State against domestic violence, in face of a nation of forty million of people, that nineteen men could invade a great State to liberate a despised and hated race, was to the average intellect and conscience, too monstrous for belief. In this respect the vision of Virginia was clearer than that of the nation. Conscious of her guilt and therefore full of suspicion, sleeping on pistols for pillows, startled at every unusual sound, constantly fearing and expecting a repetition of the Nat Turner insurrection, she at once understood the meaning, if not the magnitude of the affair. It was this understanding which caused her to raise the lusty and imploring cry to the Federal government for help, and it was not till he who struck the blow had fully explained his motives and object, that the incredulous nation in any wise comprehended the true spirit of the raid, or of its commander. Fortunate for his memory, fortunate for the brave men associated with him, fortunate for the truth of history, John Brown survived the saber gashes, bayonet wounds and bullet holes, and was able, though covered with blood, to tell his own story and make his own defence. Had he with all his men, as might have been the case, gone down in the shock of battle, the world would have had no true basis for its judgment, and one of the most heroic efforts ever witnessed in behalf of liberty would have been confounded with base and selfish purposes. When, like savages, the Wises, the Vallandighams, the Washingtons, the Stuarts and others stood around the fallen and bleeding hero, and sought by torturing questions to wring from his supposed dying lips some word by which to soil the sublime undertaking, by implicating Gerrit Smith, Joshua R. Giddings, Dr. S.G. Howe, G.L. Stearns, Edwin Morton, Frank Sanborn, and other prominent Anti-slavery men, the brave old man, not only avowed his object to be the emancipation of the slaves, but serenely and proudly announced himself as solely responsible for all that had happened. Though some thought of his own life might at such a moment have seemed natural and excusable, he showed none, and scornfully rejected the idea that he acted as the agent or instrument of any man or set of men. He admitted that he had friends and sympathizers, but to his own head he invited all the bolts of slaveholding wrath and fury, and welcomed them to do their worst. His manly courage and self-forgetful nobleness were not lost upon the crowd about him, nor upon the country. They drew applause from his bitterest enemies. Said Henry A. Wise, "He is the gamest man I ever met." "He was kind and humane to his prisoners," said Col. Lewis Washington.

To the outward eye of men, John Brown was a criminal, but to their inward eye he was a just man and true. His deeds might be disowned, but the spirit which made those deeds possible was worthy highest honor. It has been often asked, why did not Virginia spare the life of this man? why did she not avail herself of this grand opportunity to add to her other glory that of a lofty magnanimity? Had they spared the good old man's life—had they said to him, "you see we have you in our power, and could easily take your life, but we have no desire to hurt you in any way; you have committed a terrible crime against society; you have invaded us at midnight and attacked a sleeping community, but we recognize you as a fanatic, and in some sense instigated by others; and on this ground and others, we release you. Go about your business, and tell those who sent you that we can afford to be magnanimous to our enemies." I say, had Virginia held some such language as this to John Brown, she would have inflicted a heavy blow on the whole Northern abolition movement, one which only the omnipotence of truth and the force of truth could have overcome. I have no doubt Gov. Wise would have done so gladly, but, alas, he was the executive of a State which thought she could not afford such magnanimity. She had that within her bosom which could more safely tolerate the presence of a criminal than a saint, a highway robber than a moral hero. All her hills and valleys were studded with material for a disastrous conflagration, and one spark of the dauntless spirit of Brown might set the whole State in flames. A sense of this appalling liability put an end to every noble consideration. His death was a foregone conclusion, and his trial was simply one of form.

Honor to the brave young Col. Hoyt who hastened from Massachusetts to defend his friend's life at the peril of his own; but there would have been no hope of success had he been allowed to plead the case. He might have surpassed Choate or Webster in power—a thousand physicians might have sworn that Capt. Brown was insane, it would have been all to no purpose; neither eloquence nor testimony could have prevailed. Slavery was the idol of Virginia, and pardon and life to Brown meant condemnation and death to slavery. He had practically illustrated a truth stranger than fiction—a truth higher than Virginia had ever known—a truth more noble and beautiful than Jefferson ever wrote. He had evinced a conception of the sacredness and value of liberty which transcended in sublimity that of her own Patrick Henry and made even his fire-flashing sentiment of "Liberty or Death" seem dark and tame and selfish. Henry loved liberty for himself, but this man loved liberty for all men, and for those most despised and scorned, as well as for those most esteemed and honored. Just here was the true glory of John Brown's mission. It was not for his own freedom that he was thus ready to lay down his life, for with Paul he could say, "I was born free." No chain had bound his ankle, no yoke had galled his neck. History has no better illustration of pure, disinterested benevolence. It was not Caucasian for Caucasian—white man for white man; not rich man for rich man, but Caucasian for Ethiopian—white man for black man—rich man for poor man—the man admitted and respected, for the man despised and rejected. "I want you to understand, gentlemen," he said to his persecutors, "that I respect the rights of the poorest and weakest of the colored people, oppressed by the slave system, as I do those of the most wealthy and powerful." In this we have the key to the whole life and career of the man. Than in this sentiment humanity has nothing more touching, reason nothing more noble, imagination nothing more sublime; and if we could reduce all the religions of the world to one essence we could find in it nothing more divine. It is much to be regretted that some great artist, in sympathy with the spirit of the occasion, had not been present when these and similar words were spoken. The situation was thrilling. An old man in the center of an excited and angry crowd, far away from home, in an enemy's country—with no friend near—overpowered, defeated, wounded, bleeding—covered with reproaches—his brave companions nearly all dead—his two faithful sons stark and cold by his side—reading his death—warrant in his fast—oozing blood and increasing weakness as in the faces of all around him—yet calm, collected, brave, with a heart for any fate—using his supposed dying moments to explain his course and vindicate his cause: such a subject would have been at once an inspiration and a power for one of the grandest historical pictures ever painted. . . .

With John Brown, as with every other man fit to die for a cause, the hour of his physical weakness was the hour of his moral strength—the hour of his defeat was the hour of his triumph—the moment of his capture was the crowning victory of his life. With the Alleghany mountains for his pulpit, the country for his church and the whole civilized world for his audience, he was a thousand times more effective as a preacher than as a warrior, and the consciousness of this fact was the secret of his amazing complacency. Might with the sword of steel, he was mightier with the sword of the truth, and with this sword he literally swept the horizon. He was more than a match for all the Wises, Masons, Vallandighams and Washingtons, who could rise against him. They could kill him, but they could not answer him.

In studying the character and works of a great man, it is always desirable to learn in what he is distinguished from others, and what have been the causes of this difference. Such men as he whom we are now considering, come on to the theater of life only at long intervals. It is not always easy to explain the exact and logical causes that produce them, or the subtle influences which sustain them, at the immense hights where we sometimes find them; but we know that the hour and the man are seldom far apart, and that here, as elsewhere, the demand may in some mysterious way, regulate the supply. A great iniquity, hoary with age, proud and defiant, tainting the whole moral atmosphere of the country, subjecting both church and state to its control, demanded the startling shock which John Brown seemed especially inspired to give it.

Apart from this mission there was nothing very remarkable about him. He was a wool-dealer, and a good judge of wool, as a wool-dealer ought to be. In all visible respects he was a man like unto other men. No outward sign of Kansas or Harper's Ferry was about him. As I knew him, he was an even-tempered man, neither morose, malicious nor misanthropic, but kind, amiable, courteous, and gentle in his intercourse with men. His words were few, well chosen and forcible. He was a good business man, and a good husband and father: a man apparently in every way calculated to make a smooth and pleasant path for himself through the world. He loved society, he loved little children, he liked music, and was fond of animals. To no one was the world more beautiful or life more sweet. How then as I have said shall we explain his apparent indifference to life? I can find but one answer, and that is, his intense hatred to oppression. I have talked with many men, but I remember none, who seemed so deeply excited upon the subject of slavery as he. He would walk the room in agitation at mention of the word. He saw the evil through no mist or haze, but in a light of infinite brightness, which left no line of its ten thousand horrors out of sight. Law, religion, learning, were interposed in its behalf in vain. His law in regard to it was that which Lord Brougham described, as "the law above all the enactments of human codes, the same in all time, the same throughout the world—the law unchangeable and eternal—the law written by the finger of God on the human heart-that law by which property in man is, and ever must remain, a wild and guilty phantasy."

Against truth and right, legislative enactments were to his mind mere cobwebs—the pompous emptiness of human pride—the pitiful outbreathings of human nothingness. He used to say "whenever there is a right thing to be done, there is a 'thus said the Lord' that it shall be done."

It must be admitted that Brown assumed tremendous responsibility in making war upon the peaceful people of Harper's Ferry, but it must be remembered also that in his eye a slaveholding community could not be peaceable, but was, in the nature of the case, in one incessant state of war. To him such a community was not more sacred than a band of robbers: it was the right of anyone to assault it by day or night. He saw no hope that slavery would ever be abolished by moral or political means: "he knew," he said, "the proud and hard hearts of the slaveholders, and that they never would consent to give up their slaves, till they felt a big stick about their heads."

It was five years before this event at Harper's Ferry, while the conflict between freedom and slavery was waxing hotter and hotter with every hour, that the blundering statesmanship of the National Government repealed the Missouri compromise, and thus launched the territory of Kansas as a prize to be battled for between the North and South. The remarkable part taken in this contest by Brown has been already referred to, and it doubtless helped to prepare him for the final tragedy, and though it did not by means originate the plan, it confirmed him in it and hastened its execution.

During his four years' service in Kansas it was my good fortune to see him often. On his trips to and from the territory he sometimes stopped several days at my house, and at one time several weeks. It was on this last occasion that liberty had been victorious in Kansas, and he felt that he must hereafter devote himself to what he considered his larger work. It was the theme of all his conversation, filling his nights with dreams and his days with visions. An incident of his boyhood may explain, in some measure, the intense abhorrence he felt to slavery. He had for some reason been sent into the States of Kentucky, where he made the acquaintance of a slave boy, about his own age, of whom he became very fond. For some petty offence this boy was one day subjected to a brutal beating. The blows were dealt with an iron shovel and fell fast and furiously upon his slender body. Born in a free State and unaccustomed to such revolted at the shocking spectacle and at that early age he swore eternal hatred to slavery. After years never obliterated the impression, and he found in this early experience an argument against contempt for small things. It is true that the boy is the father of the man. From the acorn comes the oak. The impression of a horse's foot in the sand suggested the art of printing. The fall of an apple intimated the law of gravitation. A word dropped in the woods of Vincennes, by royal hunters, gave Europe and the world a "William the Silent," and a thirty years' war. The beating of a Hebrew bondsman, by an Egyptian, created a Moses, and the infliction of a similar outrage on a helpless slave boy in our own land may have caused, forty years afterwards, a John Brown and Harper's Ferry Raid.

Most of us can remember some event or incident which has at some time come to us, and made itself a permanent part of our lives. Such an incident came to me in the year 1847. I had then the honor of spending a day and night under the roof of a man, whose character and conversation made a very deep impression on my mind and heart; and as the circumstance does not lie entirely out of our present observations, you will pardon for a moment a seeming digression. The name of the person alluded to had been several times mentioned to me, in a tone that made me curious to see him and to make his acquaintance. He was a merchant, and our first meeting was at his store—a substantial brick building, giving evidence of a flourishing business. After a few minutes' detention here, long enough for me to observe the neatness and order of the places, I was conducted by him to his residence where I was kindly received by his family as an expected guest. I was a little disappointed at the appearance of this man's house, for after seeing his fine store, I was prepared to see a fine residence; but this logic was entirely contradicted by the facts. The house was a small, wooden one, on a black street in a neighborhood of laboring men and mechanics, respectable enough, but not just the spot where one would expect enough, but not just the spot where one would expect to find the home of a successful merchant. Plain as was the outside, the inside was plainer. Its furniture might have pleased a Spartan. It would take longer to tell what was not in it, than what was; no sofas, no cushions, no curtains, no carpets, no easy rocking chairs inviting to enervation of rest or repose. My first meal passed under the misnomer of tea. It was none of your tea and toast sort, but potatoes and cabbage, and beef soup; such a meal as a man might relish after following the plough all day, or after performing a forced march of a dozen miles over rough ground in frosty weather. Innocent of paint, veneering, varnish or tablecloth, the table announced itself unmistakably and honestly pine and of the plainest workmanship. No hired help passed from kitchen to dining room, staring in amazement at the colored man at the white man's table. The mother, daughters and sons did the serving, and did it well. I heard no apology for doing their own work; they went through it as if used to it, untouched by any thought of degradation or impropriety. Supper over, the boys helped to clear the table and wash the dishes. This style of housekeeping struck me as a little odd. I mention it because household management is worthy of thought. A house is more than brick and mortar, wood or paint; this to me at least was. In its plainness it was a truthful reflection of its inmates: no disguises, no illusions, no make-believe here, but stern truth and solid, purpose breathed in all its arrangements. I was not long in company with the master of this house before I discovered that he was indeed the master of it, and likely to become mine too, if I staid long with him. He fulfilled St. Paul's idea of the head of the family—his wives believe in him, and his children observed him with reverence. Whenever he spoke, his words commanded earnest attention. His arguments which I ventured at some points to oppose, seemed to convince all, his appeals touched all, and his will impressed all. Certainly I never felt myself in the presence of a stronger religious influence than while in this house. "God and duty, God and duty," run like a thread of gold through all his utterances, and his family supplied a ready "Amen." In person he was lean and sinewy, of the best New England mould, built for times of trouble, fitted to grapple with the flintiest hardships. Clad in plain American woolen, shod in boots of cowhide leather, and wearing a cravat of the same substantial material, under six feet high, less than one hundred and fifty lbs. in weight, aged about fifty, he presented a figure straight and symmetrical as a mountain pine. His bearing was singularly impressive. His head was not large, but compact and high. His hair was coarse, strong, slightly gray and closely trimmed and grew close to his forehead. His face was smoothly shaved and revealed a strong square mouth, supported by a broad and prominent chin. His eyes were clear and grew, and in conversation they alternated with tears and fire. When on the street, he moved with a long springing, race-horse step, absorbed by his own reflections, neither seeking nor shunning observation. Such was the man whose name I heard uttered in whispers—such was the house in which he lived—such were family and household management—and such was Captain John Brown.

He said to me at this meeting, that he had invited me to his house for the especial purpose of laying before me his plan for the speedy emancipation of my race. He seemed to apprehend opposition on my part as he opened the subject and touched my vanity by saying, that he had observed my course at home and abroad, and wanted my cooperation. He said he had been for the last thirty years looking for colored men to whom he could safely reveal his secret, and had almost despaired, at times, of finding such, but that now he was encouraged for he saw heads rising up in all directions, to whom he thought he could with safety impart his plan. As this plan then lay in his mind it was very simple, and had much to commend it. It did not, as was supposed by many, contemplate a general rising among the slaves, and a general slaughter of the slave masters (an insurrection he thought would only defeat the object), but it did contemplate the creating of an armed force which should act in the very heart of the South. He was not averse to the shedding of blood, and thought the practice of carrying arms would be a good one for the colored people to adopt, as it would give them a sense of manhood. No people he said could have self-respect or be respected who would not fight for their freedom. He called my attention to a large map of the U. States, and pointed out to me the far-reaching Alleghanies, stretching away from the borders of New York into the Southern States. "These mountains," he said, "are the basis of my plan. God has given the strength of these hills to freedom; they were placed here to aid the emancipation of your race; they are full of natural forts, where one man for defence would be equal to a hundred for attack; they are also full of good hiding places where a large number of men could be concealed and baffle and elude pursuit for a long time. I know these mountains well and could take a body of men into them and keep them there in spite of all the efforts of Virginia to dislodge me, and drive me out. I would take at first about twenty-five picked men and begin on a small scale, supply them arms and ammunition, post them in squads of fives on a line of gathering recruits from the surrounding farms, seeking and selecting the most restless and daring." He saw that in this part of the work the utmost care must be used to guard against treachery and disclosure; only the most conscientious and skillful should be sent on this perilous duty. With care and enterprise he thought he could soon gather a force of one hundred hardy men, men who would be content to lead the free and adventurous life to which he proposed to train them. When once properly drilled and each had found the place for which he was best suited, they would begin work in earnest; they would run off the slaves in large numbers, retain the strong and brave ones in the mountains, and send the weak and timid ones to the North by the underground Railroad; his operations would be enlarged with increasing numbers and would not be confined to one locality. Slaveholders should in some cases be approached at midnight and told to give up their slaves and to let them have their best horses to ride away upon. Slavery was a state of war, he said, to which the slaves were unwilling parties and consequently they had a right to anything necessary to their peace and freedom. He would shed no blood and would avoid a fight except in self-defence, when he would of course do his best. He believed this movement would weaken slavery in two ways—first by making slave property insecure, it would become undesirable; and secondly it would keep the anti-slavery agitation alive and public attention fixed upon it, and thus lead to the adoption of measures to abolish the evil altogether. He held that there was need of something startling to prevent the agitation of the question from dying out; that slavery had come near being abolished in Virginia by the Nat. Turner insurrection, and he thought his method would speedily put an end to it, both in Maryland and Virginia. The trouble was to get the right men to start with and money enough to equip them. He had adopted the simple and economical mode of living to which I have referred with a view to save money for this purpose. This was said in no boastful tone, for he felt that he had delayed already too long and had no room to boast either his zeal or his self-denial.

From 8 o'clock in the evening till 3 in the morning, Capt. Brown and I sat face to face, he arguing in favor of his plan, and I finding all the objections I could against it. Now mark! this meeting of ours was full twelve years before the strike at Harper's Ferry. He had been watching and waiting all that time for suitable heads to rise or "pop up" as he said among the sable millions in whom he could confide; hence forty years had passed between his thought and his act. Forty years, though not a long time in the life of a nation, is a long time in the life of a man; and here forty long years, this man was struggling with this one idea; like Moses he was forty years in the wilderness. Youth, manhood, middle age had come and gone; two marriages had been consummated, twenty children had called him father; and through all the storms and vicissitudes of busy life, this one thought, like the angel in the burning bush, had confronted him with its blazing light, bidding him on to his work. Like Moses he had made excuses, and as with Moses his excuses were overruled. Nothing should postpone further what was to him his only apology for existence. He often said to me, though life was sweet to him, he would willingly lay it down for the freedom of my people; and on one occasion he added, that he had already lived about as long as most men, since he had slept less, and if he should now lay down his life the loss would not be great, for in fact he knew no better use for it. During his last visit to us in Rochester there appeared in the newspapers a touching story connected with the horrors of the Sepoy War in British India. A Scotch missionary and his family were in the hands of the enemy, and were to be massacred the next morning. During the night, when they had given up every hope of rescue, suddenly the wife insisted that relief would come. Placing her ear close to the ground she declared she heard the Slogan—the Scotch war song. For long hours in the night no member of the family could hear the advancing music but herself. "Dinna ye hear it? Dinna ye hear it?" she would say, but they could not hear it. As the morning slowly dawned a Scotch regiment was found encamped indeed about them, and they were saved from the threatened slaughter. This circumstance, coming at such a time, gave Capt. Brown a new word of cheer. He would come to the table in the morning his countenance fairly illuminated, saying that he had heard the Slogan, and he would add, "Dinna ye hear it? *Dinna* ye hear it?" Alas! like the Scotch missionary I was obliged to say "No." Two weeks prior to the mediated attack, Capt. Brown summoned me to meet him in an old stone quarry on the Conecochequi River, near the town of Chambersburg, Penn. His arms and ammunition were stored in that town and were to be moved on to Harper's Ferry. In company with Shields Green I obeyed the summons, and prompt to the hour we met the dear old man, with Kagi, his secretary, at the appointed place. Our meeting was in some sense a council of war. We spent the Saturday and succeeding Sunday in conference on the question, whether the desperate step should then taken, or the old plan as already described should be carried out. He was for boldly striking Harper's Ferry at once and running the risk of getting into the mountains afterwards. I was for avoiding Harper's Ferry altogether. Shields Green and Mr. Kagi remained silent listeners throughout. It is needless to repeat here what was said, after what has happened. Suffice it, that after all I could say, I saw that my old friend had resolved on his course and that it was idle to parley. I told him finally that it was impossible for me to join him. I could see Harper's Ferry only as a trap of steel, and ourselves in the wrong side of it. He regretted my decision and we parted.

Thus far, I have spoken exclusively of Capt. Brown. Let me say a word or two of his brave and devoted men, and first of Shields Green. He was a fugitive slave from Charleston, South Carolina, and had attested his love of liberty by escaping from slavery and making his way through many dangers to Rochester, where he had lived in my family, and where he met the man with whom he went to the scaffold. I said to him, as I was about to leave, "Now Shields, you have heard our discussion. If in view of it, you do not wish to stay, you have but to say so, and you can go back with me." He answered, "I b'l'eve I'll go wid de old man"; and go with him he did, into the fight, and to the gallows, and bore himself as grandly as any of the number. At the moment when Capt. Brown was surrounded, and all chance of escape was cut off, Green was in the mountains and could have made his escape as Osborne Anderson did, but when asked to do so, he made the same answer he did at Chambersburg, "I b'l'eve I'll go down wid de ole man." When in prison at Charlestown, and he was not allowed to see his old friend, his fidelity to him was in no wise weakened, and no complaint against Brown could be extorted from him by those who talked with him.

If a monument should be erected to the memory of John Brown, as there ought to be, the form and name of Shields Green should have a conspicuous place upon it. It is a remarkable fact, that in this small company of men, but one showed any sign of weakness or regret for what he did or attempted to do. Poor Cook broke down and sought to save his life by representing that he had been deceived, and allured by false promises. But Stephens, Hazlett and Green went to their doom like the heroes they were, without a murmur, without a regret, believing alike in their captain and their cause.

For the disastrous termination of this invasion, several causes have been assigned. It has been said that Capt. Brown found it necessary to strike before he was ready; that men had promised to join him from the North who failed to arrive; that the cowardly negroes did not rally to his support as he expected, but the true cause as stated by himself, contradicts all these theories, and from his statement there is no appeal. Among the questions put to him by Mr. Vallandigham after his capture were the following: "Did you expect a general uprising of the slaves in case of your success?" To this he answered, "No, sir, nor did I wish it. I expected to gather strength from time to time and then to set them free." "Did you expect to hold possession here until then?" Answer, "Well, probably I had quite a different idea. I do not know as I ought to reveal my plans. I am here wounded and a prisoner because I foolishly permitted myself to be so. You overstate your strength when you suppose I could have been taken if I had not allowed it. I was too tardy after commencing the open attack in delaying my movements through Monday night and up to the time of the arrival of government troops. It was all because of my desire to spare the feelings of my prisoners and their families."

But the question is, Did John Brown fail? He certainly did fail to get out of Harper's Ferry before being beaten down by United States soldiers; he did fail to save his own life, and to lead a liberating army into the mountains of Virginia. But he did not go to Harper's Ferry to save his life. The true question is, Did John Brown draw his sword against slavery and thereby lose his life in vain? and to this I answer ten thousand times, No! No man fails, or can fail who so grandly gives himself and all he has to a righteous cause. No man, who in his hour of extremest need, when on his way to meet an ignominious death, could so forget himself as to stop and kiss a little child, one of the hated race for whom he was about to die, could by any possibility fail. Did John Brown fail? Ask Henry A. Wise in whose house less than two years after, a school for the emancipated slaves was taught. Did John Brown fail? Ask James M. Mason, the author of the inhuman fugitive slave bill, who was cooped up in Fort Warren, as a traitor less than two years from the time that he stood over the prostrate body of

John Brown. Did John Brown fail? Ask Clement L. Vallandigham, one other of the inquisitorial party; for he too went down in the tremendous whirlpool created by the powerful hand of this bold invader. If John Brown did not end the war that ended slavery, he did at least begin the war that ended slavery. If we look over the dates, places and men, for which this honor is claimed, we shall find that not Carolina, but Virginia—not Fort Sumpter, but Harper's Ferry and the arsenal—not Col. Anderson, but John Brown, began the war that ended American slavery and made this a free Republic. Until this blow was struck, the prospect for freedom was dim, shadowy and uncertain. The irrepressible conflict was one of words, votes and compromises. When John Brown stretched forth his arm the sky was cleared. The time for compromises was gone—the armed hosts of freedom stood face to face over the chasm of a broken Union—and the clash of arms was at hand. The South staked all upon getting possession of the Federal Government, and failing to do that, drew the sword of rebellion and thus made her own, and not Brown's, the lost cause of the century.

(1881)

My Escape from Slavery

In the first narrative of my experience in slavery, written nearly forty years ago, and in various writings since, I have given the public what I considered very good reasons for withholding the manner of my escape. In substance these reasons were, first, that such publication at any time during the existence of slavery might be used by the master against the slave, and prevent the future escape of any who might adopt the same means that I did. The second reason was, if possible, still more binding to silence: the publication of details would certainly have put in peril the persons and property of those who assisted. Murder itself was not more sternly and certainly punished in the State of Maryland than that of aiding and abetting the escape of a slave. Many colored men, for no other crime than that of giving aid to a fugitive slave, have, like Charles T. Torrey, perished in prison. The abolition of slavery in my native State and throughout the country, and the lapse of time, render the caution hitherto observed no longer necessary. But even since the abolition of slavery, I have sometimes thought it well enough to baffle curiosity by saying that while slavery existed there were good reasons for not telling the manner of my escape, and since slavery had ceased to exist, there was no reason for telling it. I shall now, however, cease to avail myself of this formula, and, as far as I can, endeavor to satisfy this very natural curiosity. I should, perhaps, have yielded to that feeling sooner, had there been anything very heroic or thrilling in the incidents connected with my escape, for I am sorry to say I have nothing of that sort to tell; and yet the courage that could risk betrayal and the bravery which was ready to encounter death, if need be, in pursuit of freedom, were essential features in the undertaking. My success was due to address rather than courage, to good luck rather than bravery. My means of escape were provided for me by the very men who were making laws to hold and bind me more securely in slavery.

It was the custom in the State of Maryland to require the free colored people to have what were called free papers. These instruments they were required to renew very often, and by charging a fee for this writing, considerable sums from time to time were collected by the State. In these papers the name, age, color, height, and form of the freeman were described, together with any scars or other marks upon his person which could assist in his identification. This device in some measure defeated itself—since more than one man could be found to answer the same general description. Hence many slaves could escape by personating the owner of one set of papers; and this was often done as follows: A slave, nearly or sufficiently answering the description set forth in the papers, would borrow or hire them till by means of them he could escape to a free State, and then, by mail or otherwise, would return them to the owner. The operation was a hazardous one for the lender as well as for the borrower. A failure on the part of the fugitive to send back the papers would imperil his benefactor, and the discovery of the papers in possession of the wrong man would imperil both the fugitive and his friend. It was, therefore, an act of supreme trust on the part of a freeman of color thus to put in jeopardy his own liberty that another might be free. It was, however, not unfrequently bravely done, and was seldom discovered. I was not so fortunate as to resemble any of my free acquaintances sufficiently to answer the description of their papers. But I had a friend—a sailor—who owned a sailor's protection, which answered somewhat the purpose of free papers—describing his person, and certifying to the fact that he was a free American sailor. The instrument had at its head the American eagle, which gave it the appearance at once of an authorized document. This protection, when in my hands, did not describe its bearer very accurately. Indeed, it called for a man much darker than myself, and close examination of it would have caused my arrest at the start.

In order to avoid this fatal scrutiny on the part of railroad officials, I arranged with Isaac Rolls, a Baltimore hackman, to bring my baggage to the Philadelphia train just on the moment of starting, and jumped upon the car myself when the train was in motion. Had I gone into the station and offered to purchase a ticket, I should have been instantly and carefully examined, and undoubtedly arrested. In choosing this plan I considered the jostle of the train, and the natural haste of the conductor, in a train crowded with passengers, and relied upon my skill and address in playing the sailor, as described in my protection, to do the rest. One element in my favor was the kind feeling which prevailed in Baltimore and other sea-ports at the time, toward "those who go down to the sea in ships." "Free trade and sailors' rights" just then expressed the sentiment of the country. In my clothing I was rigged out in sailor style. I had on a red shirt and a tarpaulin hat, and a black cravat tied in sailor fashion carelessly and loosely about my neck. My knowledge of ships and sailor's talk came much to my assistance, for I knew a ship from stem to stern, and from keelson to cross-trees, and could talk sailor like an "old salt." I was well on the way to Havre de Grace before the conductor came into the negro car to collect tickets and examine the papers of his black passengers. This was a critical moment in the drama. My whole future depended upon the decision of this conductor. Agitated though I was while this ceremony was proceeding, still, externally, at least, I was apparently calm and self-possessed. He went on with his duty—examining several colored passengers before reaching me. He was somewhat harsh in tone and peremptory in manner until he reached me, when, strange enough, and to my surprise and relief, his whole manner changed. Seeing that I did not readily produce my free papers, as the other colored persons in the car had done, he said to me, in friendly contrast with his bearing toward the others:

"I suppose you have your free papers?"

To which I answered:

"No sir; I never carry my free papers to sea with me."

"But you have something to show that you are a freeman, haven't you?"

"Yes, sir," I answered; "I have a paper with the American Eagle on it, and that will carry me around the world."

With this I drew from my deep sailor's pocket my seaman's protection, as before described. The merest glance at the paper satisfied him, and he took my fare and went on about his business. This moment of time was one of the most anxious I ever experienced. Had the conductor looked closely at the paper, he could not have failed to discover that it called for a very different-looking person from myself, and in that case it would have been his duty to arrest me on the instant, and send me back to Baltimore from the first station. When he left me with the assurance that I was all right, though much relieved, I realized that I was still in great danger: I was still in Maryland, and subject to arrest at any moment. I saw on the train several persons who would have known me in any other clothes, and I feared they might recognize me, even in my sailor "rig," and report me to the conductor, who would then subject me to a closer examination, which I knew well would be fatal to me.

Though I was not a murderer fleeing from justice, I felt perhaps quite as miserable as such a criminal. The train was moving at a very high rate of speed for that epoch of railroad travel, but to my anxious mind it was moving far too slowly. Minutes were hours, and hours were days during this part of my flight. After Maryland, I was to pass through Delaware—another slave State, where slave-catchers generally awaited their prey, for it was not in the interior of the State, but on its borders, that these human hounds were most vigilant and active. The border-lines between slavery and freedom were the dangerous ones for the fugitives. The heart of no fox or deer, with hungry hounds on his trail in full chase, could have beaten more anxiously or noisily than did mine from the time I left Baltimore till I reached Philadelphia. The passage of the Susquehanna River at Havre de Grace was at that time made by ferry-boat, on board of which I met a young colored man by the name of Nichols, who came very near betraying me. He was a "hand" on the boat, but, instead of minding his business, he insisted upon knowing me, and asking me dangerous questions as to where I was going, when I was coming back, etc. I got away from my old and inconvenient acquaintance as soon as I could decently do so, and went to another part of the boat. Once across the river, I encountered a new danger. Only a few days before, I had been at work on a revenue cutter, in Mr. Price's ship-yard in Baltimore, under the care of Captain McGowan. On the meeting at this point of the two trains, the one going south stopped on the track just opposite to the one going north, and it so happened that this Captain McGowan sat at a window where he could see me very distinctly, and would certainly have recognized me had he looked at me but for a second. Fortunately, in the hurry of the moment, he did not see me; and the trains soon passed each other on their respective ways. But this was not my only hair-breadth escape. A German blacksmith whom I knew well was on the train with me, and looked at me very intently, as if he thought he had seen me somewhere before in his travels. I really believe he knew me, but had no heart to betray me. At any rate, he saw me escaping and held his peace.

The last point of imminent danger, and the one I dreaded most, was Wilmington. Here we left the train and took the steam-boat for Philadelphia. In making the change here I again apprehended arrest, but no one disturbed me, and I was soon on the broad and beautiful Delaware, speeding away to the Quaker City. On reaching Philadelphia in the afternoon, I inquired of a colored man how I could get on to New York. He directed me to the William-street depot, and thither I went, taking the train that night. I reached New York Tuesday morning, having completed the journey in less than twenty-four hours.

My free life began on the third of September, 1838. On the morning of the fourth of that month, after an anxious and most perilous but safe journey, I found myself in the big city of New York, a *free man*—one more added to the mighty throng which, like the confused waves of the troubled sea, surged to and fro between the lofty walls of Broadway. Though dazzled with the wonders which met me on every hand, my thoughts could not be much withdrawn from my strange situation. For the moment, the dreams of my youth and the hopes of my manhood were completely fulfilled. The bonds that had held me to "old master" were broken. No man now had a right to call me his slave or assert mastery over me. I was in the rough and tumble of an outdoor world, to take my chance with the rest of its busy number. I have often been asked how I felt when first I found myself on free soil. There is scarcely anything in my experience about which I could not give a more satisfactory answer. A new world had opened upon me. If life is more than breath and the "quick round of blood," I lived more in that one day than in a year of my slave life. It was a time of joyous excitement which words can but tamely describe. In a letter written to a friend soon after reaching New York, I said: "I felt as one might feel upon escape from a den of hungry lions." Anguish and grief, like darkness and rain, may be depicted; but gladness and joy, like the rainbow, defy the skill of pen or pencil. During ten or fifteen years I had been, as it were, dragging a heavy chain which no strength of mine could break; I was not only a slave, but a slave for life. I might become a husband, a father, an aged man, but through all, from birth to death, from the cradle to the grave, I had felt myself doomed. All efforts I had previously made to secure my freedom had not only failed, but had seemed only to rivet my fetters the more firmly, and to render my escape more difficult. Baffled, entangled, and discouraged, I had at times asked myself the question, May not my condition after all be God's work, and ordered for a wise purpose, and if so, Is not submission my duty? A contest had in fact been going on in my mind for a long time, between the clear consciousness of right and the plausible make-shifts of theology and superstition. The one held me an abject slave—a prisoner for life, punished for some transgression in which I had no lot nor part; and the other counseled me to manly endeavor to secure my freedom. This contest was now ended; my chains were broken, and the victory brought me unspeakable joy.

But my gladness was short-lived, for I was not yet out of the reach and power of the slaveholders. I soon found that New York was not quite so free or so safe a refuge as I had supposed, and a sense of loneliness and insecurity again oppressed me most sadly. I chanced to meet on the street, a few hours after my landing, a fugitive slave whom I had once known well in slavery. The information received from him alarmed me. The fugitive in question was known in Baltimore as "Allender's Jake," but in New York he wore the more respectable name of "William Dixon." Jake, in law, was the property of Doctor Allender, and Tolly Allender, the son of the doctor, had once made an effort to recapture *Mr. Dixon*, but had failed for want of evidence to support his claim. Jake told me the circumstances of this attempt, and how narrowly he escaped being sent back to slavery and torture. He told me that New York was then full of Southerners returning from the Northern watering-places; that the colored people of New York were not to be trusted; that there were hired men of my own color who would betray me for a few dollars; that there were hired men ever on the lookout for fugitives; that I must trust no man with my secret; that I must not think of going either upon the wharves or into any colored boarding-house, for all such places were closely watched; that he was himself unable to help me; and, in fact, he seemed while speaking to me to fear lest I myself might be a spy and a betrayer. Under this apprehension, as I suppose, he showed signs of wishing to be rid of me, and with whitewash brush in hand, in search of work, he soon disappeared.

This picture, given by poor "Jake," of New York, was a damper to my enthusiasm. My little store of money would soon be exhausted, and since it would be unsafe for me to go on the wharves for work, and I had no introductions elsewhere, the prospect for me was far from cheerful. I saw the wisdom of keeping away from the ship-yards, for, if pursued, as I felt certain I should be, Mr. Auld, my "master," would naturally seek me there among the calkers. Every door seemed closed against me. I was in the midst of an ocean of my fellow-men, and yet a perfect stranger to everyone. I was without home, without acquaintance, without money, without credit, without work, and without any definite knowledge as to what course to take, or where to look for succor. In such an extremity, a man had something besides his new-born freedom to think of. While wandering about the streets of

New York, and lodging at least one night among the barrels on one of the wharves, I was indeed free—from slavery, but free from food and shelter as well. I kept my secret to myself as long as I could, but I was compelled at last to seek someone who would befriend me without taking advantage of my destitution to betray me. Such a person I found in a sailor named Stuart, a warm-hearted and generous fellow, who, from his humble home on Centre street, saw me standing on the opposite sidewalk, near the Tombs prison. As he approached me, I ventured a remark to him which at once enlisted his interest in me. He took me to his home to spend the night, and in the morning went with me to Mr. David Ruggles, the secretary of the New York Vigilance Committee, a co-worker with Isaac T. Hopper, Lewis and Arthur Tappan, Theodore S. Wright, Samuel Cornish, Thomas Downing, Philip A. Bell, and other true men of their time. All these (save Mr. Bell, who still lives, and is editor and publisher of a paper called the "Elevator," in San Francisco) have finished their work on earth. Once in the hands of these brave and wise men, I felt comparatively safe. With Mr. Ruggles, on the corner of Lispenard and Church streets, I was hidden several days, during which time my intended wife came on from Baltimore at my call, to share the burdens of life with me. She was a free woman, and came at once on getting the good news of my safety. We were married by Rev. J. W. C. Pennington, then a well-known and respected Presbyterian minister. I had no money with which to pay the marriage fee, but he seemed well pleased with our thanks.

Mr. Ruggles was the first officer on the "Underground Railroad" whom I met after coming North, and was, indeed, the only one with whom I had anything to do till I became such an officer myself. Learning that my trade was that of a calker, he promptly decided that the best place for me was in New Bedford, Mass. He told me that many ships for whaling voyages were fitted out there, and that I might there find work at my trade and make a good living. So, on the day of the marriage ceremony, we took our little luggage to the steamer *John W. Richmond*, which, at that time, was one of the line running between New York and Newport, R. I. Forty-three years ago colored travelers were not permitted in the cabin, nor allowed abaft the paddle-wheels of a steam vessel. They were compelled, whatever the weather might be—whether cold or hot, wet or dry—to spend the night on deck. Unjust as this regulation was, it did not trouble us much; we had fared much harder before. We arrived at Newport the next morning, and soon after an old fashioned stage-coach, with "New Bedford" in large yellow letters on its sides, came down to the wharf. I had not money enough to pay our fare, and stood hesitating what to do. Fortunately for us, there were two Quaker gentlemen who were about to take passage on the stage—Friends William C. Taber and Joseph Ricketson—who at once discerned our true situation, and, in a peculiarly quiet way, addressing me, Mr. Taber said: "Thee get in." I never obeyed an order with more alacrity, and we were soon on our way to our new home. When we reached "Stone Bridge" the passengers alighted for breakfast, and paid their fares to the driver. We took no breakfast, and, when asked for our fares, I told the driver I would make it right with him when we reached New Bedford. I expected some objection to this on his part, but he made none. When, however, we reached New Bedford, he took our baggage, including three music-books—two of them collections by Dyer, and one by Shaw—and held them until I was able to redeem them by paying to him the amount due for our rides. This was soon done, for Mr. Nathan Johnson not only received me kindly and hospitably, but, on being informed about our baggage, at once loaned me the two dollars with which to square accounts with the stage-driver. Mr. and Mrs. Nathan Johnson reached a good old age, and now rest from their labors. I am under many grateful obligations to them. They not only "took me in when a stranger" and "fed me when hungry," but taught me how to make an honest living. Thus, in a fortnight after my flight from Maryland, I was safe in New Bedford, a citizen of the grand old commonwealth of Massachusetts.

Once initiated into my new life of freedom and assured by Mr. Johnson that I need not fear recapture in that city, a comparatively unimportant question arose as to the name by which I should be known thereafter in my new relation as a free man. The name given me by my dear mother was no less pretentious and long than Frederick Augustus Washington Bailey. I had, however, while living in Maryland, dispensed with the Augustus Washington, and retained only Frederick Bailey. Between Baltimore and New Bedford, the better to conceal myself from the slave-hunters, I had parted with Bailey and called myself Johnson; but in New Bedford I found that the Johnson family was already so numerous as to cause some confusion in distinguishing them, hence a change in this name seemed desirable. Nathan Johnson, mine host, placed great emphasis upon this necessity, and wished me to allow him to select a name for me. I consented, and he called me by my present name—the one by which I have been known for three and forty years—Frederick Douglass. Mr. Johnson had just been reading the "Lady of the Lake," and so pleased was he with its great character that he wished me to bear his name. Since reading that charming poem myself, I have often thought that, considering the noble hospitality and manly character of Nathan Johnson—black man though he was—he, far more than I, illustrated the virtues of the Douglas of Scotland. Sure am I that, if any slave-catcher had entered his domicile with a view to my recapture, Johnson would have shown himself like him of the "stalwart hand."

The reader may be surprised at the impressions I had in some way conceived of the social and material condition of the people at the North. I had no proper idea of the wealth, refinement, enterprise, and high civilization of this section of the country. My "Columbian Orator," almost my only book, had done nothing to enlighten me concerning Northern society. I had been taught that slavery was the bottom fact of all wealth. With this foundation idea, I came naturally to the conclusion that poverty must be the general condition of the people of the free States. In the country from which I came, a white man holding no slaves was usually an ignorant and poverty-stricken man, and men of this class were contemptuously called "poor white trash." Hence I supposed that, since the non-slaveholders at the South were ignorant, poor, and degraded as a class, the non-slaveholders at the North must be in a similar condition. I could have landed in no part of the United States where I should have found a more striking and gratifying contrast, not only to life generally in the South, but in the condition of the colored people there, than in New Bedford. I was amazed when Mr. Johnson told me that there was nothing in the laws or constitution of Massachusetts that would prevent a colored man from being governor of the State, if the people should see fit to elect him. There, too, the black man's children attended the public schools with the white man's children, and apparently without objection from any quarter. To impress me with my security from recapture and return to slavery, Mr. Johnson assured me that no slaveholder could take a slave out of New Bedford; that there were men there who would lay down their lives to save me from such a fate.

The fifth day after my arrival, I put on the clothes of a common laborer, and went upon the wharves in search of work. On my way down Union street I saw a large pile of coal in front of the house of Rev. Ephraim Peabody, the Unitarian minister. I went to the kitchen door and asked the privilege of bringing in and putting away this coal. "What will you charge?" said the lady. "I will leave that to you, madam."

"You may put it away," she said. I was not long in accomplishing the job, when the dear lady put into my hand *two silver half-dollars.* To understand the emotion which swelled my heart as I clasped this money, realizing that I had no master who could take it from me—*that it was mine—that my hands were my own*, and could earn more of the precious coin—one must have been in some sense himself a slave. My next job was stowing a sloop at Uncle Gid. Howland's wharf with a cargo of oil for New York. I was not only a freeman, but a free working-man, and no "master" stood ready at the end of the week to seize my hard earnings.

The season was growing late and work was plenty. Ships were being fitted out for whaling, and much wood was used in storing them. The sawing this wood was considered a good job. With the help of old Friend Johnson (blessings on his memory) I got a saw and "buck," and went at it. When I went into a store to buy a cord with which to brace up my saw in the frame, I asked for a "fip's" worth of cord. The man behind the counter looked rather sharply at me, and said with equal sharpness, "You don't belong about here." I was alarmed, and thought I had betrayed myself. A fip in Maryland was six and a quarter cents, called fourpence in Massachusetts. But no harm came from the "fi'penny-bit" blunder, and I confidently and cheerfully went to work with my saw and buck. It was new business to me, but I never did better work, or more of it, in the same space of time on the plantation for Covey, the negro-breaker, than I did for myself in these earliest years of my freedom.

Notwithstanding the just and humane sentiment of New Bedford three and forty years ago, the place was not entirely free from race and color prejudice. The good influence of the Roaches, Rodmans, Arnolds, Grinnells, and Robesons did not pervade all classes of its people. The test of the real civilization of the community came when I applied for work at my trade, and then my repulse was emphatic and decisive. It so happened that Mr. Rodney French, a wealthy and enterprising citizen, distinguished as an anti-slavery man, was fitting out a vessel for a whaling voyage, upon which there was a heavy job of calking and coppering to be done. I had some skill in both branches, and applied to Mr. French for work. He, generous man that he was, told me he would employ me, and I might go at once to the vessel. I obeyed him, but upon reaching the float-stage, where other calkers were at work, I was told that every white man would leave the ship, in her unfinished condition, if I struck a blow at my trade upon her. This uncivil, inhuman, and selfish treatment was not so shocking and scandalous in my eyes at the time as it now appears to me. Slavery had inured me to hardships that made ordinary trouble sit lightly upon me. Could I have worked at my trade I could have earned two dollars a day, but as a common laborer I received but one dollar. The difference was of great importance to me, but if I could not get two dollars, I was glad to get one; and so I went to work for Mr. French as a common laborer. The consciousness that I was free—no longer a slave—kept me cheerful under this, and many similar proscriptions, which I was destined to meet in New Bedford and elsewhere on the free soil of Massachusetts. For instance, though colored children attended the schools, and were treated kindly by their teachers, the New Bedford Lyceum refused, till several years after my residence in that city, to allow any colored person to attend the lectures delivered in its hall. Not until such men as Charles Sumner, Theodore Parker, Ralph Waldo Emerson, and Horace Mann refused to lecture in their course while there was such a restriction, was it abandoned.

Becoming satisfied that I could not rely on my trade in New Bedford to give me a living, I prepared myself to do any kind of work that came to hand. I sawed wood, shoveled coal, dug cellars, moved rubbish from back yards, worked on the wharves, loaded and unloaded vessels, and scoured their cabins.

I afterward got steady work at the brass-foundry owned by Mr. Richmond. My duty here was to blow the bellows, swing the crane, and empty the flasks in which castings were made; and at times this was hot and heavy work. The articles produced here were mostly for ship work, and in the busy season the foundry was in operation night and day. I have often worked two nights and every working day of the week. My foreman, Mr. Cobb, was a good man, and more than once protected me from abuse that one or more of the hands was disposed to throw upon me. While in this situation I had little time for mental improvement. Hard work, night and day, over a furnace hot enough to keep the metal running like water, was more favorable to action than thought; yet here I often nailed a newspaper to the post near my bellows, and read while I was performing the up and down motion of the heavy beam by which the bellows was inflated and discharged. It was the pursuit of knowledge under difficulties, and I look back to it now, after so many years, with some complacency and a little wonder that I could have been so earnest and persevering in any pursuit other than for my daily bread. I certainly saw nothing in the conduct of those around to inspire me with such interest: they were all devoted exclusively to what their hands found to do. I am glad to be able to say that, during my engagement in this foundry, no complaint was ever made against me that I did not do my work, and do it well. The bellows which I worked by main strength was, after I left, moved by a steam-engine.

(1881)

The Race Problem

Members and Friends of the Bethel Literary and Historical Association: I esteem it a great privilege to be with you and assist in this your first meeting since the close of your last winter's term. The organization of your association was an important step in the progress of the colored people in this city. It is an institution well fitted to improve the minds and elevate the sentiments not only of its members, but of the general public. Nowhere else outside of the courts of law and the Congress of the United States have I heard vital public questions more seriously discussed. The men selected to address you know very well that what they may utter is subjected to close scrutiny and severe discussion. Mere rant, bombast, and self-inflation may pass elsewhere, but not here. For this reason, and for my own self-respect, I shall endeavor to say only what I believe to be the truth upon what is popularly called "The Negro Problem."

My first thought respects the importance of calling things by their true names. This importance cannot be over-estimated or over-stated. Truth is the fundamental, indispensable, and everlasting requirement in obtaining right results. No department of human life can afford to dispense with truth. The carpenter cannot join his timbers without having the parts of contact perfectly true to each other. The mason cannot build a wall that will stand the test of time and gravitation without applying the plumb and making the wall vertical and true. No train or cars is safe on the road where the relations of the rails are not true. No shot is certain of its aim where the gun-barrel is not true. As in mechanics, so in politics, morals, manners, metaphysics, and philosophies, nothing can stand the test of time and experience that does not stand on the unassailable, indestructible, unchangeable, foundation of true. Considering how important this truth is, it seems strange that falsehood should hold such sway in the world. One main advantage by which error is able to darken, blight, and dominate the minds of men is the skill of its votaries in using language deceitfully, in pandering to prejudice by misstating and misapplying terms to the existing relations of men. It has been well said that in an important sense words are things. They are especially such when they are employed to express the popular sentiment concerning the Negro: to couple his name with anything in this world seems to damage it and damage him likewise. Hence I object to characterizing the relation subsisting between the white and colored people of this country as the Negro problem, as if the Negro had precipitated that problem, and as if he were in any way responsible for the problem. Though a rose by any other name may smell as sweet, it is not in good taste to give it a name that suggests offensive associations. There are, on the other hand, things that are in themselves revolting, and should not be given fair-seeming names. The slaveholders understood this principle well enough. Slavery lost something of its offensive aspect when it was called a domestic institution or a social system and other like names. Emancipation was made to look dangerous when it got itself called an experiment, although slavery itself was an experiment, and liberty is the normal condition of man. "The Negroes were the cause of the war," said Mr. Lincoln, and straightway the loyal soldiers of the Republic began to kick and beat the poor Negroes on the banks of the Potomac, and the Irish began to hang, stab, and murder the Negroes in New York. It is dangerous even to a dog to be given a bad name. I am, therefore, in favor of employing the truest and most agreeable names to describe the relation which at present subsists between ourselves and the other people of the country.

Again, another advantage to error and one which is often employed with marked skill and effect in the presentation to the minds of men of what may be called half truths for whole truths, and thus making a sweet and wholesome truth the cover for a bitter falsehood. A counterfeit nearest in likeness to what is genuine is always most likely to impose upon the unskillful. A lie ceases to be very dangerous when it parts with its ability to deceive. The devil is less dangerous as a roaring lion than when transformed as an angel of light.

The application of these homely truths and familiar examples will become apparent in the discussion I propose of what is popularly but improperly called the race problem. It seems that the American people have a special liking for this mathematical formula as applied to the Negro. They seem determined to keep his brain forever employed and his time forever occupied in solving a great variety of problems, and generally to his disadvantage. As soon as he solves one another is propounded to him, and when he thinks, good, easy soul, his work is done he finds a new one invented, a new burden imposed, and a new hardship inflicted. There may be rest for the weary, but there seems at present no rest for the Negro. He has been solving problems during all his history.

I have before referred in this place, I think, to the fact that the Negro was confronted 200 years ago by what was considered a great religious problem, one which was very difficult of solution. That problem was: Ought the Negro to be baptized in water and admitted to membership in the Christian church? This was, as I have often said, considering time of it, a tremendous problem. As in our day in regard to Negro problems, the opinions of the wise and great were strongly pronounced and much divided. The right of the Negro to baptism was fiercely disputed, especially by those who owned them as slaves. What is plain to all now was dark and doubtful to many then. It is easy to fancy that men spoke of it with bated breath, and saw in the Negro's baptism a menace to the peace and stability of society, as well as of slavery. For to baptize the Negro and admit him to membership in the Christian church was to recognize him as a man, a child of God, an heir of Heaven, redeemed by the blood of Christ, a temple of the Holy Ghost, a standing type and representative of the Saviour of the world, one who, according to the apostle Paul, must be treated no longer as a servant, but as a brother beloved. Viewed in this light, his admission to baptism, and to the church was a matter for the gravest consideration. It touched the money nerve of the Christians of that day, for their wealth was largely invested in Negro flesh and blood. It was well said that the proposition was novel, extraordinary, and full of danger. It would impair the value of the slave, and it would put in jeopardy the authority of the master: they were right, and if the Negro is to be regarded as a Christian, he could not be regarded as a heathen, and as the Bible sanctioned only the enslavement of heathen, the Negro Christian could not be bought and sold, enslaved and, whipped, according to the requirements of the relation of master and slave. From every view they could then take of the proposition to baptize the Negro was rank radicalism and deserved stern resistance at its inception.

To the credit of the church and its ministers, it must be said that one learned and able divine, in the person of Dr. Godwin, was equal to the situation. He met the arguments of the opposition to Negro baptism in a book of 200 pages, in which he endeavored to show that baptism would not impair either the value of the slave or the authority of the master. His argument was a curious one. It divided the Negro into two separate parts, giving one to the Lord and the other to the slaveholder, and leaving nothing whatever of soul, body or spirit to himself. Baptism, he said, freed the Negro from the bondage of the devil, but not from the bondage of his earthly master. The controversy over this problem was long and furious, and the Negro only won a partial victory after all. The matter was finally settled, as usual, by a kind of compromise. The Negro was baptized and admitted to the church, but a sort of second table was set for him. He could take the Lord's supper only after his white brethren had finished eating the bread and drinking the wine. He was not even allowed to enter the same door of the sanctuary by which his white brethren entered. A separate door was cut for him in the wall, a sort of hole in the wall, leading to a high and dark place in the gallery, where his presence could give no offence to the Lord's white children on the floor.

It is strange that this state of things did not disgust and repel the Negro, make him an infidel, and drive him from religion altogether, but it did not. He clung to religion all the same. Believing that half a loaf was better than no bread, he took what he could get of the church, kept on praying and singing, and sometimes shouting. He could pray as fervently for the conversion of the scoundrel who tore his flesh with the lash, as for his best friend. He was made to think that his offensive black skin on earth would be changed for a white one in Heaven. It was a strange fancy, but quite a natural one when we see the importance given to color in the problems before us in our day.

Another problem greatly disturbed the conscientious during the time of slavery. It was this: Can a Negro contract a valid marriage? If he could, and could enforce his right to his wife and children, it would prove an inconvenient limitation on the power of his master. If what God has joined together no man shall put asunder, the right to sell the wife from the husband and the husband from the wife must cease. In the minds of the men who had to deal with it no such limitation in the right of the master could be allowed or tolerated for a moment. The master must have the right to buy and sell as he pleased, was the solution of that problem. One terrible evil of this solution of the marriage question is still seen in our land. Unable to contract valid marriage, the Negro felt himself unrestrained, and licensed to do as he pleased. He was not expected to limit his conduct by any rule or principle of morality or decency, but took to himself the freedom of the beasts of the field and the fowls of the air. He had in law no wife, no family, no children, and did not own himself. The consequence of this state of things may be seen very often in our own city at the police court and elsewhere, and the strange thing is, the very people who are responsible for this immorality and crime make merry over our wretchedness and talk solemnly about the terrible Negro problem

Happily for us, and happily for our common country, as we shall see later on, the Southern solution of this Negro problem has now been unsolved by the act of emancipation and the superior civilization of the loyal American people over the people of the old slaveholding States.

Another troublesome problem presented to our Christian country was whether the Negro should have the help of the Bible with which to get to Heaven; whether, in fact, the command to search the Scriptures imposed any obligation or duty on him. Our Southern brethren, with whom we have always been profoundly sympathetic even unto this day, decided this problem against the Bible, and against the Negro, as usual. They made it a crime, to be punished with banishment, imprisonment, and stripes, for anyone to teach the Negro to read. Yet the descendants of these same men, with the education of their fathers, and with the antecedents of their fathers, are now asking us in piteous tones to allow them in their superior wisdom and goodness of heart to solve what they are pleased to call the Negro problem of today. They are crying out lustily to the nation, like demons tormented before their time, "Hands off! We want no Federal authority, and want only local self-government. We want to be let alone!" They tell us that they know the Negro, and that they can manage him better than anybody else. They can manage his wages, his voting, and his education, and all that pertains to him. I hope the nation will not let them do any such thing. They have shown a strange inaptitude for such a task. The point with them is not what is right, but what will best suit themselves.

But again, in the history of the Negro we had another perplexing problem. It was this, and this was in some sense a national problem: Can the Negro be made a soldier? This, too, was very serious problem for the country, for it was a matter of Union or no Union, of life or death. For at one time it needed all the material which the nation could command to settle the problem of our national existence. It will be remembered that at the beginning of the war it was given out that no Negro need apply. He was not to be allowed to shoulder a musket, carry a knapsack, or wear a Union uniform. The glory of the battle-field was to be won wholly by white men. The Negro might dig but not fight. He might be a servant, but not a soldier. He might carry a pick-ax, but never a musket.

In considering this problem the nation, strangely enough, shut its eyes to the fact that in the history of the Revolution the Negro fought bravely for American independence, and in the war of 1812 he even extorted praise for his valor from the stern lips of General Andrew Jackson. His fighting qualities were nobly admitted by the hero of New Orleans. In spite of this it was insisted that the Negro was a born coward; that could never make a soldier: that he would run at the sight of a gun. Time and events however helped the Negro and the Nation in the solution of this problem, as I think they will help in the solution of any others that may arise. Fort Wagner, Port Hudson, Vicksburg, James Island, Olustee, Petersburg, Richmond—a cloud of witnesses rise before us to solve the problem of the Negro's soldierly qualities.

Whether the Negro could be educated, was another problem, and I think this has been solved to the satisfaction of all candid men. He would be a dishonest man, or an amazingly stupid one who, in the face of the thousands of Negro teachers, the hundreds of Negro preachers, doctors, lawyers, authors, and editors, with which the country is now studded, should insist, as it was once insisted, that education was impossible to the Negro.

But the greatest problem for the Negro was whether he could with safety be made free. Good men knew that slavery was wrong, but how to get rid of it was the great question. Neither the pulpit, nor the press, nor the statesman could see a solution of the great problem, and yet that problem has been solved. The Negro is free, and the country is cleansed of its greatest curse, crime, and scandal.

There were terrible things to happen upon the passing away of slavery. The freedom of the slave was the signal of ruin. There was to be no more cotton, no more sugar, no more work done by the Negro, and the South was to become a howling wilderness. But against all these dark forebodings, these pictures of dismal terror, the late was made short work of the whole problem. That sturdy old Roman, Benjamin Butler, made the Negro a contraband, Abraham Lincoln made him a freeman, and General Ulysses S. Grant made him a citizen, and not one of these terrible things have happened.

But now, though all this has been done, though slavery has been abolished, though the Negro has been freed, though he has become a citizen, though the Union has been saved, in part by his valor, the

Negro is not to be let off quite yet. He is to be made the victim of a new deal by precipitating upon the country a false issue. He is to face another problem.

Now that the Union is no longer in danger, now that the North and South are no longer enemies: now that they have ceased to scatter, tear, and slay each other, but sit together in halls of Congress, commerce, religion, and in brotherly love, it seems that the negro is to lose by their sectional harmony and good will all the rights and privileges that he gained by their former bitter enmity.

This, it is found, cannot be accomplished without confusing the moral sense of the nation and misleading the public mind; without creating doubt, inflaming passion, arousing prejudice, and attracting to the enemies of the negro the popular sympathy by representing the negro as an ignorant, base, and dangerous person, and by presenting to those enemies that his existence to them is a dreadful problem. With their usual cunning, these enemies of the negro have made the North partly believe that they are now contending with a vast and mysterious problem, the mere contemplation of which should cause the whole North to shudder and come to the rescue. The trick is worthy of its inventors, and has been played for all that it is worth. The orators of the South have gone North and have eloquently described this terrible problem, and the press of the South has flamed with it, and grave Senators from that section have painted it in most distressing colors. Problem, problem, race problem, negro problem, has, as Junius says, fitted through their sentences in all the mazes of metaphorical confusion.

In speaking of this subject in another place, I said what I say now, that these Southern people have outwitted the North in this problem business. Like skillful prestidigitators, they have turned the attention of the spectator to a distant object while they have manipulated the thing in hand. They imitated the cunning of the hunter who draws a red herring across the path of the game to divert the hounds.

The true problem is not the negro, but the nation. Not the law-abiding blacks of the South, but the white men of that section, who by fraud, violence, and persecution, are breaking the law, trampling on the Constitution, corrupting the ballot-box, and defeating the ends of justice. The true problem is whether these white ruffians shall be allowed by the nation to go on in their lawless and nefarious career, dishonoring the Government and making its very name a mockery. It is whether this nation has in itself sufficient moral stamina to maintain its own honor and integrity by vindicating its own Constitution and fulfilling its own pledges, or whether it has already touched that dry rot of moral depravity by which nations decline and fall, and governments fade and vanish. The United States Government made the negro a citizen, will it protect him as a citizen? This is the problem. It made him a soldier, will it honor him as a patriot? This is the problem. It made him a voter, will it defend his right to vote? This is the problem. This, I say, is more a problem for the nation than for the negro, and this is the side of the question far more than the other which should be kept in view by the American people.

What these problem orators now ask is that the nation shall undo all that it did by the suppression of the rebellion and in maintenance of the Union. They ask that the nation shall recede from its advance in the path of justice, liberty, and civilization. They boldly ask that what was justly and gratefully given to the negro in the hour of national peril shall be taken from him in the hour of national security. They ask that the nation shall stultify itself and commit an act of national shame which ought to make every lover of his country cry out in bitter indignation and unite as one man to oppose. A demand so scandalous and so shocking to every sentiment of honor and gratitude.

And from whom does this demand come? Not from who gave their lives to save the nation, but from those who gave their lives to destroy it. Not from the free and loyal North, but from the rebellious and slaveholding South. Not from the section where men go to the ballot-box with the same freedom from personal danger as they go to church on Sunday, but from that section where personal safety is endangered, where Federal authority is defied, where the amendments to the Constitution are nullified, where the ballot-box is tainted by fraud, and red-shirted intimidation makes a free vote impossible. It comes from the men who led the nation in a dance of blood during four long years, and who now have the impudence to assume to control the destiny of this Republic as well as the destiny of the negro.

And what are the reasons they give for demanding of the nation this retreat from its advanced position? They are these: They tell us that they are afraid, very much afraid: they are alarmed, very much alarmed, by the possibility of negro supremacy over them. This is the calamity from which they would be delivered, and with eloquent lips and lusty lungs they are calling out: "Men and brethren, save us from this threatened and terrible danger!"

My reply to this alarm is easy. It is that the wicked flee when no man pursueth: that the thief thinks each bush an officer: that the thing they pretend to fear can never happen, and that blank absurdity is written upon the face of it. The eagle, with fierce talon and bloody beak screaming in terror at the approach of a harmless black bird would not be more absurd and ridiculous. The superior intelligence of the whites, the comparative ignorance of the blacks, the former dominion of the whites and the former subjection of the blacks, the habit of bearing rule of the whites, and the habit of submission by the blacks make black supremacy in any part of our common country utterly impossible.

But supposing such an occurrence possible, what hardship would it impose? What wrong would it inflict? Who would be injured by it? If the blacks should get the upper hand, their rule would have to be regulated by the Constitution and the laws of the United States. They could not discriminate against white people on account of race, color, or previous condition without findings the iron hand of the nation laid heavily on their shoulders. The white people of the South are the rich, the negroes the poor; the white people are the landowners, the negroes are the landlers. The white people of the South are numbered with the ruling class of the nation. They have behind them every possible source of power. They have railroads, steamships, electric telegraphs, the Army and the Navy. They have the sword and the purse of the nation behind them, and yet they profess to be shaking in their shoes lest the 8,000,000 of blacks shall come to rule over them and their brethren, the 50,000,000 of whites.

Now I am here to say that there is nothing whatever in this supposition. I can hardly call this invention a cunning device, for the pretense is too open, too transparent, too absurd, to rise even to the dignity of low cunning. It is an old ragged pair of trousers, and an old mashed and battered hat of the last century stuck upon a pole in a field where there are neither crows nor corn. It is the cry of fire by the thief when he would divert the officer of the law. It is as I have said, a red herring to divert the hounds from the true game, and the strange thing is that any class of our citizens, white or black, can be deceived by it.

But black supremacy is not the only string on the harp of a thousand strings upon which our Southern brethren play. They are not merely afraid of black supremacy, but they are afraid of ignorant black supremacy. Now, this danger is just the one to appeal to the sympathy of the North. The Northern people are not in love with ignorance or illiteracy. They deplore it; they hate it, and take every means in their power to banish it from their States. They naturally sympathize with any people in deploring it and who are making honest efforts to remove it from among them. Hence they are pouring out millions of dollars to aid the South, and are sending competent teachers there to enlighten the ignorant and to lift up the black man and white man alike from the darkness and ignorance to which they had been doomed by slavery and by those would-be negro problem solvers.

But it is worthy of emphatic remark that the men in the South who are loudest in their outcry against the ignorance of the negro are not those who wish to have him instructed, but those who would make his ignorance a reason for depriving him of the rights secured to him under the Constitution.

But again, when before in the history of the Southern people have they been alarmed by the presence of ignorance among them? When before did they ask the nation to assist them in stemming the tide of ignorance? The whole history of the legislation of the South—by the South I mean the ruling class of the South—is on the side of ignorance. Their laws have made it a crime to enlighten the black man's ignorance. It has been the policy of the ruling class there to oppose education not only for the blacks, but for the poor whites as well. But as I have said, this cry is raised not for help to educate the negro, but as an excuse for taking from him the right of suffrage, by which he can in some measure promote his own education and the education of those about him.

But admitting what I do not admit, that the ignorance of the negro is recognized by the South as a source of danger, and admitting the sincerity of Southern men who are professing to deplore it, I have to say to them: If you could stand the negro when he was a slave, you can stand it now that he is free, at least a reasonable length of time for his education. Clearly enough, the remedy is not in the abridgement of his rights, but in the education of his mind. It is not in evading the plain provisions of the Constitution, but in teaching him the duties imposed by the Constitution; not in taking away his vote, but in teaching him how to use it.

To me there is something very audacious and insolent rather than pathetic and persuasive in the language employed by Southern men on this question. There is something of the old-time Southern swagger and assumption in their tone and bearing—a tone and bearing which is entirely out of date, out of place, and out of harmony with the age body of our time—a tone and bearing which invites rebuke rather than sympathy, disgust rather than approbation.

Such men as Senator Butler, of South Carolina, should remember that there is such a thing as modesty as well as decency for men of such antecedents as theirs and that it is neither modest nor decent for them to coolly propose the expulsion of citizen innocent of crime from the State of South Carolina, or from any other State in the American Union. It is only a little while ago that Senator Butler and his class were in arms against the Government which these same negro citizens loyally and bravely endeavored to save from their disloyal hands.

But let me say again, the South neither really fears the ignorance of the negro, nor the supremacy of the negro. It is not the ignorant Negro, but the intelligent North that it fears; not the supremacy of a different race from itself, but the supremacy of the Republican party. It is not the men who are emancipated but the people who emancipated them that disturb its repose. In other words the trouble is not racial, but political. It is not the race and color of the vote. Disguise this as it may, the real thing that troubles the South is the Republican party, its principles, and its ascendancy in Southern States and the nation. When it talks of negro ignorance, negro supremacy, it means this, and simply this, only this. It uses the word negro simply as a means to the end of awakening popular prejudice and enlisting its influence in favor of its bad cause, a cause for which they have shown themselves capable of committing every description of frauds the most scandalous, and cruelty the most barbarous. We all know that the negro problem would vanish into thin sir, would utterly disappear like the mist before the morning sun, if the intelligent negroes of the South would renounce their connection with the Republican party and support only the Democratic party. What the South wants, and what it means to have peaceably if it can, or forcibly if it must, is a solid Democratic party South and Democratic rule in the nation. There is not an intelligent man at the South that does not know this, and there is not an honest man at the South, who, if he would speak candidly on the subject, would deny this. The trouble is that the people of the North do no see this in its true light. Honest themselves, they cannot readily believe that others are not alike honest. It is in some sense creditable in them that they have never believed in the story of outrages committed against the negro voters of the South, because they themselves would not be guilty of such outrages, they have been easily imposed upon by the pretended fear of a negro supremacy professed by the South.

But let me be more intelligible. My idea about the problem business is this When a case has been in litigation before a court of highest resort, and that case has been solemnly adjudicated in that court, that case is finished and all the parties to it must submit to the decision or become law-breakers and criminals. The case goes into history henceforth *res adjudicata*. It is settled. If this beneficent rule did not exist there would be no end to litigation and no repose for the public mind.

To make my meaning still more clear: When in England a few years ago Northampton saw it fit to send Mr. Bradlaugh, an infidel, to represent it in the British House of Commons, and he was not allowed to take his seat, the admission of an infidel to the House of Commons was a problem: but when he continued to knock at the door of the House till he was finally admitted the infidel problem, so far as the right of membership of that House was concerned, was solved. Again, we are not the only people whose rights have been denied on the ground of race. Our brother Shem has had a taste of proscription as well as ourselves. No Jew was at one time eligible to membership in the parliament of great Britain, but after long years of agitation of the question, Mr. Baring, an eminent Jew, was admitted to a seat in parliament. The Jewish problem, when Mr. Baring was seated, was ended, I mean this: When the American people declared their independence of Great Britain and made good that declaration by victory in a seven years war, the problem of American independence was solved, and there was never anything afterwards concerning it which could be called problematical. It was a fixed fact, and has remained such until now, and will remain so, I trust, forever.

There is a grand agitation now in progress in Great Britain for local self-government, at the head of which are Mr. Gladstone and Mr. Parnell. If Great Britain shall grant home rule to Ireland, the Irish problem will be solved, and it will be nonsense thereafter to speak of it as an unsolved problem. Our American women are asking for a sixteenth amendment to the Constitution, whereby they may vote. They ought to have it. If the American people shall adopt such an amendment, the women problem will cease to exist.

In like manner, when the Negro was declared free by the highest authority in the land, when the whole system of his bondage was broken up, when he was invested by the organic law of the land with the title, dignity and immunity of an American citizen, and when it was declared that any discrimination made by any State against him on account of race or color was unlawful, I hold that his race condition could no longer be consider a problem. The thing was done: it was finished. The nation had taken its position and all the parts of the nation must ultimately adjust themselves to the whole. The individual States may be great, but the United States is greater. The mountain will not and cannot go to Mahomet, so Mahomet must and will in the end go to the mountain. Herein is the ground of my hope. The trend of civilization, the power of large bodies to attract small ones, the force of national greatness, the inclination to the stronger rather than to the weak in human forces will ultimately bring the individual States in line with the Federal body. I affirm that while the National Government shall remain in the hands of the Republican party and under the principles of that party, no State will or can permanently disfranchise any of its citizens because of race or color or previous condition. Attempts may be made to do this, but the race problem in that respect is solved, and the case cannot be permanently reopened.

But I am asked, what of the future? and will the various peoples of this country ever be thoroughly assimilated? or, to speak more plainly, will they ever intermarry? My answer is, "Sufficient unto the day is the evil thereof." We should not cross the stream till we have come to it. Whether such marriages will ever become common or not is no matter of vital concern to anybody at this day. It is mere speculation and is utterly without practical importance, so far as the rights of the American people are concerned. It touches no question of politics, statesmanship, or religion.

Individual interests, personal preferences and public sentiment may be safely left to regulate the relations of the races in respect of intermarriage. Such, I think, is the view that common sense will take of it, but such does not seem to be the view taken of it by some of our people—white, black and mixed. There seems to be a fascination about the subject which makes it impossible for men to let alone. They thrust it into our faces on all occasions, in season and out of season, and seem distressed because we cannot solve the problem for them. Some of them say that the repugnance of the white race of the black makes marriages between them impossible, and yet they proceed with great warmth and eloquence to denounce it as a thing to be closely watched and guarded against, and by no means encouraged. If the thing is impossible to happen no one should be afraid that it will happen.

I noticed while at my post in Haiti that even the Senate of the United States was compelled to listen to a learned disquisition upon this subject of race intermarriage from the lips of the eloquent, learned, and distinguished Senator from Kansas. I have always entertained for that gifted gentleman the highest respect. When he is right he is very right and when he is wrong he is very wrong. There is no halfness is his character and composition. He is either all or he is nothing. In the present instance he happens to be not only all wrong, but very wrong. His argument against the admixture of the race in intense but narrow, brilliant but unsound, learned but inconsistent and illogical. He not only contradicts the facts and the science of the case but contradicts himself. He asserts that only the bad qualities of each race inherited by a mixed race, and at the same time he permits himself to say that he attributes whatever ability I happen to possess to the Caucasian side of my parentage. So good a logician as Senator Ingalls should not have allowed himself, almost in the same breath, to knock down the whole superstructure of his argument. Mr. Ingalls is a brave and a generous man, and I am surprised that these qualities were allowed to forsake him on the occasion referred to. Had he listened to the manly side of his character he would have never allowed himself to slay with his brilliant rhetoric a million of his colored fellow citizens. He took advantage of his position on the floor of the United States Senate to deal us a blow which we had no means of parrying. His advantage was great, and the ignoble character of his attack must be measured by the greatness of his advantage. Had any colored man of spirit and ability been a member of the Senate to reply to his assault. Mr. Ingalls would not have been inconsistent with his well-known chivalric qualities. But the case was otherwise.

If it be true that good qualities are not transmissable in such unions; if it be true that only evil, and that continually, must descend to the children of such parents, it may be well asked why any of the mulatto or quadroon children and grandchildren of our earlier statesmen are found anywhere outside of the thick walls and iron-barred windows of our prisons. Why are they walking our streets and employed in our houses as trusted servants and stewards? Why are they our teachers, professors, and preachers? Why are they respected and treated as gentlemen and Christians in every part of the world except our own? Oh, no, Mr. Ingalls! Your argument will not hold. It will not bear the test of either reason or experience. Your language is the language of alarm, and the question you should put to yourself is. What if, in a nation of a hundred millions there should occasionally happen a marriage between two different varieties of the human family? Who would be hurt by it? Who, outside the parties themselves, should give themselves any trouble about it? The sun would not cease to shine, the rain to descend, nor the grass to grow. Men would not cease to go to and fro in the earth, or knowledge cease to roll onward. If the country has endured, during 240 years, lawless relations on a broad scale between the two peoples, it should not go into paroxysms of alarm over what may possibly take place under lawful conditions.

And now comes Mr. Isaiah Montgomery, of Mississippi, with his solution of the pretended Negro problem. I have spoken of him elsewhere, and I take back nothing that I have said either of this remarkable man, or his remarkable address. He has surrendered to a disloyal State a great franchise given to himself and his people by the loyal nation. He has taken the work of solving the nation's work of the nation's hands. He has virtually said to the nation:

"You have done wrong in giving us this great liberty. You should give us back a part of our bondage." He has surrendered a part of his rights to an enemy who will make this surrender a reason for demanding all of his rights. He has conducted his people to a depth from which they will be invited to a lower deep, for if he can rightfully surrender a part of his heritage from the National Government at the bidding of his oppressors, he may surrender the whole. The people with whom he makes this deal are restrained in dealing with the rights of colored men by no sense of modesty or moderation in their demands. They want all that is to be had, and will take all that they can get. Their real sentiment is that no Negro shall or ought to have the right to vote. Yet I have no denunciation for the man Montgomery. He is not a conscious traitor though his act is treason: treason to the cause of the colored people, not only of his own State, but of the United States.

I wish the consequences of his act could be confined to Mississippi alone, but I fear this cannot be. Other colored men in other States, dazzled by the fame obtained by Mr. Montgomery through the Democratic press, will probably imitate his bad example. I speak of this Montgomery business more in sorrow than in anger. I hear in the plaintive eloquence of his marvelous address a groan of bitter anguish born of oppression and despair. It is the voice of a soul from which all hope has vanished. His deed kindles indignation to be sure, but his condition awakens pity. He had called to the nation for help—help which it ought to have rendered and could have rendered but it did not—and in a moment of impatience and despair he has thought to make terms with the enemy, an enemy with whom no colored man can make terms but by a sacrifice of his manhood. There is no need here of an analysis of Mr. Montgomery's address. Its character is known and it has nothing to commend it but its ability and plaintive eloquence and the man, the place, and the circumstances under which it was delivered. The logic of the speech would have conducted magnanimous men to a prompt rejection of the surrender, for it was an appeal to all that was noble, grateful, and generous in hearts of Mississippians. They should have said, "No, Mr. Montgomery: your people have been our best friends when we needed friends, and we scorn to take from you the franchise accorded to you by the wisdom and magnanimity of the National Government."

Ladies and gentlemen: I have been requested to say an encouraging word to our people before I leave for my post of duty at Port-au-Prince, and if I have not already said such a word I find it quite easy to do so now. From every view I have been able to take of the moral and political situation of our cause, before and since my arrival in the country, I am hopeful. I have no doubt whatever of the future. I know that there are times in the history of all reforms when the future looks dark; when the friends of reform are impatient and despondent; when they cannot see the end from the beginning; when the truth that is plain to them compels them to reject the honesty of all who receive it. When they meet with opposition where they expected co-operation; when they met with treachery where they expected fidelity, and defeat where they expected victory. I, for one, have gone through all this. I have had fifty years of it, and yet I have not lost either heart or hope. It is true that we have been sadly disappointed in the action, or rather non-action, of the Fifty-first Congress. The platform of the Republican party adopted at Chicago plainly committed the Republican party to some measure of protection to the Republican voters of the South. We had right to expect the pledge there given would find fulfillment in the action of this Republican Congress. We have been disappointed, sadly disappointed. Following the advice of a new leader from Pennsylvania, but a leader not of the Thaddeus Stevens and Charles Sumner mold, this Congress has preferred protection to commerce and property to protection to personal and political liberty. We had hoped that it would adopt either the Federal election bill or the Blair educational bill. It has done neither. The omission is, on the face of it, discouraging. But what then? Shall we get mad and denounce and renounce the Republican party? Has that party sinned away its day of grace? Are there no remaining reasons for giving it our confidence? I entertain no such thought. The Federal election and educational bills are not dead, nor are their Senate and in the House may permit delay but they will not suffer defeat. The president of the United States is true to his trust. No man since General Grant has stood by us more firmly than has General Harrison. He has let it be known openly and emphatically that he is for stepping to the very verge of constitutional limitations to secure honest elections, a free vote, and a fair count in every State in the Union, and he is not the man to take any steps backward.

I admit that during many years to come the colored man will have to endure prejudice against his race and color, but this constitutes no problem to vex and disturb the course of legislation. The world was never yet without prejudice. There exists prejudice in favor of and against classes among men of the same race and color. There is prejudice between religious sects and denominations; between Catholic and Protestant; between families and individuals. The time may never come this side the millennium when men will not ask "Can any good thing come out of Nazareth?" But what business has government, State or National, with these prejudices? Why should grave statesmen concern themselves with them? The business of government is to hold its broad shield over all and to see that every American citizen is alike and equally protected in his civil and personal rights. My confidence is strong and high in the nation as a whole. I believe in its justice and in its power. I believe that it means to keep its word with its colored citizens. I believe in its progress, in its moral as well as its material civilization. Its trend is in the right direction. Its fundamental principles are sound. Its conception of humanity and of human rights is clear and comprehensive. Its progress is fettered by no State religion tending to repress liberal thought: by no order of nobility tending to keep down the toiling masses: by no divine right theory tending to national stagnation under the idea of stability. It stands out free and clear with nothing to obstruct its view of the lessons of reason and experience.

It may be said, as has been said, that I am growing old, and am easily satisfied with things as they are. When our young men shall have worked and waited for victory as long as I have worked and waited, they will not only learn to have patience with the men opposed to them, but with me also for having patience with such. I have seen dark hours in my life, and I have seen the darkness gradually disappearing and the light gradually increasing. One by one I have seen obstacles removed, errors corrected, prejudices softened, proscriptions relinquished, and my people advancing in all the elements that go to make up the sum of general welfare. And I remember that God reigns in eternity, and that whatever delays, whatever disappointments and discouragements may come, truth, justice, liberty and humanity will ultimately prevail.

(1890)

AMERICAN LITERATURE

Little Women – Louisa May Alcott
The Last of the Mohicans – James Fenimore Cooper
The Red Badge of Courage and *Maggie* – Stephen Crane
Selected Poems – Emily Dickinson
Narrative of the Life and Other Writings – Frederick Douglass
The Scarlet Letter – Nathaniel Hawthorne
The Call of the Wild and *White Fang* – Jack London
Moby-Dick – Herman Melville
Major Tales and Poems – Edgar Allan Poe
The Jungle – Upton Sinclair
Uncle Tom's Cabin – Harriet Beecher Stowe
Walden and *Civil Disobedience* – Henry David Thoreau
Adventures of Huckleberry Finn – Mark Twain
The Complete Adventures of Tom Sawyer – Mark Twain
Ethan Frome and *Summer* – Edith Wharton
Leaves of Grass – Walt Whitman

WORLD LITERATURE

Tales from the 1001 Nights – Sir Richard Burton
Don Quixote – Miguel de Cervantes
The Divine Comedy – Dante Alighieri
Crime and Punishment – Fyodor Dostoevsky
The Count of Monte Cristo – Alexandre Dumas
The Three Musketeers – Alexandre Dumas
Selected Tales of the Brothers Grimm – Jacob and Wilhelm Grimm
The Iliad – Homer
The Odyssey – Homer
The Hunchback of Notre-Dame – Victor Hugo
Les Misérables – Victor Hugo
The Metamorphosis and *The Trial* – Franz Kafka
The Phantom of the Opera – Gaston Leroux
The Prince – Niccolò Machiavelli
The Art of War – Sun Tzu
The Death of Ivan Ilych and Other Stories – Leo Tolstoy
Around the World in Eighty Days – Jules Verne
Candide and *The Maid of Orléans* – Voltaire
The Bhagavad Gita – Vyasa

BRITISH LITERATURE

Beowulf — Anonymous
Emma — Jane Austen
Persuasion — Jane Austen
Pride and Prejudice — Jane Austen
Sense and Sensibility — Jane Austen
Peter Pan — J. M. Barrie
Jane Eyre — Charlotte Brontë
Wuthering Heights — Emily Brontë
Alice in Wonderland — Lewis Carroll
The Canterbury Tales — Geoffrey Chaucer
Heart of Darkness and Other Tales — Joseph Conrad
Robinson Crusoe — Daniel Defoe
A Christmas Carol and Other Holiday Tales — Charles Dickens
Great Expectations — Charles Dickens
Oliver Twist — Charles Dickens
A Tale of Two Cities — Charles Dickens
The Waste Land and Other Writings — T. S. Eliot
A Passage to India — E. M. Forster
The Jungle Books — Rudyard Kipling
Paradise Lost and *Paradise Regained* — John Milton
The Sonnets and Other Love Poems — William Shakespeare
Three Romantic Tragedies — William Shakespeare
Frankenstein — Mary Shelley
Dr. Jekyll and Mr. Hyde and Other Strange Tales — Robert Louis Stevenson
Kidnapped — Robert Louis Stevenson
Treasure Island — Robert Louis Stevenson
Dracula — Bram Stoker
Gulliver's Travels — Jonathan Swift
The Time Machine and *The War of the Worlds* — H. G. Wells
The Picture of Dorian Gray — Oscar Wilde

ANTHOLOGIES

Four Centuries of Great Love Poems

BORDERS® CLASSICS

The text of this book is set in 11 point Goudy Old Style, designed by American printer and typographer Frederic W. Goudy (1865–1947).

The archival-quality, natural paper is composed of recyclable products made from wood grown in sustainable forests; the manufacturing processes conform to the environmental regulations of the country of origin.

The finished volume demonstrates the convergence of Old-World craftsmanship and modern technology that exemplifies books manufactured by Edwards Brothers, Inc. Established in 1893, the family-owned business is a well-respected leader in book manufacturing, recognized the world over for quality and attention to detail.

In addition, Ann Arbor Media Group's editorial and design services provide full-service book publication to business partners.

®